THE SPELL'S THE THING. . . .

At least it is if you're a sorcerer's apprentice. And in this highly original collection of brand-new stories, you will indeed find many sorcerer's apprentices. But you will also find a number of apprentices who practice far different but equally spellbinding trades. So whether you're thinking of a career change, or just can't resist a truly fantastic tale, you're certain to find what you're looking for in such magical adventures as:

"Homework"—As a prince and a hero, surely he could turn a Dread One's nephew-apprentice into a hero-in-training. . . .

"Final Exam"—He was born with Talent, a Talent that had saved his own life at the expense of his mother's. But he was no longer an innocent infant. Now he must pass a magical test by his peers—or pay a price beyond imagining. . . .

"When the Student Is Ready"—She'd never planned on cutting classes. But her dad was away, and a seemingly insane street person was offering to take her on as his apprentice. . . .

APPRENTICE FANTASTIC

APPRENTICE
FANTASTIC

Edited by
Martin H. Greenberg
and Russell Davis

DAW BOOKS, INC.
DONALD A. WOLLHEIM, FOUNDER
375 Hudson Street, New York, NY 10014
ELIZABETH R. WOLLHEIM
SHEILA E. GILBERT
PUBLISHERS
www.dawbooks.com

First Printing, November 2002
1   2   3   4   5   6   7   8   9

ACKNOWLEDGMENTS

Introduction © 2002 by Russell Davis.

The Augustine Painters © 2002 by Michelle West.

Sign Here © 2002 by Charles de Lint.

Till Voices Drown Us © 2002 by Tim Waggoner.

Homework © 2002 by Esther Friesner.

The Last Garden in Time's Window © 2002 by Dean Wesley Smith.

Final Exam © 2002 by Jane Lindskold.

The Sorcerer's Apprentice's Apprentice © 2002 by David Bischoff.

Zauberschrift © 2002 by David D. Levine.

When the Student Is Ready © 2002 by Tanya Huff.

What Has to Be Done © 2002 by Fiona Patton.

Flanking Maneuver © 2002 by Mickey Zucker Reichert.

The Muses' Darling © 2002 by Sarah A. Hoyt.

Blood and Scale © 2002 by John Helfers.

CONTENTS

INTRODUCTION

by Russell Davis

THIS is a book of stories about apprentices, and I'm sure that somewhere in the *Almost* Unofficial Speculative Fiction Editor Handbook there is a rule that I don't dare violate: any volume of stories pertaining to, dealing indirectly with, or touching on apprentices in any way, shape, or form must contain a reference to "that lovable mouse who knew enough to get the brooms started, but not how to get them to stop." So there, now that I've mentioned it, we can all move on with our lives and this anthology of apprentice stories in particular.

As a writer and an editor, I've long been fascinated with the notion of apprenticeships. When I was younger (and much more naive about how most writers and editors spent their time) I had a notion that perhaps one day—if I were lucky enough—my talents would capture the eye of a master in the field. Perhaps my high school creative writing teacher would, in a veritable fit of enthusiasm, send one of my finely honed horror stories to Stephen King, who would, in his own veritable fit of enthusiasm, invite me to come and live in his garage—an apprentice to all things horrific in nature. Perhaps one of the talented editors in our field would take note of how skillfully I had helped turn our school newspaper into a marvel that *The New York Times* would envy, and call to encourage my dream or ask me to fill in for him or her for a short time while she or he took a brief break to pursue a seminar on the finer points of rejection letters.

Alas, these apprenticeship dreams turned out to be just . . . fantasy. The professionals in our field are far too busy writing to take on a full-time apprentice, which in my own case is probably just as well. The stories in this book are fantasy as well, no doubt of that . . . well, maybe a little doubt.

One of my chief joys during the editing of a theme anthology is experiencing the myriad ways that the writers take the theme and make it their own. I never get exactly what I expect, and, in turn, the reader gets a book full of surprises. This collection is no exception, and the writers have once again delivered tales that exceeded my expectations and took the theme of apprentices in directions I might never have imagined.

Michelle West's "The Augustine Painters" is a tale about a young orphan girl with a magical touch on canvas, while Sarah Hoyt's "The Muses' Darling" is a story that envisions a young William Shakespeare apprenticing under Kit Marlowe. Jane Lindskold's story "Final Exam" explores a more modern sorcerer, while Tim Waggoner's "Till Voices Drown Us" explores an apprenticeship to the dead. Each of these authors, and all of the others, has delivered a tale of apprenticeship—be it in magic, literature, combat, or even, as Mickey Zucker Reichert's story "Flanking Maneuver" explores, love and sacrifice.

So, if you've ever imagined learning a new craft under a master fair or foul, or signing on the proverbial dotted line to take your chances with the mysterious or the magical, then these tales are for you. And to be certain I've covered all the rules in the "Handbook," I will close this introduction by asking you, as you read these stories, to remember what the mouse learned: once the brooms have gotten loose, your world is never really the same.

THE AUGUSTINE PAINTERS

by Michelle West

Michelle West is the author of a number of novels, including *The Sacred Hunt* duology and *The Broken Crown, The Uncrowned King, The Shining Court,* and *Sea of Sorrows*, the first four novels of *The Sun Sword* series, all available from DAW Books. She reviews books for the online column *First Contacts*, and less frequently for *The Magazine of Fantasy & Science Fiction*. Other short fiction by her appears in *Knight Fantastic, Familiars, Assassin Fantastic,* and *Villains Victorious*.

THE canvas, stretched and restretched, primed and reprimed, moved into the light of the open bay windows, and then moved again, and again, as the light's slant grew distant, lay waiting.

Beside it, on a three-legged table, the palette, and beside that, paint, oils, rags, and most of all the brushes, cleaned and cleaned again over years of use, the sediment of old masterpieces still visible at the edges where hair met metal and disappeared beneath it.

"Are you going to start, Camille?"

His tone was rough and impatient, the tone of an Augustine Master Painter. She was so familiar with it, he might have chosen not to speak at all. But he had spoken, and speech demanded words in return. Or action.

She offered words. "Yes, Giavanno."

"Good. You should start soon; you know that the light is fading."

"I can work in the dark."

"You can work," he said gruffly, "in the light. But we're not made of money. Use the sun."

Not made of it, no, but not lacking. She wisely said nothing; his lecture on the virtues of thrift was one of his favorites, and if allowed, he would go on at length, while she, captive audience, was forced to acknowledge his wisdom.

She had prepared water and oil, solvents for the brushes; had already blended the base colors into those muted and suitable for portraiture. But she hesitated, her hand hovering over the slender wooden handles, her critical eye upon the canvas.

"I'm not sure it's ready," she said at last, letting her hand drift toward her side. It rose again as he glowered, smoothing wild strands of hair curled by the humidity in the high summer of the city of Augustine.

He stood, his glower deepening, the familiar cracks of skin around his eyes a warning. She ducked her head, although he sat in a rickety chair half a wide, wide room away. Old habits, foundling habits.

It irritated him.

"You are hardly a child," he barked, "to be remonstrated with a simple slap."

She lifted her head, straightening the line of her shoulder, her cheeks pink.

"I'm not asking you to paint the battle of the gates of Augustine; I'm asking you to paint a picture of a tired, old man."

She shook her head, which was as much of a lie as she dared; such a task would be beyond most of the apprentices of the Augustine Painters.

And especially this one.

"Camille. Look at me."

Obedient, she raised her head.

"In a week's time," he told her, the gruffness in his voice

gentling, "You *will* be asked to Paint the battle of the gates of Augustine."

"P–pardon?"

He did not return to the confines of his favorite chair; instead, he paced a half circle in front of it. The floorboards in the apprentices' studio were worn with just such pacing; it was part of the ceremony of his art. But the floorboards in the west tower studio had obviously seen little use; they retained no memory of his circular passage.

"You heard me."

"But—"

He rolled his eyes. "We will *all* be asked to Paint that battle. Have you paid attention to nothing that's happened beyond these walls in the last five years?"

Camille lifted a brush as her Master spoke. It was an old brush, its handle of bone, thin and hollow. Her Master had cast it aside because the strands of hair were bent in such a way that they could not longer produce a clean line—but although he had cavalierly ordered her to burn it, for the brushes of the Master Painters were never merely discarded, she had kept it for her own.

It amused him. He did not understand that these muddied lines fascinated her; that she could use those stray hairs, avoiding the bulk of the brush itself, to paint the thinnest of lines, the evocation of color. Her art and his were not the same.

"Yes, sir." The battle at the gates. "But that means . . ."

All impatience left his face; she liked it better than the gravity that settled there in its place. "Yes. He is coming. And if the Augustine Painters are not up to their task . . ."

She was sixteen years of age.

Sixteen, that is, by best guess. The Master Painters of Augustine were renowned for the acuity of their observations. She had come to him, as all apprentice Painters did, from the halls of foundlings, in this case the Westerfield foundlings. Westerfield was not impoverished; it had produced, for the benefit of the Painters, some several Masters of great repute, and those Masters, grudging but mindful, paid their respects in cold, hard bars of gold. She had delivered them herself, when the Master was too busy to run such errands—which was pretty much always.

No one knew what drove a Master Painter to seek apprentices, although Camille had learned, over the years, not to ask. She was not the only apprentice in the House of Giavanno. Nor was she the oldest. But of those he had selected, her hands—after the first of many trials—remained steadiest.

Or so he told the Westerfield woman who was in charge of the foundlings. The truth was darker and much more complicated than that.

"Camille!"

She jumped and set the brush aside, but he had seen the expression on her face.

His own grew grim and severe. His smiles were reserved for his paintings, and occasionally for hers.

"You are thinking about Felix."

Felix, the oldest of the apprentice Painters, the jolliest, the loudest, and in Camille's decided opinion, the most talented.

At eighteen, he had seemed so much older than she, so much more confident of his place and his future. She could see him that way, if she struggled. She could remember that boy.

"Camille," he said gently, "I understand. But we have no time for indulgence, not even when it is earned. This painting must be complete."

Better to nod than argue; Camille nodded.

His expression shifted, a subtle movement of lip and eye. "Camille, the armies have crossed the border. Do you understand?"

She did. But she knew that he had told Felix these same words, and Felix was . . . gone.

He read the accusation in her mute features. "You've wasted the sunlight, just as I said. I won't waste the crown-age on more light for careless girls. Go on, then. Go to your rooms."

She bowed to him, and when she rose, she fumbled with the knotted bow of her apron. It was dense with oil, with charcoal, with the silver lines of lead; her own.

When she had first gained it, it had been perfect, blank as new canvas. He did not allow her to clean it; instead, he designated its place upon the wall, as if it were another work of art, an abstract, something that was uniquely hers.

She found its place, the fourth peg on the student wall, and put it there.

Turned just a shade too quickly to see that her Master was inspecting it, his face softening into lines that suggested age. Impossible, that he could look old, his hair so dark, his beard unblemished by anything other than flecks of paint, of chalk, of the tools of his trade.

Will you court madness in order to learn this art?

The halls of the Westerfield foundlings were cold and bare. There were paintings along wide, windowed walls in the wing that the dignitaries visited, their signatures all the accolade that the orphanage required when it, thrice a year, sought money from its patrons. But those paintings were seldom seen by the boys and the girls who lived behind the closed doors of the foundling halls, in their tiny rooms, with windows so high and so small they served best as perches for the pigeons that resided beneath the gables and the overhang of the shingled roofs.

Each of the small rooms had four beds, one stacked upon the other and placed against the wall; each of these had two sets of dressers, and a basin for water. There were tin jugs for water as well, and part of the early morning routine—after the rigorous bathing and combing and starching of clothing—was fetching that water from the West Southwest Well.

Camille loved that early morning trudge. She hated rain, for when it rained, the overflow barrels provided what the orphans required, and that task was sharply curtailed.

But when it did not, she would yoke herself to the buckets that dangled when empty, and she would be allowed out the back door with strict instructions not to dawdle and not to talk to strangers.

But what, after all, was a stranger? A person she didn't know.

And on the road, in the early morning, there were no people she didn't know. The farmers in the Southwest market made stalls out of the backs of their wagons near the well, for the well was the heart of all morning commerce. Everyone needed water. Everyone needed food. She learned their names, and they—those who were not above speaking with a gangly orphan girl—learned hers.

Oakley was the man she loved best, with his shock of red hair and his black, black beard. His eyes were great, wide things, open as if in perpetual surprise; he had all his teeth, and showed them frequently when he opened his mouth to emit his great, whooping laugh. He had big hands, and when he had finished setting up his stall, he would slide them under her arms and send her flying in a mad, mad spin above his shoulders, her feet dangling over the radishes and the beetroots, the cabbages, the dirty heavy sacks of potatoes and carrots.

It was for Oakley that she drew her first picture. While the other children were experimenting with circles and squares, with lines, with colors and shapes, she was playing with the long rods of charcoal. She liked it; some of it was hard, and some so soft you could just draw it away, as if it were melting into paper and leaving its essence behind.

But the picture was not what she had thought it would be; she had tried to draw his smiling face, and she had ended up, instead, with something leaner and more frightening. And more complicated, as well. His whole body was in the picture, shaded in gray and black, and he held his hat over his chest, while at his side, a man she had never seen before—and so, she thought, she had invented—was laughing. It was not a kind laugh. Camille had heard enough cruel laughter to know it, even deprived of sound.

In his hands were papers, curling in the wind; the words were smudged and dark; she could not read them. There was also a woman in the picture, thick as an old tree, bent, her hands in her face. There was a boy just older than Camille, and two much younger.

She did not like the picture, and because she did not like it, she hid it when the teacher walked past. The Sisters of the Westerfield Hall emphasized grace and beauty in all things.

"If you are lucky, you may prove worthy of the Master Painters in the city of Augustine. Do you understand what that means? But they are interested in the creation of things of beauty; they are looking for children who strive for *perfection*. Is that understood?"

Well understood.

And Camille's rough sketch would be beneath the notice of even the Sisters.

It rained the next day, and so the day after she was kept in, but on the third day, she was sent to the well, same as always.

On impulse, she took the picture from its hiding place and shoved it down the front of her apron dress, and then she scurried out into the sunlight like a frightened mouse.

Oakley was there, at the market. He smiled as he caught sight of her, and then frowned as she drew close enough that he could see her face.

"What's wrong with my lass?" he asked, frowning, his voice a deep bass. "Have they been mistreating you at the foundling hall? It won't do, girl, if they have. 'Fess up."

She shook her head. She loved it, most days, when he talked to her as if—as if he was kin, as if he was family. Had always wanted to ask him if she could come and live on his farm, for any farm that he owned must be a wonderful place, and she was used to hard work.

But she knew that he would say no; if he'd wanted her, he'd have asked, and the foundling hall would have been happy to see her go; they were always happy to find placements for the children left, year after year, on the grand, flat stretch of their steps.

"Then where's my smile, Cammy? What's clipped the wings of my flying girl?"

She shook her head again, holding back.

And then, although she could not, years later, say why, she reached into the folds of starched cloth and dragged out her picture, her folded, bent picture, charcoal smudged at the unintentional creases she had put there. She held it carefully; charcoal on her smock was not to be forgiven by the severe mistress of the hall in which she lived.

"What's that, there?"

"It's a . . . picture. I drew a picture."

"You drew, eh?" He shook his head. "What they think of at that place. Do they teach you anything useful?" But he knelt when she didn't answer, and his voice was gentle. "What did you draw, girl?"

"I—I wanted to draw a picture of you."

He smiled. There was a wealth of pride and pleasure in the smile, something that put gold to shame. She loved the smile, and it made her hate the picture even more.

"Let's see it, then. Cammy?"

She shook her head, holding back.

"What's wrong?"

She was afraid he wouldn't like it, and after a few minutes, and one glare at a customer who had the wit to step back, she told him so.

He laughed. "I'm not handsome enough to be vain, girl. And if you drew it, I'll like it. My word on that."

The paper shook in the wind of her hands as she held it out. He took it gently. Turned it around; she saw the charcoal revolve until she was looking at the smudged and creased back of the large, square sheets the foundling hall gave its students.

She could not see his face for the paper, but he said nothing, and Oakley was almost never quiet.

The buckets, empty, were at her feet. Cheeks pale, she

bent over them, lifted them, and made her way to the line of
people waiting for the pump to be free.

"Lass," Oakley said.

She turned to face him.

"This picture . . . when did you draw it?"

"Days ago."

"And this . . . this man . . . where have you seen him?"

"I've never seen him. I made him up."

"And this woman?"

"I made her up, too."

"Tell me what's happening in this picture."

"I—I don't know."

"I don't look happy."

She shook her head. "No. He does, and that's just
wrong."

"Cammy, are you from Westerfield?"

She nodded.

"And did they—did they see this?"

Shook her head.

His eyes were wide, as they always were, and they looked
surprised, as they always did, but the delight was missing, and
his face seemed pale in the light of the August sun.

"I—I'm sorry, Oakley. I know it's not good. I shouldn't
have brought it."

But he shook his head. He didn't offer to spin her around,
he didn't reach down to lift her, he didn't do any of the
things he always did. She thought he was angry.

"May I keep this, Cammy?"

She nodded.

Filled her buckets. Left.

Three days later, one of the foundling Sisters came to her
room. Her knock was always different from the knocks of
the other children; sharper and harder, shorter and more
distinct. All four of the children in the room sat up at once,
and three of them breathed an obvious sigh of relief when
Camille was taken away.

She didn't wonder what she'd done wrong; she knew.

She was led down the long, narrow hallway, to the room of the woman who headed the Westerfield Hall, Madam Dagleish. Madam Dagleish never smiled. But her frown was reserved for special infractions, and she wore it now in full force.

"Camille," she said coldly, "sit."

There was a chair, indicated by a curt nod, a dip of a pointed chin. Camille obeyed instinctively, her knees folding around the hard wood of the seat's edge, her feet brushing the carpet.

"Did you give a drawing to a farmer at the West Southwest Well?"

Camille froze in place.

"I asked you a question. Darya, that will be all."

The Sister nodded and retreated with just enough grace that she didn't appear to be fleeing.

"Camille?"

"Yes."

"Did he ask you to draw that picture?"

"No!"

"When did you draw it?"

"In—in class."

"In class." Madam Dagleish strode around her desk as if it were a battlefield, the starched folds of her shirt her armor.

"We did not see that picture."

"No, Ma'am."

"Do you understand the significance of what you've done?"

She nodded. And then, thinking better of it, because she really didn't, she shook her head.

"I see. You are relieved of your duties at the well until further notice. You may go."

There was no argument with such an edict. Camille knew it. But she had to try. "But the water—"

"The water can be fetched by someone else. Are you arguing with me?"

She shook her head. Better that than speak.

"Go to your rooms. You are to consider yourself in confinement for three days."

Three days. She had been confined before; there wasn't a foundling in the Westerfield Hall who hadn't been. But an end to confinement this time didn't meant an end; she was no longer to be allowed her one freedom. Oakley must have come to the hall. He must have spoken with the Mistress of its vast wings, its multitude of unruly children. She wondered what he said. Daydreamed about it, sheets tucked beneath her chin as she tried—and failed—to sleep the days away.

But she didn't find out that day; instead, she received a summons from the ward Sister. It was one of the few times she was happy for it.

She was led to the Mistress' office, and there, seated beside the forbidding and dour Madam Dagleish, was a man she had never seen before. He was obviously noble—or so she thought then—for he dressed very, very finely, and his clothing was not the severe and durable linen that enwrapped every other person who walked these interior halls. She wondered why he had been brought here; all the important guests were entertained in the halls lined with paintings.

He frowned as she entered. "Honestly, Marianna, what you do to these children?"

"I?"

"They might be appealing if you didn't insist on starching them. Well, come here, girl, and let me have a look at you."

She didn't need to "come there" to be appraised; she knew it because his gaze, unblinking and undeterred by the possible disapproval of Madam Dagleish, had never wavered. But she knew that if she disobeyed, she might face another confinement. As always, at the end of days staring at nothing but walls and empty beds, she was pathetically eager to please.

She crossed the room.

"Marianna, if you would be so kind?"

"I am not in the habit of being kind."

"It was a figure of speech."

"A poor one." She rose, shedding the buttressed wall of her ironwood desk. "However, you are a busy man, and even, in your fashion, a respectable one." The emphasis on respectable sounded more like a warning against future behavior than a compliment. "I will not waste your time. Do not waste mine."

She led the way out of the room, and he followed. But Camille had the sense to wait until she turned back and said, "You are to accompany us."

They went, not back to the ward, and not to the many classrooms the Westerfield foundlings toiled in, but rather, out through the plain doors and into the wing reserved for dignitaries. There, where the halls were lined with works of art that would enrich the foundling hall for decades, she paused.

She was caught by the beauty of the paintings that had been donated to the foundling hall—although not to the foundlings themselves, who were never granted leave to study them. Each of the Painters had captured the essence of light, of life, of movement, in a way that defied their medium. Her own meager sketches were now an embarrassment.

But one day, she thought, with a sudden determination, she would paint, and she would be *perfect.* As perfect as these.

The stranger did not seem to see the same beauty that moved her; he scanned the paintings with a critical eye, and the occasional derisive snort. "Where is it, Marianna?"

"You are prejudicing the experiment."

"I do no such thing. I am simply following your request and attempting to use as little of your time as possible."

No one spoke to the Mistress in that tone of voice, and certainly she seemed to think so, because she gained an extra two inches of height. But he was unperturbed.

"It is in the upper hall," she said at last.

He immediately left them standing there. "Camille," she said with the severity of a frown that the stranger had earned but was impervious to, "why are you standing there gaping? Go on."

Camille nodded, her hair flouncing as her head jerked up and down. She was almost too shocked to be excited, and she kept out of range of Madam Dagleish's hands just in case, but she did follow.

The stranger had stopped his frenetic pace, and now stood with his hands behind his back, his fingertips touching. "Well, girl, what do you think of this one?"

She looked up at it.

It was much like the other paintings that she had seen before she was forced to speed up a staircase so wide she felt dwarfed and insignificant. Landscapes often figured prominently in the paintings, although one or two were portraits of famous people—emperors, empresses, people whose names were engraved in memory in much the same way the names of the gods were. Or the days.

But in this one, the clouds were dark, their undersides tinged with a gray-green that she had seen on the wildest of storm days, in the haven of her room, through a window high enough that only the sky was visible. Beneath and against these roiling clouds were men in armor, but their armor, unlike the gleaming perfection of the Imperial portraits, was dented and stained; dirt clung to surcoats, where surcoats had not been too torn and bloodied to hold shape and form. Around these beleagured knights were men who wore no armor, or none that the painter had chosen to depict; they carried spears, wooden shafts with stone heads, broken poles. They also wore bandages, scant pieces of cloth that were incapable of staunching the flow of wounds' blood; bright scarlet, brighter than emblems, a testament to their courage or their foolishness.

As she stared at the painting, she realized that not all of the men in it were on the same side; that some of the armored knights were swinging their great swords at others, their faces twisted by the strain of the exertion. She had never lifted a sword. Had never realized just how heavy they were. There were horsed men in the distance, upon the crest of the hill. The battle itself was girded round by folds of earth, mud now, although the texture of the open ground suggested that grass had once covered it.

It would get worse. The storm clouds were heavy with rain, with lightning, with the voice of elemental anger.

One of the men on horseback moved forward; the others stood their ground, their hands upon the pommels of their swords, their faces obscured by the lowered visors of great helms.

He lifted his visor, and for a moment, the clouds seemed to part; his face itself was covered in golden light, his eyes gold, his lips gold; all natural color had stepped aside for the splendor of this moment. He lifted a horn to his lips, and the sound of its music was worse than the thunder that answered it.

Storm. Rain.

In the valley—the basin, she thought, in growing horror—rain fell. But only there.

She cried out a warning to the men who toiled in their closed lines, as their blood fell, their arms wavered, the weight of the fight descending upon them.

And they lifted their faces, as one, and they looked up. At her.

She was horrified by it, fell silent at once. But their eyes were not the only eyes that had turned toward the sound of her voice; eyes of gold did as well, as the sound of the horn died. They scanned the horizon beyond the picture's frame.

She froze in place, silent now, still and small, as a Westerfield foundling learned to be when faced with the ire of their keepers.

And the stranger lifted a hand, dropped it on her shoulder.

"Look away!" he shouted, his lips very near her ears. But his voice was not as loud as the thunder that rolled into the valley. She did not know what his face looked like; she could not turn away.

"Girl, look away! Look away, damn it!"

She tried. She did try. But the painting had swallowed even the edges of her peripheral vision; it existed. It was *real*.

And then, it was gone.

Suddenly, it was gone.

She heard Madam Dagleish's outraged shriek, and she looked up, her vision returned to her by an act of vandalism so profound, she had time to wonder about it only later.

The painting was on fire.

The stranger caught both her shoulders and turned her around until she was facing him; his long nose was an inch away from hers, and his eyes were a very strange color, like light on water. "Who are you?" he asked her.

She tried to pull away.

"Girl, answer me. Who are you?"

"C–Camille. Of Westerfield."

"And who is she?"

"A n–nobody. A foundling. I fetch—I used to fetch—the water."

"Marianna?"

"It is true."

He let her go. "You are also a very lucky young lady." He turned to face the Mistress. "Why did you wait so damn long to call me? Or am I not the first Painter you called?"

"You are the first, Giavanno."

"Do you realize what you risked?"

"She has shown no signs."

"None?"

"Until the drawing she gave to the farmer, none at all. She has none of the . . . particular compulsion toward perfection and beauty. And she is a full three years from the age at which—"

"Age be damned. If she had chosen a different subject—a farmer, you say?—you might not now have her here. And we would all be in greater danger for it."

Madam Dagleish said nothing for a long moment. And when she did, her voice was her own; cold and severe. "Do you mean to imply that the painting in question—which I

assure you, Master Giavanno, you *will* replace—is actually
a danger?"

"It was."

"Then you must look to your own for culpability here; if
I had known, I would never have allowed it to grace these
halls." She turned.

"I will take her," he said.

And she nodded.

Just like that.

In the morning, Camille knew that she would stand in
front of the easel again, the paints spread before her, the
brushes readied. And Master Giavanno, much older now
than he had been that day, would sit in his favorite chair.

She did not want to do this.

"This is how it is done in the House of Giavanno," her
Master told her, over a quiet meal. It was not quiet because
they were alone; there were five apprentices, all now younger
than Camille, at the long table. It was quiet because
Camille now occupied the chair that had belonged to Felix.
Of all the signs that had been given the younger students—
all foundlings, all like Camille—this was the most concrete: Felix was gone.

Camille pushed food around her plate. The Master, unlike the Sisters of her former home, did not carefully moni-
tor the disappearance of food on the plates of the children;
he did not comment. But she noticed that he, too, ate little.

"In the House of Giavanno, you earn your title by painting a portrait. I have chosen the portrait; you will paint it."

She said nothing. She wasn't certain why she was afraid.

After dinner, instead of retiring to the studio with the rest
of the children, she retired to her room. It was a much
larger room than she had had in Westerfield Hall, and it
possessed a single bed, a large window, a tall, ornate shelf
which held her brushes, her palette, the curled fold of her
smock, with its years of sediment. The armoire held her

clothing, and in the last two years, the Master had seen fit to gift her with fine dresses and robes, suitable for the company of nobility; she often accompanied him when he went to work on the commissions he accepted. There had been fewer of those in the last year.

She lay on the bed in silence as the sun descended; the window framed a sunset that she could capture in spirit, but never in substance. She watched shadows lengthen, watched colors fade; the curtains were seldom drawn in this room.

But sleep eluded her.

Felix was gone.

Felix. Gone. She rose, spoke three words; the room was lit from above. Only in Giavanno's house did such nonsense yield results, but they were potent. She remembered the fire that had taken canvas and gutted it on the day her future had been decided. She found her smock, her palette. Hesitated for just a moment and then set the palette aside, reaching instead for the closed tin box that held such a special place in her heart. Charcoal, in strips of various thickness, was ordered as neatly as it could be; pencils, some hard enough to tear paper, some soft enough to almost be worthy of charcoal, were also there. She held the box carefully, because dropping it could be so catastrophic, and made her way to the studio.

At this hour, it was empty. She spoke a different series of words, a longer one, that she had never spoken before. She had heard them, though; Master Giavanno spoke them in his sonorous, musical bass. The studio was much larger than her room, but it, too, responded to words, as light filled the shadows with color. Not day colors, not exactly, but not the grays that silver moon made of everything.

She found the paper she had made—in House Giavanno such tasks were not left to outsiders—and set it out flat against the tabletop. She set the box beside it, lifting the lid, its creaking hinges familiar as a favorite conversation.

She began.

*   *   *

"Do you understand why the Augustine Painters are so revered?"

Camille shook her head.

"Answer the question, Camille. Or did they cut out your tongue in Westerfield? If they did, they've become more severe since *my* day."

"No, sir."

He rolled his eyes. "It is always easier to take in boys," he said with a snort. "They have a much more obvious spirit." He dropped his hands on the tabletop with a loud *slap*. "Very well. The Augustine Painters do not simply paint insipid and flatteringly untrue portraits as adornments for the halls of vain men. Those who do well do not paint them at all. You will understand why in a little while, and I think it is best—for your sake—that you abjure portraiture. I will teach you the basics of anatomy; I will teach how to handle paints in such a way that you *could*, should you prove a disappointment, make your living on such foolishness. But you will promise me, today, that you will not undertake such a sitting at the behest of anyone but me. Is that clear?"

"Yes, sir."

"Good. The Augustine Painters are often asked to paint history. Sometimes it is the history of a thing—like the great tower occupied by the Senate; sometimes it is the history of a place. But understand, child, that it is a history that has not yet unfolded."

"You mean the future, sir?"

"Good girl. No, that is precisely what I do not mean."

"But—"

"Let me finish; you can ask your questions later. I assure you there are not many that I have not heard, no matter how vapid or how poorly thought-out.

"When I choose to accept a commission—and I do not do it out of the goodness of my heart, not even at the behest of the Emperor himself—I must understand the shape of the place that I will paint. I will often go, for a week, and live there, if at all possible. If the place is to be something that is not yet created, I will request—and be given—the designs for its construction. And then, having read them, having understood them—often by drawing them in rough from several perspectives, or in several seasons, I will walk the streets in which such construction is to take place. I will observe the people, I will pay attention to what must be destroyed in order to build, or rebuild. Am I being clear?"

She nodded hesitantly.

"That is not an acceptable answer in this house."

"Yes, sir."

"Good. All places have a sense of history. A sense of what unfolded in the moments, the hours, the years, before you chose to stand within it. That history is the foundation for all that follows, do you understand? Without that past—which is fixed and unchanging, as much a truth as can exist—there is no future."

She nodded. Swallowed and said, "Yes."

"No 'sir,' this time, eh? Well, good. So we paint history as it unfolds. We paint a continuity of events, a possibility.

"It is not for possibility that we are paid, of course. The Augustine Painters are renowned for the *accuracy* of their understanding, of their depiction. They are known for the perfection of their work, their ability to handle nuance and detail; they create a reality that is *also* a visual splendor; to wit, a work of art. You may never become an artist to your own eye; you will *always* see the flaws and the weaknesses inherent in your own work. And you will strive, girl. You will put the whole of your mind into the task of *becoming* that artist. You will work toward the day when you will create that one defining masterpiece of which you might be proud. You may never achieve that greatness—but if you struggle to achieve it, if you constantly improve, you will always be considered one of the Augustine Painters. If you survive your apprenticeship."

She did not understand, then, what he meant by that. In Westerfield Hall, children did die. The summer season was the time of the crippling disease, and the winter, of the

endless cough, and many of the smaller or weaker children
died. She assumed that his house would be no different.

"There is a magic in Augustine," he continued, his voice
softer now, his gaze distant. "It seems centered here. We do
not entirely understand it, and many, many experts have
come to study the paintings, the Painters, and the city in an
attempt to gain for themselves some of that magic. They
have failed."

This, she did know.

"You have it, already."

"But . . . But I—"

"The drawing that you gave to that farmer was an Augustine picture, child." His voice was gentle, now. "It was
rough. I understand why the Sisters did not see it; you did
not feel that it was worthy of their attention. Is this not so?"

She swallowed and nodded.

"And although Madam Dagleish would never counte-
nance my saying so, you did the farmer a great favor. He
had been about to enter into business with the man you por-
trayed in your painting, against the wishes of the woman
whose face was hidden by her hands—his wife. Had he, he
would have lost what little livelihood he now possesses. He
is not a slow man; nor is he a stupid one. He understood the
significance of what you gave him instantly. He came to
Westerfield Hall with that drawing, and he spoke with Marianna at length."

"Did he . . . ?"

"Did he what?"

"Did he ask for me?"

"You mean, did he ask if he could take you home?"

She nodded. She could not find voice for the words.

He met her eyes. "It has not been so many years," he said
softly, "since I dwelled in the halls. I know why you ask,
child. I will not ridicule you. But I will answer you truth-
fully. No, he did not ask."

Her gaze fell to the tabletop in silence.

"I told you, he is no fool. If you do not understand the

history of the Augustine Painters, he does. To my surprise,"
he added gently. "Yes, I spoke with him. I had to. He is
fond of you, and I cannot speak for what might have happened had you not delivered him your drawing. But when
he had it, when he understood what you were capable of, he
knew that he could never keep you in safety upon his farm.
And he knew, as well, that you might be in need of safety.
He came to Westerfield Hall. He spoke with Madam Dagleish. And then he spoke with me.

"I came at once. The Sisters of Westerfield Hall—of any
of the foundling halls—keep an eye on the children who
dwell within the wards. There is a reason that art is taught,
and taught early; it is the only clear measure of a child's
ability."

"But—"

He sighed. "But?"

"Why the foundling halls? You—all of the Augustine
Painters—are men of power. You're important. You have . . ."
she looked around at the high ceilings, the great windows,
of the studio, "more money than the Churches. What about
your children? What about—"

"We have no children," he said quietly.

The way he said it stopped her. "None?"

"None of the Augustine Painters has ever proved fertile.
We may marry, if we can find anyone tolerant and forgiving
enough to spend a whole life in a place like this, but that
marriage produces no children."

"But . . ."

"Find the words, Camille. You have left Westerfield, and
the only way you will ever return to it now is to gift its
great hall with a painting of your own, as a sign of your
gratitude."

"But *we* were born. We *had* parents."

"That is a mystery of Augustine," he said quietly. "Not
all of the foundlings will become painters. Most of them
will find other work—accounting, perhaps, if they've a
mind for numbers. I think one or two of them have gone on

to become lawyers of great repute. But the few who come
to the Painter Houses belong in them. Do you think that
those parents, who left children on the steps of that hall,
would not claim them after their rise to power? You have
seen too little avarice, child." He rose. "The foundlings are
of the city. We have tried, all of us, at one time or another,
to find our parents. Our mothers, perhaps our fathers.

"We have, to a person, failed."

She wanted to cry. Years of Westerfield training held her
in good stead; she was silent, her eyes dry.

His voice was surprisingly gentle. "All of the foundlings
dream of parents," he told her. "Of belonging, of family. I,
too, had those dreams. It is the loneliness," he added, "that
makes men mad. Any man. But Camille, the gift of the painting itself is this: When you work, you will never be lonely.
You will forget about the desire to find family, to find home.
You will be possessed, instead, by the desire for greatness, the
pursuit of perfection. It will be your only true freedom.

"But understand, child, that you at least will have that
freedom. Many, many of your foundling siblings will never
have that peace, and they will be driven to foolishness, time
and again, in an attempt to assuage what they falsely believe they would never have felt had they kin." He rose.
"Felix!"

A boy of ten stood up. He had been almost hidden by the
great easels that were strategically placed windowside, for
light, or she would not have missed him; he was tall for his
age. His hair was brown, but the sun had trailed sunset fingers through its strands. His eyes were brown and wide,
framed by lashes and high cheeks.

"Master?"

"Show Camille where we keep our smocks and our supplies. We will go out in the streets in exactly forty-five minutes, and I wish you to accompany us."

He smiled brightly.

"What about me?" an older boy said, peering from
around another easel in this forest of easels.

"What about you?"

"Yes, Master."

"Good."

Felix was a gangly bundle of energy. He talked nonstop from the moment the House doors opened, and it seemed that everyone in the street knew who he was, because everyone had a word or two to exchange for his hundred. He was a little too tall to be treated as a child, but everyone treated him that way anyway; his hair was thoroughly tousled before Master Giavanno chose to stop.

"Felix," he said dryly, "is much loved, and not only by himself."

Felix grinned brightly. "Yes, sir," he said.

The Master rolled his eyes. "Luckily he has not yet earned the right to use the name of *my* House; people do not expect such friendly nonsense from *me*. Felix, attend."

"Yes, sir."

"Attend with a little less bounce, please."

"Yes, sir."

"This, Camille, is paper. We use it for watercolors and rough sketches. You will learn to make it, but for now understand that it is costly."

She nodded. And then, as he glared, said, "Yes, sir."

"Understand, as well, that I *have* money. Do not let petty considerations get in the way of your art."

"Yes, sir."

"Good. Did you bring pencils, Felix, or only a hundred thousand words?"

"Pencils, sir."

"Good. Sharp ones?"

"Uh, mostly, sir."

"Good. Give some of them to Camille."

Felix smiled. "You see these letters?"

She nodded. "The A is softest. It's almost pure charcoal, I swear. We used them at lot at East Holly Hall."

"You weren't in Westerfield?"

"No. But I wish I were—East Holly was sort of like all those stories about hell, but worse."

She laughed.

"Do not, please, laugh," The Master said. "He has the entire city encouraging his ridiculous claims."

"The B is a little bit harder. That one, the H, is hardest of all. I don't like it much, that's why it's so long. See the knife there? You can sharpen the points any way you like,." Felix said.

"We had charcoal, at the hall. And some pencils. Not as many as this. Lots of chalk, though."

"Oh, chalk," Felix said, with dramatic disdain. But he winked.

"We will draw the fountain today. Camille, what do you know about the fountain in Hasting Park?"

"Nothing, sir."

The Master sighed. "Of course. Felix—tell her about the fountain."

"All of the pigeons in Augustine crap on it."

"Felix!"

"Yes, sir." He started to speak, and his words ran together in a stream not unlike the tendrils of water that fell from their height in the fountain's center. After a moment, he shrugged. "I can show you better than I can tell you. Can you give me the C?"

She handed him the pencil and he began to draw.

He drew as quickly, and as generously, as he spoke, the pencil creating wide, arching lines in its rapid wake. They made more sense than his words, although at first, they looked like simple lines.

But she saw the curve of the fountain's basin in them, and after a moment the only words he used took the form of letters, like a foundling code. "A. D. E." She handed him the pencil he requested.

She saw the shadows of flying birds over the flat stones that led to the fountain, saw the droop of the leaves of the great weeping willows that protected it from the gusts of

wind that swept through the city's center. She saw children
with willow switches, chasing each other at the base of
those trees, saw an elderly couple, at home among the pigeons, their hands outstretched.

He smiled, when he saw them appear. "That's Elva," he
told her quietly. "And her husband, Willem. They've been
together forever, near as I can tell, and they've even been
happy about it. They like the birds, the fountain, even the
really obnoxious little kids."

But the picture wasn't complete. She touched the paper,
and Felix smiled, nodding. Without a word, her hand fell
into the pencil box and came up with a letter, a designation
that made no sense in this rapidly unfolding sketch. She
began to draw.

In class, in the hall, drawing had been contained. Circle.
Square. Triangle. And then, oval, diamond, straight line.
Beyond that, a collection of these shapes, and beyond that,
a sharp rap on the desk for not paying enough attention.

This was nothing like that. No one spoke; the need for
words fell away. Confinement was almost inconceivable,
and it was forgotten. She could not say, as their hands
touched and crossed, who had drawn shape from the silver-
gray of pencil lead, who had made the face of the weeping
man, of the silent woman at his side; who had, by rapid,
sweeping line, suggested the shape of a passing carriage, its
emblem bright and shiny upon the moving blur of its body.
Horse hooves kicked up a spray of water, not unlike the
splash of the fountain, shadowing ground.

And in front of those flying hooves, another shape
emerged, a child's form, small and bent, face obscured by a
tangle of hair, attention absorbed by a roadside puddle.

She could see the convergance of lines now, although the
carriage lay beyond the fountain at the center of the drawing. Could see where the hooves and the child ran parallel,
as if they were one thing.

She reached out, dropped the pencil, as the carriage continued to move.

"Not that way, Camille," Master Giavanno said quietly. His voice was soft, but it was not at all gentle. The gruffness had left it entirely.

"Felix?"

At the sound of his name, she turned; Felix was still. "I can't see her face," he said quietly.

"Ah. Let me."

Camille watched in confusion as one of the most respected of the Augustine Painters chose a pencil from Felix's humble box. He frowned a moment, and then his pencil touched the paper. He began to work.

She watched him as carefully as she could, trying to see the drawing, trying not to see the collision that she was absolutely certain was about to happen.

Wind blew through the square, lifting willow leaves; wind fell low, traveling west, toward the carriage. The child's hair rose, and her face, three-quarter and in shadow, was clear for a moment.

"Got her, sir," Felix said quietly.

"Good. The time?"

"This afternoon, I think, by the shadow."

"And not tomorrow afternoon?"

He frowned. "That's Mr. Wainson, and his wife, Elva. They come once a week. This afternoon, sir. Or a week, but . . ."

"But you think it soon?"

He nodded.

"Good. Well done. Go and speak with the child's mother, and take the . . . sketch . . . with you. Tell her when you think this might happen. Camille?"

She was staring at them both. "Yes, sir?"

"Go with him. He'll talk for hours on the way, and he doesn't have the time. If he says more than three words to anyone on the street, kick him."

Her first picture.

The pencils that she had laid out in a neat row, letters up, were not the same pencils, of course. But the box was the same; Felix had given it to her, on impulse, when they had returned from the grateful woman's house. She hadn't had to kick him; she remembered that clearly. He didn't speak at all to the people who stopped him on the street; he simply held up the rough paper, waved it forward like a flag, and they fell away respectfully and let them both pass.

They had, with pencils and paper of Felix's construction, saved that child's life.

It was not to be the last time that it happened. There were others, and they started—always—in the same way: an outing into the streets of Augustine with paper and pencil. Charcoal, the Master said, was all very good, but the lines were too muddy to be of use when identifying the details that were truly at the heart of the drawing, rather than at the heart of its composition.

Yet it was charcoal that she reached for in the false light.

The first time that Camille worked with paints should have been memorable, but she could not clearly recall it. She loved the colors, bright and vivid; hated the length of time it took to dry, the care with which one had to move, to lift brush, to lift canvas once the day's exercise had been completed. She grew in fits and starts, and always, along with inches, came spates of pure clumsiness which she was certain the whole of Augustine—at least anyone who passed within a mile of the House at the time—knew about.

Painting with oils, as opposed to drawing with pencils, was a type of confinement. Felix, years her senior—almost three, in fact, although that seemed so much less significant now—loved paints with the happy fecklessness that he loved words, and it was to Felix's care that she was given. Roger, the oldest of the Master's pupils, was more stern and more severe; he was, he said, destined for greatness, and he did not wish that greatness to be stained by foolishness and childish pranks.

The Master, for some reason, tolerated this unbelievable

arrogance, but he was kind enough to Camille—to all of the new students—to make Felix her senior.

The exercises were *not* paintings. They were, according to the Master, an attempt to teach the young their craft; the art itself was already there.

."Understand," he said softly, "that your pencil work has been very fine—and it has done more than simply appeal to men with a few extra coppers in their pockets; it has saved lives; it has made a subtle difference in the streets of Augustine.

"But you—or at least Felix—know the people in the streets we travel. When you have such knowledge, even charcoal will do. Imagine that you had to recognize, from one of your drawings, the small child who was about to be crushed by a horse, when neither of you had ever seen her. You could not tell the color of her hair; you could not tell the color of her eyes; you could not even tell the color of her clothing.

"When the emperor calls upon you—and he will; he will have need of all his Painters soon—he will require colors. The standards that hang upon the field. The swatches of clothing that serve as crude armbands for the levies. The colors of the trees in their season, the color of the sky, the river. You will learn this, Camille. Love your pencils, if you must; love your charcoals. But this, this is the weight of your responsibility."

And so she struggled.

Felix helped, of course, and when they painted together, she loved the colors because she could see them, briefly, through his eyes.

That year, there was the first rumbling of a distant war. The Augustine Painters were summoned, and the Master returned with books, more books, letters in a script so strange that no one but he could read them. Men came to visit, with skin dark as copper. He did not spend time in the studio with the children, and as was so often the case, Felix was told to mind them.

Felix.

* * *

"Master?"

"What?"

She had grown used, by this time, to the curtness of his speech. "The day that you met me in Westerfield Hall."

"What of it?"

"Why did you burn the painting?"

He looked up. "Ah. It's taken you long enough, child, and I am busy at the moment, but it is a good question. Come."

He led her to his offices, the three rooms that he occupied with his work, his scribbling, his vast library. She expected him to tell her to take a seat—had almost, in fact sat down, when he shook his head and reached for the ring of keys he often wore on his belt.

"Do not touch anything you see," he told her quietly. "And do not speak of it outside of these rooms."

She nodded. "But—"

"Camille, you must learn to preface a sentence with a less odious word."

"I didn't touch the painting in Westerfield Hall, sir."

"You did."

"I didn't."

"You were not aware of what you were doing, child," he told her gently, "But you did; you touched the canvas."

"And you knew what I saw."

"I . . . did not know . . . what you would see, or I would not have taken you to that painting. No Master would be so careless. But, yes, when I saw your reaction, I did know. The man who painted that picture died sixty years ago," he added quietly. "But he did not die in the painting. Had he, that picture would have been gathered and hidden away."

"Not burned."

"Not burned, no. We do not fire what we create unless the need is great." He spoke, and the interior of this windowless room was lit from above. "Look," he said quietly.

"But give me your hands while you do so. The compulsion is often strong."

She obeyed almost without thought, for the room itself was like the storage room of a great gallery. Paintings, unframed, lay against the walls in great stacks, their edges inscribed with names, with dates, with numbers. Most were not visible, but some, those recently dated, were among the most prominent.

"Part of the reason," he told her gently, "that we often choose an apprentice to accompany us, when we at last begin, can be seen here. There are some works that are not meant to be finished. Some that cannot in safety be finished.

"This," he said quietly, gesturing with his chin, "is the clearest example."

"I don't recognize the name."

"No, you wouldn't. It is twenty years old. It was painted by one of the students here." He closed his eyes. "It was meant to be a portrait of a local merchant. You can see, by the clothing, that it was even started in that fashion. Safe enough; an example of craft, no more. But the boy was strongly gifted. I arrived late," he said quietly. "I went to the merchant's house when he had not returned for dinner.

"He had been painting for hours. Hours; he painted without his subject; he painted without any volition at all. We had to break two of his fingers to remove the brush from his hand."

She stared at the painting.

At the golden color of the man's skin, the shape of his exquisite eyes, the curve of his lips.

"You recognize him."

She nodded. It had been a number of years since she had seen his face, but she remembered it clearly. "Who . . . is he?"

"That," the Master said, "is the question that Augustine Painters have been asking almost since the founding of the city."

"What happened to . . . the student?"

"He was completely mad," the Master replied. "He would not eat, or drink; we could have forced either, but the end result would have simply taken longer. It was . . . difficult. He was the first student that I had lost in many years, and I was . . . unprepared for the difficulty."

"How could you have been prepared?"

"These paintings . . . happen most frequently . . . in times of war."

"There was a war?"

"Oh, yes," the Master said softly, as he stared at the face of the man who seemed to be much, much more than oil and canvas. "But we were unaware of its progress; it did not start within the borders of the Empire. It came upon us slowly. But it did come." He shook his head; freed her hand a moment to rub his eyes. But even in this he was careful; she stood too far away to reach out and touch anything.

"Then—"

"Yes," he said softly. "As in the last one, the war that is coming started well beyond our borders."

"War happens all over," she said quietly.

"Yes, child. It does. But it is only the conquest of Augustine that is reflected in the paintings you will see in the room; if Augustine is to have no part in the final outcome of the fray, he is absent from our work."

"But who is he?"

"Who? I don't know. I told you, no one does." He reached out and moved one of the canvases, catching it by the edges. The stacks were shifted, until he had uncovered a painting that was cracked with age and the conditions of its storage.

"This is the oldest. I believe that the House of Ceville has one that is older." She knew this was serious, for he spoke of Ceville in a tone that was entirely free of his usual rancor.

It was not a portrait. It was an entire landscape, similar to the one that she had seen in the Westerfield Hall. But there

was no battle here; it was a simple slaughter, in grays and
blacks, in dark, dark reds, bright oranges, pale yellow
hearts of flame.

. Those flames were his carriage, his chosen method of ar-
rival; there was no horse, no cavalry.

"The man who painted this?"

"He died of it."

She nodded.

"When I feel that you are ready, child," he told her, although his gaze was weighted by the painting before them,
"you will paint. A portrait, a simple work. If you can do
that, you will be called upon to serve the Emperor.

"If you cannot, and I am present, you will paint *nothing*
until the course of the war is decided for this generation."

And if you aren't present? She didn't ask. He hated point-
less questions, and she already knew the answer: it was
here, in this hidden, windowless room.

It had been just over half her life—by Westerfield Hall's
count—since she had last been a foundling, but some skills
never left. She wasn't breaking his rules—no one who
wanted a home did that. She wasn't *painting*.

Paint, its vibrant colors, its immediacy, its subtlety, were
too new. She went back to her roots. She went back to their
roots. Pencil. Charcoal. Paper. This paper, she had made on
her own. It was her gift.

Felix had been absent from the hall for three days. Three,
and she had counted every waking minute in a numb daze,
afraid to ask the Master for any details. Afraid to ask him if
she could see what he had painted, his last painting. She
knew it was that. The oils would be dry enough to move,
but not to touch.

*If you know the person, or the place, well enough, you
need no study; experience is the best teacher. It is why the
Augustine Painters learn so many languages, read so many
books, see so many plays; it speaks to experience. It helps
us to perceive. To observe.*

It is why you could draw a picture for your farmer.

It was not the farmer she drew now.

She had never touched Felix's face. This was as close as she had come, this broad curve of dark line against paper. Too hard. She softened the line by smudging it carefully. That much, she could still do consciously.

Felix, where are you?

She drew his chin, the broad, generous line of his mouth, the height of his forehead, his cheekbones, his eyes; she left the prominent features as a white, clear haze around which she built the shadows of his face. He was no longer ten years old. No longer twelve, or fourteen; he was no longer a child, although some of his youth remained in his smile, the curve of his eyes, the crinkle at their corners a reminder of his habitual smile. Although he worked as hard as any of the other students for the Master's approval, Felix was the one boy in the halls who did not need it.

Roger, older, more adept at his craft, had needed far more. She saw that now, although she couldn't say why; the arrogance of that face was a mask, one that Felix had no need, no desire, to wear.

She wondered how he saw her, if he saw her at all; wondered how he would draw her, if he came to this room in the dark, summoned light, and worked in the secrecy of the sleeping hall. Wondered how they might draw themselves together, their hands moving over and around each other's in a constant state of near-collision that never quite attained visual disaster.

She drew him. From memory. From experience. His face emerged, smaller than she had intended, and she realized that this was a work, an Augustine work. It was the only moment at which she could have set the pencils aside, closed the box on charcoal, let the studio retreat into nightfall.

But she let it pass by.

He held a piece of paper, clenched in his hands, the image turned toward his chest. His smile was absent, his eyes narrowed with purpose, his shoulders a straight stretch. Before him, she saw that she had drawn children, and behind him, the fountain at the heart of the square. She saw Elva, her Elva, subtly different from his own, alone on the bench; her husband had passed away last year. She fed the pigeons quietly, age her mantle.

And he held the picture out, toward her, as if, of all people present, she was the one who needed it most.

But she wasn't, Camille thought. Her vision was blurred now; she could not tell if it was the charcoal's soft lines or her tears, and it didn't matter; her hands moved, and moved again, picking up and discarding pencils, the box opening and closing, the hinges a creaky whisper.

She could not say later how many hours she had sat in this room, drawing, compelled by what she created, what she remembered.

And then she was finished. She looked at the picture. There was something about it that was wrong, something missing.

"Camille."

She started, but she did not look back; she recognized the voice.

"Camille, come away, child. It is well past your bedtime." He spoke; the studio dimmed, its darkness falling across the easels, the night sky, the table upon which her things lay scattered.

She grabbed the drawing in shaking hands; held it to her chest with as much care as she could.

"I want to see him," she said.

"You don't."

"I do. He's not dead. He's not dead yet."

"Camille, whatever he was, whatever you remember, it is gone. He will not recognize you. Do you understand? He will not know who you are."

"I don't care. I want to see him."

She heard Master Giavanno's weary sigh, and she rose,

knocking her chair over. He spoke again, and the lights returned.

"What are you holding, child?"

She shook her head.

"Camille. What are you holding?"

"A sketch."

"Let me see it."

No. No. No. But she could not say the word. Mutinous, she faced him, the paper curling around her, thin and inadequate armor. He closed the distance between them; his hands met hers around the edges of the paper. When he pulled, she let go; she could feel the tension in the paper itself, and she knew that it would not survive a tug-of-war.

He turned it around.

She could not see his face for the textured white of the paper, but she could see his hands; could see that the paper shook.

"Camille." His voice was strange. She had expected anger, perhaps, or pity, even that odd gentleness that occasionally crept into his voice. This held none of those things; there was an edge in her name that she had never heard there.

He walked past her, almost as if she weren't there. Bent to retrieve the fallen chair as if it were an afterthought, and not the crime it would have been during class time. Her stammered apology came to nothing; he sat in the chair, just as she had done, and his hand reached for the box.

She wanted to run to it, grab it, close it; it was Felix's gift. To her.

But instead she watched as he took up pencil in hand. Frowned. "Paper, girl," he said, in an entirely normal—and extremely irritable—tone.

She ran to the cupboards, his cupboards. Ran back to grab the keys that he held out in the crook of one finger. She had attended him often enough that it was easy to obey the commands he no longer cared to find words for.

Her paper was not so fine, not so finished, as his, and

usually she felt a twinge of envy when she touched its smooth surface. Not tonight. Tonight, it was simply another tool. She laid it out in front of him from the opposite side of the table. There was no chair for her; the chairs were stacked neatly to the side. She almost went to get one, but he had already brought pen to paper, and his hands were a moving blur, a magician's set of arcane gestures; they produced a magic of their own.

Augustine Painter. Master Giavanno.

He drew a room. It was the room that came first. It was almost entirely empty; there was only one piece of furniture in it. A bed.

But the bed was not empty. The blankets had a shape and a form and as his hands traveled up their length, she knew whose form it was. Felix. He lay, eyes wide, lips open; she could see them moving as he struggled. Although she could not see them, she knew that restraints held him back.

She had said she wanted to see him.

But not even Master Giavanno could be this consciously cruel, and he had not yet finished his picture. Before the bed, another figure appeared, bent over the first. She recognized the uniform of a student, recognized the ties of a smock at its neck and waist.

But she had seldom seen her own back.

He did not linger over details. He finished quickly.

And then he looked up across the table to where she waited. "I do not understand," he said quietly, "and I am certain that a council of the Masters of Augustine would see me disbarred for what I am about to do. Come," he told her quietly. "Bring your picture. I will take you to Felix."

He did not speak as they traversed the silent halls. Did not lecture her, did not offer her his counsel, his brusque advice. She had taken the picture, as he commanded, but had also taken the box of pencils, hurriedly throwing everything inside. She was certain that she had heard the snap of two delicate pieces of charcoal, but it was either that or leave them behind.

"W—what did he paint?"

Master Giavanno did not glance back. But he said, "You will see it. It has not been moved."

Just that. He did not tell her not to touch it. He said nothing at all until he reached a door that Camille had seen on many occasions. It was never open.

The east tower studio.

He reached for his keys and then frowned as he remembered who had them. They exchanged hands, hers shaking, his steady; he opened two locks. They were shiny, these locks, newer by far than the door that played host to them. Her reflection slid past her eyes as the door opened into a long, empty room.

There were windows, of course; all of the studios required windows, and these were as wide and tall as any in the hall. But she did not recognize them at first because their curtains were drawn shut. No curtains were drawn in the halls of the Augustine Painters.

"Where is he?"

"There. Beyond that door."

The room was as Master Giavanno had drawn it; stark and empty. But he had not placed the easel upon the planks of the floor. She wondered if he had so much control that in the drawing he could consciously omit it. Wondered, but did not ask. She knew that had she thought to draw this place, it would have been there, and it would have been the center of the composition. She could not see what it held; it was turned from the door toward the windowless wall.

Turned from the bed, so that the boy in restraints could not see it.

His lips were moving. They were cracked, bleeding; he had had nothing to drink for three days, she thought. She felt a sudden, bright anger, a red shiny rage in the dim, muted colors of this terrible room. "Did you even *try?*" she said, wheeling on her small feet.

"The water," he replied, his tone completely colorless, "is beside the bed. You may try, if you wish."

"He can't drink lying down!"

"He cannot be made to sit in safety."

"Whose safety?"

He said nothing. She ran across the room; it was deceptively large. As she drew close to Felix, she could hear him speak, but the words were in a language that she did not know.

"W—what is he saying?"

"We do not know. We have recorded it for the better part of two days. We have," he added grimly, "always recorded what was said, to the best of our ability. Men whose skill and knowledge resides in language have been trying for years to gain information from the words."

She didn't have to ask if they had been successful.

She stopped three feet short of the bed.

"Felix?"

He did not turn; his eyes, wide, were vacant, his lips moving as if they belonged to someone else. For a moment, fear and hopelessness rooted her to the floor, as if the wood itself were still alive, as if the act of hewing it from tree had had no diminishing effect.

But she had not come all this way to be afraid.

No? *And why, then,* she asked herself, *have you come?* The Masters have worked for centuries—for*ever*—surely they did all they could do to—to . . .

No.

She lurched forward. Freed one hand, the other clutching her drawing, her tattered flag. She yanked the blankets away, and saw that he was, indeed, restrained; broad straps held his feet at the ankles, knees, and thighs; they hugged his skeletal hips, his chest, his shoulders.

"Camille, what are you doing?"

She shook her head. She didn't know. But it seemed to

her that it was wrong, wrong to bind his arms. She worked at the buckles of the restraints, all the while avoiding the sight of his terrible, hollow eyes.

His hands were weak, his limbs weak. She raised his right arm. As if that were a signal, he struggled madly, pouring an intense, insane energy into the attempt to sit up. His eyes saw through her, to where the easel lay.

She shook her head. "No. No, Felix."

His answer—and she thought it was an answer—was beyond her.

But he was not. He *could not* be. She reached into the pocket of her smock, and drew from it his pencils, his box. She put it in his palm.

Even that did not catch his attention. He gripped it, but as an infant grips a wayward finger; reflexively and without thought.

"Camille," Master Giavanno said.

"Help me. Help me with these. Just—just this one. These two. Just these."

The Master nodded after a long pause. He must have been hesitant, but it did not show at all in the steel cast of his face.

Felix sat. Wild now, but weak, he reached out with both hands to the easel. She was there, between them. She took the pencil box from his hands, and sat upon the bed; her own drawing now had two large creases and a multitude of smaller ones; charcoal would be smudged almost beyond recognition. She could fix that. She could fix it later.

"I need a board."

"Pardon?"

"A board. Just—a board. Like the ones we travel with."

She heard his steps retreating; over the urgent plea that underlay words that had never been a part of Felix's life, she heard them approach. He handed her what she had asked for, and she felt him hovering, near the bed. He did not interfere.

She laid the picture on the board. Where paper had bent,

charcoal gathered like black dust in its creases. She opened
the pencil box, all the while interposing the whole of her
body between his and the only thing in the room he desired.

And then she placed the A in his hand, and curled his fingers around it.

For her own use, she took the F, with its harder point, its
thinner line. She began to draw, to draw the picture that she
had started, that she had thought finished in the safety and
familiarity of the studio. No, she had not thought that; she
had thought it lacking. She understood what it lacked, now.
Felix.

*Camille, the gift of the painting itself is this: When you
work, you will never be lonely. You will forget about the desire to find family, to find home. You will be possessed, instead, by the desire for greatness, the pursuit of perfection.
It will be your only true freedom.*

Drawing was not painting. It was not that. Because all
she could think of, as her pencil hovered above her rough
sketch, was that desire. No: It was the falsity of that desire.
She had found family and home in Felix. Of what use was
perfection, if she lost that?

She drew.

She spoke with pencil, with pencil lines, with the charcoal that left the box. She had to make him see. This boy,
this almost-man with his paper carefully held inches out
from his chest, his eyes turned toward the face of a lonely
widow, *this* was Felix. He was not mad.

Felix, she said, in the medium that was her oldest, her
most tactile, *this is you. This is us. We saved children, old
men, young men; we stopped robberies, found lost dogs,
freed trapped birds. We did this. This is how.*

And then, as she worked, she felt the whole of the drawing shift. She saw the pencil's lines harden, saw something
appear on the back of the drawing that she had given into
Felix's care. *Lines,* she thought, *a man's body, the outlines
of a man's face.*

He did not work in paint. He could not, by simple force

of will, force pencil to offer color. But it offered shade. Complexity. Menace.

She heard Master Giavanno's voice from a great distance off. "Camille—be wary. There *is* a danger here."

But she could answer him in only one way. She drew. Where Felix seemed to concentrate in his entirety on the picture in his hands, she worked on his face, on his lips, on the shy smile, the somber cast of his features. She had hoped that he would laugh; had hoped that he would offer joy, as he so often did, fecklessly and without thought for the cost to himself. But she saw, in the tentative smile on Elva's face, that he offered more now.

He drew quickly; she drew more slowly, but she had the advantage: she had almost completed the picture before she had brought it here, and she now knew what it had to say.

And she knew what it was that Felix was offering Elva. Knew that it had to be a picture of her husband, the old man with the gentle hands and the flock of birds at his feet.

But that was not what Felix drew.

And Camille set about correcting it, seeing clearly at last. She did not lose herself in the art; although it contained the whole of her heart, it had more besides: ferocity. Intent.

Everything they had ever drawn had come together almost on its own, the cooperation an artifact of the singularity of their vision. She had never once argued about his choice, his design; he had never chastised her for her lack of care, her rough, imprecise lines.

They argued now.

All of those years of peace formed the basis for this battle. Silver lines crossed, hands collided; they reached for the same pencils, the same letters, the same pieces of charcoal.

In the silence of their skills, they argued; they drew over each other's pictures. Camille wondered if the paper would take such a punishing exchange; the pencils were not as soft as charcoal, and her paper-crafting had never been equal to his.

But she saw that she would lose; that his vision was

stronger than hers, his hands quicker, his desperation greater. And how could it be? What had he to lose?

She stopped for a moment. Felt a hand on her shoulder.

"Camille."

It was heavy with her momentary resignation.

No, she thought. *Not yet. Not yet.*

She could not compete with him; not that way.

Instead, she turned her eye to Elva's face. And she began to rework what she had drawn there. Lines darkened the old woman's eyes; lines narrowed them, lines smudged the corners of her lips, giving them less definition. She worked best with people, had always worked that way; she brought out the grief and the sorrow that Elva felt after a lifetime of companionship had inexplicably ended.

And she found a truth in this that was keener than the truth she had attempted to draw in her duel with Felix: This sorrow, this loss, was an echo of her own. With shadow and light, she made *Elva* the heart of the picture.

And she felt the board in her lap still.

Had he finished? Had he finished the drawing that occupied the whole of his attention, the few square inches a miniature paean to what lay on the easel, hidden from view.

She did not dare to look beyond the lines of Elva's face. Did not dare to stop working.

But she saw his hands move, jerking now, the pencil lines a part of no picture, no drawing, no classroom. He cried out in fury and rage; the pencil flew from his hand, its lead broken within the case of its wooden body.

"Felix," she whispered.

He looked up. Looked *at* her.

He was weeping. "It was my best work," he told her, his hands empty. "I will never *ever* capture such a perfect beauty again. I will never *ever* have that chance." His hands covered his face; his breath came out in terrible, coughing sobs.

She caught his hands, setting her pencils down for a moment, although the picture was not finished. Because he was weak from lack of food and water, it was possible—barely—to pry them away.

"And what would that perfection do for Elva?" she asked him. "What would that beauty do for the little girl who was almost killed by a careless driver?"

"You can't understand—you will never ever understand." He was crying.

She said, "I don't want to."

"I can't—I can't work with pencils. Camille, give me paints, and I'll do whatever you ask. Just give me my palette. Give me my tools. I can't work with pencils."

"You can. Look, look at this: when is it?"

He looked down; she wasn't certain that he could see through his tears. But he did see. Enough to say, "Next week."

"Why next week?"

"It's just . . . next week. Elva will be there."

He didn't know. He didn't know how many days he had been here, in this terrible room. "And will you take her that painting? Will you offer it to her, while she sits by the fountain and thinks that in a year or two she might not even remember her husband's *face?*"

She could have slapped him with less effect. She opened the pencil box. She placed the B in his hand. And then she looked down at the picture he had been drawing, and her own eyes clouded with tears.

Felix had drawn Willem. Idealized, too perfect, perhaps too beautiful, but recognizably Willem to Camille's eyes. "But . . . but I don't understand," she said, although it was hard to get words out of the closing walls of her throat.

"She was crying," he told her, crying as well. "She was crying because she thought—she thought I had brought her—a picture. Of her husband. Of the man she's afraid she won't be able to remember a year from now.

"An old man. One old man." He covered his face again. "An ugly old man." And then he wept, and he wept, and he wept.

* * *

In the morning, eyes heavy with lack of sleep, and dark with lack of food, lack of water, Camille of House Giavanno rose. She climbed the stairs to the west tower studio, understanding the significance of its isolation; she had seen Felix in the east tower, and understood why the Master had chosen the west for her test.

Master Giavanno sat in his favorite chair. His head was bowed as she entered; she thought he was sleeping, and turned to creep out of the room. But the door was not well-oiled; after all, the room saw use only once every few years.

"It's about time you arrived, girl."

She turned and shut the door firmly behind her back.

"How is he?"

"He is recovering. He cries almost as much as a foundling."

"Master Giavanno."

His brows rose. "You know, girl, you sound a little too much like Madam Dagleish for my liking." But he smiled wearily. "He is well. He is asking for you."

She nodded. "I'll see him," she said quietly. "After."

"After?"

"I finish your portrait."

The old man nodded almost regally. "Nothing unflattering, girl," he told her primly.

She laughed. "I will make it as true to what I know as possible."

He frowned.

"To what I feel," she added. She was tired; it was a good tired. She knew that she would paint, but she felt no fear of that task now.

No fear of the battle for the Augustine gates.

SIGN HERE

by Charles de Lint

Charles de Lint is a full-time writer and musician who presently makes his home in Ottawa, Canada, with his wife MaryAnn Harris, an artist and musician. His most recent books are the collections *Waifs & Strays* and *Tapping the Dream Tree*. Other recent publications include the trade paperback edition of *The Onion Girl* and a hardcover reprint of *Wolf Moon*. For more information about his work, visit his web site at http://www.cyberus.ca/~cdl.

1

"YOU'LL never guess who came over last night."

"You're right. I won't."

"Come on. You could at least try."

"Why do you want me to work for this? Just tell me already."

"It was Brenda."

"Bullshit."

"I'm serious."

"I thought she dumped you."

"No way. *I* dumped her. Nobody ever dumps me."

"Whatever. So what did she want?"

"Cheap sex."

"Now it really is bullshit."

"I'm kidding. She wants us to get back together."

"What did you say?"

"What do you mean?"

"Are you getting back together? Maybe you dumped her, but you're always talking about her."

"She was a great kisser."

"But?"

"No buts. I just don't know. I didn't say yes or no."

"So what did you do?"

"Nothing. We just talked."

"About getting back together."

"No. More about what we've been doing, old times, stuff like that. We must've been up until almost three."

"And then you had sex."

"No. Then she kissed me good night and went home."

"Still a good kisser?"

"She was always the best. We're supposed to get together again tonight."

"So it's semiserious."

"I don't know what it is."

"You know what I did last night?"

"Jumped your own bones?"

"Oh, very funny. No, I met this guy in the Crossroads Bar and he showed me this trick. Look at this."

"How'd you do that?"

"I figure it's mostly a mental thing."

"What, like, you only hypnotized me into seeing it?"

"No, the flame's real. Good trick, isn't it? Be a great way to pick up a girl in a bar—just light her cigarette with a snap of your fingers."

"How'd you do it really?"

"It's this way of, I don't know. Seeing things differently. Like, you can actually see the molecules of the air and you just kind of convince them to be something other than what they are. Apparently, when you get good at it, you can do it with anything, and not just a tiny flame like this. But air to fire's supposed to be one of the easier ones, so that's why he started me out with it."

"And he just showed it to you, out of the blue."

"Pretty much. He said he's been looking for someone he can teach all this stuff he knows, and that I looked like the right kind of guy. He said I was 'receptive.'"

"More like gullible."

"Hey, this is real."

"Let me—ow!"

"I told you."

"So what's he get out of it?"

"Nothing, really."

"Come on. He's got to want something."

"Well, he had me sign this piece of paper . . ."

"Jesus, what did you sign away?"

"My soul."

"Get real."

"That's all it said. He gets it when I die."

"This is too weird."

"Don't go all Catholic on me. I don't believe in souls and neither do you. Hell, when was the last time you were in a church?"

"Yeah, but think about it. That was based on limited knowledge."

"What are you talking about?"

"Well, souls are kind of like magic, right? And this trick the guy showed you is like magic."

"So."

"So if one kind of magic can be real, maybe other kinds can, too. Maybe we do have souls."

"You think?"

"Well, I'm leaning more to the affirmative right now."

"I've screwed myself, haven't I?"

"I guess it depends. What did he look like?"

"I don't know. Kind of normal."

"No horns—no tail?"

"Oh, for Christ's sake."

"You're the one he taught to make a flame by snapping your fingers."

"That's real."

"I know it's real. I saw it."

"I guess he looked kind of like Elvis, circa the Vegas years, only older."

"Elvis."

"Not exactly like him. More like Harvey Keitel sort of playing him in that movie we rented a while ago."

"*Finding Graceland*?"

"Yeah, that's the one."

"And you just up and traded him your soul to be able to light smokes for women in bars without using matches or a lighter."

"I don't own a lighter."

"I know you don't. I'm making a point here."

"I don't get it."

"The point is, how stupid can you be?"

"Hey, he's going to teach me other stuff. I'm going to be his protégé."

"Until you die and he gets your soul."

"Something like that. If I even have a soul."

"The more I think about it, the more I'm betting we do. I mean, why else would the guy ask you to sign it over to him? But the difference between you and me is, I still own mine."

"I am so screwed."

"Maybe, maybe not. We're smart guys. Maybe we can figure a way out of this. Hell, maybe we can even come out ahead."

"I'd settle for having my soul back."

"It's not gone yet."

"You know what I mean."

"Let me think on this."

2

"So did you ask him how to live forever?"

"Yeah. He said, if I can't figure it out for myself, then I don't deserve to know. But he showed me another good trick. All I have to do is concentrate, sort of like you do with the air molecules, except this is with molecules of time."

"I don't get it."

"It lets you predict the future."

"Get out of here."

"No, really. But it's a bitch. I can only look ten seconds or so ahead and it gives me a headache that makes a hangover feel good. But it's like the other thing, he said. The more I practice, the easier it'll get and the farther ahead I can see."

"So you could predict lotteries and horse races and all kinds of crap."

"I guess."

"Did you get a name from this guy?"

"He said I could call him Mr. Parker."

"Meaning, it's not really his name. That's just all he'll give you."

"I guess."

"Well, I've figured out the living forever bit."

"Bullshit."

"No, he was right. It's pretty simple, really. Here. Look at these."

"What are these?"

"Souls."

"How'd you get them?"

"Well, I figured I'd try buying them. So I went into Your Second Home and kept offering the losers drinking in there five bucks if they'd sign over their soul to me. You'd be surprised at how many people who swear they don't believe in God will balk at signing over their soul, but I got a few takers."

"Yeah, well, I wish I'd been smart enough not to sign away mine."

"Doesn't matter now. You've got these."

"I don't get how it works."

"I don't either. Not yet. But there's got to be a reason your Mr. Parker wanted your soul, and I figure this has to be it. You must be able to use the souls you acquire to prolong your own life. And if you don't die, then he doesn't get yours."

"I don't know."

"Just take them. Ask him if you can trade for yours. Only don't offer them all at once."

"I won't."

3

"So how'd it go?"

"He didn't want them. He says there's varying grades of souls. The ones you got are only worth a year or so because the people that signed them over don't really care about their lives anymore."

"He could tell that just by looking at pieces of paper?"

"Apparently. He says you need higher quality ones to buy you a decent amount of time."

"But we're on the right track."

"I suppose. But it doesn't feel right."

"What doesn't?"

"Trading people's souls like this."

"Hey, they didn't have to sign them away."

"But they didn't know."

"So what are you saying? I should give them back?"

"I don't know. It's just . . . after signing away my own, I can feel for them."

"I was just trying to help."

"I know. And I appreciate it."

"So what did he teach you today?"

"Nothing new. He just showed me some meditation techniques to make it easier for me to narrow my focus. You know, so that when I practice, it's more productive."

"Figures. He's already got you hooked."

"It's not what you're thinking. Maybe he conned me with the soul business, but the rest of what he's showing me's on the level. Here, look how hot I can make this flame."

"Jesus, it's like a tiny blowtorch."

"Cool, huh?"

"Sure, if you ever want to weld anything really, really small, I guess."

4

"Mr. Parker?"

"Yes?"

"My name's Robert Chaplin."

"Oh, yes. Peter's friend. The one who's trying to help him break his deal with the devil."

"*Are* you the devil?"

"The devil is rather a recent conceit. I'm much older than that."

"Which doesn't really answer my question."

"It's not really relevant. Was that all you wanted to know?"

"No. I . . . this stuff you're teaching Peter. Is it all just going to be parlor tricks?"

"What I've taught him, and will teach him, are hardly tricks. They are lessons that will help him to understand the underpinnings of the world. The more proficiency he gains, both in understanding the makings of the world and in manipulating them, the closer he will come to achieving the potential I see inside him."

"Unless he dies first."

"Everyone dies, Mr. Chaplin. Everything has an expiration date."

"Except for you."

"Even me. I'm long-lived, not immortal."

"So why Peter?"

"He has a bright fire in his soul. He has so much potential."

"But what's that to you?"

"I like to help people."

"By stealing their souls."

"That isn't how I'd phrase it."

"Then how would you phrase it?"

"I'm bound to help others. It's . . . part of the bargain I made."

"Of course. You had to make a bargain, too. Who'd you sell your soul to?"

"What exactly is it that you want from me, Mr. Chaplin?"

"Can you teach me?"

"Teach you what?"

"Everything."

"That depends. What can you give me in return?"

"I guess I've only got one thing you want."

"If you're referring to your soul, I'm afraid not. Even knowing you have it, does not make you value it any more than you did before you gained that knowledge."

"And Peter did? Valued his soul, I mean?"

"He did, indeed."

"He didn't believe any more than I did."

"I assume that's simply what he led you to believe. Your friend has hidden depths that it appears he never shared with you."

"Whatever. So I'm out of the loop."

"Not necessarily. Offer me the soul of someone who values what they have and perhaps we can do business."

"And once it's accepted, the contract can't be broken?"

"Not so long as both parties adhere to its conditions."

5

"I've got this weird idea, Brenda."

"What's that?"

"Well, things didn't work out so well before, did they? Between us, I mean."

"I don't blame you. Neither of us were pulling our weight. It takes two to make a relationship work."

"I know that. But I was just thinking . . . if we're really going to try to make it work this time, maybe we should, I don't know, put it all down in writing. Make it official."

"You want to get married?"

"Not this minute or anything, but that's certainly something to work toward. For now I was thinking more of a kind of contract—something to show that we're taking all of this seriously."

"A contract."

"Yeah. We each write down what we're putting into this and what we expect from the other person. We keep it simple."

"How do you think that will change things?"

"I don't know. It'll be a commitment in black and white. Something we can reread if we start to get frustrated or antsy. To remind us of how we really feel so that we don't say or do anything stupid."

"Like writing our own wedding vows."

"Sort of. Except this would be more our relationship vows."

"You're right, it is weird."

"Yeah, I thought it was. Too weird, right?"

"No. I actually like the fact that you're taking the time to think about this sort of thing."

6

"This is really nice."

"Thanks. But I can see I got a little long-winded, now that I'm reading yours."

"It's not about the length, Brenda. It's about what we mean."

"But you were able to put it so succinctly. 'If you give

me your soul, I will always honor, cherish, and respect
you.' That's beautiful."

"Thanks."

"Only why do you say 'soul' instead of 'heart'?"

"I don't know. Heart didn't seem to encompass everything that we should be giving to each other."

"You know, I never saw this side of you before."

"I've had a lot of time to reflect since we broke up. Is it
something you can sign? I can certainly sign yours."

"Hand me the pen."

7

"So? What do you think, Mr. Parker?"

"She has an extraordinary spirit. Strong and true and full
of grace."

"You can tell that just by holding the paper up to your
face and smelling it?"

"Hardly. But her essence permeates the paper. I was simply admiring its potency."

"That good, huh? Well, she always was a looker and she
kisses like you wouldn't believe—though I guess you
wouldn't be into that kind of thing."

"Let's just say I'm selective. I certainly appreciate your
bringing her to my attention."

"Well, I know the best way for you to show that appreci-
ation."

"I'm sure you do, Mr. Chaplin."

"So, do we have a deal? Her soul for what you can teach
me?"

"I think an agreement can be made."

"Great. So where do we start? With the little flame business, or can we cut right to the living forever trick?"

"Patience, please. You haven't simply dialed an 800
number."

"Hey, I delivered. I expect you to do the same."

"And so I will. But first I need you to go home and reflect on your place in the world—where you are now and where you would wish to be in, oh, let's say start with five years from now."

"What for?"

"Then, when you return to me, we will have a better understanding how to begin your education."

"That's not how it worked with Peter. You just started right in on showing him stuff."

"Indeed I did. But each of us is different, and so the paths we need to take to reach the same goal can also be very different. Peter doesn't jump into a new thing, so the best way to begin with him was by doing just that. You, on the other hand, are already an impetuous individual. So for you, we need to balance that higher energy with elements of a quieter meditative process. It all has to do with balance."

"So I just think about who I am, what I want?"

"Indeed."

"Okay. I guess I can live with that. Only tell me this. It's not all going to be this mumbo jumbo, right? You're going to show me something practical, too."

"I believe, Mr. Chaplin, that you will find that I can be the most practical of men."

8

"I can't believe you did that, man."

"Did what?"

"Tried to trade off Brenda's soul to Mr. Parker."

"Oh, please. What the hell was she doing with it?"

"You just don't get it, do you?"

"What's to get?"

"It's not about taking people's souls and using them to live longer yourself. It's about giving. It's only by helping other souls reach their full potential that your own lifetime is extended."

"Is that what Parker told you?"

"He didn't have to. I've been working on those meditative exercises he gave me and damned if I'm not starting to
see connections between everything. There's not a thing we
say or do that doesn't have repercussions. The smallest
kindness can blossom into an age of renaissance while one
cruel deed can bring down an empire."

"Jesus, did he see you coming or what?"

"Yeah, I think he did. But not the way you think. I'm
honored that he felt I already had such potential."

"And what about his not taking the souls of all those
losers I offered him because they'd only give him a year or
so more of life?"

"It's because they require too much work, Robert. There
are so many people in the world that it's better to work with
those that have the higher potential because if you can win
them over, then they'll start doing the work, too."

"Work, work—what the hell are you talking about?"

"An enlightened world where everyone takes care of
each other and the planet they live on."

"Right. That's why he was so happy when I traded him
Brenda's soul."

"You didn't trade her soul. It wasn't yours to trade."

"Bullshit. I handed it over to him, signed and delivered."

"You're missing the point. If you don't keep up your side
of the bargain, then the contract is void."

"I haven't had time to keep up my side."

"You had time enough to try to trade her soul."

"Then why was he so happy to get it?"

"He wasn't happy about that. He was happy because
she's such an advanced soul. Waking her up to her full potential will take a fraction of the time it would normally
take with others."

"Like you?"

"Sure, like me. I'm not ashamed to say I've got a ways to
go. But at least I'm on the road."

"And I'm not?"

"I don't know what you are, Robert. I guess I never did.

You're a hell of a lot darker than I could ever have guessed. I mean, what do you even care about, besides yourself?"

"Wait a minute here. If Parker's helping people, why does he need them to sign over their souls to him?"

"It's just to make a connection. A powerful connection. Yeah, it's sort of freaky when you realize that you really do have a soul and you've just signed it away. But the more you work at what he gives you, the quicker you come to understand that he couldn't possibly keep it. If he did, he wouldn't advance anymore. He wouldn't be able to help other people anymore."

"This is such a load of crap."

"Let me tell you about this thing I found, Robert. It's a void. You know, a place where none of your senses can come into play because there's nothing there for them to sense."

"Am I supposed to be listening to this?"

"There's a place like that inside each one of us. I think it's where we go when we need to mend, like when you go into a coma."

"And your point is?"

"I think you need to go there. Not just because you're hurting yourself, but because you're hurting others."

"Hey, keep back."

"I'm not going to hit you. I'm just going to touch you—here."

"Where . . . what the hell did you do? I can't see anything . . ."

"Mr. Parker says that sight goes first, hearing last."

"I'm going to kill you, you—"

"You're not going to do anything. You're not going anywhere."

"Christ, I can't feel anything. Don't do this to me, Peter."

" . . ."

"Peter."

" . . ."

"Come on. Quit screwing around."

" . . . "

"I'm not a bad guy."

" . . . "

"Peter?"

" . . . "

"Oh, Jesus. Anybody . . . ?"

TILL VOICES DROWN US

by *Tim Waggoner*

Tim Waggoner has published more than sixty stories of fantasy and horror. His most current stories can be found in the anthologies *Civil War Fantastic*, *Single White Vampire Seeks Same*, and *Bruce Coville's UFOs*. His first novel, *The Harmony Society*, is forthcoming. He teaches creative writing at Sinclair Community College in Dayton, Ohio.

THE roads were narrower than he remembered; twistier—if that was a word—and rougher. The ditches on either side of the road were overgrown with weeds, tall grass, and stalks of Queen Anne's lace. There weren't many homes out here, mostly farmhouses set back a ways from the road, fields of corn and soybeans forming green barriers between their planters and the world.

Thomas Wolfe said you can't go home again, but Michael knew that he'd got it wrong. You could go home, but who in their right mind would want to? But that was the problem: he *wasn't* in his right mind, and so he had no choice but to return to Ashton.

"I'm hearing a K word. It's a first name, I think. Kevin? Karl?"

"Could it be Clint?" The woman was soft-spoken, almost

timid, but as soon as she said the name, he knew that was it.

"Yes, Clint. He's . . ." Michael frowned. He tried to ig-nore the audience, the lights, the cameras, and the crew, and concentrate on the almost inaudible voice whispering in his head. "He's related to you, that's definite. Close. Not a brother or father. Husband. He's your husband."

Ashton was a dirt-poor town in the middle of southwest-ern Ohio farmland, equally close to the Indiana and Ken-tucky borders. Houses with flaking paint, drooping gutters, yards that always needed mowing, rusted-out cars up on blocks in the driveway, and too much junk on porches. The main employer in the town, a bicycle factory, had closed its doors when he was a boy, and those foolish enough to stay in Ashton worked what subsistence-level jobs they could find, dull-eyed fish swimming in a river of alcohol and un-fulfilled dreams, marking time until they died.

Except not everyone was content to wait for the in-evitable. The grinding despair and hopelessness of life in Ashton took their toll, and every year more than a few folks decided to give the Reaper a helping hand. Gunshots to the head were a popular choice, as was driving your car at full speed into a tree. But the most common method of commit-ting suicide in Ashton by far was jumping off the Old Mill Run Bridge into the rolling water of the Bluerush River.

He remembered an old joke from his childhood. What's the most popular sport in Ashton? Diving.

In his mind, Michael saw the image of a sunflower grow-ing in a garden. The flower was top-heavy and drooped to-ward the ground, causing the stalk to bend. He wasn't sure what the image meant—he often wasn't—but he knew it didn't matter. His aunt had taught him that.

"You don't need to understand everything the dead show you," she'd said. "You're just their mailman; all you have to do is pass the message along."

He focused his gaze on the woman, on Clint's wife.

Michael described the image of the sunflower, and the woman began to cry.

"I had a sunflower just like that in my garden. My husband teased me about how ugly it was, he . . . he used to say he was going to go out and cut it down, but of course he never did. Then one day—"

Another image came to Michael. "He took an old broom handle and used it to straighten the sunflower. He tied the stalk to the wood with a piece of twine so it would stand upright."

The woman's eyes grew wide, and she smiled in delight and disbelief. "Yes! But how could you know that?"

It was Michael's turn to smile. "Because he just told me."

He'd never had many friends growing up. To most of the other kids, he was the boy who lived outside of town in the trailer with the "old witch woman." Luckily, that reputation had kept him from getting beaten up more than once or twice, but that was about all it was good for. Ashton was a lousy place for anyone to grow up, but for someone of his abilities, the psychic atmosphere of the town was stifling and oppressive. He had no idea how his aunt endured it. When he at last reached adulthood, he joined a traveling carnival as a medium and got the hell out of Ashton. He'd returned only a handful of times since, and then only to visit his aunt on holidays.

Even though it wasn't that hot out for late June, Michael kept the windows of his BMW rolled up and the air conditioner running. He told himself it was because he didn't want to set off his hay fever, but in truth, he just didn't want to breathe the air, didn't want to fill his lungs with the smells of grass, corn, and manure. He'd spent a decade and a half purging his system of this place, and he wanted to limit his exposure to it as much as possible.

As the applause began to die down, he felt a tingling at the base of his skull. Clint, trying to get his attention. Michael redoubled his concentration, attempting to clear his mind and be open to the spirit's energy. He could feel Clint's presence grow stronger, as if the man had been standing a dozen yards away a moment ago, but now had stepped to within arm's length. He felt the man take one step closer, lean forward and whisper in his ear . . .

But instead of words, a new image appeared in his mind. A field of darkness rushing toward him, so deep, so utterly devoid of light that it pulled everything toward it; a complete, profound emptiness demanding to be filled. Then, as the blackness drew nearer—or as Michael was sucked toward it—he saw that what he had first taken for nothingness was instead something far worse. And it reached for him with a million-million grasping ebon claws.

Michael's eyes flew open and a scream tore free from his lips—a scream that might have been his, but just as easily might have belonged to a dead man named Clint. The studio lights spun in his vision, his knees buckled, and he felt himself begin to fall toward the floor.

He had a Beethoven CD playing—the "Symphony No. 9 in D minor"—the volume turned up so high he could feel the steering wheel vibrating in time with the music. But as loud as it was, the symphony couldn't drown out the whispers that tickled the inside of his ears. Whispers that grew louder and clearer with every mile he put behind him.

He knew other tricks to shut the voices out, though. Lots of them.

★ ★ ★

"You want to touch it, don't you? Go ahead; it can't hurt you, child."

Michael was six years old, and he had never touched anything dead. Not unless you counted food that had once been alive, like hamburgers and fried chicken, but Aunt Lena said that wasn't the same.

Once an animal's been killed, reduced to hunks of meat, and then cooked, the tie to its spirit has been well and truly severed. Even then, if you're sensitive enough, you sometimes catch an echo of its life when you eat it. That's why a lot of folks like us are vegetarians.

Michael looked down at the dead toad. It was tiny, little more than a baby, really. It lay on its back in the middle of the dirt path that led up to the front door of Aunt Elena's trailer. Michael was responsible for the animal's death. He'd been skipping down the path, singing the ABC song to himself, and hadn't seen the little toad. Without meaning to, he'd stepped on the poor thing, mushing its guts to one side of its belly, leaving the other side flat. The toad had writhed for half an hour before it died. Michael had watched the entire time, on the verge of tears, but also morbidly fascinated. When the toad had finally passed on, he'd gone to get his aunt. She'd know what to do with it.

He looked up at his aunt for confirmation, and she smiled, crow's-feet becoming deeper and more pronounced as she did. She was really his great-aunt, and while he didn't know exactly how old she was, she was the oldest person he knew, which as far as he was concerned meant she was pretty old.

Michael stretched his index finger toward the dead toad—he was nervous, but his finger didn't tremble, remained rock-steady—and gently touched the bulging side of its abdomen. Its skin was soft, leathery, and still warm.

His vision went gray, and he felt a small hot pinprick of pain between his eyes. He gasped, but he didn't remove his finger from the toad.

"What you're feeling is its anger," his aunt said softly. "It blames you for its death, and it's trying to get back at you the only way it knows how, by hurting you. 'Course, it's a small spirit without much power, and so it can't do much damage. Hurts less than a bee sting, doesn't it?"

Michael nodded. "I didn't mean to kill it, though. It was an accident."

"You and I know that, but the toad is just a poor, dumb animal. All it knows is that its life has been taken away and you were the one that did it."

The pain between his eyes began to grow more intense. He tried to pull his fingers away from the toad, but he couldn't. It was like he was glued to the animal.

"It's starting to hurt worse, Aunt 'Lena." He couldn't keep the fear out of his voice.

"Don't you worry. A little old toad spirit can't do you any real harm. And you can make it go away anytime you want."

"I can?"

Aunt Elena nodded. "Close your eyes and imagine that your head is covered by something. A blanket, or maybe a hat."

"How about a helmet, like the kind my army men wear?"

"That'll work fine. Now go ahead: close your eyes and imagine you're wearing a thick, green army-man helmet. A helmet so strong that nothing can get through, not even the pain that little toad ghost is sending you."

Michael did as his aunt instructed. It wasn't easy to ignore the pain between his eyes—it was starting to spread, and felt more like a headache now—but he did it, and imagined the helmet so well that he thought he could actually feel its weight on his head. Within seconds, the pain began to lessen, and soon it vanished entirely. Michael was able to withdraw his finger from the toad then.

He looked up at Aunt 'Lena and smiled. "I did it!"

She grinned, wrapped her fleshy arms around him, and gave him a hug. "You sure did, Mikey! And anytime you're pestered by a spirit that you don't want bothering you, you go ahead and imagine up your army-man helmet, and you'll be just fine. Now let's see about giving this little toad a proper burial, all right?"

★ ★ ★

Over the years, Michael had learned that his army-man helmet only worked so well. If a spirit was strong enough and determined to make itself heard, there was only so much you could do to shut it out. But the spirit-whispers that were plaguing him at the moment were primarily background noise, and the helmet image worked well enough in concert with the music. And if the whispers didn't recede entirely, at least they were muted enough to ignore.

He continued on toward Ashton.

He pulled his Beemer to a stop a dozen yards from Elena's trailer, parked, and cut the ignition. He sat behind the wheel for several moments, making himself ready. The trailer—which Elena had named Holly, for reasons that had never been clear to him—sat at the end of a dirt path not quite wide enough to be called a driveway. Its green-and-white siding was tinged with rust at the edges, and the wooden front porch, which he had built and painted over one summer between seventh and eighth grade, was weathered and seriously in need of repainting. The grass was high; it had been a while since she'd mowed, but not so high that the yard looked neglected. Trees surrounded the property on all sides, taller and thicker than he remembered. When he was a child, the trees had made the place seem cozy, safe, and protected, but when he'd become an adolescent, they'd been stifling, a cage made of brown, gray, and green. Now, they were just trees.

He took a deep breath, held it for a count of three—just as Elena had taught him—and let it out slowly. Telling himself that he felt calmer now, though in truth he didn't, he got out of the car and started for the porch. Branches swayed in the summer breeze, their leaves shusssshing against one another, the sound overlaid by birdsong and cicada-thrum. He listened for the whispers, but heard none.

It was almost as if the dead had paused in their eternal gossiping, watching and listening to see what would happen next.

He walked up the front steps and onto the porch, turned toward the screen door, half-expecting Elena to be standing there waiting for him. After all, she had to have been aware that he was coming home. But she wasn't there. He started to knock, then paused. Elena would chide him for knocking, would tell him that no matter how long he'd been away, no matter that he hadn't called in months, this was still his home, and he didn't have to knock as if he were some stranger come to sell her something.

He opened the screen door and stepped inside.

The heat hit him first. Elena hated air-conditioning, said it made the air taste wrong, but she didn't like to open the windows in summer, said the humidity made everything feel damp and caused mildew. Next came the smell, a mingled odor of cooked meals, flowers on the verge of rot, and lemon-scented furniture polish. Last, he heard the low tones of a television program drifting from the living room. A man's voice, the cadence rising and falling, almost like he was chanting. Michael couldn't make out the words, but he didn't need to. Elena only ever watched religious programs on TV, and the man was undoubtedly a televangelist.

The trailer's front door opened on a small dining room that Elena hardly ever used. The dining table was covered by framed pictures of family, the older pictures to the rear, the more recent ones in the front. In back were photos of his mom and grandparents, and Aunt Elena's husband—all long deceased. There were no pictures of his father. The man had taken off months before he was born, and had never returned to Ashton. There was a good chance he was probably dead now, too, not that Michael gave a damn. If the man's spirit ever tried to talk to him, Michael would give him the old army helmet treatment. If his father hadn't wanted anything to do with him in life, Michael sure as hell wasn't going to start a relationship with him in death.

To the left of the dining room was the kitchen, to the right the living room. Michael went right.

Elena sat in the recliner he'd bought her with money he'd saved from his first job as a professional medium when he was sixteen. He'd worked as a "spirit-reader" at the county fair one summer, though he'd told Elena that he was cleaning horse stalls at the Johnstons' farm. Elena didn't believe in using their gifts for personal gain, and while she had clearly disapproved once she'd found out where the money for her new chair had come from—and he'd suspected she'd known all along—that hadn't stopped her from accepting his gift.

He wondered how she felt about what he did now. His television show, *The Other Side,* was one of the most popular programs on cable, its ratings high enough to impress the networks, and there was serious talk of syndication. Since Michael was a cocreator of the show, that meant *mucho dinero.* And though his aunt had never said anything, he was pretty sure that in her mind, it counted as exploiting his gift for personal gain.

She sat staring at the TV. A white man in an expensive suit with a mound of blow-dried blond hair atop his head stood behind a wooden lectern, talking about the glory of serving Jesus. His face and voice exuded an overly practiced sincerity that couldn't disguise his true message: Give me money.

"Don't be so cynical," she said.

Michael smiled. As irritating as it was never to be able to hide his feelings from her, it was also comforting in its way. No one else in the world knew him as well as she did, and no one ever would.

She was thinner than when he last saw her, though not exactly a scarecrow. Her white hair was cut short and straight, the edges a bit uneven. He wondered if she'd taken to cutting her hair herself. The whites of her eyes were tinged yellow, and he wondered if that was a sign of some serious medical condition. Liver trouble? Gall bladder?

Her hands rested on the arms of the recliner, the joints of her fingers bulging from arthritis, or as she'd always pronounced it, ar-thur-itis. She wore a simple striped shirt which left her arms bare and a pair of orange shorts. Her legs were a road map of varicose veins, so thick and discolored it looked like a colony of fat, purple earthworms had burrowed beneath her skin.

She gestured toward the couch without taking her gaze from the television screen. "Go ahead and sit down. Unless you're not planning on staying."

Michael did as she ordered, having to pass between Elena and the TV to do so. He sat down, wishing he'd worn something lighter than the black shirt and slacks he had on. He'd only been inside the trailer for a few minutes, but already his skin was slick with sweat, and his clothes stuck to him like a second layer of flesh.

Time passed without either of them saying anything. Michael found himself watching the televangelist so he wouldn't have to stare at his aunt's face. Finally, after what seemed like a long time, but which Michael knew had only been moments, Elena spoke again.

"You've seen it, haven't you? The darkness."

Michael nodded.

Elena took a deep breath, held it for a three-count, just as she'd taught him to do, then released it slowly. When she was done, she turned to Michael, gave him a smile and held out her arms. "Well? Are you too big a TV star to come give your old auntie a hug?"

"So what was it? I mean, I've made contact with the other side hundreds of times, but I've never experienced anything like that before." Even now, outside in the light of the late afternoon sun, the thought of that awful darkness made him shiver and raised goose bumps on his flesh.

Elena didn't answer at first. They walked side by side, his aunt holding on to his elbow with her left hand. Her feet were covered by a pair of slippers that were hardly appropriate for outdoors, but she'd refused to put on shoes, saying they pinched her feet. They were walking through the woods, on a well-worn path that Michael knew as well as the layout of his condo back in the city, even though he hadn't set foot here in almost fifteen years. He wasn't sure where they were going. After they'd chatted for a bit, mostly small talk about nothing in particular, words designed to get them used to each other again and to stave off discussion of the real reason he'd come home, she'd suggested that they go for a little walk. Michael, without saying so directly, had hinted that maybe it was too hot out for someone of Elena's years, but she'd ignored him, and now here they were, walking in the woods, Michael fearing that his elderly aunt would have a heart attack or a stroke any minute.

At least it was cooler here than inside that oven of a trailer.

"The departed ever give you any sense of what the other side was like?" she asked.

Elena had never referred to them as *dead* or, worse yet, *ghosts*. She'd always used terms like *spirits* and *departed,* the latter always sounding to Michael as if they'd just stepped out for a quart of milk or a pack of cigarettes, and they'd be back before long.

"Sure. People ask all the time when I do readings." It was one of the most common questions he got. After someone asked if their loved one was okay on the other side, they always wanted to know what the afterlife was *really* like. "I always get a sense of peace and togetherness from . . . the departed, as if on the other side we're reunited with our loved ones that have passed over before us, and everything is all right."

He looked at his aunt. "Do *you* know what it's like? I mean, you never said much about it, but I always assumed you believed in the Christian version of heaven—angels and saints and all."

Elena smiled. "And you didn't, which is why you never asked me, isn't it?"

Michael felt himself blush. It was almost as if his aunt had told him that she'd known all along what he was doing in the bathroom with the water running so long when he was a teenager. "Well, it just never felt right to me, you know? And you always told me that I should trust my feelings."

"That I did." They walked in silence a bit before Elena went on. "I wish I could believe in the storybook version of heaven. I wish I was like most other people in the world: blind, deaf, and dumb to anything 'cept what's in front of my nose at the moment. But I'm not."

The trees began to thin, and Michael knew they were coming to the edge of the woods. He knew what lay beyond, but he didn't want to think about that just now.

"I knew you had the gift the first time I laid eyes on you as a monkey-faced little baby." She gave a snorting laugh. "Good thing you got handsomer as you grew up. After your mother . . . passed on, I made sure to teach you everything you'd need to know to be able to live with your abilities, and maybe be able to use them to help other people some day."

Was there a gentle rebuke in her last sentence? Elena had given readings for folks all her life, but she'd never charged them much, just enough to cover the cost of food, phone, and electricity, and even then she'd always had trouble paying her bills. Since leaving Ashton, Michael had become something of a celebrity, and while his cable TV show wasn't making him rich, he charged five hundred dollars for a one-on-one reading, more if the client was wealthy. Paying bills was not one of his problems.

"You taught me well, Aunt 'Lena."

"I did my best, and I think, all in all, you turned out okay." She grinned, but then sadness filled her eyes and her smile fell away. "But there are a few things I didn't tell you. Things you weren't quite ready to hear back then.

Things you may not be any more ready to hear now, but I don't have a lot of choice about telling you."

Elena's voice was soft, her tone cold and flat, and it cut through him like a blade of ice. "Like what?"

She looked away, and her eyes glazed over, as if she were focusing on something far in the distance, something only she could see.

"Well, for one thing, the dead are liars. Every last one of them."

They were past the woods and into a clearing, the waving grass almost knee-high. To the west a low wall of orange brick surrounded row upon row of small weathered gravestones. The wall was only three, three-and-half feet high, easy to climb over. Michael should know; he'd shinnied over it often while growing up. There were trees in the cemetery, oak and elm; tall, old things with thick branches and lush green leaves that gave shade and shelter to the dead, not that they needed it. Michael had the impression the trees were watching as he and 'Lena passed by. They seemed more curious than malevolent . . . and somewhat smug, as if they knew more than he did about what had drawn him home.

A gentle breeze blew from the north, and Michael detected a sound beneath the wind, something like an ocean wave breaking against a deserted beach. Deep, sonorous, more felt through the soles of the feet than heard with the ears. The dead weren't bound to their physical remains, but their bodies made effective focal points for contact, and places like this, where their cast-off shells were gathered, were the psychic equivalent of a strong telephone connection.

Aunt Elena chuckled. "Seems like they get noisier every time I walk by."

Michael smiled. "Maybe you just keep getting better at listening."

She laughed, a rich, hearty sound that could have originated in the throat of a much younger woman. "So now it's your turn to teach me, eh?" She grew suddenly serious. "Well, maybe it is. Maybe it is."

It had been years since Michael had been this near West Branch. It was a Quaker burial ground erected in 1864, and most of the folks laid to rest within its walls had been there so long that time and the elements had scoured the legends from their gravestones, rendering them anonymous. There had been only a few fresh graves dug over the last half century. In fact, the last one had belonged to his—

He cocked his head. He thought he heard something rising above the ocean noise of the endlessly whispering throng. A voice . . . loud, as if someone were desperate to get his attention.

"Hold up for a second, 'Lena." He stopped, and his aunt stopped with him. He closed his eyes and listened with a part of himself beyond his physical body.

Yes! He could hear it more clearly now. It sounded just like—

"Mother!" He released 'Lena's arm and started toward the graveyard wall.

His aunt called after him, but he paid her no heed, wasn't even sure exactly what she was saying. All he could clearly hear was his mother, calling, calling after so long a silence.

He reached the wall, climbed over easily, and set foot in the kingdom of the dead.

★ ★ ★

Michael, fifteen now, sat cross-legged on his mother's grave. The dirt had long since settled, no longer a mound around which mourners gathered with tear-puffy eyes and bowed heads, but simple, flat earth covered with grass. If it wasn't for her headstone—*Miranda Tays: Beloved Mother, She Served Her Maker Well*—there would have been no sign that she was buried here at all.

It was late fall, and only a few stubborn leaves still clung to tree branches. The rest covered the ground with a blanket of brown and red, leaves curled and dry like the husks of desiccated insects. Michael had had to brush them aside to make room to sit.

He'd learned much from his aunt over the years, so much so that she let him help with readings from time to time, and he'd even done a couple all by himself. She said he had a real knack for the work, as if he'd been born to it. But of all the spirits who'd whispered to him, first animals and then people, there was one he wanted to hear from more than anyone, one who had so far remained silent.

His mother had died when was he was only two years old, from cancer, Aunt 'Lena said, and what memories Michael had of her weren't real memories at all, just half-formed, fuzzy things constructed out of old pictures in photo albums and stories his aunt had told him. He had no true sense of his mother as a person who had given him life, taken care of him, loved him for the two years their lives had overlapped. And the one question his aunt had never been able to answer to his satisfaction was why, if he could talk to the dead, he'd never been able to talk to his mother?

Not that 'Lena didn't try to give answers. *It's like trying to see the tip of your own nose—it's just too close. Don't worry about it none. When the time is right, you'll hear from her.*

Michael was tired of waiting. As far as he was concerned, the time was now. If the dead cared at all about the living—if his mother cared at all about *him*—then today they'd make contact. And if not, he'd say to hell with being a messenger between this world and the next, and start thinking about becoming an accountant or an engineer, it didn't matter what. Any profession would do, just as long as it was boring and mundane and didn't involve talking to ghosts.

He took a breath, counted three, let it out. "Okay, Mom. Here we go."

He pressed his fingertips against the ground, digging them into the earth, shoving soil up under his fingernails. It hurt, but he ignored the pain, closed his eyes, and concentrated on breathing.

Breath is life, Aunt Elena had taught him. *To touch death, we begin with life.*

Michael imagined his fingers becoming roots, snaking down into the earth, curling through dirt and rock, down, down toward his mother's coffin. Imagined the roots touching the wood, shoots drilling through the surface, reaching inside, connecting with the empty shell his mother had left behind. A shell that might provide a touchstone between them.

He heard the dead speaking all around him, their voices the sound of dry autumn leaves rustling in a midnight wind. He sifted through the voices, searching for one in particular . . .

Mother?

A gentle breeze touched his right cheek, feeling more like warm, soft fingertips than any wind.

Then, so faint he wasn't sure if he really heard it, came a loving whisper. *It's all right, honey. Everything's okay.*

Michael stood over his mother's grave. Aunt 'Lena remained outside the cemetery, too old to climb the wall. She leaned against it, watching him, her gaze unreadable.

Two sentences. That was all his mother had ever whispered to him through the veil that separated the living and the dead. Not much, not much at all, but it had been enough. Until now, that was.

"What do you feel, Mikey?" she called to him.

He looked at the words engraved on his mother's stone, not wanting to answer. "Nothing," he said in a small, lost voice. He didn't mean that he failed to feel anything at all. Rather, he sensed a nothingness that was almost tangible, a vast unbroken stretch of blackness that was beyond such childish concepts as *shadow* and *dark* and *night* as a supernova is beyond the feeble illumination of a burning match.

And he knew he was seeing it through his mother's eyes.

"Why?" He felt tears threaten, fought to hold them back. "Why did she lie to me?"

'Lena didn't answer right away. Eventually, she said, "Remember how I told you that it's hard to contact our own loved ones because it's like trying to look at the tip of your own nose?"

His gaze still focused on his mother's headstone, he nodded.

"Well, that's true enough, as it goes. But the dead have a hard time lying directly to friends and family. That's where folks like you and me come in, Mikey. It's easier for the spirits of strangers to lie to us, to lie *through* us. But we have too strong a connection with our own departed loved ones. We can see through their lies too easily, *feel* when they aren't telling the truth, so they avoid contact with us."

He turned away from his mother's grave and walked back toward his aunt. He stopped when he reached the wall and looked deep into her eyes.

"But when you get good at talking with the dead—*too* good—none of them can lie to you anymore."

She nodded. "And that's what happened to you when you were taping your show. The man's spirit tried to lie to you so that you could pass that lie on to his wife . . . just like your mama lied to you when you were a young man. Like they *all* lie to us. To reassure us, make it easier to go on with our lives and do what we have to do."

"But in the studio, I finally saw the truth."

"Oh, yes." She reached out and touched arthritic fingers to his cheek. It felt exactly like another touch, one he'd felt here in this cemetery over half his lifetime ago. Thick, viscous tears welled in 'Lena's rheumy eyes. "You poor, poor boy."

They stood side by side on the Old Mill Run Bridge, leaning on the railing and looking down at the water rushing by beneath. The bridge was old, its wood gray and weathered. It felt soft beneath Michael's hands, as if he might sink his fingers into the wood and tear away great chunks as easily as he could pull apart a slice of stale bread. The Bluerush River wasn't living up to its name today; the water was reddish brown, a sluice of tumbling, surging liquid clay.

"It's rained quite a bit the last few weeks," 'Lena said. "The river's all stirred up."

The river's not the only thing all stirred up, Michael thought.

Trees formed a canopy over their heads, branches heavy with leaves, hanging low as if bowing under the weight of the summer heat. Michael was sweaty. His shirt clung to his back and sides, and he could feel rivulets running down his face and the back of his neck. He glanced at 'Lena. The old woman wasn't sweating at all. She kept her gaze fastened on the water, an expression of profound sadness on her face.

"This is the one place I never brought you, Michael."

Not *Mikey* this time, he noticed.

"It's time for another lesson. The last one." She sighed and something rattled in her lungs, deep and nasty. Michael thought that after this was over, he should take her to the doctor, just in case.

"This place, this bridge, is the reason why we're here, you and I. And when I say *here,* I don't mean just in Ashton. It's the reason we were put on this world and given the powers that we have." She turned and gave him a small smile. "The reason why we exist at all."

Michael stretched out his senses, tried to feel what was so special about this bridge, but beyond the ever-present whispering of the dead—which now seemed to be coming from the water flowing beneath them—he felt nothing. It was more than strange: this was a place where dozens of people had ended their lives. Despairing, feeling there was no other way out than to climb over the railing and drop into the river, letting the current take them, lungs filling with water as they embraced the final release of darkness. The bridge should've reeked of emotional turbulence and lingering suicidal thoughts, a foul psychic residue soaked deep into the wood. But there was nothing, nothing at all.

"I don't understand."

"Look down at the water," 'Lena said. Her voice was flat, toneless.

He did as she asked and saw the water had turned black. Blacker than night, blacker than sin, blacker even than death itself. It was the same darkness that he had seen in his vision back in the television studio. A darkness that was balefully alive and eternally hungry. Now he understood why he felt nothing here. Nothing—Nothing with a capital N—was all that *was* here.

As he watched, faces began to bob up from beneath the surface of the black river. Dozens, hundreds, thousands of white faces, skin bleached, eyes black holes filled with the same darkness they swam in. Mouths open wide as if shouting, but nothing came out save more maddening inaudible whispers, and try as he might, he couldn't make out what was being said. Once as a boy, Michael had seen a school of ravenous carp feeding on water insects near the bank of the river. The big, thick-scaled fish writhed and tumbled over one another, eyes cold, dead, and staring as they mindlessly fed. The faces of the dead struck him the same way, and he had an awful thought. What if their mouths were stretched wide not because they were trying to say something, but because they were *hungry?*

"I told you the dead lie, Michael. What I didn't tell you was the reason why. You know as well as I do what they tell us to pass along to the living: that the other side is a place of peace and contentment. All worries, all troubles are washed away in the passage from this world to the next.

And that's true enough, as it goes. What they don't say is that the negative emotions—all the anger, envy, lust, hatred, and dozens of others which humans haven't thought up names for yet—are carried over with them. And once those emotions are purged, they don't just vanish. Just like the spirits they were part of, those feelings are eternal. And once those emotions are free, they have to go somewhere."

Michael looked down at the river and into the deep shadows within the bleached-white eye sockets of the dead. Shadows that surged and roiled as if alive and eager to be free from the hollow prisons that held them.

"The Darkness," he said.

'Lena nodded. "The toxic waste dump of the afterlife. And it's alive, in its own way."

The bloodless faces continued to gawp like fish. And was there one face that Michael recognized? A face he hadn't seen since he was two? Maybe.

He fought to keep his voice steady. "What does it want?"

She shrugged. "What does anything want? To feed, to grow, to go on living."

One of the faces, the one that Michael thought he recognized but which he wasn't ready to acknowledge, oh no, not yet, began to rise up out of the black water, long raven hair (God, please don't let it be *her!*) trailing behind a naked, snail-flesh white body.

"'Course, what it feeds on is emotion," 'Lena said. "Negative emotion." Her voice was calm, too much so considering that the woman (*not her, not her!*) was rising upward on a fount of ebony water, white arms stretched toward them, mouth yawning open and eye sockets bubbling with living darkness. "And the dead don't have any of those feelings anymore. They got rid of them when they crossed over, so the darkness needs *us*, the living. It's too greedy to wait for us to die and feed. It wants to be fed *now*. So it comes to places like this, where the barrier between worlds is thinnest, and it pushes and pushes until it makes a tiny tear.

But that's all it needs to reach through and intensify the negative emotions of the living."

Still rising, coming closer, within a few yards now. Cracked white lips drawn into a rictus of a smile, and the hands—nails so long they were almost talons—trembled, eager, so eager . . .

'Lena went on calmly. "Ever wonder why there are some places in the world—places like Ashton—where everyone is always depressed and down on their luck? Places where people can't help taking to drink, drugs, and crime? Where they decide it's better to kill themselves than endure one more minute of the hell their lives have become?" 'Lena nodded toward the thing rising from the river. "It's the Darkness, planting seeds of itself within them, and then harvesting its crop."

Only a few yards away now. Michael could smell the stink of fetid river water on the creature's chalk-colored flesh. He couldn't take his eyes off the face that he hadn't seen in so long, a face that was in many ways as familiar to him as his own.

"The dead do their best to keep the Darkness they created at bay," 'Lena said. "They work to communicate with the living, to pass along the false message that everything is all right on the other side, that the afterlife is a beautiful place of peace and rest, where we'll be reunited with our loved ones some day. It's a lie, of course, but a beautiful, necessary one designed to give the living hope, to keep despair at bay and deny the Darkness the awful nourishment it so desperately wants."

Rising, rising ever closer . . .

"And I lied to you, too, Michael. Your mother didn't die of cancer, and she's not buried in the cemetery. I paid to have an empty coffin put into the ground, and a stone set over it so you'd believe she was there. She was like you and me, could hear the dead whisper, but she saw through their lies earlier than most, and she couldn't take it. Couldn't live with the knowledge of what truly waits for us all on the other side, and couldn't bring herself to help the dead deceive the living any more. She became depressed, convinced life had no purpose other than to feed the Darkness, and nothing I could say or do would help. In the end, she came here." 'Lena nodded toward the water below.

The fingers had drawn even with the bottom of the bridge now, and still they rose upward, clutching frantically, like the multijointed legs of some crustacean. Above the whispering of the dead in the river below, Michael could make out a high-pitched keening, as if of an infant crying to be fed.

Michael's mind was reeling. He wanted to deny what was happening, to ignore his great-aunt's words and pretend he'd never come home, never learned her final lesson. But he couldn't. Part of him accepted it, as if deep in the core of his being, he had known the truth all along. When he spoke, he was surprised at how calm he sounded.

"Have you brought me here for the same reason, 'Lena? So that I can watch you feed the Darkness the same way my mother did?"

She turned to him, surprised. "Lord, no, child! I'd never do that to you." She smiled and touched his cheek with stiff, swollen fingers. "I may be old, and I might not have much hope left in me after all these years of helping to hold off the Darkness, but I still have a little."

The crustacean fingers found the railing, closed over the wood, talons digging into its soft surface. With a last heave, the thing from the river pulled itself up until it was the same height as they were, less than a foot away from them now. Michael couldn't bring himself to look into its wet, ivory face. He wanted nothing more than to get the hell out of there, to run off the bridge and down the road, screaming until his throat bled. But he knew 'Lena wouldn't follow, and he refused to leave her alone with . . . with . . .

"What I don't have much left of, Mikey, is time. I'm sick. So full of cancer that the doctors don't see any point in trying to fight it. At my age, they figure the operation's just as liable to kill me as the sickness, and if I survive that—and it's a mighty big *if*—the chemotherapy would probably finish me off."

Still smiling she withdrew her hand from his face. "I haven't come here to surrender. I've come so that I can continue my fight in the next world." 'Lena nodded toward the one who had joined them, and Michael turned to look full upon his mother's face.

The darkness remained in her eyes, and her skin was still pale as a fish that had lived its entire life in the deepest depths of the ocean. But her lips had formed a smile now— a loving, human smile, and he knew that his mother hadn't come as an avatar of the Darkness, hadn't come to feed. She'd come as an escort.

'Lena stepped toward her niece, and Michael's mother wrapped dead arms around her. She lifted the old woman off the bridge, and then the fount of water which held her aloft began to recede, bearing them both slowly down toward the black river.

"Wait! There's still so much I need to know!"

'Lena smiled. "You'll figure it out, honey. Just remember to trust your feelings."

Their feet touched the water, began to sink. The blackness, which was already edging back toward brownish red, rose up to their knees, toward their stomachs . . . The clown-white faces of the rest of the dead dipped below the surface of the river, and the whispering that had been in Michael's ears ever since he'd got near Ashton finally fell silent.

The water was up to their chests now, closing in on their necks . . .

"What do I do now?" Now that he knew the truth, now that he knew what he had done all his life—pass messages along for the dead—had been a lie.

"What else?" 'Lena said as the water touched her chin and rose toward her mouth. "Keep hope alive. And remember that we love you."

The darkness in his mother's sockets cleared like clouds dissipating after a summer shower, and her eyes became human and blue again, just the way they were in the photo albums.

He heard a single word in his mind, whispered in a soft, gentle voice.

Yes.

And then they were gone and the river had returned to normal.

For a long, long time, Michael stood on the bridge, sweating in the June heat and watching the water pass by. Thinking.

"Can I . . . ask a question?"

She sat in the last row of the risers, a bird-thin woman in her fifties, with glasses and wispy brown hair. Behind those glasses, her eyes shone with a mix of fear and hope.

Michael gave her a reassuring nod. "You can ask anything you want."

She seemed almost embarrassed, and despite the instructions the producer always gave to the audience before taping, she kept sneaking direct glances at the camera. "Ask my brother . . . ask him what it's like where he's at." Her voice was hushed, as if she thought she were breaking some divine taboo by asking. "What it's like on the other side."

He closed his eyes to shut out the crowd, the lights, and the cameras. A vision flashed in Michael's mind. Endless, ravenous Darkness clawing at the barrier between worlds, desperate to get in, desperate to feed. But now he could see, dwarfed by the Darkness' unimaginably vast night but still very much present, tiny pinpricks of light. Billions upon billions of souls, everyone who had ever lived and died, struggling to hold the Darkness at bay, to keep it from getting at their children.

Michael opened his eyes. He knew one of the camera operators was zooming in on his face for a close-up, so he forced a smile and prayed it was convincing.

"It's wonderful."

HOMEWORK

by Esther Friesner

Esther M. Friesner is no stranger to the world of fantasy, having created, edited, and written for the *Chicks in Chainmail* series. Her son, daughter, husband, two cats, and warrior-princess hamster treat her with accordingly appropriate awe which has nothing to do with the thirty novels she has had published, the two Nebulas she has won, or the over one hundred short works she has written.

P RINCE Gallantine slowly came out of his drug-induced slumbers, his head feeling as though a thousand *suntoos* had just staged their annual mating dance on the floor of his cerebellum. The last thing he recalled was his most recent interview with Morbidius, Lord of the Ebon Empire. It had been less than fully satisfactory. Although he had been able to maintain his justly high reputation for possessing a wit as sparkling as his teeth and as smooth as his bright golden hair, Prince Gallantine had not been able to draw out Lord Morbidius as much as he'd hoped. Thus, while the Dread One had terminated their little *tête-à-tête* by stalking out of the dungeon in a huff as anticipated (brought on by Prince Gallantine's oblique reference to the sexual preferences of the Dread One's mother), he had left before revealing anything of his incipient plans for the overthrow and conquest of Prince Gallantine's own realm, Placidia Felix, to say nothing of the Lands Yonder.

Bold Prince Gallantine knew better than most that it was imperative for Lord Morbidius to 'fess up to some small scrap of preconquest information. How else might it be turned about and put to use against the Dread One after the prince's inevitable escape? An evil secret plan shared was an evil secret plan as good as thwarted, but an evil secret plan that remained a secret was thwartproof. Good hero that he was, thwarting evil was Prince Gallantine's life. He was still brooding over this thwartless turn of events (and the unsettling possibility that perhaps the Dread One was beginning to catch wise) when one of Lord Morbidius' corps of debauched eunuchs brought him his supper. It was the usual: stale bread and slimy water with a side of rat poop.

Well, that and a cookie.

"Poison?" Prince Gallantine murmured as he picked up the anomalous object. Chocolate chips glistened like maiden's tears. "No, no, it can't be. Morbidius would never kill me outright; not so soon. He's barely had the chance to taunt me, let alone subject me to a series of tortures that would break a lesser man in body and spirit. What the hell, it's food." So saying, he gobbled down the cookie (after ascertaining that those really *were* chocolate chips) and was just setting his teeth to the hunk of rock-hard bread when the dungeon began to swirl and tilt around him before finally plummeting into darkness.

He awoke to find himself shackled to the wall, which was to be expected, and to sunlight and fresh air, which was not. Lord Morbidius prided himself on ruling over keeps and castles without number, each possessed of dungeons famed for their airless, lightless, hopeless atmosphere. The only source of illumination permitted was the fitful glare of smoky torches or, in the cells of the dissident poets, the lone flame of a badly guttering candle. It was even rumored that Lord Morbidius' purchasing agents-in-the-field had commissioned artisans to manufacture candles guaranteed to burn with an especially pathetic and possibly suicide-inducing flame. Prince Gallantine would not put it past him.

But *this* place—! Shackles or no shackles, Prince Gallant had to admit he'd been in elfin palaces that were drearier. Pale buttercup-yellow walls decorated with splodges of botanical murals surrounded him, the relentlessly cheerful vista broken only by ample windows that opened onto a view of extensive rose gardens. Double doors gave onto a golden-pillared balcony where a family of chubby squirrels was enjoying a picnic lunch of acorns.

The acorns were pink. They were set out on a teensy-weensy red-checked tablecloth. There were matching napkins. It was the last straw.

"Gods of all heroic goodness, where in hell *am* I?" Prince Gallantine cried.

"'Lo," said a voice.

The prince turned his head this way and that, but could not find the source of the greeting. "Who are you?" he demanded. "Where are you? Show yourself, recreant fiend, if you're half a man!"

"'Kay."

The air before the prince's dazzled eyes shimmered. A form took shape, a form dark and sinister as the Dread One himself, provided that the Dread One had been washed in hot water and improperly dried. As Prince Gallantine stared in disbelief, a black-garbed boy of about nine years' growth materialized fully. His face was partially shadowed by a deeply belled hood, an amulet of unutterable power gleamed with a fierce blood-light from the iron chain around his neck, a demonling of hideous aspect perched upon his shoulder, and a finger of dubious cleanliness was thrust halfway up his left nostril.

"'Lo," he said again.

Prince Gallantine scowled. "Who are you?" he repeated.

The boy removed his probing finger and studied the results, then wiped it on his sable-trimmed black cloak. The hood fell back, revealing auburn hair, green eyes, and a

round, freckled face that would not have looked out of
place on any farmstead in Placidia Felix. "Count Androphagus Doomdreamer of the Raven Keep. Mom calls me
Andy."

" 'Mom'?"

The boy nodded. "Yeah. Only Uncle Morby made her
stop it. He says that Dread Ones don't have nicknames. It
makes us less dread or something. I dunno if that's true or
not. I figure that if you kill enough people and lay waste to
enough kingdoms and despoil the countryside and stuff,
you can call yourself Binky and people will still wet themselves when they hear it."

Prince Gallantine licked his upper lip slowly, digesting
what he had just heard (as well as seeking out the last few
crumbs of chocolate chip cookie. He reasoned that they
were too tiny to contain enough soporific to do him any
further harm and besides, drugged or not, chocolate was
chocolate). *So, the whispers are true,* he thought. *Much has
it been bruited about the Lands Yonder that Lord Morbidius
possesses kinfolk, even as any ordinary mortal man. This
child, then, must be his sister-son and as such the heir to all
of his dark powers. No doubt he has apprenticed him to follow in his own tainted footsteps. Apparently, I have been
drugged and brought hither much as a mother cat brings a
half-dead field mouse to her kittens, that they might hone
their hunting skills by stalking the hapless creature. Thus
Lord Morbidius must hope to give the lad a taste for human
pain and suffering by whetting his appetite with my own im-
pending torments. So be it. Perhaps this is something which
I may yet turn to my advantage. The boy is young and, as
such, impressionable. I will use this as best I may.*

"My lord," he said at last. "My lord, you speak with a
wisdom far beyond your years. Your dread uncle would do
well to heed you."

The boy's expression did not change at this flattery. In fact,
the boy's face could hardly be said to bear anything resem-
bling an expression at all, for there was nothing actually

being *expressed* by that flat-eyed stare and that gape-mouthed regard. Doormats showed more animation, road-kill more vim.

Prince Gallatine tried again: "My lord, for what dire purpose have I been brought here? What shall become of me at your all-powerful hands? Tell me, that I might tremble before you." It was pure, blatant banana oil, liberally laced with hogwash, but experience had taught Prince Gallantine that villains ate up such stuff with a spoon.

"Oh," the boy said. "I dunno. Uncle Morby said he was gonna kill you pretty soon, so I figured it wouldn't hurt nothin' if I did it."

That brought Prince Gallantine to attention. "You mean—you mean it was *your* idea to bring me here? Not Uncle Mor— Lord Morbidius's?"

"Uh-huh." In the way of ordinary children his own age, Andy crossed his eyes experimentally a couple of times while speaking, just to see if he could do it and if they really *would* freeze that way. "I mean, 'kay, so he's gonna be kinda unhappy with me when he finds out, but I don't care. I'm sick an' tired of just killin' stuff on paper."

"On paper?" Prince Gallantine echoed. He glanced down at his feet. The floor of this sunny chamber was covered with a thick carpet in summery tints with a pattern of jolly hamsters in sunbonnets. "I—I suppose that would be to prevent any blood from—from staining—" He faltered. It was difficult to speak of any means of preserving a carpet that so obviously could only be improved by bloodstains.

"Huh?" the boy said. Then: "Naaaah. That'd akshally be *fun*. For a change. Uncle Morby doesn't know about fun or else he doesn't care. He says I'm not ready to really kill anything yet, except in my stupid textbooks." He shooed the demonling from his shoulder, then clasped his hands primly before him and in a nasal singsong recited: "If you have fifty elves chained in Dungeon A and twenty dwarves shackled in Dungeon B and it takes 0.5 seconds to slit the throat of each elf and 2.5 seconds to saw through the throat

of each dwarf and the Armies of the Ineffable Effulgent
Light are battering down your stronghold's oak door (which
is five inches thick and reinforced with bands of steel) and
you have dispatched seven of your elite trollish bodyguards
to execute the prisoners using standard issue military dag-
gers, how many elves and dwarves can die before the
Armies of the Ineffable Effulgent Light burst in and spoil it
all? Include standard battering-ram-to-door-resistance ra-
tios in your calculations. Be sure to allow for the fact that
the trolls will need to fetch step stools in order to reach the
elves' throats and that it takes four trolls to hold one shackled dwarf still for long enough to have his throat cut. Show
all work."

Prince Gallantine realized that his mouth had dropped
open somewhere around the point where the boy had described the dimensions and specifics of the stronghold door.
He scarcely noticed when the demonling decided to alight
on his head. *"That's* what he has you do?" he demanded, in-
credulous. *"Examples?"*

Andy nodded. "All day. It's boring."

"You're not just whistling *Suntoo Parade,*" the prince
replied, in full agreement. The demonling gave his scalp a
vicious peck, but took flight again when the prince jangled
his shackles at it. This time it landed on top of an armoire
painted with maypole-dancing gremlins.

"Yeah. That's because he thinks I'm still just a baby."

"Clearly." Prince Gallantine's glance swept the sunny
room once more. When he blinked, he could have sworn he
felt sugar crystals crunching between his eyelids.

"So anyhow, I figure that if I had you drugged and
brought to my chambers and I killed you—after I tortured
you some and all; you know, the usual—maybe Uncle
Morby would see that I'm good enough to move on to
something a lot more interesting in my studies, you know?"
He clapped his hands and two debauched eunuchs came
waddling out of the shadows. (For there *were* some shad-

ows in the boy's room; they just happened to be a lovely pale indigo rather than the traditional murky black.)

Prince Gallantine eyed the debauched eunuchs askance. They were of first quality, being not only enormously fat but so greasy that their bald pates reminded the hero of a formal dinner where the butter was rolled into little balls. He felt certain that if he could press a finger down upon the top of the nearest debauched eunuch's head it would sink in with absolutely no resistance.

For their part, the debauched eunuchs were living up to the worst said about them, for they were cackling with unholy glee as they spread a black velvet cloth at the prince's feet and proceeded to lay out a series of metal implements upon it. Serrated edges glittered as nastily by sunlight as by smoky torchlight, as did cruelly pointed tines and keen-edged devices for . . . *scooping* things. The prince felt his throat go dry as the full horrific meaning of this display engulfed him.

"The gods defend me!" he gasped. "That's *tableware!*"

Andy squatted down at one edge of the velvet cloth and poked a grapefruit spoon until it flipped over. "Well, *duh*," he replied. "Like Uncle Morby'd ever let me get my hands on the *good* torture stuff." He selected a fish fork, his gaze shifting between the puny utensil and Prince Gallantine's massive iron thews. He bit his lip, put down the fish fork, and opted for a salad fork instead. The cackling of the debauched eunuchs reached a pitch commonly associated with psychotic poultry as the boy approached his helpless captive. The salad fork gleamed with the promise of pain.

"Look here, young man," the prince began, trying to sound reasonable. "Those are not torture devices. They're utensils. They might make an oyster on the half shell squirm, but that's about it. If you try to use them on me, you'll only be wasting your time and mine. This isn't the first time I've been a prisoner. Your ghastly uncle put a price on my head ages ago, and his filthy flunkies have been trying to collect on it ever since. Why, last year alone

I was thrown into the dungeons of Earl Plagueworthy,
Baron Somberdrear of the Sickly Marshes, and the mad
Lord Ahk-Ahk, Viceroy of Tandoori. Now *there* was a man
who knew what torture's all about!" A peculiarly fond look
touched the prince's eye, but as quickly vanished. "I have
withstood the barbarous ministrations of some of the most
direly talented torturers in all the Ebon Empire. I have been
restrained by fetters made from every substance imagin-
able, from silk to steel, including *suntoo* fur." There was
that odd *look* again. "If you want to make me suffer, then
for the sake of all the gods combined, at least use the
proper equipment. Perhaps your uncle won't let you near
his first-rate tools, but couldn't you make the effort to steal
a few second-string thumbscrews? How difficult is it to
scare up a used Wreath of Infinite Weeping in a place *this*
big? And by the four heavens, this stronghold has a library.
There are at least ten excellent sourcebooks on how to
make your own garotte, and those are just the editions that
are still in print! Do the words 'be prepared' mean *nothing*
to you?"

The boy shrugged. "I don't care. I got time. As long as
I'm torturing you, I don't have to do my real homework,
and if Uncle Morby catches me, I can show him I was
doing something constructive." He tried the points of the
salad fork against the ball of his thumb gently. Then he
tried them a bit harder. Then he attempted to stab himself in
the fleshy part of his palm. All three essays yielded the
same results, or lack thereof. Andy snorted in disgust and
flung the salad fork aside. This time he settled on a dinner
fork, though only after pausing long enough to nip a teaspoon which he hung by its breath-warmed bowl from his
nose. "*Now* you'll be sorry," he informed the prince. He
took one step forward and the teaspoon dropped.

"Oh, for—!" Prince Gallantine rolled his eyes in exas-
peration and then, with a single flex of his abounding muscles, tore his shackles from the wall. Bits of pastel-colored
plaster flew like confetti. The debauched eunuchs shrieked

and ran, but they did not get very far. Pouncing upon the place setting of doom before him, the prince nabbed a pair of butter knives and flung them after the retreating minions with such force and precision that they lodged in the soft spot at the base of the skull, killing them instantly. They fell face-forward with a massive *thud,* underscored by the tinny **doooiiiinnnnng** of the still-vibrating cutlery.

"Wow," Andy breathed. A gap-toothed grin stretched itself out from ear to ear. "Neat." His green eyes shone with a tender and adoring light as he gazed at Prince Gallantine and begged: "How'd you do that? Wouldja teach me, huh, wouldja, huh, pleasepleasepleasepleaseplease? I mean, golly, that was just so—so—so *super.* Honest. I mean . . . *wow!*"

Prince Gallantine instantly recognized the force transforming the Dread One's nephew-apprentice. It was nothing new to him. He had seen it many times, on the faces of many boys of about Andy's age when they learned that the supposedly humble wayfarer spending the night in their family's wretched cottage—often with their family's comeliest daughter—was in fact *that* Prince Gallantine of whose exploits the bards all sang. (They had better; he paid them enough for their hero-worshiping warbles, the lyrical leeches.)

Now, studying the lad's doting looks, Prince Gallantine rubbed his chin in thought as a fresh inspiration struck him. *Hmmmm. Perhaps the gods have chosen to smile upon me in sooth. Now might I readily effect the destruction of the Dread One and all the heinous abominations for which he stands. Aye, and single-handedly, what's more! No need to call upon the Resplendent Alliance, no need to pay off the legions of dwarvish mercenaries nor share the honors of conquest with those glory-hog elves. And when the bards sing about* this *little picnic, I won't even have to bribe them to get my name right. They'll get it right for free.* His grin was wide, but cold as an edge of tempered steel. *They'd better.*

He let his smile warm and soften like lard in the sun as he turned it upon Lord Morbidius' nephew-apprentice. "Son," he drawled, "would you *really* like to learn how I did that?"

The boy's head bobbed like a duckling in a whirlpool.

"Good. I could *use* an apprentice."

Andy's expression went from worshipful to wary in a flash. "Apprentice?" he repeated. "You mean like with *homework?*" He pronounced the word with a loathing that grown men usually reserved for tax collectors.

Prince Gallantine waved away the lad's mistrust, his broken shackles jangling. "Heroes don't do homework," he said. "And neither do our apprentices. Textbooks are for the forces of evil. We prefer learning-by-doing."

The boy's face brightened once more. "Yeah? Swell. When do we start?"

Prince Gallantine hunkered down to eye level and tapped the balefully glowing amulet depending from Andy's neck. It hissed at him. "We start," he said, "by sharing. That's your first lesson as my apprentice, son: Heroes always share."

Sword in hand, Prince Gallantine strode through the secret passageway linking Andy's quarters with Lord Morbidius' throne room. After the cumpulsory chipperness of the boy's chambers, the gloom and reek now surrounding the hero was almost a relief, to say nothing of the spiderwebs and the occasional human skull or rib cage crunching underfoot. In short, the secret passageway was everything a secret passageway in a Dread One's stronghold should be. Better still, it was everything Prince Gallantine had *expected* it to be. He was not a big fan of surprises.

He smiled grimly as he watched young Andy lead the way through the satisfactorily dark shadows ahead, the amulet around the boy's neck giving off a sulky scarlet light. Prince Gallantine was pleased: his new apprentice was working out perfectly. Granted, it was the first time he'd ever heard of a hero taking on an apprentice—pages, yes; squires, yes; faithful old family retainers, yes; sidekicks, *duh*—but he was willing to go with what worked at the moment.

It wasn't as if he was going to be saddled with the kid forever. As soon as he'd used Andy to effect the utter defeat and preferable destruction of Lord Morbidius, he'd hustle the kid off to the fabulous dwarven mines of Underpinning-upon-Edgewort. After all, even with Lord Morbidius annihilated, there would still be several grand battles to be fought until the Dread One's subordinates got the message that their leader wasn't going to be backing them up anymore. An epic battle for the future of Placidia Felix and all the Lands Yonder was no place for a child.

Or so he'd tell the child in question.

Prince Gallantine sucked his teeth thoughtfully, extracting the last strings of demon flesh from between his bicuspids. As a token of his unqualified devotion, Andy had turned the power of his amulet upon his own pet demonling, roasting it with a single, fiery blast of power from the glowing red jewel so that his new master might eat and refresh himself before their confrontation with Lord Morbidius. Such loyalty was a rare thing in this sorry day and age. It was almost a pity to sell the lad into captivity as a mine worker once they reached Underpinning, but the prince needed the money. (Hiring bards to sing his praises did not come cheap, and the rapacious rhymsters *would* insist on being paid by the stanza.)

But it won't be real *captivity,* he thought, seeking to salve his conscience. *It will be a valuable learning experience for the boy, a welcome respite from all those musty old textbooks Morbidius had him study, hands-on work, honest manual labor, a top-notch opportunity to get some much-needed exercise. You can't beat dwarvish mine overseers for giving a body a good workout. It'll toughen him up wonderfully, get some muscle on him.* He grinned as the ultimate comforting thought struck him: *Why, it's not* captivity; *it's a brand new* apprenticeship!

He was still basking in the glow of self-congratulation when they reached the end of the passageway, a wooden panel set into the stone wall of the stronghold's inner warren. Andy laid one hand on the planks and turned to Prince Gallantine, his eager young face painted with bloody shadows from below, cast upward by his amulet.

"'Kay, this is it," he said softly. "Uncle Morby's throne room is on the other side."

"Are you sure he'll be there?" the prince asked. As already noted, he didn't like surprises, and there was no worse surprise than bursting in upon one's unsuspecting enemy with a loud *Die, recreant fiend!* on your lips, only to discover that the recreant fiend in question was nowhere in sight. There was simply no way of making such a blunder look like something you *meant* to do.

Andy nodded. "He's always in there. He says it's the best place in the whole stronghold for brooding over the fate of his enemies, or laying evil plans, or gloating. He likes gloating. Used to be he left it sometimes, to eat and sleep, but ever since he overloaded the Heart of Helvorash and it blew up, he can't eat or sleep anymore. He says it's better this way, saves lots of time, which is 'specially useful when he gets behind in doing his paperwork."

"What's the Heart of Helvorash?" Prince Gallantine asked, nervously thumbing the hilt of the huge broadsword which his new apprentice had so considerately provided. Whenever a Dread One owned an object that was named the Random Body Part of Someplace No One Ever Heard Of, it boded ill for the forces of Good.

"Nuthin'." The boy twiddled with the chain around his neck. "Not anymore. It *was* a big ol' red rock twice my size, burning with a hellish and, um, uncanny radiance. He got it as ransom for releasing this real important demon prince he summoned and bound. He *says* he was a whole year younger'n me when he did it." The skepticism in the lad's voice was immeasurable. "Anyway, if he *did,* which he didn't, maybe it's a good thing he waited all that time until he tried to harness its power to blast you and all your armies and allies and stuff off the map, 'cause like I said, when he tried that, it blew up." He tapped the seething face of his amulet. "This is the biggest chunk that was left and it don't do much of anything, so he gave it to me. I mean, sure, it could maybe kill an elf at fifty paces, but what can't?"

"Ah. Well, that's all right, then." Self-confidence restored, the prince pushed young Andy aside and stated, "You have done passably, Apprentice. Now watch and learn." With that, he kicked open the door and sprang through.

It all came off like a charm. Lord Morbidius was taken entirely unawares, with the utmost ease. The only reason that he did not perish instantly was that his capture *was* so effortless. One minute he was standing on a *suntoo* skull, hunched over a cauldron full of something nasty, the next he was huddled on the floor with Prince Gallantine's foot on the small of his back, his face crushed to the basalt slabs. Gazing down upon his vanquished foe, the doughty hero felt a pang of disappointment.

Is that all there is? he mused. *I could slay him where he grovels, and yet— Curse it all, this is supposed to be the final showdown between Good and Evil! It ought to play itself out a* little *longer!*

Trying to save the situation, Prince Gallantine cleared his throat and declared, "So, Lord Morbidius, to this low estate have come all your wicked plots and plans for the subjection of the Free-Range Peoples! A pity that you shall not be able to hear the cheers that shall rise up from the massed armies of the Resplendent Alliance when I ride back into our main encampment with your severed head dangling from my saddlebow."

"Do not kill me, noble Prince Gallantine!" Lord Morbidius implored, thumping his forehead against the stone floor repeatedly in a gesture of abject submission. Catching sight of Andy, he cried, "Oh, my beloved nephew Androphagus, has he taken you hostage, too?"

"Naaah," said the lad. "I'm *his* apprentice now." He puffed out his chest mightily.

"What? You treacherous cur! Perfidious swine! Cursed and double-cursed and thrice-cursed be the day your slut of a mother coupled with a leprous *suntoo* and gave birth to you!" Slick as a snake, he threw off Prince Gallantine's foot and leaped up, his palms filling with crackling green fire. But when he hurled the balls of dire sorcery against the boy, the crimson-stoned amulet automatically cast up a shielding counterspell that deflected them. Lord Morbidius was knocked on his hindquarters by the rebound effect and found himself looking down the full length of Prince Gallantine's broadsword before he realized what had happened.

"Don't try that again, Morbidius," the prince drawled.

"Ha!" Andy crowed. "He better not or you'll—you'll—you'll chop off his head and—and do what you said." He was so worked up that he seemed to be having a hard time getting his words out. "You know, ride back to where the Splendid—no, wait, the *Re*splendid Alliance is waiting for us!"

"*Resplendent,*" the prince corrected him gently.

"Yeah!" The boy began to hop from one foot to the other in a way that set the prince's nerves on edge. "And they'll cheer us so loud that it'll cause a big ol' landslide and maybe kill a few horses and stuff, but—"

"There will be no landslide," Prince Gallantine said, a trifle more firmly.

"Why not?" Andy sounded cheated. "You guys are camped in the passes of the Distant Prospect Mountains, right? I mean, that's what Uncle Morby's raven-spies said. There's *always* landslides in the Distant Prospect Mountains!"

"Silly child, don't you think we know that? Those troops are merely an illusion cast by our best wizards." If the prince wanted to talk down to Andy any farther, he would have to get up on a ladder. "The main force of our armies is actually located along the banks of the Hushamuk River, with Pigeon's Hill and the Sundry Morass at our backs."

"Oh." The boy stopped bouncing, but Prince Gallantine's relief was short-lived, for he immediately began to crack his knuckles as he said, "Well, I betcha two hundred thousand warriors can cheer real loud."

Prince Gallantine gave a deprecating laugh. "If you're going to be a hero's apprentice, your first lesson must be never to use ravens as spies. They can't count worth a damn, and they can't tell the warriors from the camp followers. We have perhaps five thousand fighters in camp, though more stand ready to rush to our aid as soon as the line of signal fires from Pigeon's Hill to Thrushmeadow Parva is lit."

"Five . . . thousand," Andy repeated slowly. His fingers moved in the time-honored fashion favored by children everywhere who had been told to do the math in their heads but wouldn't. "About two hundred seventeen roadstaves from Pigeon's Hill to Thrushmeadow Parva as the raven flies . . . one signal fire every eleven . . ."

"What are you doing, lad?" Prince Gallantine asked.

"Sh!" Andy scowled and resumed his mutterings: "Two ravens to carry one bucket of water between them . . . allow for wind resistance, spillage, weather conditions . . . Got it!"

He looked at a very perplexed Prince Gallantine. Then he smiled and laid one chubby finger to the center of his amulet.

After the great Battle of the Hushamuk River, it was sung by the few surviving bards that Prince Gallantine never knew what hit him. This was not true. He knew, all right. He knew that he was hit by the same blast of pure, merciless, searing energy that had transformed a demonling into cutlets, medium-rare. Whether he had any time to *react* to this knowledge, to *apply* it to some purpose, however briefly (besides shrieking with the hideous pain of it all) remained a mystery for the ages.

It simply went to prove what he'd always said: He did *not* like surprises.

Lord Morbidius stood beside his nephew on the throne room balcony and watched with deep satisfaction the never-ending line of captives trudging down the road that led them inexorably through the black iron gates of the stronghold. Their groans and lamentations were so heart-rending that the Dread One himself deigned to smile.

"Very good, Androphagus," he said, patting the boy on the head. "Once we had the information about the siting, numbers, and communications system for the Resplendent Alliance, destroying them was easy. That was a very original plan you concocted. I think that your mother will be pleased to hear that I have decided to give you a grade of—" He fell into a short bout of contemplation before concluding: "—B-plus."

"B-plus!" Andy squealed. "B-*plus!* But I planned it all! I gained and betrayed the confidence of your archenemy! I got him to reveal all that stuff you needed to know, and then I *barbecued* him! Thanks to me, we *won!* Totally! Everything! All the marbles! The Ebon Empire's spreading out all over Placidia Felix and the Lands Yonder like a big ol' puddle of *suntoo* barf! How come all I get is a stinkin' B-*plus?*"

"Simple," his uncle replied, turning his back on the boy to return to the dismal shadows of his throne room. "You failed to show all work."

He never knew what hit him.

THE LAST GARDEN IN TIME'S WINDOW

by Dean Wesley Smith

Dean Wesley Smith has sold over twenty novels and around one hundred short stories to various magazines and anthologies. He's been a finalist for the Hugo and Nebula Awards, and has won a World Fantasy Award and a *Locus* Award. He was the editor and publisher of Pulphouse Publishing, and has just finished editing the *Star Trek* anthology *Strange New Worlds II*.

THE sun beat through the window over the sink, making the small main room of the trailer feel degrees too hot. In my memory, as far back as being a young boy, this trailer always felt hot and stuffy. In the summer, Grandma and Grandpa never opened the doors. In the winter, the gas stove just put out too much heat for the tiny eight-by-twenty trailer.

I turned and blocked the door open, then threaded my way past my grandfather's stuffed armchair to the small kitchen and forced open the window there. A faint summer breeze took some of the heat, but left the smell of my grandparents. The lingering odors of his cigars, her perfume, were embedded in every pore of the space.

It was almost as if they were still there, Grandpa in his chair, Grandma in the small kitchen behind his chair. She always did all the talking when I visited, asking me about

work, about which woman I was dating. Except for an occasional grunt or laugh, Grandpa had very seldom made a
noise or spoken an entire sentence to me.

I stood near the dark gas heater, trying not to touch anything. I didn't want to accidentally trigger a memory spell.
Dirk, my master, had told me a dozen times to be careful,
repeating it over and over right up until I got on the plane.
He didn't think my magic was ready to be used or controlled without his watchful eye. I was just an apprentice
and I should damn well remember that.

I did think about his warning, but now standing in my
grandparents' old trailer home that sat tucked back in a
shabby trailer park in Boise, Idaho, I was having trouble
caring. This was a different world, far more distant than the
thousand miles that separated me now from the world
where I learned to control my magic with Dirk in Scottsdale, Arizona.

Boise was where I grew up and where I now had to try to
understand what happened to my grandparents. Why I had
stared at two caskets side by side at the funeral today. Oh, I
knew the "how" of their death. The police said the gas
stove had finally leaked, filling the trailer and killing them
while they slept. A neighbor had noticed the smell and
called the fire department.

But I just couldn't bring myself to believe it had really
happened. Not after all these years of the two of them living in this trailer. An accident like that wasn't something
they would ever allow to happen, no matter how old they
got. Or at least that was what I wanted to believe.

After the service at their graves, I had thought about calling Dirk, asking him to come and help me, but I knew what
his answer would be. He would smile and shake his head, his
perfectly-combed hair not mussing. I could almost hear his
voice say the words, *When you are ready, you can find the
answer to their deaths. But first you must learn the control
and the discipline of your magic.*

More than likely he would have been right. I had learned

to trust the guy who looked like a golf pro in his Izod shirts and golf slacks. Dirk seemed to know everything there was to know about magic. He was rumored, among the other apprentices I was on-line with, to be one of the most powerful magicians in the world. Considering there were thousands of full magicians around the world and thousands more apprentices like me, that was saying something.

But sitting in my grandparents' old, tiny trailer, I didn't much care or want to listen. Something had taken the two most important people in my life from me, and I was going to find out what.

I stood, and without touching anything, tried to really look at the trailer around me, to see if anything was missing or out of place. One big armchair that had been my grandfather's sat in the center of the room, another smaller one on the other side of the gas stove had been Grandma's place. A tiny, blanket-covered couch under the room's one window had always been for guests. I remembered sitting on that couch a thousand times. The space was so small that half the time I had to keep my legs tucked under me to keep from kicking Grandma.

Behind Grandpa's chair was a tiny kitchen, beyond that a bathroom I could barely even turn around in, and then a bedroom taken up completely by a queen-sized bed. A closet with a few drawers was across from the bathroom and what few clothes the two of them had were still hanging there.

I hesitated before pulling the drape aside and going in to the bedroom where they had died. I still didn't understand how they could have lived like this. My single dorm room in college had had more room. Yet they never seemed to be hurting for money, and had no desire, even during the days I had worked for Microsoft and had a ton of money, to take my offer of moving them to a house. Grandma had just smiled every time I had offered, patted me on the hand, and said, "We're fine here, dear. We have more than enough room. Thank you."

So after a few years I had quit offering, then when the magic started to show itself, Dirk appeared at my door in Seattle, took me under his wing, told me that what was happening to me wasn't my imagination, or a deadly disease, and convinced me to move to Scottsdale to train and learn control. He flat-out told me that I had hidden magic talents and Microsoft was no place for me.

So I quit and went with him.

Now, six months later, a day after my thirty-fifth birthday, both my grandparents were found dead on their bed.

I took a deep breath of the stuffy air and carefully pulled aside the curtain that sheltered the small bedroom. Two indents were clear on the bed. One short and not very deep: Grandma. One a little taller and smashed into the mattress: Grandpa.

The police were not talking to me at all. The paper had said they had died of unknown causes which were under investigation. But the trailer had been open for me to come and go as I wanted. And I saw no signs of an investigation, no police tape, nothing. Clearly the police thought they died of some old-age thing and didn't care.

But to me nothing made sense. Granted they were both in their late eighties, but both were healthy and active.

I stared at the two body marks for a moment, then turned back to the front part of the trailer. If I was going to discover what killed them, I would have to start slow and move carefully and remember every ounce of magic training Dirk had given me so far.

I moved so that I stood in the middle of the tiny living room and faced my grandmother's chair. Then spelling the word "d-i-s-c-o-v-e-r," I sat down.

For me, magic always started with a tingling in my fingers that quickly ran up my hands into my head, making me so dizzy that I had to close my eyes. It was what had sent me to the Seattle hospital half a dozen times, and what Dirk said had led him to me. He told me that after a few years of practice, the "ignition effects" as he called the tingling and dizziness, would go away.

I closed my eyes as the tingling raced up my arms and into my head.

Then it was gone, much quicker than normal.

I found myself in a wonderful-smelling kitchen. I knew, intellectually, that I was actually still sitting in Grandma's chair in the trailer, but around me was a massive kitchen that was all white and stainless steel. Someone had been baking and the smell of cherry pie filled the air. Through the kitchen window I could see blue sky and pine trees.

I walked around the room, not touching anything. The place looked familiar. The table and six chairs against one wall covered by a checkered red-and-white tablecloth finally gave me the clue. This was a vastly expanded version of my grandmother's kitchen back in their old home. They had owned the home for forty years before selling it and moving into the small trailer. I could remember, as a kid, sitting at the kitchen table while Grandma baked. Clearly, my magic had brought me back to one of my own memories. This wasn't going to help me.

I opened my eyes.

As if someone had snapped off a television picture, I was back in the trailer.

I stood and moved over to Grandfather's chair. Spelling the words "d-i-s-c-o-v-e-r G-r-a-n-d-f-a-t-h-e-r," I sat. The tingling started, I closed my eyes, and this time found myself outside, in a mountain forest of pine and brush. The air was biting cold and very crisp.

Slowly I looked around, trying to take in every detail. There was nothing to see but pine trees, rocks, and brush. The air felt like morning and the sun was low on the horizon. There was a slight dew on the ground in places.

What looked like a game trail moved off down the slight hill, so I followed, moving easily through the brush and marveling at how real the discover walk felt, right down to the branches scratching my arms. This magic was still so new to me, it often surprised me.

After a hundred paces the trees thinned and I could see a 1950's pickup truck with an old camper on the back. A canvas tent was set up to one side, and three rifles were leaning against the back of the camper. A deer had been skinned and was hanging on a pole between two trees, cooling.

I knew instantly that I was in another of my own memories. The smallest gun leaning against Grandpa's old camper was mine. I got to carry it back the first time my father had let me go hunting with him and my grandparents. The deer hanging was the last one my dad shot before he died that winter in a car accident. I had never gone hunting with my grandparents again, even though they always asked me to go.

I opened my eyes, snapping the vision of that old camp away, replacing it with the hot little trailer. It almost felt good after the cool mountain air in the last memory vision.

I stood and moved outside, tying to get some fresh air. My magic clearly wasn't strong enough to overpower the memories of my own childhood. It was clear I really didn't have any choice. I was going to have to button up the trailer, get back on the plane, and go back to Scottsdale and Dirk and keep learning until I had enough skill to do this right. I had enough money to pay the rent on the space in this crummy little park, so that wasn't a problem.

But leaving was. I needed some closure, and going back wasn't going to give that to me. I needed to know why my grandparents had died. Suddenly and together, in the same bed.

The beep of my cell phone startled me. I flipped it open. "Yeah?"

"You all right, kid?" Dirk asked, his rich voice filling my mind with the image of his face. That was a phone-magic trick to give his words more power. I had worked on it a few times but didn't do it naturally yet.

"I've been better," I said.

"Come on back," Dirk said, the image of his face smiling at me in my mind. "I'm sorry about your grandparents. I'll help you get this worked out."

"I know you would," I said. "Thanks."

"The discover spells are not going to work," Dirk said, his mental image in my head frowning. "Not worth your time trying them anymore at your ability. They'll just get overwhelmed by your own memories, as you have discovered."

I felt stunned and sick to my stomach. I should have known that a powerful magician like Dirk would know everything his apprentice was doing. More than likely he knew my every thought.

"So besides coming back there, what can I do?"

"Nothing," Dirk said, his voice firm and seeming to echo in my mind. But it seemed a little too strong. Along the edges of the answer I could sense a half-truth. It was a skill I had picked up while working in corporate jobs. I tended to always know when someone wasn't telling me the entire truth. Dirk had told me it was part of my untrained magic power.

"You know that's not possible," I said. "At least not now. I need to know why this happened."

"It was an accident."

"If it was," I said, "I need to find out why. Something like this just doesn't happen to my grandparents. I was hoping my magic would help me understand."

"And it will, given time."

I stood, silent, thinking, listening to what wasn't being said more than what was. Finally, I told Dirk, "I've got one more thing to try, then I'll be back."

I snapped the phone closed before he could tell me not to do what I was thinking.

I felt very alone, as if by hanging up on him I had cut off a safety net that I needed to get through this. Or maybe that feeling was coming from the fact that my grandparents were gone. They had always been there for me, a sort of

stable, safety net of human caring and love. They had always accepted me for what I was, never judged, never criti-
cized. They had only given support and worried about me
being well fed and healthy. Right now I was missing that
support a great deal.

I stepped back up into the trailer and moved down the
short hall to the bedroom. The imprints of their bodies on
the bed seemed like ghosts to me. In this place they were
still here, yet not. This was their private place. I had no
memories in this room.

I eased along the tight space between the wall and the
bed until I stood over impression that had been Grandma's
final resting place. There was one spell I had read about on-
line, but never asked Dirk about. All the apprentices I
talked with had used it at one time or another to find people
or things. I had not.

At least not until now.

I took a deep breath, leaned down and just before touching the place on the bed where my grandma used to sleep, I
spelled the words, "f-i-n-d G-r-a-n-d-m-a."

I had no idea what a find spell would do when looking
for a dead person. More than likely I would end up at the
cemetery, but at least I had to try.

The tingling in my fingers snapped into a sharp pain in
both arms that threatened to break bones and twist my
wrists off. I snapped my eyes closed as the pain streamed
up my arms, through my shoulders, and smashed into my
head, knocking me back against the wall.

Then I found myself, the pain gone, in a beautiful rose
garden that seemed to stretch forever. A woman was kneeling, her white hair in a bandanna, clipping at a bush.

"Grandma?" I said, knowing from the back that it was
her.

She looked around, startled. "What?" She stood, dropping her clippers as she moved toward me.

It was clearly Grandma, only about twenty years younger
and looking very healthy.

"Bob!" she shouted for my grandfather as she got near me. She had a very clear look of worry on her face. The last time I had seen that worry-look directed at me was the night she told me my father had died.

From behind a row of rosebushes my grandpa stood, shook his head, then laughed. He had a lit cigar in his mouth and a twinkle in his eyes.

"Where are you right now?" Grandma asked, clear worry in her voice.

I glanced around at the garden of fantastic roses. In the distance were tree-covered mountains. The air smelled fresh and slightly warm. "I don't recognize this place."

She shook her head as my grandpa moved up and stood beside her. "No, how did you get here?" she asked as she looked me directly in the eyes. "Where is your body?"

Now I was even more confused. I hadn't told them about my magic, or why I had moved to Arizona. So how would she know I was using magic to find her? Did that knowledge come after death?

"He's in our bedroom, I'll bet," Grandpa said. "Healthy as an ox."

I looked at him and nodded. "How did you know?"

Grandma looked relieved, checking me out as if I were a side of beef.

"Your finding spell is thin and unpracticed," she said. "That's how he knew."

Grandpa laughed and nodded.

"I can see it around the edges, dear," Grandma said to me, patting my hand. "That's all right, you'll get better."

Grandpa laughed. "And only an apprentice would use a finding spell to look for a dead person. I don't want to have your headache when you get back."

I stared at him, stunned at the words he had just said. Not only were they amazing, but it was the longest sentence I had heard him speak in twenty years.

"This is the first time he has ever tried this," Dirk said.

"He doesn't know there are better, and less painful, ways of getting here."

I spun around as my master walked up behind me. He was frowning, clearly not happy. And he looked very out of place in the rose garden with his golf shirt, slacks, and polished shoes.

"Gave him a boost, huh?" Grandpa said, chewing his cigar. "Good."

"Couldn't convince him to not come looking for us, could you?" Grandma asked Dirk, smiling as my master moved over and stood beside my grandparents.

At that moment I was more confused than I had ever been in my life. Clearly, I was imagining all this in my head. I hadn't really gone and found my dead grandparents. This was just my spell going wrong and my guilt at not following Dirk's instructions clogging up the vision.

"He's your grandson," Dirk said, laughing. "What do you think?"

Grandma laughed, her voice light and carried away on the breeze.

"Well, you found them," Dirk said to me. "Now can we get back to your training?"

I stared at him, then at the smiling faces of my grandparents. Nothing was making sense at all.

"I don't think he's ready to end this visit just yet," Grandma said. "Come on, I have some cherry pie cooling."

"Ice cream?" Dirk asked.

"For you," Grandma said, "always."

The next moment the garden was gone and I found myself with them back in the massive kitchen. Grandpa moved over and sat in one of the kitchen chairs. Dirk took another, leaving me to stand in the center of the big room with my mouth open and a thousand questions all jumbled together in my head.

"Sit down, dear," Grandma said. "I know you like cherry pie."

I looked at her as she worked to cut the pie. I had watched her as a kid do the same thing, in her old kitchen.

"Okay," I said, turning to face Dirk and my grandfather. "My memory is winning again, isn't it?" Then I realized just how silly I was talking to an image I was superimposing in an old memory.

"Actually, no," Dirk said, smiling at me. "You were here just a little bit ago."

"You were?" Grandma asked, surprised. "Well, good for you."

I nodded. "I sat in your chair and did a discover spell."

She laughed. "That would explain it. I came here a lot from that chair."

"And the old hunting camp?" I asked, glancing at Grandpa.

"All yours, that one," Grandpa said.

"Actually," Dirk said, "I blocked you on that spell, trying to get you to give up and let your grandparents get settled here in peace."

I looked at my master. "You can do that from Arizona?"

With that all three of them laughed. Obviously, there was a great deal I didn't know about magic. Then, finally, I realized what Grandma had said. She had come to this kitchen from her chair in the trailer.

"You both have magic powers?" I asked as Grandma put a piece of cherry pie in front of Dirk.

"Of course," Grandma said. "You get your talents from our side of the family."

Now I understood why they had been able to live in that small trailer all those years. They had this world to come to, a cleaner, nicer version of their own past made up of memories and magic and a wonderful garden.

"Good pie, as always," Dirk said.

"You've had my grandmother's pie before?" I asked.

"In this kitchen dozens of times over the years."

Grandma eased me by the arm toward a chair at the table, then slid a piece of hot cherry pie in front of me as I sat.

"So you all have known each other?" I asked. I looked at my master. "That's how you found me in Seattle when the magic started?"

"Sure," Dirk said. "Your grandparents asked me to take you on and train you, as your grandfather did for me."

I looked in shock at my grandfather who only raised an eyebrow and then went back to eating. Dirk had been an apprentice of my grandfather? My mind was reeling.

"So have a bite to eat," Grandma said, patting my hand as she used to do when I was a young boy.

I eased a wonderful-tasting bite of cherry pie into my mouth and tried to get my thoughts in order. I still wasn't really believing that any of this was more than my mind making up what I wanted to feel and hear.

"So ask them your question, apprentice," Dirk said, "and you can get back to Arizona and back to your studies."

I looked at Dirk for a moment, trying to understand what question he meant, then it hit me. I looked at Grandma, then Grandpa. "Why did you die?"

Grandpa chuckled.

"Do we look dead to you, dear?" Grandma asked, smiling at me.

"I buried you this morning," I said, the images of those two caskets clear in my mind.

"You buried our bodies, dear," Grandma said.

"Nice funeral, too," Grandpa said, then took another bite of pie.

"We're right here, same as always," Grandma said.

"But what if this is all just part of my imagination?" I asked.

Again they all three chuckled, clearly understanding something about my question that I did not. And not understanding was making me more and more frustrated.

"Apprentice," Dirk said, "would it make a difference?"

"Yes," I said, disgusted at the question.

"Really?" Dirk said, pushing his empty pie plate away and facing me directly. Every time he did that, I knew I was in for a lesson. "When you were in Seattle, did you see your grandparents every day?"

"Of course not," I said. "But they were alive and I could—"

Dirk held up his hand for me to stop. "You could not see them or touch them, could you? They lived only in your memory when you were in Seattle. Correct?"

"But I could go see them, or call them."

"And what are you doing now, apprentice?" Dirk asked.

"Giving himself a hell of a headache," Grandpa said, then chuckled.

Dirk laughed as well.

"There is much to understand about your magic, dear," Grandma said. "And much to understand about life, both in the living and the dying. You will learn."

"I will see you in Scottsdale tomorrow," Dirk said.

With that the pain smashed through my head and I found myself slouched on my grandparents' bed. I lay there, hoping the pain would ease before I died. Slowly the pounding was replaced with a dull ache.

But it was the ache of missing the two people I had cared most about in the world. I would never again come to this trailer to talk with them, and I didn't believe in my own magic enough to really believe what I had just seen had reality to it.

I moved over into the center of the bed, so that I wouldn't be lying in either of their places. In the morning I would go back to Arizona and work with Dirk to figure out what had been real, what had been magic, and what had been a dream.

But for now I belonged here, where they had lived and died.

I closed my eyes and let my memories of them flood back in naturally.

And for the moment, that was as it should be.

FINAL EXAM

by Jane Lindskold

Jane Lindskold has both taken and given more final exams than she chooses to remember. Her current life as a full-time writer frees her from this necessity. She is the author of many novels, including *Changer*, *Legends Walking*, and *Through Wolf's Eyes*, and more than forty short stories. "Final Exam" is her fourth story featuring the Albuquerque adepts.

IT"S not easy having your entire family think you're a goof off. Then again, easy isn't really what I want or need. It's taken me—Danny Bancroft—a long time to learn that. Now that I have, though, I still have a few ghosts to lay to rest.

I was born with Talent, raw Talent, gifts so strong that they killed my mother as I was being born. It happened like this:

Prenatal me had a hole in one of the big arteries that feed the heart. When I was being born, the strain tore open that hole. My heart pumped as hard as it could, but it wasn't enough. I was dying as I was being born.

I remember it.

It felt like smothering. I'd never breathed, but that's what it felt like. I knew I couldn't get enough air.

For the first time ever, I started thinking—up till then, everything had been unfocused. I'd heard, felt, moved, swam in the warm darkness, but I didn't really think. Now I did. They weren't brilliant thoughts, more like emotion given construct. I was scared and I knew it!

That's when my Talent snapped into focus. That makes it sound like it was a separate part of me, but it wasn't. My Talent is as much a part of me as an arm or a leg. Just like an arm or leg will catch you when you're falling—sometimes even before you know you're falling—so my Talent reached out to catch me.

It pulled those artery walls together, tried to suture them, to make them hold blood. But an infant not yet born doesn't have much Power and that mending took more than I had to give. So my Talent reached out and sucked. I was still connected to my mother then. I pulled the life right out of her and into me.

I never knew my mother, but I sure knew when that warm comforting haven which had been my world went away.

They tell me that it was a miracle I survived that strange labor, for my mother was dead before I was born. The doctors had to do an emergency Caesarean, hauling me back out of the birth canal I'd already slid partway down.

My mother's death certificate gives her cause of death as heart attack. It's true. I attacked her to save my heart.

I grew up spoiled rotten.

Two years after I was born, my father married my mother's sister. Auntie Mom, as I called her, had come to take care of me when her sister died. Pictures of her and my mom at the same age show them as looking much alike. I guess it's not really surprising that my father fell in love with her.

Auntie Mom gave me at least as much love as she did her own children—my half brother and sisters. Maybe she even gave me a bit more, to make up for the fact that I wasn't completely hers. My dad lavished even more love on me, grateful that if fate had to take my mother, he hadn't lost me. I was his miracle boy, his darling. He even called me his Cupid, because of how he and Auntie Mom had got together.

To me, all that love was a stolen sweet. I knew I didn't deserve it, because I never forgot that I had killed my mother. I figured if they knew what I'd done, they'd stop loving me.

Despite this fear, unable to bear the guilt, I tried to tell them the truth, first when I was about three, again when I was ten. They didn't understand. Another attempted confession, this one when I was fifteen, got me put into counseling. The counselor was a thoughtful, gentle man. He was also one of the Talented.

An aside here.

There are all types of levels and kinds of Talent, lots of groups that initiate, rank, teach. Lately, they've got sort of affiliated, but they're not all friendly. It's like professional sports. The teams play together, agree to rules together, even set up boards to arbitrate disputes, but that doesn't mean they're not competitors.

Just like with sports, there are scouts, those who go out there and seek the Talented. One of the better ways to find them is by getting into counseling. This is because there are two things that activate Talent. One is stress. The other is adolescence—which now that I think about it is sort of a biologically programmed megastress.

Obviously, not everyone becomes Talented at adolescence, but more dormant powers awaken then than at any other time. In modern society, adolescents who get out of line—bad temper, drug use, lack of focus, whatever—are quite likely to be offered counseling, even if all that's available is some well-meaning high school guidance person.

And if those kids are lucky and their problems are

associated with awakening Talents, there will be someone pres-ent who will understand.

That's what happened to me. My counselor was a private guy, hired by my folks. Mr. Wyse had been recommended by a friend of a friend, understood kids, got into their worlds . . .

Man, did he ever!

I'd like to say that Mr. Wyse looked like Gandalf or Merlin or somebody really cool with a flowing white beard and long hair and all, but I have to be honest. He didn't.

He wasn't short—maybe a finger shy of six feet tall—but he was so enormously overweight that it always came as a shock to realize he had height as well as girth. His hair was dark, swept in a side part, left to right. Even though his eyes were kind of buried in surrounding flesh, their gaze was amazingly intense. I could never remember the color of Mr. Wyse's eyes, though. After a while, I decided he could change it at will.

If Mr. Wyse looked like anyone famous, it was Nero Wolfe, that fat detective Rex Stout created back in the early part of the twentieth century. I think Wyse knew about the resemblance and cultivated it. He'd even adopted Wolfe's habit of closing his eyes when he wanted to think hard, and pursing his lips in and out.

Now it hadn't only been my morbid-sounding attempts to confess to my mother's murder that had got me put into counseling. There had been other stuff, too. Remember how I said I was spoiled rotten? Well, the older I got, the more I thought that getting my own way was my right, not a privilege. I bullied my younger siblings until they avoided me. I acted like a pig to most of my schoolmates. Worst of all, I abused my Talent to get my way.

It's probably for the good of everyone that the prenatal strain of saving my life snapped my Talent into a form from which I couldn't alter it. If I'd been able to throw fireballs or stuff like that, someone would have been killed. As things shaped up, my first gift was altering biological functions. My second was altering moods. My third—and this one is hardest to admit—was siphoning off other people's energy. Basically, I was a psychic vampire.

This has got to be hard to believe for those of you who've met me through my friends' versions of the events we've been through together. They see me as sweet, gentle Danny—maybe a bit of an idiot when it comes to finishing college, but otherwise their leader from behind, the encouraging one. Fixer of broken ankles and healer of torn souls.

They didn't know me before. I grew up in Colorado. I came to UNM for college on Mr. Wyse's suggestion, but, wait . . . I'm getting ahead of myself.

Even without fireballs or lightning bolts, I was pretty dangerous. I could make someone's heart beat faster or their breath come up short. Stealing energy from them made them light-headed and vaguely nauseated.

Moods were harder—I think because I didn't really believe anyone other than me had feelings—but I could enhance what a person was feeling. When I was little, I enjoyed making someone laugh really hard or act silly. Later, I learned that making them angry and then having them be blamed for losing their temper could be pretty effective, too.

Then I nearly killed my brother Joel. I was going on fifteen, and maybe the shadow of my birthday—always a hard time for me—made me a bit crazy. Maybe I would have lost it anyhow. I don't know.

I'm not going into the details. That's not part of this story. Leave it that I used my Talent on Joel and after he came 'round, he blamed me. My parents probably wouldn't have believed him, but I knew I was guilty and broke down. I started sobbing that I was damned, I'd killed my mother, now I'd almost killed Joel . . .

And they sent me to Mr. Wyse.

Again, I'm going to spare you the details of therapy. Mr. Wyse laid a lot of groundwork before letting on that he knew there was something different about me. Funny thing was, he really was a good counselor, not a mere Talent scout. That made a difference—all the difference.

Thing is, the job isn't done. That's what this story is about. . . .

Winter break my third senior year. The last eight months had been hell, literally.[1] I'm not going to bother with the details since they don't matter here except in one way. I'd been through a lot, and I wasn't really in the mood for the annual inquisition.

Dad starts it, though, just as he always does.

"Joel's sending out applications to law school."

"Like that's what the world needs," I say. "Another lawyer."

Dad grins.

"There's some truth to that," he admits. Then the grin fades. "At least he's planning on graduating, though. How long do you plan to stay an undergraduate, Danny?"

"What does it matter to you?" I retort with a rudeness that would shock my friends. "It's not costing you anything."

It isn't, either. Mr. Wyse has friends who've arranged a scholarship that covers my tuition and basic expenses. I've learned to live pretty well between that and what I earn summers.

"It's not costing me anything," Dad says, "but it's costing you, Danny. It's costing you years and opportunities."

Our argument has a ritual quality, like a ballet. We've had this argument three times a year ever since I was a junior. I don't think either of us even hears the words any-

[1] See "Hell's Mark" in *Wizard Fantastic,* edited by Martin H. Greenberg, DAW 1997, and "Hell's Bane" in *Battle Magic* edited by Martin H. Greenberg and Larry Segriff, DAW 1998, for the details.

more. It doesn't do any good either—except that maybe Dad thinks he's done his job as a parent.

That afternoon I make my usual visit to Mr. Wyse. By now it's a friendly thing, not a professional thing. I drop in at his home rather than his office, slouch on a sofa rather than sit up straight in a hard-backed chair. At least I like to think of it that way. Today, I feel a difference in the air.

I can't figure it out. Mr. Wyse greets me in his usual, friendly manner, offers me a drink, sets out a tray of these wonderful gourmet cookies he and his cook make every year, leans back in his enormous custom-built chair and smiles.

We shoot the breeze for a bit. He wants to know about my friends. They're an unusual group—all magically talented in one way or another. The existence of this group in its continually mutating form is why Wyse wanted me to go to UNM. I finish telling Wyse about what happened to us that past term and he expresses suitable awe and admiration, then he asks:

"And how is Vanessa?"

"Good, I guess. She's gone to California to grad school. I haven't seen her for a while."

"And Tony?"

"In Tibet studying something—meditation, I think."

"And Ian?"

"Don't know. Last I heard he was in Africa."

"And Danny?"

I stare at him, confused, thinking for a moment that he means someone else, someone who was in the group before I joined it. Those colorless eyes pin me like a bug on a card.

"Huh?" I ask.

"And Danny?" he repeats remorselessly. "How's he?"

I try to believe he isn't doing the Dad thing. I grin and thrust the fingers of my right hand up under my hair, casu-allike.

"Well, I don't know what to do about Lucy. She's got a

big-time crush on me, but I don't think we'd work out long-term, and I don't think it'd be fair to break her heart."

"That's kind of you," Wyse says. Is there a trace of mockery in those level tones? "You're very handsome in a long-haired rock-star kind of way. The leather bomber jacket and dark colors you wear really add to the effect."

I shrug. I'd be denying what I know if I said I couldn't understand why women like how I look. I've got dark brown hair that I wear long, a bit past my shoulders. Dark eyes, dark brows—firm and strong but not really big or bushy. Good skin, thanks to sunscreen and an end to rioting hormones. A decent build—not skinny, not beefy, kinda like the eyebrows, masculine without being overbearing or threatening.

The dark clothes and leather jacket go with the look. It's easier, too, to match things when you don't overdo the color thing.

I expect him to say something about Lucy, something about girls, or my looks. Maybe that's because that's what I want him to say. What he does say shocks me in a way my arguments with my father never do.

"Inertia, Danny," Mr. Wyse says. "I wanted you to know what peace felt like—you who had fought yourself since before you saw light. You've taken it too far."

I stare at him disbelieving. He goes on.

"Your scholarship will not be renewed after this year."

"It won't?" The words tumble out before I can stop them. "But what will I do!"

"You got yourself out of the womb once," Wyse says. "I guess it's time to see if you can do it again—without exacting the same price."

That hurts. That hurts worse than hell. If I hadn't ever forgotten, I'd felt . . . I don't know what . . . forgiven?

Mr. Wyse clears his throat. For the first time in this increasingly awkward interview he looks uncomfortable.

"I'm afraid that's not all," he says. "There was a condition on your taking that scholarship."

"I don't remember any conditions," I say in increasing panic.

"The condition," he shifts, a mountain moving, "wasn't so much on you as on me. I didn't think I needed to mention it to you."

"Yeah?"

"I never expected the terms to be activated," he says and I realize with a trace of shock that he's pleading with me.

"Yeah?" I say again, but more gently.

"There are members of the board, Danny," Mr. Wyse goes on, "who insist that you haven't proved yourself sufficiently to be trusted with . . ."

He trails off. I'm getting really weirded out. This isn't like him.

"With . . ." I prompt.

"With your Talent," he says. Then he finishes in a rush. "When you came to me, you were more dangerous than you knew. The only way I could secure you the scholarship to UNM and some of the special education you've had since was to agree to place a binding on your Talent. It's rather like a posthypnotic suggestion, and if I speak the key word . . ."

He clears his throat, forces himself to meet my eyes.

"Your Talent and power will be sealed."

"Sealed?"

"Cut off. Effectively, you won't be able to do magic anymore."

I can't even argue. What he's saying is that someone wants to blind me. Maybe it would be more like having skewers thrust into my eardrums so that I couldn't hear anymore.

Involuntarily, my mouth opens in a silent scream.

"There may be a way around it," Mr. Wyse says quickly. "Not everyone agrees with the assessment of the board. Your friend Lucy's mother, for one, insists you be given a chance to prove yourself—sort of a final exam."

"And you," I ask angrily, "did you insist?"

His anguished expression is too much. I relent.

"Of course you did," I say.

I try to make light of the whole damnable thing.

"So, do I get time to study or is this a pop quiz?"

"Pop quiz," he replies, adopting my tone. "It's more like a practical than a written. Do you remember when you were tested for your initiate's rank?"

I nod.

"This will be similar. However, that time they sought to press you so hard that any and all Talents you possess would be forced to their limits by the stress. This time, you will need to survive by not using all of your Talents."

I stare at him with an inkling of what's coming.

Mr. Wyse frowns, then continues with the delicacy of someone discussing a terminal illness, "The board worries that we have no proof that under stress you will not revert to old habits."

I didn't ask what he meant. We both knew. It's dangerous letting a vampire loose—especially one that drains power rather than blood. The bloodsucker, at least, drinks in order to survive.

"So," I say, trying to make light of it, "all I need to do is get through whatever obstacle course they set up for me without using any other power than what I already have in reserve. I can deal with that."

But I wonder if I can. There'd been no such restrictions on the last test. They'd *wanted* to see everything I could do. I'd done it, too, knowing there were controls so that I wouldn't kill anyone the way I'd nearly killed Joel . . . the way I'd killed my mother.

I get to sweat for a few days while arrangements for this final exam are made. It's to be back in New Mexico, since that's where those who have been observing my training— or as some of them see it, my lack of training—in the mystical arts are located.

Mr. Wyse and I drive down there together, our excuse

being that he's going to talk to the dean and see what we can do to work out a schedule that'll let me graduate at the end of this term. My folks are so astonished that they don't even protest my leaving before Winter Break has ended.

Although Mr. Wyse doesn't share Nero Wolfe's aversion to travel—actually, I think he enjoys it, especially when he doesn't need to drive—he doesn't have a lot to say as the hours unroll the blacktop in front of us. A couple of times he comments on the weather, like wondering if we'll get through Raton Pass or if it'll be blocked with snow, but mostly he's quiet.

I glance to the side from time to time, see his lips doing pushups in and out, and keep quiet. If he's thinking that hard, I doubt it's about whether we can get the dean to accept an anthropology credit in place of a philosophy one or whether I can test out of the remaining language requirements.

The weather's not too bad, and at about eight in the evening I pull Mr. Wyse's big panel van into the parking lot of the apartment complex near campus where I have my digs. The lot is half empty, traces of snow clinging to the empty spots showing that most of the student residents haven't yet returned from holiday.

Ominously, though, several cars are clustered near my building. One has a bumper sticker that reads "My Other Car is a Broom." A second's license plate says "WZRD." A third, a beat-up little sedan, is lacking these embellishments, but looks vaguely familiar. After a moment I realize why—it's Lucy's car.

Mr. Wyse turns his pale gaze on me.

"It seems you have company," he says so dryly that I realize that this is a surprise to him, too.

"Well," I reply, determined not to show how scared I really am, "you *did* say this would be a pop quiz."

They're waiting inside my apartment. That doesn't really surprise me—after all, it's cold outside and magic can make minor obstacles like locks no obstacle at all. What surprises me is the flare of anger I feel. This violation of my space seems a prefiguring of what they plan to do to me, a casual dismissal of my rights.

I manage to keep my cool, at least on the surface, but I wouldn't be surprised if none of them are fooled. Mr. Wyse, at least, is not. He looks back over his shoulder—I'd gestured him through the door in front of me—and gives me a warning look.

I don't say anything, don't even nod, just try to summon up that sleepy calm that had been so habitual a few days before. It comes easily, maybe because this is the place where I first learned to cultivate it. As I turn to inspect my guests, I feel a lot closer to the me I like being.

My guests number five: three women, two men. One of the men I recognize right off—a slightly bent, wiry little man who affects a cane and a scruffy, completely inadequate beard. He goes by the craft name Lord Whatsis. I happen to know that his real name is the much less impressive Dicky Jones.

The other man and two of the women are strangers. The third woman—a stout, rather heavyset woman of obvious Hispanic extraction—seems familiar, but for a moment I can't place her. Then memory and car come together, and I realize who she must be. I haven't ever met her, but . . . A spontaneous grin lights my face and I thrust out my hand.

"You must be Lucy's mom," I say, folding her warm hand in mine. "She talks about you all the time. You're the *curandera,* right?"

Mrs. Sanchez smiles back at me.

"Better *curandera* than *bruja,*" she answers with a slight chuckle, automatically translating in case I don't know the Spanish terms. "Better a good witch—a healer—than a bad witch. *Sí?*"

I nod. Her words are underlaid with a musical Spanish accent, something Lucy lacks entirely. I wonder at that, filing it away as something to ask. Suddenly I'm struck by how little I've bothered to learn about people—like Lucy—

who I consider my closest friends. I've been content to know them in the context of their relationship to me, but haven't bothered to learn much about their lives beyond where we meet.

A chill twists my guts. Is this part of that failure to learn my scholarship board had detected?

I don't have time to think further. Lord Whatsis, stuffy and affected, has risen from his chair and is waiting to introduce the remaining three.

"In order to be completely fair and unbiased, this examination board was drawn from both the local area and from outside."

Mr. Wyse, still standing a few paces inside my front door, clears his throat in protest.

"Dick," he says, "I realize there's a certain advantage to taking the candidate off-balance, so I didn't say anything, but since it's clear you're not launching immediately into the test, how about giving Danny and me a moment to take off our coats and get comfortable."

Lord Whatsis frowns, but he can't deny the reasonableness of Mr. Wyse's request. There's an intermission of maybe fifteen minutes while we get settled. Someone—I'd bet anything it was Lucy's mom and maybe the guy I don't know yet—brought refreshments. I have the makings for coffee.

By the time Lord Whatsis starts again, we're all a lot more relaxed and the air in my apartment, rather than smelling stale and flat, is warm with the scent of fresh-brewed coffee and rich chocolate cake.

"This examination board," Lord Whatsis says, beginning about where he'd left off, "was drawn from both the local area and from outside. Mr. Wyse is already familiar with all of them and has agreed as to their fitness to participate in this test."

Mr. Wyse, now comfortably ensconced in the huge recliner I'd bought at a secondhand shop so he'd be comfortable when he visited (though I've got to admit it makes a great place to watch TV or read), nods around the room. He looks much happier with a thick slab of chocolate cake balanced on a plate in one hand and a mug of coffee at one elbow.

"The gentleman on your right, Danny," Lord Whatsis continues, "is Gerard Ruvola. He is visiting from Wyoming and has graciously given up part of his vacation to be part of this."

Gerard Ruvola looks exactly like my idea of a ski instructor. He's big but lean, muscular without being the least bit bulky. His fair hair might have been bright gold once, but is now faded to a shade somewhere between blond and white. As Lord Whatsis finishes speaking, Ruvola thrusts out a long-fingered hand.

"Call me Gerry," he says.

"Sitting beside Gerry," Lord Whatsis says, clearly not liking the informality, "is a new resident to our area. She is called Moonshine Yarrow."

Moonshine Yarrow—no way that's her real name—looks a whole lot less flaky than her craft name might indicate. She's of medium height, neither old nor young. Her silver hair is cropped in that short, almost mannish cut that it seems about half the women I've seen get into when they get older. I'd bet anything that when Moonshine Yarrow was young her hair flowed down past the middle of her back and she wore tie-dye.

She doesn't offer me her hand, but her nod is polite and correct, not warm, but not cold either. I settle for a friendly bob of my head, not a bow, a polite acknowledgment.

"Completing the circle," Lord Whatsis says and something in his tone says that even his pomposity is impressed, "is Indira Yansi. Like Gerry Ruvola, she's visiting from out of state."

Indira Yansi is the perfect movie Indian—not like Native American—like from the continent. She's wearing a red sari embroidered with the colors of flame and even has a caste mark on her forehead. I can't come close to guessing her age. Her long hair, swept up into some complicated knot, is jet black, but her eyes hold wisdom that wasn't learned over any short period of time.

I don't look for Indira Yansi to put out a hand, but offer a deep bow so automatically that I don't even feel weird about it. As I'm rising from it, I hear the ringing of bangles and see her slim brown hand is extended toward me.

She smiles.

"Such old-fashioned manners," she says and her voice has that wonderful music that is British English transformed by ears that hear all the vowels slightly differently than they're heard anywhere else.

I don't have time to ponder this, for when her fingers touch mine, the world as I know it swirls and is transformed. I have neither time nor focus to think about what is happening to me, certainly no time to wonder or analyze. All I can do is react, and react I do.

A field filled with wildflowers, a stream running down one edge spreading into a beaver pond overflowing at the dam. Someone is sprawled on the dam, hung up along with the bits of drifting bracken and trash.

Face up, though, face up, and I wade out into water so cold that it neuters me and immediately removes my feet from consideration. Stumbling, I haul the person—a really ugly mountain-man type—onto the bank. He's breathing, barely, and I use artificial respiration first, but nothing in the modern medical kit is going to warm him in time.

The meadow's damp, anyhow, I don't have anything with which I could kindle a fire. There's a fire in me, though, and I tap it, channel the heat into the man, feel satisfaction as color flows back into that ugly face under that untrimmed grizzled beard.

A suburban shopping mall, the parking lot in the evening. A boy right on the edge of being a man. He's lying on the ground, his leg crushed and bleeding. A car has backed over it and the driver is standing to one side alternately making panicked excuses—"God, I didn't see him! I didn't see him!"—and shaking the cell phone he holds next to one ear as if he can make someone answer his call faster.

I can see that even if his 911 call goes through in record time, it's going to be too late for the boy. Craft rules, drilled into us until we're ready to vomit, say that you don't use your Talent where anyone can see you, where anyone will know. If I do, I'm destined for review, for censure, maybe some huge penalty. If I don't, this boy is going to die.

I kneel down and wrap my fingers around that bloody mess, willing the veins and arteries to mend, the worst of the fractures to close. Energy flows out of me even as the blood does out of the boy. Still, I can feel my Talent working. He'll make it.

If I'm lucky, they'll say it was a miracle.

That same parking lot. Even in my vague, dream state I feel slightly confused, like someone has made a mistake.

I'm coming out of the mall, my arms full of packages. In the back of my mind I'm aware that it's late and the place is pretty empty. I'm relieved when I hear the tapping of hard-soled shoes behind me and see a man walking crisply toward his Mercedes Benz. I turn away to where my own car is parked.

Out of the corner of my eye I see a shadow loom silently from behind one of the concrete pylons, a lithe figure, hand raised to strike, but not at me, at the man with the Mercedes. The mugger misjudges something out of my sight. Maybe he slips in pooled oil or water, but his blow falls short and his momentum brings him down onto the ground.

The man backs his Mercedes over the mugger's leg. The boy's leg is crushed. I run over, drawn by the screams as if by an unbreakable nylon cord. As I slide to the pavement next to the boy, I see his mugger's weapon, a tire iron. If he'd hit, he'd have killed the man. For what? An expensive car, maybe?

I kneel, thinking of the risk I'm taking, wondering if this nasty, vicious creature—this weasel in human form—is worth it. Then I wrap my hands around his leg, willing the injury away, feeling my energy drain from me like it's flowing down a drain, wondering all the while if I'm doing the right thing.

It's dark, perfectly dark. Wet, close, and warm. A contradictory sense of silence and noise. My ears feel closed, like when you fold the lobes to plug them, but I'm still aware of noise, a rhythmic beating—lub-dub, lub-dub—and a gurgling, and other sounds not so easy to define, some close, some muffled.

I'm being crushed. My head is being squashed so hard that my skull is bending. My neck is scrunched and my chin is thrust into my chest. Forced by unseen pressures, my shoulders are twisted to fit into an opening that is too tight.

I stick in place and my panicked heart beats rapidly. I have an uncanny awareness of my own innards—like they're all I really know and all I have ever known. With that awareness I realize that something has burst a leak.

I'm being crushed, but this time from inside. A faint trickle of life is being fed to me from my center, but what I need to carry that life through me is broken.

Something within me stirs. It's a part of me that's been there, but, like so much of me, has never been used. It shifts, moving along my interior landscape, trying to fix what's broken.

It almost succeeds, doesn't have enough energy. I reach back through me, to my center, to that point where life trickles into me and pools, unable to feed my dying system because the way into my heart is broken. I tap the pool. There isn't enough here. Enough to restore some energy, not enough to mend the broken part.

There's more energy there, through that link. I course along it, begin to suck . . .

* * *

A frozen moment. I'm two Dannys, the dying baby, the twenty-four-year-old. For the first time since Indira offered me her slender hand, I am aware that this is a test.

Yet it isn't a test, not only. If I refuse to save that baby, I could die for real. That happens in situations like this. The body doesn't know what's a hallucination. To the body, this is all too real.

I don't want to die, but Danny-now realizes what Danny-then had not. Just because I have the ability, it's not right to steal life to preserve my own.

"What about self-defense?" something in me argues.

"Who's attacking?" I respond. "That pain-racked young woman who thinks that in a few minutes the pain will have vanished and she'll hold her baby in her arms? Is she attacking?"

"She'd want me to live," that other part argues. "Mothers always want their babies to live."

"We're losing him! We're losing him!"

I don't really understand the words, but I understand the panic. Life is there, right on the other side of the umbilical cord.

This time, I don't reach up it. This time, I die.

"We're losing him! We're losing him!"

It's Mr. Wyse's voice. I hear a crash as an end table goes over, feel a splash of coffee lukewarm against my cheek. From all sides there's a confused babble of voices, cutting through it all, a thin, wailing chant.

Someone is pounding on my chest. Even in my pain, I realize that mere CPR isn't going to be enough. Then a hand, impossibly hot, grasps my wrist. I feel raw energy in that touch, even recognize the technique. It's a *curandera* one that Lucy has often borrowed. Mrs. Sanchez is trying to feed me energy, trying to jump-start a heart that believes it has died.

Like the CPR, it isn't going to be enough. My Talent clamors to snake up through that warm contact, to borrow more power. Mrs. Sanchez is stronger than my mother. She can spare the power. She's trying to bring me back. Is there anything wrong with helping her?

I don't know, but I don't want to take the risk. Once again, I die.

Death has many faces. There's that classic, the cowled skeleton. There's a cute girl with Egyptian eyes. There's a pale woman in evening dress, a crocodile monster with dripping fangs, a withered old man with a ragged beard, a woman with four arms, infinite others. The faces and forms buzz past, like the images on playing cards barely glimpsed when you shuffle.

When the shuffling stops, Death has my face. I always knew he did. After all, didn't my life begun with a death?

Danny-Death leans back against a wall and studies me. He's wearing my leather jacket, but then, so am I. His hands are thrust into the pockets. Mine are resting limply in my lap.

"Want to go back?" he asks.

I don't need to ask where. I know. He's offering me life.

"Sure," I say with a casualness I don't feel.

"You'll need to abide by the rules I set," Danny-Death says, "and sometimes do my bidding. Not everyone can be saved. Hard as it is for the living to believe, sometimes death is a mercy."

I nod. I like the idea of rules. I can guess what form they might take. Heal those you can if you can do it without harm to themselves or to others. Soothe those who are in crisis. Maybe borrow a little power, but only when you aren't going to cause more harm. That last one seems a bit ethically gray, but I'm sure I can learn the refinements.

"Name your rules," I say.

Death smiles my own sleepy smile.

"No rules but the one," he says, "and that's not a rule,

only a reminder. Remember death isn't the worst thing that can happen, and use your gifts to sustain the living when you can't save the dying."

"That's it?" I ask, appalled. "I want . . ."

"More," Death interrupts. "I know, but you can't have more. The Talent is yours; so is its guidance. You can learn from others, but ultimately the decisions—as with the Talent itself—belong to you alone. Still want to live?"

For a moment I'm not at all certain. Dying was terrifying, but it seems a whole lot easier than facing a life filled with decisions—like coasting along in college is a whole lot easier than graduating. . . .

"Sure." I manage a grin. "I'll give it a try."

"He's coming around!"

The voice is Gerry Ruvola's, and the joy and relief in it is so great that I feel myself tearing up. The hands that have been thumping on my chest stop their rhythm. A warm ear surrounded by silky hair presses against my chest. I don't need the spicy scent of some exotic perfume to tell me that it's Indira Yansi.

"Heart rate is normal once more," she says, those sultry accents making her clinical pronouncement sound like a spell.

"And his life energy is growing stronger," say the very different accents of Mrs. Sanchez. "Thank God!"

They lift me up onto the sofa then, spoon hot milk into me, take turns watching me. One at a time they file off into my study. I don't need to be told that Lord Whatsis is in there along with Mr. Wyse, reviewing my test results.

I'm not really surprised when Lord Whatsis comes out and announces, almost more to the others than to me, that I've passed. He leaves immediately afterward.

The others depart over the next half hour or so, each stopping to chat for a bit. None are as cool as Lord Whatsis, though their moods vary from guilty relief that I pulled through (Moonshine Yarrow) to a sort of bluff welcome to the club manner (Gerry Ruvola). Mrs. Sanchez is the last to go, and when I ask if I can come visit her and maybe learn something of *curandera* ways, she smiles a warm welcome.

"I will make enchiladas," she promises. "And Lucia will be so glad to see you."

There's something so knowing in her laughing brown eyes that I have the grace to blush.

One thing really bothers me, though. Each of the board members had told me what part he or she had in designing the tests. Not one of them had admitted to coming up with the Death-thing, even though it had been the most decisive test from my point of view.

I look over at Mr. Wyse who, now that I'm comfortable, has settled into the lounge chair again, a fresh cup of coffee and a new slice of cake near at hand.

"So what was your part?" I ask. "I know that Gerry was responsible for the drowning mountain man and that Lord Whatsis, Moonshine Yarrow, and Indira Yansi collaborated on the two-part mall story. I was surprised to learn that Mrs. Sanchez came up with the flashback—that was brutal."

"Healers often need to be brutal," Mr. Wyse says. "To answer your question, I didn't design any of the test. I was the moderator only. How could I be more? You have been in my charge for ten years now. I am hardly unbiased."

I stare at him, but there's no guile in those pale eyes, no deception in that smooth round face.

"Oh, my God," I say. "I really died."

Mr. Wyse stares at me, but I don't have any answers for him, just as Death had no answers for me.

THE SORCERER'S
APPRENTICE'S APPRENTICE

by David Bischoff

David Bischoff has been a professional writer now for twenty-five years, and the number of his books is nearing the century mark. He has written teleplays and nonfiction and has recently been called "the best wrestling writer in the world" by the *Washington Post* for his article work for *Rampage Magazine*. His new novel is *Philip K. Dick High*. His new story collection is *Tripping the Dark Fantastic*. He can be reached at: davebisch@sff.net

EXCRETION is the better part of valor.

I can hear the Ye Olde Farte bellowing that corny old line, clear as a bell down all these years. He'd take a drink out of his tankard, the suds would run down his gray and greasy beard and he'd bellow in that baritone and wake up all the roosters within earshot of the tavern. Ye Gods, the bastard could get drunk, Sir Harry Springraff. He taught me how to drink, eat, cheat, beat the retreat, and be merry.

Aye—get that spelling right there, Grompole, you lice-ridden dung-priest and take care not to spill that damned ink again. I'm trying to write me memoirs, not paint the solar floor black.

Where was I? Oh, right. Springraff. Yes, and I suppose I should just take the recollections as they roll, because at my creaky age you take what you get, Grompole—and if you want to see another wedge of wormcheese and bottle of wortwine, you'd best scribble this tale down correctly. Can't do damned much in my dotage, but I do enjoy taking out my royal execution ax, and it takes my shaking hands a few whacks to hit the neck . . .

Excretion! Aye, and this story of I, Vincemole White-viper, and Harry Springraff and how we plumbed the depths of Beyond and I lost what little innocence I had left to me.

So, yes! That better part of valor, excretion. This story starts with that fundamental product.

No . . . not the Harry saying it.

Harry in the latrine, making it.

"Zounds!" said Sir Harry.

"Are you all right, m'lord?" I said, obsequious little cur as usual. Springraff enjoyed these little niceties, even though he knew as well as I they were as packed with heated air as his own to superiors.

"Just freezin' my arse off. Hand me another wad."

I had a pile of daintily scribbled manuscript, complete with monkish illuminations on their margins. I crumpled one up and handed it through a window in the latrine to m'lord to aid him in his nether wipes.

There was a long silence.

"Zounds!" The bellow shook the wooden rafters of the outhouse.

"Another, m'lord," I said, teeth chattering. I was starting to feel like handing him a leaf of the prickly-pine trees growing behind the inn.

The door banged open. Sir Harry billowed out, surrounded by winds of less than glory. He clenched the manuscript page I'd just handed him and waved it toward the heavens as though in praise. "Ah ha! Viper, we shed misfortune!"

I held my nose and grimaced.

Of course we had to depart the inn under the cloak of night, for we owed a week's worth of back rent to say nothing of Sir Harry's jug fees. However, Sir Harry was nothing but smiles and flashing teeth and comparative sobriety.

"What is it?" I had asked in a nasal voice as I backed away from the malignant outhouse.

"Prime pickings, Vincey Viper. An ancient doddering sorcerer lives some hundred leagues away in a dilapidated manse filled with treasure," said Sir Harry, thumping the vellum with a forefinger.

"And you know, Vincey, I am a mongoose around sorcerers. A mongoose!"

I confess my own bowels felt a little loose at these words, for I'd heard many a dread tale about sorcerers' wrath, and those that I'd experienced had not left me with feelings of warmth and love. In fact, I rather loathed sorcerers—a feeling that had not diminished. However, in truth, we had no money and I had not allied myself to this thief and cutpurse to learn how to sit in a tavern all day and guzzle brew. It would seem that the next phase of my lessons were dawning.

We found a carriage in a livery outside of town which I stole with the burglary skills I'd learned the year before. Sir Harry boarded it like royalty and thumped into the back seat, immediately blessing me with his snores as we pulled off into the night toward the Southwestern Road. There were two close calls with whickersnipes along the way, but say this about Sir Harry, lazy as he is, when in a jam, he can toss knives or slash a sword better than any man I'd seen before. No better way to distract whickersnipes than to disembowel one and then send it back to its fellows to devour. A few changes of carriages later (and a gift of the last carriage to a final lucky livery) and we were in the town

mentioned in the manuscript, one Ogreton. Sir Harry and I
took lodgings at the local inn, The Plucked Rodent. Sir
Harry employed his stately airs and Brick-in-the-Box scam
to win the innkeeper over, and we were soon at our
trenchers with a goodly amount of princely honey air and
goose stew, relaxing from the journey.

"A day or two of bed rest for *moi,* Vincey, I think," said
Sir Harry, mopping up a puddle of succulent grease with a
bit of bread. "Nothing better to calm the nerves after a long
journey. Meantime, you might employ some of the skills I
have taught you to inquire about a certain manse near the
Hellmouth Mountains."

I was happy for the rest but not happy about the name.
Hellmouth Mountains? Springraff had not used that name
before, but having glimpsed the jagged peaks and dark
foreboding shadows of that mountain range as we neared
this town, I could not argue with the appellation. Nor did
the distant black clouds, nor the thunder and lightning
grumbling and spitting like an angry demon. Nor the smell
of dead leaves and touch of premature winter.

All this could have been a sunny day near a mild lake for
all of Sir Harry's concern. He was simply principally interested in diving inside a tavern's keg. And he was well into
one, as it happened, when who should make an appearance
but none other than our sorcerer—along with that sorcerer's
apprentice—making themselves known in a most magical,
but alas, startling way that caused Sir Harry to nearly choke
and his moon of a face to go purple as cheap wine.

Have I spoken yet of Sir Harry's appearance? Perhaps,
perhaps not. Nevertheless, I should, as just considering him
brings back those long lost days, and as I think of that
moon face, I see the scene better. The Sir Harry Springraff I
knew then was a tall, round bluff man with long curly hair
that he took care to wash and groom even when the rest of
him was unbathed and stained with food and drink. He was
fat, but he was strong, too, as though for all his wasted days
somehow he still got in enough adventure to exercise

him—usually running away. He wore long leather boots that it was my chore, as apprentice, to black and buff to a shine, and he wore a uniform of the Northern Hussars, not because he was particularly proud of his days belonging to their number but because he liked the epaulets, the shiny buttons, the flummery. A large leather hat he wore was made to hold a feather. Sometimes it did. Sometimes it did not. Now, as it straddled the oaken table where we sat, it did not as the ostrich plume it had sprouted had been lost in the tussle with those whickersnipes on the Southwestern Road.

It was upon this grand hat that Sir Harry spewed his mouthful of ale. Fortunately, I was not eating or drinking, but to tell you the truth, with the event, I was looking not to vomit up the victuals of which I had just partaken.

We had not noticed the sorcerer and his apprentice when they entered. After all, it being the dinner hour, many locals and travelers had entered and were enjoying the repast with us.

Actually, come to think of it, that was not entirely true. I had noticed the apprentice, for she was a beautiful young girl and though only age fourteen, what Harry hadn't taught me about attractive females I sensed with the baser parts of my nature which even then already offered a wide arena.

She had long corn-silk hair, immaculately combed and aflow down perfect shoulders, bowing a bit over comely breasts, and framing a soft and perfect complexion, a perfect home for azure eyes, full mouth, and a diminutive nose. It was I who first noted the beginning of the events that nearly sent me straight to hell.

The man she was with seemed old and bent and wore a dark hood and robe, so I could not see his features. The two had taken seats so that I had no view of the old man, but saw enough of the girl to keep my interest piqued. They were supping and speaking in quiet voices when a drunk approached them, weaving and slopping a goblet of brandy. I did not hear the discourse, but I did notice that the drunk leered at the girl as coarsely as did my heart. He wobbled and hovered and wobbled and hovered for some time and then he made a grab for the girl's beautiful breasts. She shrieked and pushed him away, prompting M'Lord Harry's attention—

Then the man in the robe hoisted a wizened finger, aimed it at the man—and let forth a blast of dazzly white energy that crackled and cracked like a flaming whip. The bolt bored straight through the man's cuirass, through his chest, and out his back. The drunk stood there for a moment with a hole so big in him I could see through to the wall—then he keeled over leaving only a ghost of smoke in his wake and the rapidly spreading smell of charred flesh and magic.

I turned away, the image of the mage-blasted spine stump and cauterized heart half burned into my eyes. I looked up to Sir Harry—and he was grinning.

"I believe, my friend, that we have found our sorcerer," Sir Harry took another drink while I digested this information and looked back at the scene of destruction. The man in the cowl barked a quick order to his beautiful assistant, and they immediately settled back to finish their supper, the man speaking urgently to the girl in soft tones. The room returned to its general conversational hum while the inn-keep and a barman pulled the dead drunk off the floor and dragged him outside.

I could not eat or drink. I could only think, *This is the individual who is going to provide us with treasure.* The thought made me so frightened I wanted to run up to my room and take to my bed—but I saw again the beautiful face of the girl and again I was transfixed.

"Hmm. You like that lass, eh?"

I sighed. I turned back to the mug of ale, which I sipped. "She has beauty and grace, Sir Harry. She is angelic."

"Pah! The sap in you sings pretty songs. She's just a woman, no better or worse than any other—with a fetching face and form perhaps. You're a young strap though, Vincey. You'll come to understand soon enough." I saw dazzles of thoughts dancing in his eyes. "But I see she is very young. And you, Viper, you are not without your charm."

Now, Grompole, you must understand—was up to dastardly deeds already at age fourteen—but I was still wet behind the ears at that time and my experience with women had been limited to the tramps and whores that hung about Sir Harry and diddled with me from time to time for nothing. The sight of such astonishing beauty made me quite weak about the knees and between the ears.

"What! Sir Harry, I could never approach such a fair maiden without falling on my face with clumsiness!"

The dazzles in Sir Harry's eyes paraded into a calculation, procured a sum. "Oh, you are filled with inspiration, sirrah. We must act fast, however, before they take their leave . . . and Vincemole . . . please do not take these next moments personally."

"Pardon—" I began, but before I could say one more word, Sir Harry slapped me across the face. I was hurled back out of my chair, and I rolled arse over elbow onto the floor.

"Knave!" bellowed Sir Harry. "Scoundrel!"

My lord got up and bellied toward me. He bent over and he hoisted me up and put his face to mine, his voice trumpeting all over the room so that not one ear could have ignored it.

"You'll listen to me and take orders, you pile of worthless skeecrunk's dung." He dragged me a few yards. "And I'll get some honor and craft and intelligence into you if I have to kick it up your bum!"

Thereupon, Sir Harry turned my dazed self around, bent me over in a particular direction and kicked me in the backside with great power. I was still in a state of shock, and the added impact sent me deeper. The next thing I knew I was windmilling forward, trying to keep my balance—and then, the next moment, I was crashing into a wooden table. Plates of stew and containers of drink dashed all about, but mostly onto me. I was flung over the table and onto the ground, where I lay on my back, staring up mutely, gasping. I found myself staring up into a dark cowl and into the red eyes of a bald man who looked none too happy about all this. It was when I recognized him as the sorcerer who had just tunneled a wide channel in the drunken pest that I started to beg.

"Oh, sir! Don't blast me! I'm so sorry. Please accept my ardent apologies!"

"Uncoordinated sprout!" grumbled the sorcerer, squinting down at me through his dark and wrinkled face.

"Bah!" crowed Sir Harry. "Apologies, apologies. Send him to hell if you like, Sir Magician—but take my word, he's not worth the effort."

The sorcerer sniffed. "Good help is hard to find." He seemed to be glowering toward the young girl.

"Aye. Here—let me take you to the barman. We'll clean you off, I'll buy you a drink—and get you a fresh plate of stew."

The sorcerer nodded slowly. "You are lucky to have a good-hearted master, young worm."

With that, he lifted his robe like a dainty skirt and followed the friendly face of M'Lord Sir Harry Springgraff, whose Hail and Well Met Demeanor always put men and women and even sorcerers at ease.

I groaned and tried to get up, even as the rest of the room, laughing derisively, went about their business.

"Are you all right?"

I blinked. It was the beautiful girl, kneeling beside me. This close I could see that she was a few years older than me, perhaps eighteen, wearing young womanhood perfectly on her chest and hips. This close I could also smell her— cherry blossoms and rose hips and ginger and femininity— and her beauty and warm eyes were so intense I could barely breathe.

"Not really. Bit winded, I confess," I said, and I realized

that Harry's blows had put me in that respiratory dilemma—not my new friend.

"Here. Let me help you up."

I took her hand and managed to get to my feet.

"I'm drinking ginger beer—very bracing. Would you like some?"

She held a glass forward to me that she'd managed to save from my plunge. "Thank you."

I sipped it.

"You have a harsh master—just as I do," she stated simply. "There must be some sympathy for such as us occasionally—or we go mad or became as harsh and nasty as our employers."

"Thank you."

"You are a servant?" she asked.

"An apprentice, actually," I said. "Same difference, I suppose."

She smiled. "Yes, I can agree with that. I am an apprentice myself, and it is no easy position." She sighed and looked away wistfully as if gazing into dreams grown murky and distant. I felt a richness, a depth to her soul—a beauty about this young woman so much deeper than just her earthly shell. I wanted to rip off her clothes right there and have her!

Or did I? Was there a soft spot that blossomed in Vincemole Whiteviper's heart then? Of course not, you nincompoop. It was in his head!

Aye! She was a looker, all right and I was all aquivery just being close to her. But even at fourteen I knew what was up about sex—and what was up in my nethers! Treasure is all very well, but there's nothing like pleasure.

"We both have hard taskmasters," I said sorrowfully. "But I just study to be a knight! Yours is a sorcerer. Do you study, then, to be a magician of some sort?"

"Yes. I am an apprentice to the lore of magic. I cannot hope to become as great as my master—but I have my reasons to be as good as I can be." Again, those eyes seemed

shielded in mystery and regret. Suddenly, though, they
came alive, flickering with interest. "You, though. A
knight! How exciting. You must have many more adventures than I could ever dream of!"

"Adventures! Oh, yes! Lord Harry and I have great adventures in lands far and near!"

"Yes! What sort of adventures? What do you do? Quest
for the Holy Quail? Destroy evil punsters preying on innocent peasants?"

"Oh, yes," I said, already my master's student. "And we
regularly save fair maidens from their prisons, under the
control of evil ogres—and take them out for picnics in the
sunshine. In fact, I would do a good deed now as a knight's
apprentice and take you out tomorrow by the river!"

She shook her head. "That is very kind of you, but my
ogre would never allow it. You are a sweet young man,
though. I enjoy talking with you . . ."

Damn, I thought. The fish was on the hook—and who
should be approaching now but the sorcerer, glowering at
me as though he'd like to be able to see the wall through
my smoking chest.

"Relfalyn," he said. "Do not consort with this baggage.
He is below you!"

"What's your name?" she whispered, smiling apologetically at me.

"Vincemole."

"You are sweet, Vincemole. I shall always remember
you."

She squeezed my hand, and then she got up and moved
obediently to the sorcerer's side.

"Stay away from him," said the sorcerer. "And his master as well. They are thieves. I caught the bastard with his
hand in my purse!" The sorcerer took hold of Relfalyn's
arm and guided her toward the door in a flurry of robes and
mutters of curses in a language I'd never heard.

Still bemused, still hurting from the boot I'd taken and
unable to get up for fear of showing off the length of my

arousal for Relfalyn, I remained on the bench. Just at the door the young woman turned around, looked at me, and bade a faint good-bye with a gesture of her fingers.

A moment after the door slammed, Sir Harry strode up, looking pleased with himself. He set the table up in front of me, waved at a barkeep for a couple of flagons of drink and then set beside me. I sulked a bit.

"You talked to her, then, eh? A pretty piece—wish I'd got a peek down her robe!" he said jovially.

"You're lucky, m'lord, you're not on the floor burned to a crisp!" I said. We'd known each other well enough after these years that I could speak my mind.

"Pah! He shot his stuff with the drunk," said Sir Harry. "Didn't mean to try a pilfer but couldn't help meself. Did get the information I needed—as well as a doubloon." He flashed me a shiny gold coin. "Chap's name is Beeulberdun the Visage, Sorcerer Rank Aqua. He's got that pile near the mountains, all right, and he's cookin' something up, I feel it in these wizened bones. 'Course that's neither here nor there for us, then, is it? We're after more of this!" The coin flashed as he flipped it, caught it, and placed it safely in a hidden sealed bag where he kept his valuables. "Aqua's the sorcerer claque that explore the Scintillant Dimensions."

"After a pickpocketing, you think he's going to let you within a league of his castle?" I said.

"Oh, I should think not, which is a shame. However, I don't think I had any intention of going." He winked at me and nudged me with a chunky elbow. "She's a beauty all right. Do I espy the mopey adolescent pangs of ardor in my apprentice's face! Why, I approve. We shall be here for as long as we like. I showed the innkeep my doubloon, so he knows we have money." He smiled evilly. "Plenty of time for a man of the world to teach his young crony the Way of the Woo!" He eagerly grabbed his flagon and drank deeply. He licked his lips clean. "Plenty of time, dear Vincey Whiteviper, for a young pair of pants to chase a young skirt!"

* * *

I confess I was a roil of emotion, and therefore most likely did not use my head. Although the danger was quite clear and I would have very much liked to simply leave this place, I could not get the lovely face of Relfalyn out of my mind. And so, the next thing I knew, a new day had dawned. Sir Harry was sleeping off his keg of spirits, and I was legging up the pathways through a forest which led to the mountains and a certain sorcerer's castle—my head teeming with beery instructions on pursuing true love's ardorous whatever.

The forest thinned, giving way to a field of boulders as the path narrowed. As I passed a hill that hid my view of the town, daintily tucked away down in the valley, I was given a good view of my destination.

The castle looked like a copse of mushroom trees, with ragged canopies, balustrades, balconies, and crenellations more like nature's bumps and lumps than the work of mankind. Cupolas angled out at jagged junctures, connected by webs of spun rock and mineral. I would not have been surprised to see giant spiders hanging down, waiting for innocent prey—although, come to think of it, I was soon to encounter much worse than giant spiders. As I approached the castle, the air seemed to thicken with cold and the very nature of the atmosphere seemed to distort the angles of the structure. Or perhaps, I thought as I puffed along, perhaps it was clearing up the true view of this monstrosity.

It was all I could do not to simply turn tail, scurry back, and inform Sprigraff that ferocious dragons guarded the gates to the castle and it was a hopeless cause. However, though already cowardly, I was also much younger and dumber at that age, and also my master well knew how to motivate all three legs of an apprentice. In truth, I could not get Relfalyn out of my mind.

No dragons or any other unearthly guardians were here, I noted. There were, however, several doors. One grand gothic entrance stood central. However, so imposing was this that some instinct told me to try another. Around the side I went and found another door of oak, set against the stone. I knocked, and when there was no reply, I knocked again.

With a sigh, I was about to leave and try another door when a spy hole opened. "Vincemole!" said a voice. "What are you doing here?"

"I wanted to see you. We barely had a chance to speak, and I thought we should talk. It is a heavy burden to be an apprentice. I thought, for a short while, Relfalyn, I might help you and be your apprentice!"

It was a speech that Sir Harry had given me and it worked. She laughed. "Oh, but you shouldn't be here."

"Is your master about?"

"Up in his tower. I'm doing some chores down here."

"When will he descend?"

"At dusk."

"Then there is plenty of time. I can help you at your chores!"

There was a moment of silence. Then the door opened.

"Very well, Vincemole. I hope you enjoy being an apprentice sweeper."

She was wearing a simple dress and had her hair tied up by a kerchief, trying her very best to look like a maid. However with her perfect complexion and her slender and yet vital figure, she still looked like a princess to me.

"You are a funny one, Vincemole," she said as she found me a broom. "but I confess I am rather lonely and you are not hard to look at." She giggled. "Besides you are rather sweet."

She led me to a room which appeared to be a large dining hall. She gave me a broom, which was made of straw tied around a long stick. We swept and we chatted. I soon learned that Relfalyn was an orphan and the castle was all she knew. There was an older servant woman who lived in the castle who had helped raise her. Now she was away for

a few months, visiting distant relatives. So far, she informed me, she hadn't learned very much at all about
magic and felt frustrated, although she had been very well
schooled, could read and write, and knew a number of languages. Now she served as Beeulderdun's secretary as well
as maid and cook, positions which she did very well at,
though she was becoming bored and wished to see more of
the world than the occasional jaunts to the village.

Sir Harry had said that there was no hurry and that I
should not be aggressive about anything upon the first visit,
which was to start gaining her trust. However, upon finishing sweeping and putting the brooms back in a large closet,
I soon found out that Relfalyn was not as shy as she'd
seemed at the inn.

"Dear Vincey, do not think me coarse and awful. I know
that you are young, but we must all grow up," she said,
putting her arms around me. "Kiss me, Vincey. I would
know what it is like to kiss a boy!"

The next thing I knew her lips were on mine, and her
tongue was in my mouth and I wasn't doing the kissing. In
truth, I'd stolen kisses before from a very young age, at the
instruction of my master, so I knew what was what, although it took me a moment to get my bearings. Soon
enough, I had my elder youth moaning and sighing and
breathing hard, and although now I realize I was quite
clumsy, the girl acted as though she'd been gifted with a
godling's lovemaking. As I have mentioned, I had my share
of didling with drunken whores, but let me tell you, I was a
virgin to pure youthful ardor. Relfalyn whispered things
she'd read in books and was delighted to discover that once
we'd accomplished one of these and lay naked on the closet
floor in each other's arms, once a few minutes of rest had
elapsed, the necessary bits of me were ready for other ac-
tivities. By the time she set me back on the path for home, I
was exhausted—but my head was spinning with love.

Later, Sir Harry held his nose when he beheld me and
bought me a hot bath. Then we had a man-to-boy talk and I

knew a little more about what I needed to know to delight young maidens. "Aye, Vincemole. You'll have her wrapped around your little Whiteviper!"

The next day I returned to the castle. Relfalyn advised me that Beeulderdun was in the tower again, but that there were floors to be mopped. If I helped her to mop, we might have time together in the broom closet again.

I mopped. We mopped another large room, this one some kind of function room empty of furniture save for a great couch and two chairs by a fireplace, so it was easy enough. I asked about the other rooms, for Sir Harry had suggested that I explore for caches of treasure. However, she told me I shouldn't go anywhere she wasn't, for there were "shadowgasms" in the castle that could be dangerous to strangers. We then went to the closet and found some other sorts of "gasms."

I attempted the maneuver Sir Harry had suggested. For a moment I thought I had killed Relfalyn, for she screamed and then she passed out. She revived, however, but was too exhausted for further play, which gave me the opportunity to inquire about the sorcerer and the castle. I learned soon enough that Sir Harry had been right . . . Beeulderdun the Visage was the sort of sorcerer who explored different "dimensions"—that is, worlds unlike ours that are somehow connected to ours by membranes impermeable to normal beings, but accessible through various levels of the proper magic. She herself had been utilized as a youngster to squeeze into small apertures, obtain objects, gems, and geegaws according to the instruction of her master. I suggested that there must be much of interest that had been obtained by Beeulderdun over the years and she said that he indeed kept much of it, and she supposed by her reading that it was worth many fortunes. The sorcerer from time to time would journey away with a box, cash it in, trade for what he needed, and then return. In fact, as it happened, he was leaving the very next day—which, she suggested, would give us much time not only to clean the castle but also to perfect our maneuvers. In fact, she said, she knew of a book she might study this very night—

When I returned to the village inn, I tingled all over, as much because of what would happen tomorrow as what had happened today. Sir Harry was overjoyed to hear that the sorcerer was leaving and that indeed there was treasure to be had.

"I told ye! I told ye, lad!" He patted his bulbous nose. "The nose knows!"

He restrained his drinking that night, and arose the same time as I did and accompanied me to the castle. Relfalyn was startled to see him, but I explained that Sir Harry was particularly good at polishing furniture, the task for much of the sorcerer's period of absence, and that he had volunteered to help us so that we could spend much time together. Sir Harry's charm and smile quickly allayed other suspicions, and her own eagerness to apply her own book discoveries to our persons overcame any trepidation. Sir Harry fortunately had charms, he said, that would protect him against any "shadow-gasms" while he went about the task of polishing furniture.

I confess, Relfalyn did not do much of that. Her breast was heaving so with eagerness, and I responded with ardorous glances to the degree that when Sir Harry suggested over his pot of polish and cloth that he had things under control and we should take a break, we dashed for the closet.

Relfalyn's discoveries involved a great deal of exercise and contortions on my part, but they were not without reward. I thought at times I would burst with passion—and other times I was sure exactly that was happening. It was betwixt the one and the other when the closet door suddenly opened and an amazingly bright light fell upon parts of me where light usually never shone.

Relfalyn gasped—but not for the right reason. I scrambled off her and stood up, embarrassing myself further, shielding the light with a hand.

"How dare you!" I cried. "I'll have you know," I said, "I am skilled in both fighting and magical techniques!"

"Oh, excellent!" said the sorcerer. "You'll be needing both where you'll be going soon!"

I managed to get some clothes on, as did Relfalyn, and we followed Beeulderdun out to the kitchen, per his terse instructions. There we found Sir Harry in a chair, tied securely by a number of ropes.

The sorcerer looked remarkably different from what I remembered. Instead of old and craggy and sour, he seemed spry and strong and vital. His glower was becoming a satisfied smirk as he told me to sit in another chair. The moment my rear touched wood, ropes rose up and tied themselves around me, fastening unnecessarily tightly. Relfalyn looked confused and embarrassed and fearful—but withdrawn once more, as she had looked when I first saw her.

"Relfalyln," said the sorcerer. "Go and prepare for a Crossing."

Her eyes filled with alarm.

"But you said . . ."

"And bring sufficient supplies for two companions who will be joining you."

She looked about to object, but the eyes of the sorcerer held such anger and force, she did not bother. She turned and scurried away. To think that one moment I was in her arms—and now I was in the arms of coarse hemp!

"I am still confused, sir!" said Sir Harry, his tone and demeanor bluff and dignified. "As I told you, I was here merely to help my young friend polish furniture."

"You were here to steal, villain!" said the sorcerer. "I caught you in my treasure room."

"There was much to polish there, sir!" said Sir Harry haughtily. "And as for my companion—clearly your apprentice seduced him. Have you no shame! He is barely into puberty. Abuse! I say. You are lucky if I do not bring this before a court of law somewhere. Now let us both go

and I shall not make an issue of it—although a small mone-
tary remuneration would not be amiss, under the circumstances."

The sorcerer actually smiled. "Oh, I have bagged exactly
what I need. I knew it! I sensed it." His gaze slashed across
us both. "You an old tub of cowardly lard—but with cunning and experience." The eyes stopped on me. "And
you—more of the same, yet with a remarkable potential
destiny. I knew I could make good use of you. Alas, you
may well die in the process, but at least you'll know it was
in an excellent cause."

"Die?" said Springraff in a high-pitched squeak. He
cleared his throat and went for another stab at his usual imposing tenor. "Die? I'll have you know, sirrah, that as ser-
vants of the King of Hubbubnia, should we not report, a
garrison of soldiers will be dispatched with orders to execute instantly anyone who has visited harm upon us."

"Indeed!" I said, trying to appear as bluff and haughty
but withering again under that serpentine stare.

"Save your nonsense. I know who you are! Do you forget I am a master of arts dark and light and magical? Do
you not think that even without my many years of experience I cannot see into your larceny, your chicanery. Why,
you stink not just of ale, Sir Harry—you stink of theft. You,
you scoundrel, perhaps have even stolen your personality
from your betters."

"Nonsense," said Sir Harry. "You merely shake your
spear!"

"In any case, let me give you the bright side of this situation you are in. We might all benefit. You see, you could
well come out of this with your pockets bulging with jewels
if you do as I say and follow directions. I knew I could
never get you up here to help me without your greed lead-
ing you, but I knew, you see, that treasure tasted best with
treachery—and you, Sir Harry, run in the opposite way of
danger."

"I take it," said Sir Harry, not without a gulp in his voice.

"That we have a task ahead of us. And danger to our persons is involved."

"Danger to your persons, danger to your souls—" said the sorcerer. "And that seems too mild a word for what awaits you."

Sir Harry turned to me. "I should never have followed your dastardly plan, evil midget. But I am stupid and helpless under the thumb of your power!"

Beeulderdun the Visage smiled and shook his head.

My legs ached, and the rope around my arms itched. I leaned against a wall watching as the sorcerer leaned against the opposite wall, running a hand over the surface of a stone wall opposite. Beside him was an open window with a view of distant jagged mountains, dark and filled with spurts of lightning.

Relfalyn stood beside the still half-tied Sir Harry and myself. She had changed into leather jerkin and boots and looked every inch a strong adventurer. Only her face revealed a reluctance and a fear as though she well knew what was ahead, and was not confident of the future.

"Need I explain?" the sorcerer said as he worked. "Perhaps not, but I shall exercise my tongue anyway. You are quite correct, Sir Harry Springraff. I am a Dimension Diver. I quest for the secrets of neighboring dimensions. Oh, the riches in knowledge and power that therein lie! Alas, I do not often venture into many of the dimensions, for to do so would be possible doom for myself. And so I employ assistants to do my work for me—and engage freelancers for special tasks. And every once in a while I come across a scintillant dimension in time and space congruent with our own that even the bravest, the boldest, the heartiest of adventurers cannot or will not explore properly." He raised an eyebrow significantly. "I have found one such!"

I looked over to Sir Harry. His usual red complexion had become the color of a drowned earthworm. "I fear, Sir Sorcerer," he said, "that I am allergic to other dimensions. I fall into catatonic states the moment I step into one and am of no use to anyone. The medallion around my neck indicates this and other allergies, if you care to look."

"Pah. Stuff and nonsense." The sorcerer found the space he was looking for. From his robes he took out a small crooked dagger. The pointed end of this he inserted into a chink in the stones. He twisted. He turned. He dug. He then extracted from his voluminous robes a crowbar. This he pushed halfway into the crack. He applied pressure. Suddenly, a door-shaped shiver of sparkles spread out upon the wall. A ghost door opened and I could see through it and through the solid rock into another world.

That it was another world, another dimension if you will, I did not doubt, as I noted profound differences betwixt here and there. However, much more immediate was the sight that stretched directly in front of us. Between this world and on the cusp of the other there appeared to be an antechamber. Of marble were its arches and full filigreed were dazzling tapestries picturing amazing elongated representations of fantastic beasts. On the floor were a number of human corpses in various stages of decomposition. Flung about were shattered swords, shields, and armor.

"You will be given weaponry and supplies to last for two days as we count time," said the sorcerer. "You will have better luck than these hapless fellows, be sure, for not only have you more cunning and talent—you shall be accompanied by my apprentice, Relfalyn, who is well versed in the odd angles of the Outer Scintillants, having survived many herself."

I looked at my darling one. She looked back blankly, gnawing on a lip. She did not look particularly self-confident despite all that experience and the thought of spending two days with me clearly did not excite her one jot.

As for Sir Harry, the bastard son of a bar-sponge looked as though he were about to faint. Nor could I much blame him. Not only was the smell of the dead adventurers in this antechamber a bit much for those who favored the easy life, but the angles and textures and colors of this dimension were askew. I would call it somewhat of a double-vision effect, only at once more subtle and more outrageous. The immediate sense, however, was of the oblique, the obtuse, the alien, containing a heavy malignant element.

Sir Harry's mouth was quivering. I asked the question that he was doubtless attempting to ask.

"Just what is it that you want us to procure from this place?"

The sorcerer's smile increased. "Intelligent lad! I almost forgot the most important part! Well, now, this dimension seems to be a series of boxes. Boxes connected to boxes. Boxes within boxes and boxes without boxes. In fact, a maze of boxes. Now somewhere—and not all that far by my instruments and reckoning, there is a chamber wherein there will be an altar. Now upon this altar will be a book, and its printing is done in the blood of the Eldest Ones. It is this volume I seek and nothing more. Any baubles or oddments that you pick up along the way, you shall be free to keep. The book, however, you shall bring to me."

"And once we bring it to you, you will let us be on our way."

"Oh, yes. You must only promise to pay in full your innkeeper, for he is my friend. Then you may go spend your money far away—and the farther away, mostly likely the better. In the meantime, good luck."

He pulled Sir Harry up to the entrance of the dimension and pushed him over the edge with his foot. Then he dragged me into the same position and I rolled in. As soon as I hit the floor, the ropes came loose and limp. By the time I was able to kick myself up and free, however, Relfalyn stepped through, our supplies were tossed in, and the door began to close again.

"You are hasty, sir!" said Sir Harry. "There are many other questions we need to ask to effectively complete this vital mission. Perhaps over dinner and a bottle of port—"

"Ask Relfalyn. She is my apprentice and she will speak

to me," said the sorcerer. With that, the portal shut tight, with the sound very much like the sticking of a cork in a wine bottle.

At my age now, it seems foolish to lie about the past. However of all the things I've done over the years, the vile things, the nasty things, the deliriously awful things—I'd much rather blather about them than this.

So what are you looking at, you miserable excuse for a cretin? Very well! I cried, Grompole. Mind you, I didn't blubber. And you have to remember I was still just a boy, only fourteen years old. Standing there amongst those rotting bodies and skeletons with Gods know what kind of horrors awaiting me in this box dimension, I was upset. I felt trapped and betrayed. All I had wanted to do was to get close to another human being—not another damned world!

"Oh, Vincey," said Relfalyn. "I'm so sorry." She put her sweet arms around me, and I could feel her warm tears touch my cheek. I felt a touch of comfort assuage my vulnerable heart.

The next thing I heard was a loud honk. I looked up and who should be blowing their nose into a handkerchief but Springraff. Springraff had sprung a leak himself and now was sobbing away pitifully. "We're going to die. We're all going to die." He came and put his arms around us in a miserable little huddle of boo-hoos.

This lasted perhaps one full second. The next thing I knew, Relfalyn put a hard elbow into Sir Harry's midriff and he backed off. "Keep your hands to yourself, lecher!" she said.

She stepped back, suddenly dry-eyed and starchy. "And get yourselves together. What sort of successful thieves and cutpurses are you? Take it from me," she said, her voice as steely as the sword she drew. "We'll have plenty of time to bawl if we make it to the end of this nonsense. We all have talents for survival. You think we brought you up here because you were total losers?"

I confess, I was stunned. I was a stranger to the quixotic in women and how fast their emotions can flash from disintegration to cold resolve. I also admit that I had fallen for the impression that Relfalyn was an innocent party to this tender trap.

"You—You knew Beeulderdun would be back!"

"I thought it a possibility." She shrugged. Then she smirked a bit. "We had our fun. Perhaps there'll be more. But I was raised for this kind of thing, Vincey." Her eyes glinted with a diamond hardness beyond her age. "And there are rewards. This is a difficult dimension, however. Look at the fools who never even made it out of this room."

"Why is that?" said Sir Harry, his voice quavering.

"Survival skills afore," said the suddenly soldierly maiden in leather. "Here comes the reason, Sir Harry. And the first barrier to our goal."

Through the door stepped a giant woman with long silver hair, carrying a double-edged ax. "Halt!" she said.

"We're going nowhere," said Sir Harry.

"Who dares to enter our world from the riffraff quadrants?" snarled the woman.

Sir Harry put his handkerchief away. His chest puffed out. "Riffraff? You see before you scholars. We journey for enlightenment. Is there a crime in that!"

"Scholars?" The giant woman seemed confused.

"We seek *The Book of the Eldest*."

Her eyes narrowed. "Ah. Not scholars then in search of knowledge for its own sake or for the sake of selfless enlightenment. No, the usual trash in search of power and riches as viewed through your particular perspective. Right! You shall then have to answer a riddle. Give me the correct answer and you will gain entry.

"What rises when the head is taken away?"

"Oh, yes! I have the answer," said Sir Harry approaching the woman. "I can only think it must be a sword. Yes, that would seem to be the only solution."

Before the giant woman could think to even raise her ax,

with a snicker-snack Sir Harry jumped up and cut off her head. Such was the suddenness of this fat and normally torpid, slothful man that it caught the Guardian of the Dimension totally off guard.

"Hmm," said Sir Harry. "Not you, 'twould seem."

"A pillow," said the head. "That's the answer. You didn't have to get literal."

Then it died.

"Now, madam," said Sir Harry. "Would you care to direct us onward?"

Relfalyn was looking at Sir Harry in an odd and perhaps newly appreciative way. "Your guile and cunning has a ruthlessness about it!"

"Ale is sweet and life is sweeter," said Sir Harry. "Stand not in my way blocking me from either."

Respectfully, Relfalyn gestured and we were on our way, stepping over the cooling giantess.

The next room looked much the same as the other, save that there were no bodies upon the floor. Alas, there were no treasures either. Each of the walls held a door. Relfalyn guided us to the one on the right and bade me open it. I did and immediately regretted it. I found myself staring pupils to pupil with the eye of some gigantic lizard. A roar reverberated through the room.

I hastily slammed the door shut.

"Wrong door," said Relfalyn apologetically. We tried another, and this led us down a corridor to another room. Somehow I had imagined these supernatural rooms to be strewn with rubies and diamonds and alien jewels that would dazzle my eyes. No such luck. It was a most curious journey. We entered one doorway and found ourselves coming up through a trapdoor. We went through another doorway and found ourselves dropping down from a vent in the ceiling. All these rooms were bare of furniture and contained tapestries featuring different scenes of cavorting alien beings. Finally we came upon a room without a room. Or was it a room containing a room? In any case, it was a room not unlike the other room with a wooden cube float-ing in the middle. The closer we got, the larger it got. It contained doors in its side.

"This is a difficulty," said Relfalyn. "This, I believe, is as far as warriors get. They are too big to squeeze through the door. I would, but I lack defensive skills."

It would be a squeeze, but I could see that at age fourteen I was still runty enough—smaller than Relfalyn—to just be able to make it through the small door. I was not thrilled at the notion at all, but then I was informed that this was the point where horrible monsters showed up and consumed strangers within the half hour. Needless to say, this moti-vated Sir Harry to motivate me.

"Aye," he said. "Perhaps there was some sort of other en-trance. Look for a lever or switch or somesuch, lad. Now be off with ye!"

I pushed my sword through the door and wiggled it about. Then I pushed myself through as well. A small drop, a small konk on my head, and I was through. I was sur-prised to find myself in a very large chamber, filled with shadows and flickering torches. As my eyes adjusted to the dim light, I discovered that I was in a room with a large altar, laden with necklaces, crowns, and bracelets, all agleam with precious gems. On the very top of this altar there was a large leather-bound vellum book, bracketed by two dripping candles. The pages were gilt-edged and all around this marvelous tome hovered the aroma of rare and mysterious magic.

"I think I've got it!" I said.

"Would you pass it through, then?" said Sir Harry. "Yes, pass it through, so we'll be done with this and be on our way."

If I smelled magic here, I also smelled danger. I was young and stupid, yes, but not so unintelligent as to think that I could just jump up onto that dais, whip that book shut, and haul it away with no consequences. What could a

fourteen-year-old lad with a sword do though against any
sort of ancient trap or invisible guardian?

There was no time to muse on the subject, so I pulled a
trick that Sir Harry had taught me, a simple feint with the
point of my sword. I patted the dais with the sword where I
had to stand to pick up the book. I touched the book itself
with the sword blade. When nothing undue occurred, I
stepped up, grabbed the book, and hustled it off the shelf. It
was when the eyes opened in the cover of the book that I
realized exactly what I was holding on to. The eyes were
joined by a nose and a wide set of razor sharp teeth that
snapped where my hand had been. I let the book flop onto
the floor. Cowardice is not all flight with no fight, and so I
took my sword and instinctively jabbed it down into one of
the eyes. Blood and a white serum squirted. An unholy
yowl let me know that I had struck home. Cowardice also
takes immediate advantage, and so I immediately pulled
my sword out and stabbed down again into the other eye.
The yowling grew outrageously loud, and a wind from between the stars blew through the room, snuffing the candles. Shadows about me began to converge, black and
ominous.

"The book!" cried Relfalyn.

I pulled the book, streaming with blood, up and pushed it
through the door. I felt a claw scratch at my back. I followed and rolled out the door, slipping in the gore.

"Close the door!"

I could have saved my breath, for Sir Harry was already
in the act of shutting it. A nasty clawed hand was caught in
the closure. Sir Harry lopped it off at the wrist, and it flew
off somewhere, disappearing.

Relfalyn held the bloody book in her hand. It was rising
and expanding, breathing heavily, stunned but not dead. "Oh,
yes, this must be it. We must leave this room before—"

Before the monsters arrived, but already I could see we
were too late to avoid a sighting. I knew it was Sir Harry
who spotted them first, for it was he who let go a squeal.

And well he should, for they were frightly things, collections of fangs on stalky legs slashing the air like clockwork mechanisms. Relfalyn spared no time going through the door. Sir Harry squeezed through. I tossed my sword at one and followed. The door slammed shut behind me, only to sprout a garden of blades.

"Onward!" said Relfalyn.

For such a mass of blubber, Sir Harry moved quite fast, easily keeping pace with Relfalyn. Once I thought I even saw him try and trip her to get ahead—but surely that must have been an optical illusion. It seemed a long scrabble back, but soon enough we were again in the stench-filled room with the decomposing questers. No sooner had I stepped in, closing the door behind me, stomping on the dead giantess with a "squosh" than the door to our dimension opened with a sparkling. There stood Beeulderdun the Visage, eyes twinkling.

"Give the book to me!" he said, holding out his hand into the room with eagerness.

"Do nothing of the sort," piped Sir Harry. "He can easily close the door and we'll be trapped. Stand aside, sorcerer, for our job is done and we would be removed from this place."

Sir Harry bellied through, and though the sorcerer frowned heavily, he did not try and stop him. I took the opportunity to leap myself, for I heard the distant banging of doors, signaling pursuit by unpleasant beings. This left Relfalyn alone in the room with the bleeding book.

"It is alive," she said. "Can it survive in a separate dimension, though wounded?"

"Give it here. I know how to heal it," said the sorcerer.

Relfalyn did so, then casually brushed past him.

In truth, I was more than happy to be back, but that door still made me nervous. "Perhaps you can close that door up," I said. "I believe there are things pursuing us."

"Terrible draft as well," said Sir Harry.

The sorcerer waved his staff, and it was done. I breathed

a little easier and in truth was happy to be breathing at all. The sorcerer then set the ailing book down in front of him. He intoned an alien language and set the end of his staff to it. A rippling coruscation spread over the pages. The seeping of blood ceased. The ruined eyes drew back into the body as did the other facial features. And the book was again just a book.

"The task is done!" said Sir Harry. "We only ask for our reward and we are gone."

"We found no gems or baubles along the way," I said.

The sorcerer smiled grimly. "No matter. You would not leave with them anyway. I do not need tongues as busy as yours are to wag about the world. Therefore I will still them."

I was alarmed to see the man's hands pulsing with a fulsome light the exact shade of the bolt that killed the drunk in the tavern. That pointed fingers were headed my way did not make me feel better.

However before any kind of deathblow could be dealt in my direction or I could even start to duck, the sorcerer gasped. From his breastbone emerged the end of a sword, bloody. Blood bloomed from his mouth. He turned, aghast, and got one glimpse of his attacker before he crumpled onto the stone floor.

Relfalyn stood before us, looking down at her handiwork.

"That felt good," she whispered.

She stepped over and picked up the book, which she tucked under her arm, stroking it. She smiled at us. "I'm not certain how losers of your ilk helped me accomplish this—but I thank you."

"Any kind of reward would be helpful in that communication," said Sir Harry.

She waved her hand. "Plunder what you like from here, now that it is vacant of its ruler. However, I would warn you that the sorcerer's traps are still armed."

I could not help but notice that she was changing, her

face first. From a creamy complexion, a picture of feminine beauty it become mottled and full of suckerlike appendages. Her back twisted, and the arms that held the book became tentacles. A rancid smell began to exude from her, and I noticed that buboes, like plague polyps began to grow on every bare bit of flesh.

"You're not . . . not a . . . woman!" I gasped, and I will tell you right now, not without horror.

She puckered her lips and blew me a kiss. "Oh, I quite assure you Vincey—I'm all woman . . . I'm just not human." She leered. "Do you still love me, Vincey? I hope so."

She drew some sort of wand from her robes and described a circle in the air. She inserted a set of fingernails into the air and drew back the edge of this circle like a bit of backdrop scenery in a play. Beyond I could see geometric designs and sparklings abuzz in crazy quilt patterns.

"You're . . . you're from a different dimension yourself!" I cried.

"You think?" She chuckled throatily and started to step through the aperture, holding the book closely to lumpy breasts.

"I hope we meet again, Vincey. You were a most enjoyable lover."

Then she was gone and the hole in this world was sealed again.

But alas—not the hole in Vincemole Whiteviper's heart.

What are you staring at, fool? Yes, of course your master once had a heart, and I'll happily eat yours for supper if you don't get these words down correctly.

The castle? Full of rubbish, absolutely nothing much to plunder at all. The "treasure room" turned out to mostly contain gems of cut glass and fool's gold. There was enough of the stink of evil magic to make us both want to depart quickly. We'd found some coins in the sorcerer's purse. With these we paid our bills and bought passage on a coach to a seaside port where I could learn to pick the pockets of drunken sailors, a sport at which I became quite adept.

Now pour yourself some wine. And refill my chalice again. I'm not drunk enough.

Did I ever encounter Relfalyn again? Not in person, I confess. But with every woman I've ever entered, and I've entered many, I think of her eventually, for always, always I find myself in strange and dangerous and alien dimensions!

ZAUBERSCHRIFT

by David D. Levine

David D. Levine is an apprentice writer moving
into journeyman status, with a Second Place win
from Writers of the Future and four stories sold
this year. He is a graduate of Clarion West, class
of 2000, and his story "Wind From a Dying Star"
is in the sff.net anthology *Bones of the World*. He
holds various software jobs in the Pacific North-
west, coedits the fanzine *Bento*, and serves as
household sysadmin and cat substitute. He says,
"This story is based on my first summer job."

A CRUEL wind tugged at Ulrich's cloak and threw rain
in his face as he topped a small rise. The weather had
worsened steadily as they neared the village, and the mood
of his traveling companions Agnes and Nikolaus had
soured along with it. But now, as they emerged from the
trees, Ulrich's spirits rose as he recognized the ragged clus-
ter of buildings that had been his home nearly twenty years
ago.

"Welcome to Lannesdorf," said Agnes, her expression
grim.

At first it seemed that little had changed. There was the
mill, its wheel turning rapidly in the swollen creek; there
the tiny church, there the cottages of Konrad and Georg.
But as they approached, Ulrich saw how badly the village

had been battered by months of constant rain and wind.
Several houses had collapsed completely. From those that
remained, thin ribbons of smoke rose only a short distance
before being shredded by the relentless downpour. A few
dispirited goats stood in the street, their ears drooping and
their wool hanging soddenly. No people were visible.

The feeling that lodged in Ulrich's throat was a strange
compound of nostalgia, hope, and despair. He prayed he
would be able to find some way to help.

Ulrich had barely recognized Agnes when she had first
appeared at his shop in Auerberg. The ample, jolly woman
he had called "foster mother" during the three years of his
apprenticeship had become thin and stooped, her face lined
and most of her teeth gone. Behind her, the young man she
had introduced as Nikolaus the pastor clutched his hat to
his chest; he was as thin as she, and his shaven cheeks were
sunken. Ulrich was keenly aware of their worn and smelly
clothes, and hoped they would leave before any of his more
prosperous customers saw them.

"Why have you come all this way to ask *my* help? I am
no wizard—I never even finished my apprenticeship. I am
just a dyer."

"I know," said Agnes, "but Johannes always said you
showed great promise."

A twinge went through Ulrich at those words—the pain
of lost opportunity. He had been making excellent progress
in his apprenticeship when his father and three older brothers had been taken by the bilious fever. Suddenly, unex-
pectedly, he had found himself in charge of his father's
business. It brought him a tidy income, to be sure, but also
a thousand spirit-sapping tasks that left him exhausted at
the end of each day.

"Tell Johannes I thank him for his generous words."

"Alas, we cannot," said Nikolaus, "for he passed away
twelve years ago."

"May God keep his soul," Ulrich said. "But what of his partner Heinrich?"

Agnes' face was bitter. "He and Johannes had a great argument, and he left Lannesdorf not long after you did. In any case, he, too, has passed on."

"Have you asked your lord for assistance?"

"Graf Erhart sent soldiers, but they could do nothing against the weather. This is wizards' business."

Ulrich began to appreciate their predicament. "And no wizard will help you?"

"We lack the money for a master wizard, and no ordinary wizard will touch another's spell. But you were Johannes' own apprentice; surely that gives you some special connection with his work?"

"Perhaps . . . I don't know. It's been twenty years."

"Please, sir," said Nikolaus. "Our crops are drowned. Men and beasts alike are sick with hunger. Please. You must help us."

Ulrich turned away and pretended to busy himself with a length of dyed cloth, so as not to meet Nikolaus' miserable eyes. "I'm sorry," he said. "I have my business to tend to." Three journeyman dyers, constantly in need of instruction and correction. A roof that needed mending. Taxes to be paid. He sighed.

"There is one more thing," said Agnes. "Bechte, daughter of Wolfgang, lies grievously ill."

Ulrich's head snapped around at that name. "Bechte?" She had been too young to marry when he was forced to leave.

"Bechte. She has the lung fever." Agnes' expression was knowing, but sympathetic. "She asked specially for you."

They left for Lannesdorf that very day.

Agnes, the widow of Friedrich, lived with her family in a typical two-room peasant cottage, with wattle-and-daub walls, a dirt floor, and a roof of thatched straw. By comparison with Ulrich's three-story house in Auerberg, it was little more than a box made of sticks held together with mud. It lacked windows, chairs, and chimney; smoke from the hearth fire exited through a simple hole in the roof. "Mind the wall, there," she said as they entered. "You could put your elbow right through it if you're not careful. We keep trying to patch it up, but in this weather nothing ever dries."

Ulrich dropped his traveling bag on the table. "Take me to Bechte," he said. "I must see her at once."

Agnes' son Michel looked up at that, his eyes wide. "Oh, sir . . . you may see her, but I fear she cannot see you."

"What do you mean?" Ulrich asked, though he already knew the answer.

"She died this morning, sir."

Bechte lay in state on the table at her cottage, her weeping husband and children by her side. She was as beautiful as he remembered, though her death-pale skin was blotchy from the fever that had killed her. Weakened by hunger, she had not been able to put up much of a fight against it.

Ulrich felt a pang of envy for Bechte's husband . . . but then he realized they shared a common pain. Both of them had loved Bechte, then lost her through no fault of their own. He embraced the man and offered his sympathies.

Finally he leaned down and delicately kissed Bechte's brow. It was cold and waxy. "Rest in peace, my wife that never was," he whispered. "I swear to you I will find some way to help your village." He straightened and looked around at the thin and haggard faces of Bechte's family, Agnes, and Nikolaus. They looked back at him with expressions of hope.

But what could he do to help them? He had never even finished his studies, and had forgotten most of what he had learned.

"I will visit the wizards' house in the morning," he said at last. "Perhaps I will find something there."

They all joined hands and Nikolaus led them in a prayer for salvation.

* * *

Ulrich bedded down on a pestilential straw mattress with Agnes, her sister, her sister's husband, and seven or eight children. The smell, the constant fidgeting and sniffling, and the moist oppressive heat kept him awake at first. He was used to cool linen sheets, wooden floors, and breezy windows.

And yet . . . and yet he found the presence of those others strangely comforting. It reminded him of his apprentice days, when he had slept with the wizards and their families. His duties had been small and well-defined, then, though they had seemed enormous at the time. He not known how happy he was.

Ulrich snuggled against the warm, breathing bodies and passed into sleep.

The wizards' cottage was well away from the rest of the village, off by itself in a stand of beech. It was abandoned and weather-beaten, but showed no signs of vandalism. "People avoid this place," Agnes explained. "It's known to be haunted."

"Indeed," Ulrich replied. "Wizards rarely leave their homes or possessions unprotected. I should go in by myself first."

He pushed the crumbling door aside and ducked beneath the collapsed lintel. Inside he found dripping water, weak daylight streaming through holes in the thatched roof, and a swampy smell of mud and decay. The back half of the roof had collapsed; a heavy beam lay across the cracked hearthstone, and rotting straw lay everywhere.

For a moment he just stood, taking it in, trying to reconcile this ruin with his happy memories. Johannes' writing desk had been there, Heinrich's chest of herbs and compounds there. Now there was nothing but disorder and decay. Johannes' favorite chair lay overturned in a corner; when he tried to pick it up, it fell to pieces in his hands. He flung the rotten boards away.

Enough delay. There were problems to be solved here.

All morning he had strained his mind, trying to piece together bits of memory. He had remembered three of Johannes' *tesserae*—words of command over daemons—and hoped that would be enough. He cupped his hands to his mouth and called them out, one after another. There was no reaction to the first or second, but at the third he felt a movement in the mud and rotten straw under his feet.

Gingerly at first, careful of his fine clothing, then more and more enthusiastically he swept the mud away with hands and feet. Finally he grinned as the iron-bound lid of Johannes' coffer appeared. It appeared to be intact, and the third *tessera* had released the ward on its lock. "Nikolaus! Agnes!" he called. "Come in! I think it's safe, and I need your help!"

The three of them dragged the heavy coffer out of the sucking mud and onto the hearthstone. Ulrich cleaned the grime away from the hinges and hasps as well as he could, then rinsed his hands in a puddle before raising the lid.

The large bound volume of spells was inside, as he'd hoped. But it was covered with mold and mildew. Black and green tendrils engulfed the book in a wild profusion of corruption.

"God in Heaven," Ulrich breathed. "With the shape this thing is in, we're lucky the weather is no worse than it is."

"Demons?" Konrad the reeve cried, touching the saint's medal pinned to his doublet. They had hauled the coffer with its precious, damaged contents to Agnes' cottage for a more careful inspection, and Konrad, Graf Erhart's representative in Lannesdorf, had joined them there. His long face was very lined and hard for a man so young, and he carried himself with an authoritative swagger.

"Not demons, *daemons,*" Ulrich explained, remembering his own panicked reaction when Johannes had used the word for the first time. "The word is Greek; it is closer in meaning to *Geist,* spirit, than *Dämon,* demon. Philosophers disagree over where daemons come from, even whether or not they exist before they are bound to a task, but they are *not* devils or angels. Only God may command those, but daemons are subject to human will."

"Demons or spirits, they are still evil," said Konrad.

"Not evil. Just mindless and powerful." Johannes had been fond of comparing them to an imbecile child with the strength of a bull. "When properly controlled, they are beneficial. The daemons bound by these spells gave you twenty years of exceptionally good weather."

"It's true, Konrad," Agnes said. "Up until this year we hadn't had a crop failure since before Ulrich was an apprentice. You're too young to remember, but we used to have a bad harvest at least one year in four."

"But now they have turned against us," said Konrad.

"Not really," said Ulrich. "Look." He gestured at the book open on the table before them.

Spell books were never beautiful like illuminated Scriptures; they consisted of nothing but line upon line of the convoluted legalistic Latin called *Zauberschrift*. But this spell book was truly ugly. The center of each page was still legible, but the edges were discolored and many of the letters were unreadable.

"You see how badly damaged the words are," said Ulrich. "The daemons are still doing their best to obey these commands, but they are so garbled the results are disastrous."

Agnes looked puzzled. "But if the book was damaged by the rain, and the rain came from the damage to the book . . . which came first?"

Ulrich had to think about that. "The mold must have come first," he said after a time. "It probably started years ago, while the weather was still good. The damage to the book caused the rain, not the other way around." But something nagged at the back of his mind.

Konrad's angry voice interrupted Ulrich's thoughts. "Surely to control the weather is a violation of God's will!"

"God sends the rain," Nikolaus said, "but it is no violation of His will to wear a hat. Perhaps these daemons have been something like a hat for the whole village."

"But now they are destroying it!" Konrad replied. "And we must destroy them. Burn the book!"

"It's not so simple," said Ulrich. "The daemons will try to follow their commands even as the book burns." Ulrich recalled a demonstration Heinrich had given him. He had bound a very simple protective daemon to a yew tree, then had set fire to the spell. The tree had become a twisted heap of splinters in an instant. "These weather daemons are very powerful. I would not want to be here if you did anything to damage this volume any further!"

"There must be some way to dispel the daemons," Nikolaus asked.

"Yes, but breaking a spell is an exceedingly complex spell in itself. Only a master wizard would even attempt it."

"So what do you propose to do?" said Agnes.

"Clean away the mold, repair the vellum and binding, re-ink the damaged places. That should put things back the way they were. And then you can store the book someplace dry."

"I thought you said you were not a wizard," said Konrad.

"Only a wizard can write a new spell, but even an apprentice should be able to repair one. All I have to do is make up some ink, cut some quills, and read and write a few words of Latin. I did those things every day." *And I pray I can still remember how after twenty years,* he added silently.

There was one other thing he did not mention. The sealing of the spell with blood, and the risk of death that went with it. But he had an idea to avoid that.

"Very well," said Konrad. "But if the weather does not improve soon, I will take matters into my own hands."

Ulrich sat at Agnes' trestle table, grinding charcoal into a fine powder with a mortar and pestle he had found in the ruins of the wizards' cottage. Nearby, Agnes dipped goose feathers into a cauldron of boiling water to soften them for cutting. Ulrich's goose-bitten finger throbbed, a reminder of the eternal enmity between geese and the scribes who steal their eggs for ink and their feathers for quills.

"You said these weather daemons are very powerful," said Agnes. "Why work such great magic in such a tiny village?"

"Many villages have a weather daemon or two. But Johannes and Heinrich together were able to bind stronger daemons than either of them could alone." He paused in his grinding, lost in memory for a moment. "It's a pity they didn't stay together. Do you know why Heinrich left?"

"It was his ambition. Johannes was content to stay where he was born, and work more and better spells for the benefit of the village. Heinrich was always pushing, always reaching for more and more power. He ached to be a king's wizard. Finally it came to a huge screaming fight, and he left the village in a foul temper. But, without Johannes, he was nothing. He eventually became wizard of Mehlen, and died there."

"I do not know Mehlen."

"I'm not surprised—it is an even smaller town than Lannesdorf."

"I remember how Heinrich treated his horse—whipped the poor beast so hard I feared for her life. I wondered sometimes why Johannes put up with him."

"He told me once that he had tolerated Heinrich for the sake of the magic they could do together. But in the end it was Heinrich who left, and good riddance."

Ulrich set down his quill and rubbed his eyes. After two weeks of scrubbing, stitching, and inking, the letters seemed to swim upon the page like a thousand tiny black fish. But this was the last of it.

The sound of Agnes' family snoring in the outer room mingled with the drum of rain on the thatched roof, the hiss of wind through the cracks in the walls, the rhythmic splats from the mud puddle under the leak in the corner. The smoky flame of the tallow candle wavered in the draft. He wondered what hour of the night it might be.

He turned back over the pages, looking for any remaining spots of mold or illegible words. Here and there he touched up a letter, but he knew he was only delaying the inevitable. Finally he brought from his belt-bag the fragments of the wax seal that had closed the spell book—wax mingled with wizards' blood. He melted the fragments together in the candle's flame, let the melted wax fall onto the cord that held shut the book. Then, fingers trembling, he pressed his father's signet ring into the wax.

Nothing happened. The spell was sealed, and he still lived.

He let out a breath he had not even known he was holding, and knelt to thank God for his success. Then he dragged his weary body off to bed. He did not even bother to undress.

A short time later he was jerked from sleep by an enormous clap of thunder.

He sat up, trying to shake the sleep out of his head. A long flash of lightning showed the wide eyes of Agnes and her family, huddled together in fear—the thunder followed just a moment later, seeming to smash a lid of darkness down over the scene. Between peals of thunder Ulrich heard a tremendous rattling roar—hail pelting the roof and walls.

The youngest child wailed. Another bolt of lightning showed Ulrich her terrified face, and one tiny hand reaching out to grasp at Agnes' sleeve. Thunder rolled across the roof.

Ulrich struggled out of the bed, groped for a candle. Then the roar of hail doubled in volume as the front door was flung open. A flash of lightning revealed Konrad and a dozen other villagers, their dripping faces contorted with rage and fear.

"Enough of wizardry!" Konrad yelled. "Agnes, stoke the fire. We will burn the cursed book this very night!"

"There is no telling what might happen then!" Ulrich shouted.

"Silence!" Konrad replied. "It could scarcely be worse than this. Nikolaus, bring the book."

"No!" Ulrich yelled, and dashed into the inner room. He snatched up the spell book.

Lightning flared again, a long stroke that cast a net of blue-white fire across the scene. Nikolaus and Agnes blocked the door, their eyes hard; Konrad stood behind them. Water trickled down the windowless walls. No escape.

Ulrich clutched the book to his chest. Then, with a growl, he lowered his head and charged—straight at the wall.

The rain-sodden clay gave way, and he crashed through, feeling the sticks within the wall claw at his face and arms. He tried desperately to protect his eyes and the book at the same time. He got his head and upper body through, but then his legs met resistance and he tumbled face-first into the cold mud outside.

Hail battered his head, a sharp broken stick jabbed into his thigh, and his mouth and eyes were clogged with foul, clinging mud. He struggled blindly, writhing in the ruins of the broken wall. Hard clods of clay fell onto his back and head.

Then he felt hands grabbing at his feet. Panicked, he surged forward, finally winning free—all save one shoe, pulled off by someone inside the house. Freezing mud squelched between the toes of his bare foot.

Ulrich struggled to his feet, rubbing mud from his eyes with one hand, awkwardly juggling the heavy book with the other. He heard a confusion of voices behind him as a large section of the wall collapsed, delaying pursuit. Konrad shouted something, but his words were lost in the sounds of hail and thunder.

This was clearly no natural storm. The hailstones that seemed to pound in on him from all directions were black, not white, and had the size and twisted shape of knuckle-bones. Lightning flared again and again, blue-white flashes mingling with greenish afterimages in his eyes. The thunder was nearly constant. And there was a weird, light-headed sensation, as though he were falling, which he had experienced before in the presence of great magics.

"There he is!" A tremendous bolt of lightning accompanied the shouted words, revealing Konrad standing in the door of Agnes' collapsing house. His finger pointed directly at Ulrich, and two villagers began to move in his direction before the light faded.

Ulrich ran.

His head and shoulders were battered by the black hail as he ran, hunched protectively over the book, unbalanced by its weight. His bare foot slid painfully across the hailstone-littered mud, and he nearly fell, but he caught himself with one hand and kept going. Shouts and the splashes of feet in puddles sounded not far behind.

Another flash of lightning revealed a fork in the path. The left fork led into the woods—the natural destination for any outlaw. He could lose himself there with ease. But unless he found shelter soon, the hail would destroy the spell book as surely as any fire.

He took the right fork. Konrad and the others were right behind him.

Ulrich left the path and charged through the trees. Branches whipped his face; sticks and sharp rocks assailed his bare foot with every step. But it delayed his pursuers, and with his desperate haste he gained a little way on them.

Then the ground fell away from him.

Ulrich cried out in surprise as he slid down a muddy embankment and splashed into the freezing waters of the creek. He felt the book slipping from his arms as he regained his feet, and it was only with a frantic grab that he prevented it from falling into the rushing water. He heard shouts behind him. With an effort he hoisted the book over his head, then waded into the creek.

The chill water ripped at his legs, threatening to topple him over, but he pressed forward. Deeper and deeper he slogged, feeling the current tug at his leggings, then at his jacket. He had no idea how deep the water might be after months of rain, but he forced himself to keep going. Water splashed to his waist, his chest, his armpits, sucking all warmth from his body. He could feel nothing from his feet. His arms burned from the effort of holding the heavy book above his head. He kept going.

Finally the creek bed began to slope upward. He struggled on, feeling his body grow heavier and heavier as he rose step by step from the roaring water. At last he reached the bank and collapsed onto a log, letting the book fall into his lap. His muscles twitched from exhaustion and he trembled all over from fatigue and fear.

Another bolt of lightning illuminated the scene. Three villagers stood, pointing, on the opposite bank. Konrad was halfway across, his face set in an expression of determination and hatred.

Ulrich hauled himself to his feet and stumbled up the bank, seeking higher ground, hoping to lose himself in the trees.

He staggered through a black world, freezing cold and lit only by irregular flashes of lightning. Again and again he ran headlong into a tree or fell into the mud. Thunder roared like God's mocking laughter. Blood pounded in his ears, even louder than the thunder; breath rasped in his throat.

Then, just as he entered a clearing at the top of a small hill, his bare foot snagged on a protruding root, and he sprawled full length, the book flying from his hands. Desperately, he scrambled forward on hands and knees, found the book caught in the branches of a thorny bush. The cover was still closed; he prayed none of the pages had been damaged. He levered himself to a standing position, clutching the book to his chest.

A flash of lightning revealed Konrad's lined face not three feet from his own.

Ulrich backed away from the apparition, his free arm flailing as he toppled backward into the bush. Thorns clawed at his hands and face, caught his clothing. His own weight and that of the book pinned him to the bush, whose branches hampered his arms so that he could not rise.

Trapped.

Konrad smiled as he stepped forward. "You look tired, sir," he said. "Let me take that heavy book for you."

Ulrich struggled against the entrapping bush.

Konrad reached for the book.

And then a blue-white sheet of fire stretched across the sky, accompanied by an immediate smashing pressure of sound. It was all too huge for Ulrich's eyes, his ears, his brain to comprehend, and he lost consciousness.

Some time later—he had no way of knowing how long—he was able to see and hear again, to move his limbs, to wrench himself free of the bush. The night was still dark; the lightning and hail still raged.

Konrad lay unmoving on the ground, already covered with a layer of the black hailstones. His hat and shoes were missing; much of his clothing looked burned.

Wearily, Ulrich picked up the book and began walking.

After an eternity, he came to the mill. Its wheel groaned loud enough to be heard even over the ringing in his ears.

He splashed through the creek and into the darkness under the mill wheel's axle. Here was a small space where he had spent many a pleasant hour with Bechte. As he ducked inside, there was a sudden movement, and a fox dashed out between his legs. The space was foul and muddy, but at last he was shielded from the pounding hail.

Shivering, he wrapped himself into a ball around the

book. He would wait here until daybreak, then find a better
hiding place.

He awoke with a start to the sight of Agnes' dripping
face. Her mouth was set in a scowl, and he scrambled back
away from her, cracking his head on a projecting timber.

"Agnes!" he gasped, stupidly. "How did you find me?"
His own voice sounded peculiar to him; his ears felt stuffed
with straw.

"I grew up by this mill. You are not the only one who
knows of this trysting place."

A little wan daylight seeped through chinks in the wall,
and outside the hail had been replaced by a driving rain.
Thunder still rolled.

"I'm sorry I broke your wall."

"You should be!" she snapped. "Half the house collapsed
behind you."

"I'm sorry," he said again, and meant it. "I should never
have come here."

"Be quiet and move over. My bottom's getting soaked."

He moved away from the entrance, letting Agnes pull
herself fully inside. There was just room for the two of
them. Agnes' eyes were white in her mud-smeared face,
and Ulrich knew he must look far worse.

They sat in silence for a time. Finally he said, "Are you
going to tell them where I am?"

"I don't know. Half of them want to burn the book, and
God knows what would happen then. But I'm not sure what
else I can do."

"You can help me. I know what I did wrong. I can fix it,
I think. But I need some things."

"What kind of things?"

"A candle. And some sealing wax. And a sharp knife."

"I'll see what I can do. Are you sure this won't make it
even worse?"

"I think not. I only hope I have the courage to do it."

She began to back out of the hole, then paused. "May I ask you one question?"

"Anything."

"These daemons . . . they control the weather. Rain, wind, sun. Why could they not keep one book dry?"

"I . . . I don't know."

"No matter." And she left.

But it did matter. It tugged and tugged at Ulrich's mind while he waited for Agnes to return. She was right; keeping the spell itself safe from harm was a simple and standard part of any spell. How could a wizard of Johannes' abilities have forgotten it?

Ulrich cast his mind back over the last two weeks of work. He had not read every page—much of the *Zauberschrift* was beyond him in any case—but he did remember seeing a clause for protecting the spell book.

He broke the seal. A twinge went through him at that, but the weather did not seem to worsen, and he leafed through the book in search of the passage he recalled. The light was terrible, there was barely room to turn the pages, and his vision was blurred from exhaustion, but eventually he found it.

It was indeed, as near as he could puzzle out, a clause for protecting the spell book. But there was an addition in Heinrich's crabbed hand: *you and all your brothers shall in this, and in all things, be obedient to Heinrich the wizard above all others.*

Tired though he was, Ulrich seethed. That power-besotted bastard Heinrich had given himself personal command of all the daemons, hiding it here in this obscure clause. And worse, he had done it badly. He had inserted his text in the phrase that invoked the protective daemon, and the insertion had mangled the language of the invocation. This error had left the spell book completely unprotected. It was a wonder the book had lasted as long as it did.

Just then Agnes returned. "I brought your materials, and

something to eat. But I think they may search the mill soon. You must hurry."

Ulrich wolfed down Agnes' bread and cheese, spitting crumbs as he explained to her what he had found. Taking the knife, he scraped away Heinrich's words, replacing black treason with a pure expanse of creamy vellum. He read and reread the remaining words, trying to reassure himself that this change would have the desired effect and no other. He thought that it would, but there was much here he did not understand, would not have understood even if his ears were not still ringing.

And now came the part he had been dreading. "A spell is a compact between wizard and daemon," he explained to Agnes as he lit the candle with flint and tinder, "It must be sealed with blood. There are errors, in the spell or in the sealing, that can cause injury. Or death. So when the time came to seal the spell, before, I took the coward's way. I resealed it with the old wax. With the two original wizards' blood. I hoped that would seal the spell without involving me. But it didn't work. The false seal inverted the meaning of the spells. Brought disastrous weather instead of good." He dripped fresh wax onto the cord, picked up the knife.

"This time I use my own blood. This time I take the risk upon my own head. And may God forgive me if I have made any mistake." He pricked the ball of his left thumb with the knife, squeezed a few drops of blood onto the hot wax. Then he dripped more wax onto the cord and took up his father's signet ring.

The moment he pressed the ring into the wax, a blue light burst from the book, illuminating the dank hole like the legendary lighthouse at Pharos. With the light came a great whispering roar like the wings of ten thousand butterflies, and the flavor of cinnamon and salt.

"How will we know if you have succeeded?" asked Agnes.

Ulrich sat gape-mouthed for a moment. "Did you not see the light?"

"What light? The day does seem a bit brighter, if that is what you mean." Indeed, the light outside was stronger, and the rain seemed to be slackening.

"Yes, it does," he said. Though the light and sound had lasted only a moment, the taste of cinnamon and salt remained on his tongue and a peculiar tingling suffused his limbs. "I think that means I have succeeded."

Mud-caked and aching, Ulrich leaned heavily on Agnes as they slogged wearily back to her half-ruined cottage. The spell book lay in the crook of Ulrich's arm, miraculously clean. Clearly the protective daemon was hard at work.

The sun raised wisps of steam from the sodden ground and glinted from the puddles that lay everywhere. A hungry winter day ahead, but there might be time for one small harvest before the snows and there was the promise of an early, daemon-driven spring.

As they approached the village square, they saw that a celebration was already in progress. People danced in circles, joyous at the sun's warmth on their upturned faces.

"Ulrich," Agnes said, "it has been twelve years since Lannesdorf had a wizard of its own. Will you consider staying here with us?"

Ulrich stopped walking. He stared at the shiny red seal on the spell book. At last he spoke. "I will consider it. If I can find a wizard to complete my instruction. If my journeymen have not destroyed the shop in my absence. And if the village will build a proper house for me. One with wood floors."

"I do not know if these things can be arranged," she said. "But we will see. Come, now, let us enjoy the fine weather."

Agnes took Ulrich's arm, and together they joined the celebration in the village square.

WHEN THE STUDENT IS READY

by Tanya Huff

Tanya Huff lives and writes in rural Ontario with her partner, four cats, and an unintentional chihuahua. After sixteen fantasies, she wrote her first space opera, *Valor's Choice*, the sequel to which, *The Better Part of Valor*, is now out from DAW. Currently she is working on the third novel in her *Keeper* series, which began with *Summon The Keeper* and *The Second Summoning*. In her spare time she gardens and complains about the weather.

THE first time Isabel saw him, he was rummaging in the garbage can out in front of The Second Cup at Bloor and Brunswick. He was wearing a filthy "I love New York" T-shirt, a pair of truly disgusting khaki Dockers barely hanging from skinny hips, and what looked like brand-new, high-top black canvas sneakers of a kind that hadn't been made since the sixties—at least not according to her father who moaned about it every time he had to buy trainers. His dirty-blond hair and full beard were streaked with gray, as well as real dirt, and both skinny arms were elbow deep in cardboard coffee cups and half-eaten snack food.

She couldn't take her eyes off of him, which was just *too* weird. Having lived her entire life—almost seventeen years—in downtown Toronto, she'd seen street people before. Seen them, avoided them, given them her loose change if she was feeling flush and they weren't too smelly or too old. This guy was nothing special.

Thumbs hooked under her backpack straps, she took a step closer. Considering the heavy, after-school foot traffic, he had rather a large open area around him. Which wasn't at all surprising when the breeze shifted.

Did she know him? Was he like some old friend of her dad's who'd fallen on hard times? Breathing shallowly through her mouth, Isabel tried to recognize a familiar feature under all the dirt.

As if drawn by her regard, he rose up out of the garbage and turned, what she could see of his face wearing an expression of extreme puzzlement.

"Half a Starbuck's apricot square will last forty-six hours and seven minutes without going moldy," he said. "A muffin . . ." Glancing into the garbage, he shook his head. Then he looked up again, locking bloodshot gray eyes on hers. "There isn't much time."

Isabel could actually feel the hair rise on the back of her neck. It was a totally gross feeling. Pulling a handful of change out of her pocket, she thrust it toward him. "Here, buy a *fresh* muffin."

The two-dollar coin caught his attention. He plucked it off her palm, closed his right eye, and held it up to his left. "Twonie or not twonie. That is the question."

The coin disappeared.

She'd been watching the coin. Had almost seen it slide sideways into nothing. Had almost *recognized* the movement. She thought she heard something growl. A quick look around—no dogs. When she turned back to her streeter, he was in exactly the same position he'd been in when she'd turned away. "So, do you want the rest of this money or not?"

He shrugged and held out his hand.

Isabel dropped the change in his palm, careful not to

touch anything, and hurried away. *Maybe Dad's right. Maybe I should start taking taxis home from school.*

"Dad? You home?" She didn't expect him to be home, not at four thirty on a Tuesday, not on a day that Mrs. Gerfinleo was in, but it never hurt to ask.

Shrugging out of backpack and blazer, she dropped them on the floor, kicked off her sensible black school shoes, picked up her backpack, and headed for her bedroom. By the time she got out of the shower, her blazer was hanging brushed and pressed on the door to the walk-in closet and her newly shined shoes were aligned neatly in their cubby.

Grinning, she threw on jeans and a T-shirt and made her way to the kitchen for her biweekly lecture on how clothing didn't pick itself up.

The kitchen was as empty as the rest of the condo.

"Mrs. G.?"

A noise on the terrace, the sound of furniture being moved, caught her attention.

Well, duh. Mrs. G. was out watering the plants.

"Mrs. . . . ." Her greeting trailed off, leaving her standing silently in the open doorway staring at the biggest crow she'd ever seen. Perched on the back of a rattan chair, head cocked, it stared intently at her out of a brilliant yellow eye. And it was staring at *her*—not just in her general direction the way most birds did.

"What?"

In reply, it dropped the biggest streak of bird shit she'd ever seen down the back of the chair.

"Too gross! Go on, get out of here!" Flapping a hand at it, she added an emphatic, "Scram!"

Instead of flying away, it dropped down onto the terrace and hopped toward her.

"I don't think so, bird." Stepping back, she slammed the door in its face.

It stopped, glared up at her, ruffled its feathers into place, and said . . . well, it didn't say anything exactly. It cawed like crows did, but for a moment, Isabel was certain—almost certain—it had called her a stuck-up bitch.

"Okay. Low blood sugar. Definitely time for a snack."

Wherever she'd been, Mrs. G. had to be back in the kitchen by now.

She wasn't. But this time, Isabel saw the note.

Bella: Mr. Gerfinleo called from the emergency so I have to leave early. There was an accident with the forklift. Don't worry, he's okay if you don't count the broken leg. Your supper is in the refrigerator in the stone casserole. Ninety minutes at 350 degrees, then grate some of the parmesan on top. Tell your father, I'll call him later when I know.

Well, that explained why the condo seemed so empty. It was.

About to peer into the casserole, Isabel paused. If Mrs. G. had left early, who'd picked up her clothes?

Clothing didn't pick itself up.

She saw him the second time on her way to Gregg's Ice Cream. Seven o'clock, her dad still wasn't home, and half a dozen questions kept chasing themselves around in her head. If anything could take the place of answers, it was sweet cream on a sugar cone with sprinkles.

Her streeter was standing outside the Royal Ontario Museum, inside the security fence, inside the garden for that matter, both hands pressed flat against a floor-to-ceiling window, staring in at the Asian temple. His wardrobe had grown by the addition of a mostly shiny black jacket with the logo for Andrew Lloyd Webber's CATS embroidered across the back. Nobody but her seemed to have noticed him, but he did have the whole poor-and-homeless cloak of invisibility thing going.

About to cross to the southwest side of Queen's Park—the museum's corner—Isabel stepped back up onto the curb and crossed to the north side of Bloor instead. When she then crossed west, four lanes of Bloor Street were between them.

It didn't matter.

As she drew level with him, her streeter turned and looked directly at her.

"Time is not an illusion, no matter what they say. Spare some change for a cup of coffee, miss. We need to start soon." He didn't shout, he didn't bellow, he just made his declaration in a quiet conversational voice.

She shouldn't have been able to hear him.

Then a transport drove between them. Caught by the red light, the trailer, decorated with a hundred paintings of closed eyes, completely blocked her view of the other side of the street. Isabel crouched down, but a pair of sedans in the next lane over blocked that view, too. When she stood, the painted eyes were open, the irises a deep, blood red. As the transport pulled away, she thought she saw them blink.

The lawn at the ROM was empty except for half a dozen pigeons milling about like they'd lost something.

"Extra sprinkles," she decided, picking up her pace.

The best ice cream in the city was of less comfort than usual. She still needed answers. The light was on in her father's den when she got home.

"Hey, Dad?"

He pushed his laptop away and turned to face her, waiting expectantly.

"Have you . . ."

He was a good dad, the best dad—even if he did have a tendency to date men who weren't ready for commitment—but Isabel knew with a cold hard certainty that he couldn't help her now.

". . . heard from Mrs. G?"

If he realized that wasn't the question she'd begun, he didn't let on. "As a matter of fact, I have. She won't be in until Monday; Mr. Gerfinleo is going to need her at home. Will you be all right?"

"Me?" Did the weirdness show on her face? "Why?"

His brows dipped. "Because I've still got to leave for New York tomorrow morning, and I'll be gone until Friday afternoon."

Oh, yeah. New York. "Right. I forgot."

"You'll be on your own." He sounded less than convinced that it was a good idea.

"For less than three whole days." Isabel rolled her eyes. "I don't drink, I don't smoke, I don't have a boyfriend to bring over, I'm almost seventeen—even if I eat nothing but crap—which I won't—I'll survive and, as long as I avoid Mrs. Harris, no one's going to call The Children's Aid Society on you."

"I don't know. Perhaps you should go stay with your Uncle Joe."

"Uncle Joe thinks I should be allowed to get my belly button pierced."

He winced. "On second thought, you'll be safer here."

Four long strides took her to where she could bend and kiss her father's cheek, patting him on the shoulder in what she hoped was a comforting manner. "Have a good trip. I'll be fine."

She had no close friends among the girls at school, no one she could call and say, "Do you feel like something weird's about to happen?"

That left only one person. Isabel reached out for the phone. It slapped into her palm, and she actually had her finger poised above the numbers before she managed to stop herself. No. Things would have to get a whole lot worse before she called her mother.

Which was when she realized that the phone had been across the room on the bed.

Her fingers tightened around the red plastic. That was not normal. Hearing crows talk was not normal. Normal people's clothes didn't hang themselves up. Normal people didn't have street people talk to them across four lanes of traffic.

"Normal people," she told her reflection, "would be way more freaked about this, but I'm not. Does that make me not normal people?"

Her *reflection* looked normal enough.

She saw him the third time through the window of Dr. Chow's chemistry class. He was shuffling up and down on the sidewalk in front of the school. She was supposed to be studying ionization constants.

"Ms. Peterson?"

Isabel jerked her attention in off the street to find Dr. Chou and most of the class staring at her expectantly.

"Le Chatelier's principle, Ms. Peterson."

The blackboard rippled and she was staring at the back of Mrs. Bowen teaching Classical Literature next door. And then it *wasn't* Mrs. Bowen. And then she realized it was about to turn around.

That would be bad.

Very bad.

Its eyes would be a deep blood red.

I'm so *going to die.*

The blackboard reappeared so quickly, the front of the classroom picked up a faint fog of chalk dust.

For a moment, she couldn't breathe and then the moment passed and Dr. Chou was still waiting for an answer she didn't have. "Um, I'm guessing it's not the nice old man who was head of the school where Le Chatelier went as a boy?"

The class broke into appreciative giggles.

"Good guess. Loss of three points for being clever. Can anyone tell me the correct answer?"

Someone could. Isabel paid no attention to who. Her streeter was sitting cross-legged on the sidewalk, shoulders slumped in apparent exhaustion.

He was still there, fifty-five minutes later when the final

bell rang. Pushing past a small clump of fellow seniors, she hurried toward him.

"Hey, Peterson."

It was an Ashley. Or maybe a Britney. One of the highlights and high hems crowd, anyway. Experience having taught her that ignoring them did no good, she turned.

"I'm so glad to see you finally got yourself a boyfriend." A toss of long, blonde hair behind one slender shoulder. "What *is* that aftershave he's wearing? Or is it Eau de *toilet*?"

Isabel's lip curled. "Up yours."

Ashley—or maybe Britney—jerked, eyes wide. "You're such a total loser," she sneered, but the insult didn't have the usual vicious energy behind it. Tugging at her kilt, she turned her attention back to her friends.

Isabel had to stand directly in front of him before he noticed her. "You did that. Stopped that . . . thing."

He nodded.

"You were waiting for it. How did you know it was going to be there?"

"It was drawn to your power."

"My power?"

He smiled then, showing incongruously white teeth. "The youngest is always the most powerful."

"The youngest?"

"Youngest wizard."

She wasn't even surprised by how little surprise she felt. "You keep saying there isn't time. Time for what?"

"To teach you before the test."

Uh-huh. A test. "Is that what that . . . thing is? Was?"

"Spare some change?"

Isabel slapped her hands together an inch in front of his nose. "Hey! Let's maintain focus here!" He jerked back, his eyes clearing. "Is that . . . thing, the test?"

"No. It just wants your power."

"Great." A hundred new questions joined the earlier half

dozen. She settled on the most mundane. "What's your name?"

His brow furrowed. "I have names."

"Good. Pick one."

"Leonardo."

"di Caprio or da Vinci?"

"What?"

"Pick another."

"Fred."

"There used to be one here, but now there isn't, and so I came. The others are all still arguing over which one of them it should be, but there isn't time." Fred tapped his chest lightly with a grimy fist. "I know."

Under normal circumstances, Isabel wouldn't have believed a word he'd said, but normal circumstances had been a little absent of late. The elevator chimed, and she held up a hand as the door began to open. "Wait here until I check the hall. I'm *so* not explaining you to anyone."

The coast was clear. She got him out and moving fast; hopefully fast enough that no one—specifically Mrs. Harris—could trace the nearly visible scent trail to the door. She didn't breathe until it closed behind them. Then she learned that breathing in an enclosed space with Fred was not a good idea.

By the time she stopped coughing, Fred had left the foyer and was standing in the middle of the living room.

Isabel hurried in beside him. "Look, my father is going to kill me if this place ends up smelling like the inside of a hot dumpster. You need a shower and some clean clothes."

"Clean." His tone suggested he was searching for a definition of the word. "Okay."

All at once, he *was* clean—hair, clothes, probably breath if she wanted to get that close, which she didn't.

"How did you do that?"

"Godfry!"

"What?"

Ignoring her, Fred headed for the terrace door and tried to push it open. On the other side, a big crow hopped from foot to foot and shouted, "Pull, you idiot." When he finally pulled the door open and went through, the crow fluttered up to the top of a rattan chair.

"Well?" it croaked. "Did you tell her?"

"He said he's here to teach me," Isabel answered before Fred had the chance. "That there'll be a test. He said I'm the youngest wizard and the nasty thing with red eyes is after my power—which rather redefined the rather shaky definition of normal I'd been working with. He didn't tell me what he is, it is, or *you* are."

"Him?" The crow turned to glare at her. "He's one of the nine—same as you."

"Nine?"

"Nine wizards. There's always nine. Don't ask why, I don't know. When one finally pops—and one popped early last year—the power finds a new conduit—that's you. It's been gathering in you since Beth Aswith died, which is why you're taking this so well in case you're thinking it has anything to do with you as a person."

Isabel curled her lip, but the bird ignored her, swiveling his head to face Fred.

"Him, he's an old conduit."

"I'm a piece of O-pipe."

"Sure you are." And back to Isabel. "My name's Godfry, I'm with him. The big thing with red eyes is a bad guy—sort of an anti-wizard. You've got no control right now, so you're lit up like a Christmas tree. The bad guys want your power—well, they want everyone's power, but you're the only one they can find."

"Great." She picked savagely at a thread on her blazer for a moment. The crow's explanation, although it covered the main points, had been a little light on details. First things first. "So, if there's seven other wizards, how come I rate the dumpster diver?"

This time, Fred answered for himself. "No one else

would come in time. A wizard with an apprentice gains power. They're arguing over who should get to teach you, and so they'll argue and stop each other from coming to you until it's too late." He peered nervously around the terrace, hands wrapped in the bottom of his T-shirt. "I've seen it before."

"Haven't they?"

"Yes. But it's their own places in the web of power they're concerned with, not yours."

"Wizards, as a rule, aren't very nice people," Godfry snorted. "You should fit right in."

"Yeah, you'd fit in a roasting pan, so if I were you, I'd be careful."

"Oh, I'm so scared." Wings flapping, he hopped along the back of the chair. "Help, help, cranky teenager!"

"Stop it!" Fred's voice rang out with surprising force. "We haven't time."

"Oh, like you care," Isabel snapped. " 'A wizard with an apprentice gains power,' remember? You're in it for yourself like everyone else."

He frowned, confused. "What would I do with more power?"

She opened her mouth and closed it again. Even clean, he still had the frayed-at-the-edges look of the street. "Okay. Good poi . . ." Her eyes widened involuntarily—another physical sensation she could have happily done without—and she jabbed a finger toward the sky. "Look!"

Fred and Godfry turned just as the clouds drifted into new formations.

"I see a horsy," the crow mocked.

"There were eyes," Isabel insisted. "Blood-red eyes in the clouds."

"It was the sunset through a couple of clear spots."

"It was not." Fred's hands were rolled so high in his T-shirt she could see the hollow curve under the edge of his ribs. "The first lesson is to trust what you actually see and not what you think you should see."

"Or what I *want* should be there," Godfry muttered. "If you two want to see blood-red eyes in the clouds, be my guest, I don't."

Unwinding a hand, Fred rested it lightly on the crow's back. "What you want doesn't change anything. But what *you* want . . ." He turned to Isabel. ". . . does. You have to agree to become my apprentice. Your choice."

"Your what?"

"My student."

"I have to agree to learn to be a wizard from a skinny dumpster diver and a smart-ass bird, or I wait around for the teeth and claws to catch up with the eyes?"

"Yes."

"Great choice."

"Not really. But you might survive either way. Some people do."

Except for the nervous mannerisms, Fred looked and sounded like he knew what he was talking about. And she had to admit that given giant red eyes, nervous mannerisms weren't unreasonable. "Okay. Why don't you get something to eat while I get changed. On second thought . . ." She had a sudden vision of the two of them in the kitchen. ". . . wait here and I'll bring something out."

When Isabel returned to the terrace in street clothes, Fred had eaten a deli-pack of sliced roast beef, half a loaf of bread, and was just licking the last of the mustard off a tablespoon. "Don't put that back in the . . . Eww. Tell you what." She pushed the jar toward him. "Why don't you just *keep* the mustard."

Smiling, he shoved the spoon down until he could get the lid on, screwed it tight, and dropped the jar over his left shoulder. It never hit the terrace.

"What happened to . . . ?"

"Pocket universe," Godfry told her, hopping down onto the table and poking around in the deli wrapping. "Very handy."

"I'm sure." It would certainly solve the forty-pound backpack problem. "So what's next?"

Fred stood and wiped his hands on his pants, leaving bright yellow smears against the green. "Next we go to my workshop and I teach you how to control your power."

"Okay, where's your workshop?"

"This is your workshop?"

A short walk from Isabel's building had brought them to the alley between the Sutton Place Hotel and the insurance headquarters next to it. Given the caliber of tenants in both buildings it was a pretty clean alley, but still . . .

"The world is my workshop."

"Cliché," Godfry put in from the top of a dumpster. "But true."

"Okay." She folded her arms. "So teach me."

Fred patted the air beside her shoulder. "Learn where your skin is."

"It's on my body."

"Can you feel it?" He headed for the dumpster.

Could she feel her skin? How stupid was that. Of course she could. She could feel her socks hug her ankles, the waistband of her jeans cutting in just a bit, how warm it was under her watch . . .

"From the inside." Fred's voice echoed about the dumpster and then floated up, eerily disconnected from his body. "Oh wow. It's a good thing I kept the mustard."

"You can't feel your skin from the inside," Isabel snorted at last. They were walking along College Street, heading toward Spadina.

"I can't?"

She glanced over at Fred, but he was watching where he was putting his feet with single-minded intensity. "Okay. *I* can't."

"When you try, what do you feel?"

"I don't know." A pause while he crouched and picked

something off the sidewalk—she didn't want to know what. "A sort of a sizzle."

"Good. You found the power." He straightened, putting the something in his pocket. "That's what I wanted you to find."

"Yeah? Then why didn't you just tell me to look for the power?"

"Did you know what to look for?"

"No, but . . ."

"Now you do. Get to know it."

Isabel sighed. What a waste of time. "Is that lesson two?"

Fred started. "There was a lesson one?"

"Yeah: trust what you actually see, not what you think you should see." They'd reached the lights and, as they seemed to have been wandering without purpose, Isabel crossed north with the green.

"Good lesson." He stepped off the curb after her. "Wish I'd had a fish."

"Right." And as far as she was concerned, that was it for the night. Godfry, by far the more consistently articulate of the two, had long since disappeared. "Look, I gave it a shot but it's getting late, and I promised my dad I'd be in bed by midnight."

"You agreed to be my apprentice."

"Fine." She rolled her eyes and picked up the pace back toward Bay Street. "I'll be your apprentice tomor . . ."

The shadows moved in the way shadows didn't, drawing closer, growling softly, tiny red lights flickering in pairs. They were all around her, cutting her off.

"Find the sizzle! Grasp it. Throw it at them!"

Fred sounded kilometers away although she knew he couldn't have been more than a meter behind her. Propelled by the pounding of her heart, the sizzle raced around just under her skin. No way she could catch it. And what the hell did *grasp* mean anyway?

A louder growl. Isabel spun around to face it. Her elbow

brushed shadow. Sparks flew. She wanted to scream, but she couldn't find her voice. Wrapping her arms around her body, she tried to make herself as small as possible. Which seemed to contain the sizzle.

So she'd found it. Was grasping it. How did she throw it?

As a second shadow brushed icy terror against her.

The night exploded in light.

When she could see again, Isabel stared at the image of an elongated arm burned into the bricks of the building beside her, the talons nearly touching the shadow of her throat.

She peered through the white spots dancing through her vision. "Did I do that?"

"The youngest is the most powerful."

"So you said." There were other images burned beyond the closest one. "Cool. So, if I can do this, why do I need you?"

"Do you know how you did it?"

"Uh . . ." Icy terror. Light. ". . . no"

"Can you do it again?"

The sizzle had faded to a tingle—and in some places not even that. "Not right now."

"What if you had to? What if they attacked again?"

"More of them?" When he nodded, she moved a little closer to the streetlight. "Okay, okay, I need you. Still, can't I have a moment to enjoy my victory?"

"No." His voice dropped an octave and he held out his hand. "Teenager sets off explosion in street. Film at eleven."

"That's so retro, but I take your point." The wails of police sirens were growing closer. His hand was still basically clean. She reluctantly put hers in it.

And they were standing outside her building.

Fighting the urge to puke, Isabel staggered back until her shoulder blades were pressed against the brick. Waiting for the world to stop rocking, she sucked in deep lungfuls of air.

"Downside to everything," Fred murmured philosophically. "Can you spare some change?"

Although Isabel offered him the use of the spare room, Fred spent the night on the terrace, wrapped in a disgusting sleeping bag he pulled from his pocket universe.

"I have to be where the sky people can contact me. And you have to sleep with your head at the foot of the bed."

"Why? Will it, like, scramble my power signature or something?"

"I have Liza Minnelli's signature on my arm."

Safe within her room, Isabel checked her messages and called her father back at his hotel. Conference was going great, blah, blah, blah. New York antique dealers had a few pieces he could use, yadda, yadda, yadda.

"Izzy, are listening to me?"

"Sure, Dad. I'm just tired. I'll see you Friday. Love you. Bye." She hung up before he could answer and glared at her bed. Wondering why she was listening to someone who ate pizza crusts covered in someone else's spit, she yanked up the sheets and moved the pillows down against the footboard.

The first time she woke, gasping for breath, she turned on every light in her bedroom before going back to sleep. The second time, she stuffed a pair of jeans along the crack under the door. The third time, she shoved her mattress off the boxspring and onto the floor so they couldn't come up at her from below.

At least I don't have to worry about Dad.

Hands rolled in the sheet, she stared at the ceiling and counted backward from a hundred in French.

"You look like crap."

"You look like you'd go with cranberry sauce." Stepping past the crow, Isabel swept a searching glare around the terrace. "Where's Fred?"

"He left about sunrise."

"Contacted by the sky people?"

"Not likely," Godfry snorted. "They're just a figment of old Fred's imagination—his reason for why he goes completely buggy if he sleeps inside."

"Great."

"Hey, be glad he's not wearing the tinfoil helmet any more."

"I'm just glad he's gone." Feeling nothing but relief—the thought of getting Fred out of the building unseen had tied her stomach in knots—she headed for the terrace door. "Tell him I'll see him after school."

"He's expecting you to join him."

That stopped her cold. Turning, she frowned down at Godfry. "What, now? Are you nuts. No way I'm cutting. My dad would kill me."

"And the shadows will what? Lecture you on responsibility?" He preened immaculate breast feathers. "Still, it's your choice. You can learn to be a wizard or you can put on that little fetish outfit and learn to be a productive member of society for as long as you manage to survive."

"Fine. I'll join Fred. But he'd better teach me the spell that makes lame excuses sound convincing."

It was too much to ask that the elevator be empty.

"Mrs. Harris."

"You're not going to school today?"

Isabel glanced down at her jeans. "Casual Friday."

"It's Thursday."

"Okay, casual Thursday, then."

"I heard men's voices on your terrace last night *and* this morning. I thought your father was in New York."

"He is. You probably heard one of my CDs."

"No." A thin lip curled. "I know what *they* sound like."

"Can't think what it might have been then."

"Can't you?"

The elevator door whispered open. "Have a nice day, Mrs. Harris." Isabel charged through and across the lobby.

Half a block away, Godfry dropped out of a tree and landed on her left shoulder. He weighed a ton and his claws hurt even through her jean jacket and he was still the most obnoxious creature she'd ever met, but it was so cool to be walking around with a crow on her shoulder that Isabel didn't care.

"Who's the old broad with the pickle up her butt watching us from the door?"

"Mrs. Harris. She's always *watching*. She's totally bent out of shape that my dad's gay."

"Yeah? I'm usually pretty cheerful myself."

They found Fred back at The Second Cup at Bloor and Bay. He rose up out of the garbage as they approached, holding two half-eaten blueberry muffins. "Good morning, apprentice. Breakfast?"

"No, thanks." She flexed her shoulder as Godfry dove for one of the muffins. "I'll get my own. Then can we go somewhere less noticeable? My school's just north of here."

They ended up sitting in the concrete doorway of the TransAc Club, half a block south on Brunswick, Fred assuring her that they'd be undisturbed for a while. A while lasted two and a half hours by Isabel's watch. Two and a half hours spent chasing the sizzle under her skin while Fred gave lectures to passing ants.

They moved on just before the lunch shift showed up, heading south, then east along Dundas. Fred walked slowly, hitting up almost everyone they passed for change. When they got to Dundas and Yonge, he dropped what he'd collected in the battered old box sitting in front of an equally battered old man playing the harmonica.

"I don't need money," he explained. "And the world needs music."

"Even bad music," Isabel winced. Behind them, the harmonica wailed painfully.

"Yes."

"Is that the third lesson?"

"Sure. Why not."

"Do you have *any* idea of what you're doing?"

"Put your sizzle in your hands."

"Now?"

"The shadows don't ask so many questions."

It was hard to concentrate with the traffic and the people. "Okay."

"Put your palms together and pull them apart slowly."

Isabel rolled her eyes but did as she was told. For a heartbeat, three pale lines of light connected her palms, then they were gone.

Fred held up his hands. Even in sunlight, the multiple lines were a brilliant white. "This is control. This is what you need to be able to do before you can learn what to do *with* it. So, to answer your question . . ." The lines disappeared as he whirled to face a passing suit, grimy hand outstretched. "Spare some change, mister?"

Godfry caught up with them in the small park behind the Eaton's Center. Isabel vetoed a garbage can lunch and bought the three of them takeout. After they finished eating, she lounged back, the crow on the grass by her head, while Fred talked loudly to one of the spindly trees.

"He's got special sauce all over himself."

"Saving it for later."

"Gross."

"Hey, you're seeing him at very nearly his best. He's really into this whole master/apprentice thing."

"Master," she snorted. "As if. Godfry, how . . ."

"Did one of the nine end up a loony who sleeps on subway grates and talks to trees? Well, the other wizards think he couldn't cope with being so different, but me, I think he couldn't cope with not being able to change things."

"What do you mean?"

Godfry studied her with his left eye then his right. "When you get control of your power, what are you going to do?"

"I don't know; I haven't really had time to think about it." Plucking a few pieces of grass, she dropped them onto the wind. "Travel, I guess. Find that matching Queen Anne vase my dad's been looking for his whole life."

"Fred wanted to make the world a better place, but you can't do that with power, you can only do it one person at a time. Even if you change the outside crap, easing droughts, ending wars, that sort of stuff, you can't change the way people behave and that's where the problems really come from. After a while, the frustration just got to him."

"So he's too good to be a wizard?"

"Essentially."

"And I'm not?"

"Apparently."

"I'd be more upset about that, but . . ." She waved a hand at the topic of the conversation who was methodically sliding lengths of folded newspaper down his pants.

They spent the afternoon down by Lake Ontario, freaking out a scattering of tourists and condo owners. Isabel kept expecting someone to call the cops, but apparently these buildings had no Mrs. Harris. Lucky them.

Toward sunset, one of the waves rose higher than the others and half turned toward them, a translucent but nearly human face momentarily under the crest.

"Water elemental," Fred told her when Isabel squeaked out an incoherent question. "Don't trust them—most of the time, they work with the under-toad. But good eyes on your part. You saw what was really there."

"Rule one."

He nodded. "If that's your toaster."

Another fast food meal and an evening wandering slowly through alleys and access roads back toward Bloor. By the time they reached her building, Isabel could hold a single string of light between her palms for almost fifteen seconds. It wasn't much, but for those fifteen seconds she knew what she was doing and she knew *that* was the feeling she had to capture and keep.

She'd have been happier about it had a previous attempt not arced up and plunged three city blocks into temporary darkness.

"No shadows tonight?" she asked as Fred dragged out his sleeping bag and unfolded it under the table.

"Now they know how much power they need to use to take yours, so they're building it. Tricky for them. If they wait too long, you'll know what you're doing. They'll be back sooner than later." Hanging his CATS jacket neatly over the back of a chair, Fred smiled up at her. "But that's why *I'm* here."

Isabel was surprised to find that comforting. It was the only thing that had surprised her in days.

"One of the reasons I'm here," Fred ammended thoughtfully. "Because you're my apprentice. That's the other reason. Not that I wouldn't protect you if you were. Or weren't."

"Good night, Fred."

"Okay."

There was no way the clock in her bedroom was right. Except that it was the same time as her watch. And the microwave. And the VCR. And her computer. One oh five. A.M. An hour and five minutes too late to call her dad—who'd left three messages.

He didn't sound happy.

Until five in the afternoon, Friday was pretty much a carbon copy of Thursday. At five, Isabel managed two lines of light for twenty seconds and was so close to *knowing* what she was doing that not being able to do it was driving her crazy.

She wanted to yell and curse and throw things.

"Why are we hanging around here?" she demanded, leaping off the concrete retaining wall that separated the parking lot from the alley. "What is he *doing?*"

"What's it look like he's doing?"

"Sorting through a dumpster!"

Godfry spread his wings and methodically folded them again. "Good girl."

"He's not teaching me anything! I'm learning all by myself!"

"Hey, a few less exclamation marks and a little more remembering who taught you what you were supposed to learn in the first place."

"And has he taught me anything since? No." A snicker pulled her attention off the crow to two boys about her age crossing the parking lot. "What?"

"Weirdo," said one.

"Brain fried," snorted the other.

"Oh, yeah, like you two are going to rule the world some day. You know, I don't need him to teach me how to be unpopular," she pointed out when the boys were gone. "I can do that on my own. I'm done for today. When he gets out of the dumpster . . ."

"It's time."

The crow and the wizard's apprentice turned to see Fred holding an empty laser printer drum and staring north.

"Time for what?" Isabel asked, searching the gathering shadows for flecks of red.

"Chinese food. There's great garbage behind the noodle shop."

"Forget it," she sighed. "I'll pay."

By the time they finished eating, it was dark. Godfry had devoured half a bowl of noodles and left while he could still see to fly. They were walking through the tiny park on Bellevue Avenue, arguing the merits of egg rolls over spring rolls when the shadows attacked.

"Fred!"

Darkness wrapped around him, reached for him. He screamed and Isabel echoed it although none of the shadows had gone for her.

"*. . . they want everyone's power but you're the only one they can find.*"

And Fred was with her.

So they could find Fred.

She could barely see him inside the shifting darkness. A dozen or more glowing red eyes swirled around him. He was confused. He'd expected her to be attacked and Fred didn't change gears quickly. By the time he did, it would be too late.

She was his only chance.

And when they finished with him, they'd be after her.

Hands ten centimeters apart, Isabel fought to control her breathing.

Find the sizzle. Find the sweet spot. Find where it works.

Two strings of light stretched from palm to palm.

Oh, that's a lot of help.

How did Fred do it? He never concentrated on *anything* this hard.

Duh.

Power snapped into place with an almost audible click. Half the shadows turned as a hundred strands of light formed between her palms.

Too late.

She smacked her hands together.

It was still nothing more than a crude release of power, but this time she was doing it on purpose. With a purpose.

"Fred!" Blinking away afterimages, she dropped to her knees by his side. "Are you okay?"

After a short struggle, he focused on her face. "The rain in Spain falls mainly on the plain."

Isabel grinned. Suddenly her dad's interest in musical theater was actually useful. "Could you possibly mean, 'By Jove, I think she's got it?'"

"Okay."

*   *   *

"We rule. We rock. At the risk of sounding like the end
of every bad sports movie ever made, we are the champions
and champions deserve ice cream. There's a pint of Cherry
Garcia in the freezer." She flashed a smile at a still wobbly
Fred and reached for the condo door. "Technically, it's
Dad's, but he's not . . . Dad!"

"Isabel."

Hurrying into the foyer behind her father were Mrs. Harris, a police officer, and two large men dressed like ambulance attendants. Isabel was suddenly very aware that
behind *her* stood a skinny, grimy man who looked like he'd
just been bounced across a park and who still had folded
newspaper down his pants.

Anger and worry showed about equally on her dad's
face. No, wait, anger seemed to be winning.

"I didn't want to believe what Mrs. Harris was telling
me, Isabel, but when you weren't home last night and then
I got the message from the school about you not being in
class, and then you wander in . . . Do you even know what
time it is?"

"Uh, ten?"

"Three."

She checked her watch. Three A.M.

"Time flies when you're having shadows."

"Thanks, Fred. You might have told me that!"

Fred shrugged. "Iceberg."

Which was either an enigmatic Titanic reference or he
was gone again.

"He's probably her dealer," Mrs. Harris snorted.

Isabel ignored her, stepping between Fred and her father.
"Dad, I know this looks bad, but Fred's my . . ." Quick, a
word for what Fred was that her father would understand.
". . . friend. Okay, I cut school and I let him sleep on the
terrace, but he needs me."

"Needs you?"

"Yes! And he's teaching me so much."

Mrs. Harris pursed her lips disdainfully. "I can't imagine what."

"Try compassion," Isabel snapped. "And I'm sure you can't imagine it!"

"Isabel . . ." Her dad sighed and began again. It looked as though worry had won the final round. "Izzy, your friend has run away from a facility in Scarborough. The police have been searching for him for weeks. They recognized him the moment Mrs. Harris gave them a description. These men are going to take him to the facility and see that he gets back on his medication."

"Dad, he's not crazy."

"All right, but look at him, he's skin and bones. If he stays on the street, he'll die. I don't know why you've suddenly decided to adopt him—and believe me, we're going to talk about this—but he's a person, not a puppy or a kitten, and you can't know what's best for him." Grabbing hold of Isabel's shoulder, he moved them both to one side. Pressed up against him, she could feel the fear rolling off him like smoke.

Afraid for her? Or of something?

The ambulance attendants advanced.

"Fred! Do something!"

He stared wide-eyed at the approaching attendants. "I can macramé a plant hanger."

"Not helpful!" She had to do something. But what? All she knew how to do was make a bright light which was great at chasing shadows away, but these were flesh-and-blood men. Big men. Big scary men. Even if she temporarily blinded them, Fred would probably just stand there blinking.

But what else could she do? What else had Fred taught her?

Trust what you actually see not what you think you see.

They'd already gone after Fred once.

What will you do if they come after you again?

No wonder the ambulance attendants were so terrifying. Their eyes were a deep, blood red.

As she pulled her hands apart creating a cat's cradle of light, the closer shadow turned to face her. She froze.

"They should take all these sorts of people off the streets and put them in institutions where they belong."

Thank you, Mrs. Harris. Shadows held no terror for her; she spent her life surrounded by shadows of her own making.

For the second time that night, Isabel slapped her palms together.

When she could see again, the shadows were gone and Fred was gone—was safe, she knew that for a certainty without knowing how she knew. Unfortunately, Mrs. Harris and the cop remained.

"Well, you have your daughter home safe and sound, Mr. Peterson. I'll leave you to handle it." From the look the constable shot her, he clearly thought rather too much had been made about a sixteen-year-old girl who stayed out late on a Friday night.

Her father looked like he had every intention of making even more about it. "I'm sorry to trouble you, Officer."

"No. This isn't right." Mrs. Harris stared wide-eyed around the foyer. "Where are the others? There were other men here. A filthy one and two strong men to carry him away."

"Uh, ma'am, there were only the three of us until the young lady came home."

"No. That's wrong!"

The constable exhaled once, through his nose, and moved behind Mrs. Harris. "Just the three of us, ma'am. It's late, I'll escort you safely home."

She could walk out the door, or she could be pushed. She chose to walk.

Isabel turned to face her father. "So. How was your trip, Dad? Have a good time?"

"Apparently not as good as you did."

*   *   *

Isabel was out on the terrace at dawn, holding a three-day-old salmon steak.

With a poof of displaced air, a broad-shouldered blond in a cable-knit sweater appeared by the table. Throwing the piece of fish at him seemed like a perfectly reasonable reaction.

He frowned and deflected it with a glance. As it hit the floor, he turned his bright blue gaze back to Isabel. "Congratulations, you am passing your test."

"Am passing?"

"Are passed?"

"Let me guess. English as a second . . . Are there going to be many more of you?" she asked as a small Asian woman and a tall, distinguished looking man in a turban appeared as well.

All three of them ignored her, turning instead on each other.

"What are you doing here?"

"I came to inform her . . ."

"No, we agreed I would tell her . . ."

"I are telling her, yah."

"Oh, no, not you. Me."

Shouting simultaneously, they disappeared.

"Well, you can see how much help they'd have been to you," Godfry muttered, dropping out of the sky beside the salmon. "Is that for me?"

"Yes. Let me guess; three more of the nine?"

"Who else? Do you know what they call a group of wizards? An argument."

Made sense. She shifted her weight to one hip and waited until the crow finished eating. "They said I passed my test."

"Yep." He flew up to his regular perch on the chair. "Last night, when you didn't immediately try to save your own ass and saved Fred."

"The first time or the second time?"

"The second time. The first time you were thinking that once they finished with him, they'd come after you." Wings folded, he cocked his head up at her. "As Fred would say, the world doesn't need wizards that taste good, they need wizards with good taste. You have to be worthy of the power."

"So Fred wasn't teaching me how to pass the test?"

"Wasn't he?"

Try compassion.

Isabel sighed. "Where is Fred?"

"Having breakfast."

"At The Second Cup garbage bin?"

"Nah. Not on a Saturday. Saturdays it's the dumpster behind the Royal York. You get in much trouble with your old man?"

She shrugged and, greatly daring, stretched out one finger to stroke an ebony shoulder. "I've been grounded for a month with no TV, but Dad says he understands teenage rebellion—as if—and I can probably pay my scholastic debt with a thousand-word essay on responsibility. It could have been worse."

"You could have been swallowed by shadow. Not a problem now," Godfry continued before Isabel could respond. "You got control, so you're in no immediate danger. The rest of the lessons can wait for a month."

"The rest of the lessons?"

"Oh, yeah. A wizard's apprenticeship lasts seven years."

"What?" Stepping back, she kicked the chair leg, sending Godfry flying. "I am *not* spending the next seven years looking into dumpsters!"

"Hey, you agreed; don't take it out on the bird! Besides, there's a lot more than dumpsters—there's garbage cans, landfill sites, soup kitchens, overpasses, winters in cardboard boxes, summers in storm drains, roadkill . . ."

Isabel slammed the terrace door, cutting off the crow's litany.

It was going to be a *long* seven years.

WHAT HAS TO BE DONE

by Fiona Patton

Fiona Patton was born in Calgary, Alberta, in 1962 and grew up in the United States. In 1975 she returned to Canada, and after several jobs which had nothing to do with each other, including carnival ride operator and electrician, moved to seventy-five acres of scrubland in rural Ontario with her partner, four cats of various sizes and one tiny little dog. Her first book, *The Stone Prince*, was published by DAW Books in 1997. This was followed by *The Painter Knight* in 1998, *The Granite Shield* in 1999, and *The Golden Sword* in 2001, also by DAW. She is currently working on her next novel.

THE city of Cerchicava was a battlefield of odors in high summer; the stench of dead fish from the Ardechi docks vied with rotting fat and blood from the Orlandi abattoirs and raw sewage from the Bergo and Soffino Housing Districts. All those who could had abandoned the city as soon as the fruit trees had lost their blossoms: the rich to their vast, green estates along the south side of the river; the merchants to their garrisoned counting houses against the north walls; and the Church officials, high and low, to the expansive retreats and monasteries to the west. Those who were left gleaned what advantage they could from the emptying streets and prayed for cooler weather.

In the cellars of an abandoned warehouse on Via del Masaccio, twenty-one-year-old Coll Svedali bent over an eviscerated corpse laid out on a large, metal table. The heat and the thick odor of blood and bile made breathing difficult, but despite the feverish cast in his eyes and the sheen of sweat across his cheeks, his hands never wavered. Slowly removing each organ, he carefully compared them to the brightly painted illustrations in a large book, before setting them on a tray. Finally, the old woman seated behind him coughed impatiently.

"Well, boy? I haven't got all day."

He straightened. "Slow starvation."

"Caused by . . . ?"

"Imprisonment. Probably in the Fortenzza; it's the closest."

"Any sign of the Trade?"

He pressed one hand briefly against a small scar on his abdomen where two years before a necromantic attack had left the Death Mage who'd cast the spell dead, and Coll with a debilitating, magical wound.

"Some," he answered, feeling the scar tingle in recognition of the spell-casting.

Her walking stick cracked against the table and, despite his familiarity with her ways, he jumped at the sound.

"Not like that!" she barked. "As I taught you: a scrap of tainted flesh pressed against the lips and a drop of prepared oil between them. You should be long past squeamishness by now."

He met her rheumy, gray eyes with an even expression. In the three months he'd served as her conscripted apprentice and servant-come-bodyguard he'd learned more about necromantic spell craft from the retired Death Mage than he'd ever wanted to know and done things he'd never thought he'd have to do again. He did them because it was the only way he could become powerful enough to fight the

Trade that preyed on those as poor and desperate as he had been most of his life. But, like most citizens, he believed anyone touched by necromancy was as damned as Its practitioners. Mona Masaccio believed that was a load of horseshit. It was one of many, long-standing arguments between them.

"It's not squeamishness," he answered. "It's practicality. The wound's a better indicator, and it doesn't taint the body."

"That may be, but in my lab you do things my way, understand? Unless, of course, you think you know enough to get by on your own now," she added caustically, her eyes burning with a crimson glow.

Coll looked away. As always the need to learn fought against his revulsion for what he was actually learning, but she was right. After a lifetime's involvement in the Trade, first as a lantern holder and then as a "cutter"—a collector of organs and tissues—he should be long past squeamishness by now. He wasn't, but he should be. Wiping his hands on his leather apron, he reached for a pottery urn containing a small, square piece of preserved flesh.

He worked the spell in silence, his eyes flashing red for an instant, then turned.

"As I said, some."

"Concentrated in which area of the body?"

His shadow-darkened gaze met hers. "Veins. You Bled him first, didn't you?"

"I may have taken one or two small vials," she allowed with a dismissive sniff.

"You could at least have waited until we'd found out if he'd been touched or not. He might have been pure."

She gave a harsh bark of laughter. "We're none of us pure in this city, boy, especially the poor. You, of all people, should know that"

"Maybe so—we all do what we have to do to survive— but not everyone's been tainted by the Trade."

"There's damn few that haven't." She fished through her

shawl, searching for her flask. "It's the most powerful business in Cerchicava and I'll tell you why: it feeds people."

"It feeds *on* people; destroying the body and withering the soul."

She waved one hand dismissively. "Hunger moves faster." Taking a long swallow, she waved at the corpse. "Anyway, the state of this bugger's soul is none of your concern. You just get on with your work and prepare his body for burial. When Maria gets back from the Mercato with my dragon root, the two of you can take him to Father Andre and wipe away my *withering* touch—and yours, too, for that matter—if it makes you happy, but I'm not paying for it. It's all a lot of Priestly lies and rot, and the sooner you bring yourself to accept that, Coll of the Svedali Innocenti Foundling Home, the sooner you can live your life free of *their* touch. Which is a damn sight more damning if you ask me."

Unwilling to argue the point any further, Coll reached for a jar of burial oil. "We can't take him to Father Andre, he's fled the city," he answered instead.

"What? When?"

"Three days ago, two steps ahead of the Holy Scourge."

"Bugger it. Nobody tells me anything." Mona gave her shawl an agitated jerk. "A person could die down here from all the attention they get."

"I just found out this morning."

She frowned at him a moment, then lifted her flask with a shrug. "Well, a long life to the old fart in Pisario or wherever he ends up. Take the corpse to Brother Toric. He won't be sober, but he should remember most of the words. Good enough for the Fortenzza's leavings, or did you want to summon the Arcivescovo back from his estate?"

Ignoring the sarcasm, Coll cracked the jar's wax seal, filling the small room with the bitter odor of pallweed oil, before shaking his head. "Brother Toric's dead."

"What?"

"They hanged him last month."

She glared at the back of his head. "How long have you known about *that*?"

"I watched him swing."

"Did you have anything to do with it?"

He glanced over his shoulder at her. "I don't go after broken-down old drunks, Mona," he answered in a reproachful tone.

"Oh, yes, I forgot, just the enemies of Cerchicava's great Duc Giovanni de Marco."

"That's right."

"Informer."

"Don't you mean, 'traitor,'" he answered mildly. He began to apply the pallweed oil to each organ before gently returning them to their cavities in the body. "His Grace needs help," he continued. "He'll never free the city from the Death Mages alone. He doesn't know how."

"And you do?"

He smiled, his gaunt features suddenly skeletal in the lantern light. "I'm starting to, with your help. Now who's the informer?"

She glared back at him. "Smug little . . . You know, he doesn't care a fig whether you live or die."

"It doesn't matter. He needs me, so does the City. I'm the only one willing to do what it takes."

"Oh, oh, and aren't we all high and mighty today. Who named you Cerchicava's Protector, the ghost of Duc Leopold?"

Turning, he studied the deep lines etched across her face with a concerned frown. "Is your leg paining you?" Setting the oil aside, he wiped his hands, then picked up a jar of salve.

"This has nothing to do with my leg!" She poked him in the chest with her stick as he knelt beside her.

"But it is paining you."

"I'm old. Everything pains me."

He waited patiently, and finally she just shrugged.

"It's the heat. It always acts up in the heat."

He held up the jar and she snatched it from his hand with a growl. "Fine. I'll rub on the damn salve; you just get back to work before he," she waved her cane at the corpse, "stinks up my home worse than he already has. Find some Priest, any Priest, I don't care which one, willing to do a purification—or better yet, drop him in the river. Just get him out of here tonight."

"As you wish."

"Damn right as I wish."

She took another pull at her flask as Coll returned to his work.

After several moments of silence he heard faint snoring coming from the depths of her shawl. Setting the oil aside, he laid one hand on the dead man's forehead and the other on the scar and closed his eyes.

The ever-present tingle in his abdomen became an itch, traveled up his torso and through his extremities—following the path of Mona's collection—then suddenly shot up his spine and into his eyes as a new path asserted itself. For an instant he saw a cell door, felt the chill dampness of cold stone seep into his lungs, and tasted the fuzzy odor of rot in his mouth and nose. His vision grew dim, then the image shattered, knocking him backward with a shout of surprise.

Mona jerked awake.

"What?"

Leaning against the table, Coll waited for the room to stop spinning before answering.

"I'm don't know. Something odd just happened."

"What do you mean, *odd*?"

"I . . ." He rubbed at his eyes. "I think I had a vision."

"Only fortune-tellers and lunatics have visions in this heat." Mona studied the cloudiness in his eyes with a frown. "You mean a hallucination."

"No, I mean a vision. I was in a cell." He glanced down at the corpse. "Maybe his cell. It was damp and cold. I felt . . . weak and afraid and . . ." He looked up, his dark eyes rimmed with a dull red glow. "I think I saw his last moments of life."

Mona's frown deepened. "Are you sure they were *his* last moments and not yours?"

"His. I don't know how, but I could taste the age of it; it was the past."

"Could you identify a trigger, a spell remnant, maybe? There are scrying spells that leave trace magics in the body."

He shook his head; trying to clear it. "No. It was another path."

"What do you mean, another path?"

"A spell-caster's signature carves a path through the body that's separate from trace magics. If it's a necromantic path, I can feel it echoing through my own body when I touch someone."

Her eyes narrowed. "You mean you can feel it echoing through the scar?"

"Yes."

"I thought I told you not to do that?"

"You told me not to use it to cast for signs of the Trade. I didn't." He raised his hands as she bared her teeth at him. "The scar's going to react anyway, Mona, I might as well listen to what it has to say."

"Fine, but if you pick up some nasty residual spell, don't come whining to me." She rose with a grunt and came over to peer down at the corpse. "So what did the *scar* say about this other path of yours?"

"I'm not sure. It didn't feel like a collect signature. And it didn't feel like a practitioner's signature either."

"I should think not," she sniffed. "He was probably a marker in his youth, more likely a cutter or even a small-time contact. You're probably just feeling the remnants of an old binding spell."

"I don't think so."

"Oh, well, if you don't think so, never mind my thoughts on the matter. I've only been in the Trade for forty years or more and I'm only your master, so there's no real reason to listen to what I have to say, not that you ever do, anyway."

"That's not what I meant. I meant I've felt a binding spell path before. This feels different."

"Fine. Where's this second path concentrated, then?"

He closed his eyes, trying to remember the direction the path had taken before the vision had swept it away.

"Eyes?" he ventured after a moment.

"But you're not certain?"

"No."

She waited a few seconds, her expression expectant, then snapped her teeth together in annoyance. "Do you think you might cast another identification spell sometime today, then?"

"Oh, right."

"Idiot."

A few moments later he nodded. "Eyes. Also back brain and spine." He frowned. "But that doesn't make any sense; they're all intact." Turning the corpse over carefully, he ran his fingers along the bumpy ridges of protruding vertebrae. "Wait. Here." He pushed the tangled, gray hair to one side and they both peered down at the deep cut just below the neck.

Mona prodded it with a scalpel. "That's a collection wound," she declared, "whatever it might *feel* like."

"But nothing's been taken."

"No?" She sighed. "Try to remember that there's more to the body than organs and muscles." She pried the wound farther open. "See there?" She straightened. "Spinal fluid."

"What's that used for?"

"Nothing." She pursed her lips tightly. "No spell-casting that I know of, anyway. It must be something new."

He shook his head. "That's not possible. There's no Death Mage left in the city powerful enough to create new castings."

"Would you bet your life on it?"

After a long moment, he met her gaze. "No."

She nodded grimly. "Very well, then, get him turned over. It's time I taught you how to identify a spell-caster's signature . . . magically," she added with a snarl, "not through any ridiculous feeling. Now, pass me that box."

His fellow apprentice returned an hour later. Neither Mona nor Coll had recognized the signature on the second path, and now the old woman had fallen asleep in her chair again, leaving Coll to finish with the body. He'd just sewed up the chest when Maria put her head through the door and gestured silently at him. Tugging off the apron, he followed her through the maze of corridors and up the back stairs, feeling the tingle of Mona's binding spell react to the wards on the door as he passed. Once outside, Maria didn't speak, merely headed down the street. After taking a moment to adjust his eyes to the bright afternoon sun, he followed.

At eighteen, Maria Gervasio had been with Mona almost twice as long as Coll, ever since she and her brother Ciro had come to the old woman for help in freeing him from a necromantic spell that had turned him into the equivalent of a walking corpse. Ciro had finally been released to death, but Maria had remained, learning, as Coll did, the tools needed to fight the Trade, but for different reasons. Her motives were simple; destroy those who had destroyed her family. Coll often envied her unwavering determination.

He caught up with her at the end of the street.

"Where are we going?"

"The Derchi Mercato. There's someone there I want you to meet."

"Meet?"

"Help. To verify a purification."

Coll nodded his understanding. The most powerful business in Cerchicava might be necromancy, but the most lucrative business was simply death. The price for even a plain burial with minimal rites and protections in one of the six paupers' cemeteries around the city could run as high as

fifty soldi: the undertakers charged twelve, the grave digger
eight, the Church demanded thirty for their services on top
of their already fifteen percent tithe of the deceased's
goods. For the city's poor it might as well be a thousand.
Add a purification charge of another thirty in the case of
possible necromancy, and it was often completely out of
reach. Many had to make do with an unprotected interment
at the rapidly growing Debassino Heretics' Cemetery outside the walls until their families could come up with
enough money to have them properly consecrated and reinterred. For most, it never happened and many of these bodies ended up serving the Trade. There were, however, ways
around everything in Cerchicava if you willing.

The grave digger at San Salvi's would prepare, bury, and
ward a body for four soldi if one of the deceased's relatives
met him behind the crypts for ten minutes. But only if the
body was untainted by the Trade. If necromancy was even
suspected, the body went to Debassino's, period. And the
Priests charged thirty soldi for a purification; all Priests,
any Priest.

The Church could not tell if a body had been touched by
the Trade.

Coll Svedali could.

Coll charged five.

As they made their way through Bergo's crowded Derchi
Mercato, he ignored the stench as well as the press of bodies all around him. He'd smelled worse in his twenty years,
and even though he was neither a large nor an imposing
man, no local cutpurse would be stupid enough to pick his
pocket. He and Maria were known in Bergo. So was Mona
Masaccio.

Pausing before a dilapidated stall, Maria caught the attention of the girl waiting by the counter.

"Lucia Buca," she said, "Her family are tinsmiths. This
stall keeps eight of them in food and shelter."

Coll studied the girl as she sidled over. She was a

scrawny child of eleven or twelve, the mark of hunger stamped on her body as obviously as it had once been stamped on his and Maria's, but her clothes were clean and carefully darned, if threadbare—she had family and security if no money.

"He the one?" she asked warily.

Maria nodded.

Lucia looked him over with a suspicious frown.

"You're sure you can tell if someone's been touched? For certain?"

"You know someone who might have been?" Coll replied.

"My brother, Taddeo. He never came home last night. Ma found him in an alley off Via del Vesla this mornin'."

"And?"

"And he was kinda . . . messed up, so the Priests won't bury him without a purification. Ma ain't got the money."

"So, let him lie at Debassino's."

"Ma don't want that. She's . . ." Her face twisted as she searched for the appropriate world that would explain both her mother's feelings and her own frustration and finally settled for: "pious. If he ain't touched, he can lie at San Salvi's for four soldi."

Coll didn't ask who was going to do the negotiating. "You know that if he is touched you'll still need a purification."

"Sure, but if he ain't . . ." She fell silent with an eloquent shrug. She wouldn't beg. In their world begging was useless. She would wait, and either he would help her or he wouldn't.

He gestured. "Lead the way."

Turning, Lucia disappeared through the tattered curtain that separated the back of the stall from the front.

It took a few moments for their eyes to adjust to the gloom inside, but there was no mistaking the smell of death. The six people gathered by a body laid out on a makeshift table hadn't even tried to mask it with perfume or flowers and, as Coll drew closer, he saw why. Like Lucia they were dressed in old, threadbare clothing, their faces drawn with more than just grief. The oldest, a woman with thinning gray hair, looked up as they approached. The girl gestured.

"Ma. This is the fella who can tell if Taddeo needs a purification or not."

The woman barely glanced over.

"My girl here says you charge five soldi?" she said, her voice ragged.

"Yes."

"Then do it." Her throat worked with the effort to keep from sobbing. "He was a good boy. I want him treated right. If he has to be purified, we'll find the money somehow."

Coll nodded, then glanced over at Maria.

"Do you want to take the family outside. I'll be a few minutes."

"Sure."

She herded them through the curtain, and when he was alone, Coll approached the corpse.

Lucia's brother had been a young man near Maria's age, maybe a year or two younger. His clothes were of better quality than theirs; he'd probably been some merchant's clerk or even a junior guildsman, the one family member they'd poured all their hopes and dreams into, but not anymore. Coll drew closer and the scar on his side began to throb dully. Already knowing the answer, he glanced down.

"*Kinda* messed up?"

The man's face was a mask of blood and dried, crusted fluid tracking along his cheeks, his expression twisted into a grimace of pain and horror. The rest of his body was unmarked except for his fingers which were covered in the same blood and tissue, much of it driven under the nails. After a careful examination, Coll reached out and placed one hand gently over what was left of his mangled eye sockets.

The throbbing in his side grew, then shot into his mouth. He tasted something hot and bitter, felt it tingle all the way down into his stomach, and then suddenly he was crouched beneath a lime tree on Via Marcillo in the wealthy Carmina district. Four indistinct figures waited beside him, one holding him by the jacket as he studied the windows of a darkened palazzo and somehow he knew the owner of the grand home was going to die, alone, and soon, but not when. He could feel the others growing impatient, saw the glint of a knife's blade in the moonlight and then a small, glass object was pressed into his hand. He lifted it to his mouth, tasted the same bitterness flowing over his tongue, then suddenly a white-hot light burst into being all around him. His eyes began to burn.

A few moments later he stumbled from the stall, squinting painfully in the sunlight. The family crowded around the counter, glanced over fearfully and he shook his head.

"I'm sorry."

The old woman sagged.

"Was he . . . involved in the Trade?"

He hesitated for a brief moment. "No, just . . . attacked."

"Do you know who did it?"

"Not yet." He exchanged a meaningful glance with Maria. "But we're going to find out."

Nodding her head sharply, she pressed the five soldi into his hand. "Kill whoever did this to my boy," she hissed. "Kill them and damn their souls as his was damned. I know you can do this."

"Oh, we will," Maria promised darkly.

Drawing herself up with effort, the old woman led the others inside, leaving her daughter to make their good-byes. When she was out of view, Coll turned.

"Lucia, did your brother ever eat or drink anything unusual?"

She blinked at him. "Huh?"

"Something in a vial or a small bottle maybe, something he wouldn't have let your mother see?"

Sharing a mystified glance with Maria, she shrugged. "I dunno."

"If you find anything like that in his things, will you keep it for me?"

"I guess. Where will you be if I do?"

"Around."

"All right."

Glancing past them, Maria spotted a Priest striding purposefully toward the stall, expensive robes flapping against well-polished calfskin boots. Quickly, she drew them both to one side. He passed by without seeing them, and she released a sigh of relief. She and Coll were known to the Church as well as to the poor, and the Church was not so pleased with their interventions.

"How will you find the money for a purification?" she asked quietly, turning back to Lucia.

The girl shrugged. "Ma'll sell the stall and whatever else we have." She laughed bitterly. "Taddeo always hated it here anyway. He was always after Ma to sell out. He said we could make more money helpin' him tell fortunes and stuff in the Carmina Mercato, but Ma never liked it. Thought it was lyin' though she never woulda told him that."

Coll blinked. "Fortunes?"

"Yeah, Taddeo said he could see the future. He didn't have a real stall or nothin', so he never made too much." Her voice dropped. "He always said that with a real stall in the Carmina or Bianco markets he could make a fortune." She shook her head. "I guess he musta been lyin'. I mean if he coulda really seen the future he'd have seen this comin', huh?"

"Maybe not," Maria answered gently. "Maybe it's harder to see your own future than someone else's."

"Maybe." She turned away. "He wasn't much of a

brother," she said in a regretful tone, "but he didn't deserve this."

Maria gave Coll a meaningful look. Nodding, he held out the five soldi—probably a week's earnings from the shabby little stall. He had no doubt that the family would stand guard over Taddeo's corpse until they could raise the money to have him purified and reinterred, but that could take months, maybe even years. This wouldn't go far, but at least it would help.

Without a word, Lucia accepted them back, then disappeared behind the curtain. Maria turned.

"You should have lied to them," she said simply.

"Who says I didn't."

"What do you mean?"

"Later. I have to figure something out first."

The trip back to the warehouse took more out of him than it should have. His face was gray as he followed Maria through the wards, the binding spell radiating up through the scar suddenly making him want to vomit. The burning in his eyes had eased, but he felt so drained that all he wanted to do was sleep. But first, he had to get past Mona.

The retired Death Mage was just putting the last stitches into the old man's shroud as they entered the lab.

"Did you get the dragonroot?" she asked without looking up.

Fishing it from her tunic, Maria tossed it onto the worktable.

The older woman sniffed at the package suspiciously. "Smells stale."

"It's all they had. They got raided last week."

"That why you're so late getting back?" Catching sight of Coll, she straightened with a jerk. "What the blazes happened to you?"

Maria glanced over at her fellow apprentice as he sank slowly onto a pallet in the corner. "He came with me to verify a purification," she admitted.

Mona's lips pursed themselves into a tight, little line of disapproval. "And?" she demanded.

"And he was tainted," Coll answered weakly, "with the same signature we found on this one."

"You used the scar to track it, didn't you?"

"Yes."

She clacked her teeth together in anger. "What do I have to do to make you obey me? I swear if you don't stop running off against my wishes . . . I've told you a hundred times, it's *dangerous* to make use of a necromantic wound. It could consume you. And you," she rounded on Maria. "I should have thought you'd have learned better after Ciro."

The younger woman's eyes flashed, but when she spoke, her voice was calm.

"The family needed our help."

"Another protector." Dropping down into her chair, Mona snatched her flask from her shawl. "Fine. Did he at least have the same incision in the spine?"

Coll shook his head wearily.

"Then how'd he die?"

"He tore his own eyes out." Pulling a blanket over his head, he curled up in a ball, facing away from the light and refused to speak further.

Two days later, in the early morning, Maria drew him up onto the streets again.

"There's been another one."

This time the body lay in a crumpled heap behind a tavern off the Giardino Mercato in Carmina. A middle-aged man, he'd been professionally stripped and stuffed behind a row of empty barrels. Coll knelt, feeling the pain radiate up his side at the sight of the face encrusted with blood and tissue, eyes missing again. Touching the body lightly on the forehead, his back thumped against the wall as his legs gave out underneath him. His eyes flashed with an eerie white light, then he suddenly stiffened. Alarmed, Maria yanked his hand away just as he began to convulse.

"Coll?"

Willing himself to stop shaking, Coll wrapped one hand over his eyes and the other over the scar.

"I' m all right. Just . . . give me a moment."

"Was it the same?"

"Yes. Same . . . signature, same death. Who was he?"

"Another fortune-teller," she said meaningfully, "only a much more successful one than poor Taddeo. His name was Benito Martelli. He *did* have a stall in the Carmina Mercato, not even a hundred yards from this spot."

Peering carefully between his fingers, Coll shuddered as the aftereffects of the vision played across his sight. "He was talking to someone about a death. He was . . . *seeing* if someone was going to die. He was afraid that if he didn't tell him what he wanted to hear, the death would be his. He could see it—I saw it—forming in vision right in front of him. He took a . . ." He squinted down at the body. "If it was on him . . ." Pushing against the wall, he staggered to his feet. "It might be in his stall. We need to search his stall. Come on."

"Wait. Shouldn't we . . . ?"

"What?" His eyes rolling in his head, Coll gave her a sarcastic glance. "Carry him off so Mona can dissect him?"

"Coll!" she hissed, glancing quickly around. "Are you insane? Keep your voice down. The Watch'll be here any minute."

"All the more reason to leave. *His* family can afford a purification, and we can't learn anything more from him." He dropped his voice. "They're drinking it, Maria."

"Drinking what?"

"Some kind of necromantic infusion to see the future. And it's killing them."

"What? How?"

His jaw tightened in frustration. "I don't know, but if we find the infusion, maybe Mona can identify the source and maybe the supplier. It might still be in his stall. We have to find it before someone else gets hold of it. They won't know what they've got. If they drink it . . ." He headed for the mouth of the alley, and Maria grabbed his arm.

"It won't do any good, Coll."

"Why not?"

"Because Pira, the one who told me about Benito, will have rifled his stall already, probably even before she came to me."

"Do you know where she is?"

"I'm not sure."

"Be sure, unless you want her to die like *he* did."

"I think I might know where she'd go to sell a load of goods first."

"Then come on."

It took them most of the morning to track Pira down, and by that time it was too late. They found the ten-year-old thief curled up beneath an abandoned wharf on the Ardechi docks, the remnants of her few tattered belongings tucked about her like a nest, her face as mutilated as the others'. Maria gathered her up in her arms, her expression terrible.

"We have to find who did this, Coll," she grated.

Methodically searching the ground around her, he nodded. "We will. But first we have to find that infusion." His fingers brushed against a glass object wedged underneath a rotted saltbox and, careful not to touch the open lip with his bare hands, he wrapped it in a scrap of cloth, then glanced over.

"Do you want to bring her to the lab? To prepare her," he added quickly as Maria turned a furious gaze in his direction. "For burial?"

She nodded stiffly. "She can lie at the Gervasio Foundling Cemetery. She's still young enough. And they know me there. They'll take care of her."

"Do you need help carrying her?"

Maria looked down at the diminutive body in her arms

and shook her head. "Just find me something to cover her up with."

Taking back alleys and closes, they reached the lab a few minutes later without incident. Maria laid Pira's body gently onto the table as Coll handed the vial to Mona, admitting quickly where they'd got it. With one explosive snort, she took the vial gingerly to a side table to study the few remaining drops while Coll and Maria prepared Pira for burial. After an hour of stirring, sniffing, and muttering to herself, she finally straightened with a groan.

"Near as I can figure, the main component is pure alcohol with one or two ingredients I can't identify," she announced, pulling out her flask. "But the necromantic component is definitely spinal fluid with a pinch of brain matter added in for good measure, and the source is our old bugger from two days ago." She waggled the vial of blood in Coll's direction. "That incision must have gone deeper than we thought. Now," she continued, "you said the Mage's signature, path, or what have you, was concentrated in the back brain, eyes, and spine?"

Coll nodded.

"Why do you think that is?"

"Eyes for the visions, spine for the place of collection likely."

"And the back brain?"

He frowned. "I don't know."

She pulled one of the smaller books from the shelf and tossed it at him. "It's the visual center. The part of the brain that controls sight," she expanded as Coll looked at her blankly. "Physical sight, that is, though some think it also controls metaphysical sight."

Flipping through the pages, he peered at the many cross-sectional drawings of the brain. "You'd think it would be at the front," he noted.

"You would, but it's not. So, this Mage takes spinal fluid

and brain matter and mixes it in pure alcohol because . . . ?" Mona glanced expectantly from one apprentice to the other.

"Because alcohol is a better spell conductor than water," Maria answered woodenly without turning away from the table.

"Good girl. Now, why? You say this stuff causes visions?"

"Visions of *death*," Coll amended.

"How? Other Mages have experimented with brain matter in the past and never come up with this sort of thing."

"Because our corpse was a fortune-teller," Coll answered.

Both women turned to stare at him.

"How do you know that?" Maria asked.

"I don't, but it makes sense. Think about it. He's a fortune-teller and he's dying in the Fortenzza. Maybe he's raving about his visions, maybe he's pleading with the jailers to let him out and he'll tell their futures. Someone wonders: what would happen if you distilled the brain matter that controls these visions, adding the spinal fluid for extra potency or whatever. Suppose you rub it on your face, or dribble it into your eyes, or drink it. Would you have the same visions? You can't collect the components while he's alive, but you can after he's dead. Especially in prison. The necromantic elements would lock the visions to time of death, but so what? Death is big business in Cerchicava, especially if you want to loot a body or an empty house, hide a relative's money from the Priests ahead of time, or just kill someone and know you'll get away with it. If you don't want to risk taking it yourself, you have a built-in market in the Giardino and Derchi Mercatos."

"Maybe," Mona allowed. "But it would have to be someone who's studied anatomy. Most people don't even know these components exist, never mind to what use they might be put."

"A surgeon or a physician would know."

"The Fortenzza has a physician," Maria observed.

"The Fortenzza has a barber who fancies himself a physician. Michael Diacchi's just a glorified butcher," Mona sniffed.

Coll's eyes narrowed. "Maybe in more ways than one. He'd have access to as many bodies as he wanted to practice on, and no one would ever be the wiser. The physicians act as coroner and undertakers in prison."

"And the Trade's seen a steady stream of Its own march through the gates of the Fortenzza, that's for sure," Mona mused. "There'd be plenty willing to teach him in exchange for an easier time of it."

"It's him." Coll headed for the door.

A lock spell snapped into being around the lintel before he could cross the room. "Not so fast, boy! Without proof, you're just the Holy Scourge running around after anyone who blinks funny. I have one or two spells that can identify him for certain—it's time you both learned them anyway— if you can get me some of his hair, that is. It's a piss-poor component, but it's dead when it comes off the body, so it will do in a pinch. Now, can you find out where he lives?"

"Easily."

"First we lay Pira to rest," Maria interrupted firmly. She directed a glare worthy of the older woman in their direction then gestured at Coll. "Help me with her shroud."

The ceremony was fast and simple with Maria and Coll acting as the girl's family and Father Fiori of the Gervasio Foundling Home purifying the body and speaking the necessary words over the small, wooden casket. They stayed until the grave digger had finished his task, then, as the sun dropped below the city walls, they turned away.

Lucia Buca was waiting for them at the entrance to Via del Masaccio. Before they could ask, she held out her hand.

"I found this in Taddeo's things last night."

She held out a small glass vial, half an inch of clear liquid still clinging to the bottom. Coll almost snatched it away.

"You didn't . . . Did you . . . drink any of it?"

She gave him a withering look. "And end up like Taddeo? I'm not that stupid. That's what killed him, isn't it, not some attack by some marker or some Death Mage?"

He met her eyes. "Yes."

"And he took it on purpose, right? Nobody forced it down his throat? He tainted himself on purpose and cost us the stall and everything we own to get his lazy arse purified?"

"No."

She narrowed her eyes at him suspiciously.

"He was forced by four men. They wanted him to tell them if it was safe to rob a palazzo. They made him drink it to increase his abilities."

"So he really could see the future?"

"Yes."

Her throat worked, and she looked quickly away. "You gonna find out who they were?" she asked after a moment, her voice thick.

"Eventually, but first we have to find who sold this to them."

"When you gonna do that?"

Coll's expression darkened. "Right now."

Maria caught up with him two streets down.

"Where are you going?"

"San Albiento's."

"Why?"

He glanced back at her, his expression dark. "To verify the source."

"Mona's going to verify the source."

"After we bring back some component from Michael Diacchi, *if* we can get it without tipping him off." He shook his head sharply. "When I visit the Fortenzza's physician, it won't be to steal his hair for some necromantic working, it will be to force this infusion down his throat. The scar will tell me everything I need to know, and it will tell me now.

You can go and try to break into his home if you want to, or you can come with me. Its your choice, but I'm going now."

He headed across a small piazza, and after a moment's hesitation, she followed.

The San Albiento's Pauper's Cemetery had an air of abandoned desperation despite the crowded rows of head-stones and markers, the main mausoleum in the center, dark and still. Coll twisted the lock right off the rotting door-jamb with one swift motion, then the two of them passed inside. The Church was supposed to ward the larger crypts once a month, but neither Coll nor Maria had ever seen a Priest inside the gates. The denizens of San Albiento's were damned—if not by necromancy, then by poverty—and the Church did not concern Itself with either. Following his nose, Coll headed deeper into the main tomb.

The old man's body lay to one side, resting on the bones of several others. The pallweed oil had kept much of the rot at bay, but the stench that emanated from it was still enough to make Coll's eyes water. Gently tugging back the shroud, he laid his hand on the old man's forehead, then closed his eyes.

Nothing.

He moved his hand down directly under the neck and tried again.

Again nothing.

Looking up at the shadowy ceiling, he shook his head.

"Who'd have thought Mona'd be right?"

Maria took one step farther inside the doorway. "What do you mean?"

"I mean, we shouldn't have had him purified, it's wiped away the taint."

"Can we go, then?"

"No. I want to try one more thing." His fished into his tunic, drawing out the glass vial. Maria's eyes widened.

"Are you completely insane?"

"The infusion came from his body. If I can link to him through it, I might be able to see who collected it after his death."

"You'll join him in death. Have you forgotten what that does?"

"I'll be all right. The others died because they took too much. I'm only going to use a single drop."

"How do you know that a single drop isn't too much?"

He shook his head impatiently. "Because he's selling it. If a single drop were too much, there'd be more bodies." He reached for the cork, and Maria caught his arm.

"Coll, don't. You don't have to do it this way. Mona has a spell."

"Mona has a *necromantic* spell."

"What do you think this is?"

"This is different."

"How?"

"It just is! Look, Maria, Mona is a *Death Mage*. The spell craft doesn't matter to her, how she does it, or where she gets the components from. But it matters to me. I'm not a cutter anymore, I gave that life up, and when I did, I swore I would never make another collection from another human being, no matter how damned they already were. Especially if I could find out what I need to know another way."

"You'll be killed. You'll tear your own eyes out of your head."

"No, I won't, because you're going to stop me. You're going to hold my hands while the vision runs its course."

"And afterward?"

"Afterward, we're going to pay a visit to Michael Diacchi." With a quick motion, he popped the cork and poured a single, clear drop onto his tongue before she could form another argument.

Michael Diacchi kept the first two floors of a small palazzo in the Lambruschini District. He paid extra for specially created Church wards, but the apparition that crashed through his cellar door went through them as if they didn't exist. Its blazing eyes burning with white fire, it had him by the throat in a heartbeat before he could even blink. It raised him up with one hand, fingers driving into the soft tissue around his larynx and shook him above the collection of necromantic tools laid out on the side table. Darkness rushed in on him, but just as he was about to lose consciousness, a bolt of red fire smashed the creature aside. As he fell, he saw two women standing over the body of a slight, dark-haired man.

By the next morning the news had swept across the city. The Fortenzza's physician had been found outside his palazzo, his eyes torn from his head, apparently by his own hand. The Holy Scourge had collected up his body but would not comment on any investigation they might be conducting. The Fortenzza paid for his purification and had him quietly interred in the Piero Devanza Necropolis, and the entire affair was swiftly forgotten by all except the relatives of Taddeo Buca who, thanks to Maria Gervasio, could now afford to take his body to the merchant cemetery of Santa Anna with full rites and ceremonies.

In the warehouse on Via del Masaccio, Coll Svedali sat, wrapped in a blanket in Mona's chair, squinting in the light from a single candle. His sight was slowly returning, but the infusion-fueled assault on Michael Diacchi had damaged more than his eyes. He could feel the path the combined effect of the infusion and the residual casting in the scar had left in his body. If Mona hadn't interceded when she had, it would have burned all the way up to his brain. He was lucky to be alive. He shuddered as he remembered the first terrible streak of fire that had shot from his mouth to his abdomen.

That single drop had been enough to send the old man's last few moments of life crashing over him. The seer had

known, right to the end, what Michael Diacchi was planning to do with his body, and the helplessness and horror
he'd felt had boiled over into a killing rage that still sizzled
along Coll's nerves. He barely remembered the streets between Debassino's and Lambruschini flying past, but he remembered the sweet feel of the physician's throat under his
fingers and the need to squeeze until his eyes popped out of
his head, burning as Coll's own eyes had begun to burn.
And he remembered the bolt of necromantic magic that had
knocked him away. It had been cold, as cold as death, and
as familiar as his own thoughts. He'd almost welcomed it.

While he'd lain, retching, in a corner, Maria had made a
quick, almost professional search of the palazzo, finding
and destroying eight other vials while Mona dealt with the
physician. Coll had watched the old woman work her magics with horrifying precision. When she finished, and
Michael Diacchi had stumbled, screaming, from the
palazzo, she and Maria had carried Coll back to the lab
where she'd spent five hours battling the combined effects
of the infusion and the wound. Finally she'd won out, but
not before exhausting them both. Now, she hobbled over
and handed him a bowl of broth, peering myopically into
his eyes. Her own were red-rimmed from lack of sleep
rather than magic, and he dropped his gaze. She grunted in
satisfaction.

"You'll live."

Fishing out her flask, she took a long swallow before
pulling up another chair. They sat in silence for a long time
before she gave one, explosive snort.

"You scared Maria half to death," she said bluntly.
"You're lucky she ran for me when you lost control instead
of trying to subdue you herself. You know the last thing she
needs is for necromancy to consume another person she
loves."

"I know."

"And what would I have done if you'd died, eh?" she
continued. "I'm too old to lose an apprentice like that."

With a sniff, she tucked the flask back in her shawl. "I suppose the problem is that you aren't really my apprentice, are you? You're a man who hates everything I stand for."

He glanced curiously at her, unused to the tone of weary self-pity in her voice.

"Not everything," he allowed. "But you're right. I'm not your apprentice. I can't be. Whatever else is true, you're a Death Mage. And every time I touch a piece of tainted flesh or see a corpse defiled by necromancy, I remember what that means and I feel like I'm dying inside." He leaned forward. "I don't want to leave you, Mona, and I don't want to fight you. There must be some way we can work this out and stay together." He looked away. "I think we need each other. For company, anyway."

The old woman gave a half snort. "I'm too old to change my life." She sighed. "But my first learning came from a Physician, so I suppose if Michael Diacchi can go from Physician to Death Mage, I can teach you to go from Death Mage to Physician, or at the very least to Coroner. That way I suppose you can still follow this delusional urge to save the city from itself, since you're obviously bent on it regardless of the danger. But Maria learns what she will. We don't choose for her. Agreed."

"Agreed."

"Good. Well. I'm glad we got that sorted out. Now, get out of my chair and get some sleep; I've some lists to make up. I'm going to need books, and more supplies, that is if you two haven't spent all my money on interments and purifications while my back was turned."

"I think there might be a little left."

"Fine. Well, go on, then. I have a lot of remembering to do, and I can't do it with you sitting there."

He rose stiffly. "Thank you, Mona."

"For what?"

"I don't know, for last night, for all of last night."

"Yes, well, we do what has to be done. Sometimes that means killing an evil man, sometimes it means saving a good man. The trick is being able to do both and still sleep at night."

"And can you?"

"What?"

"Sleep at night?"

"As long as I'm still alive."

"Words to live by."

"Damn right." Fishing through her shawl, she gestured him gruffly toward the door. His last sight of her before he closed it softly behind him was of her raising her flask to toast the single, flickering candle flame. He smiled, and for the first time in years, his eyes were clear.

FLANKING MANEUVER

by *Mickey Zucker Reichert*

Mickey Zucker Reichert is a pediatrician whose fantasy and science fiction novels include *The Legend of Nightfall*, *The Bifrost Guardians* series, *The Last of the Renshai* trilogy, *The Renshai Chronicles* trilogy, *Flightless Falcon*, *The Beasts of Barakhai*, *The Lost Dragons of Barakhai*, and *The Unknown Soldier*, all available from DAW Books. Her short fiction has appeared in numerous anthologies, including *Assassin Fantastic*, *Knight Fantastic*, and *Vengeance Fantastic*. Her claims to fame: she *has* performed brain surgery, and her parents *really are* rocket scientists.

AN icy breeze glided through the woods, rattling the branches of the tightly packed *aldona* trees and sending the dying weeds into a strange, bowing dance. Dressed in homespun worn into rags, Umbert shivered and tried to focus on the words of his commander. The sweet spices of his fourteenth birthday bread were still haunting his tongue when the army demanded his apprenticeship a full year before the one prearranged with the blacksmith. The same naturally muscular thighs and upper arms that had attracted Horton Blacksmith had drawn the attention of the troop's commander as well, and the drafting age had drifted downward through the years.

Umbert ran a hand through his thick black hair, glancing around at the other Arsie soldiers. None had uniforms, and many wore clothing as tattered as his own. Though dozens strong, the unit bore little resemblance to the proud ranks he thought he remembered from his childhood, marching off to war in rigid lines with spear points gleaming and songs of victory wafting to the heavens. He wondered whether the innocence and relative smallness of youth had only made things seem so much huger, so much more glamorous than reality.

The commander stopped speaking, and the men broke off into groups. Umbert remained in place, feeling empty and chilled, realizing he had missed most of the instructions. The youngest by at least three years, he felt out of place, confused, and uncertain. The soldiers knew one another like brothers, had risked their lives together and rescued each other with desperately grim matter-of-factness. He was the newcomer, untried and untrained, dragged into a part of something too enormous for him to understand and desperately wishing for a different life for himself. He did not want to kill, did not seek the excitement of worrying for his own life or others, saw no future here.

The clusters of soldiers prepared themselves and their weapons, built fires, and shared their scant but welcome evening meal. The tribe had become urgently small, yet Umbert knew very few of these warriors. His world consisted of men and women too old, too wounded, or too feeble to fight, children, and the captured Hurrdu females who helped bear the tribe's babies, including his own mother.

An older man with ivory skin and a shock of white hair gestured at Umbert, and he gratefully accepted the invitation. The boy trotted over to where the man sat cross-legged in front of a cheery, orange campfire. "Hello," he said, motioning for Umbert to sit. "My name is Oslan."

Umbert sat. "I'm Umbert. This is my first day."

Oslan smiled kindly. "I know. We all know the new recruits."

Umbert nodded, gaze straying to the fire. They all might know, but none of the others had made the effort to acknowledge his presence in any way.

As if reading Umbert's mind, Oslan responded to the thought. "Everyone's afraid to get too close to the new guy, especially one as young as you. The inexperienced don't tend to last long. They'll get a lot friendlier once you've proved yourself."

Umbert did not understand. He rolled his gaze to Oslan's blue eyes. "Proved myself what?"

"Competent. Reliable." Oslan poked a stick into the fire and rolled something from the ashes. "A survivor."

Umbert shivered. "What if I'm none of those?"

Oslan replied without emotion. "Then you won't last long, and there's no reason to get to know you." Attention still locked on the campfire, he explained further. "It's dangerous to associate with new recruits. They make more mistakes, and in war, mistakes are fatal. You freeze up, it might mean the death of your shieldmate."

Umbert bit his lip and studied his own hands. As shocking as the revelation was, he appreciated the older man's candor. "I'm going to die, aren't I?" The words came surprisingly easily, but true contemplation of their meaning remained a distant abstraction, impossible to reach.

Oslan grasped the object he had poked from the flames, gingerly tearing it with light touches that saved his fingers from burning. "We all are, son. Some sooner than later. That's just the way it is, the way it's always been."

"Why?"

"Why, indeed." Oslan's lips formed a knowing smile that reflected all of his years. "Because we're at war. And, in war, no matter how good you are, you'll run into an enemy who's faster or stronger or more determined than you. Or into plain old bad luck. The fighting goes on; but, for you, it's over. Everyone's time comes eventually. The quick, the alert, the lucky last longest." He passed over a greasy hunk of charred grouse.

Umbert accepted the food gratefully. Like most boys his age, he could happily spend all day doing nothing but eating and sleeping. "I meant 'why' as in, why are we fighting? What's the war about?"

"We're fighting to save ourselves, our women, our flocks, and our land from the Hurrdu."

Umbert savored the warmth of the cooked food in his hands and the heat of the fire on the front half of his body. "Why do *they* fight?"

Oslan gave Umbert a patient look. "To get those things."

The explanation made little sense to Umbert. He took a bite of the grouse, considering for several moments as he chewed. "We take those things from the Hurrdu, too."

Oslan took a bite of his own share of the meager feast. "We have little choice but to kill the black devils when they attack us. We need their flocks to eat, their women to help us reproduce. And it seems only right to reclaim the lands they steal from us."

Oslan's point seemed at once logical and ludicrous to Umbert. "But if we just stopped fighting, wouldn't we each have our own flocks to eat, our own women to reproduce, and our youth back to grow crops on our share of the land?"

Oslan rose, stretched, and placed a fatherly hand on Umbert's shoulder. "Wouldn't it be lovely if life really were that simple?"

Umbert just nodded. So many things in life seemed easy and obvious to him, and grown-ups found him eternally amusing. *Will I ever get old enough to understand?* If he believed what Oslan had told him about war, it seemed unlikely.

The next day, another contingent joined them, bone-weary, disheveled, supporting their injured. They also brought a line of twenty women, roped together to prevent escape. Their leader reported to the commander; and, though Umbert could not hear the words, the deepening frown on the commander's face suggested bad news. Umbert focused on the women, who ranged in age from nearing thirty to one barely his own age. He studied her most closely. She bore the same velvety black hair as the others, but her eyes held a glint of emerald. While the others kept their heads low, she glanced about fitfully, like a deer seeking a safe place to give birth to a helpless fawn. Umbert's tea-colored skin was the darkest in his company, yet all of the prisoners, save her, were darker still. The youngest matched him and was, perhaps, even a quarter shade lighter.

The commander raised his voice above the camp hubbub and greetings, which silenced instantly. "Men, our companions won a very hard-fought battle."

Cheering followed the announcement, cut short by the commander's sudden glare. Sunlight blazed through his close-cut sandy hair, and his gray-brown gaze carved a trail of quiet through the ranks. "But they could not prevent a flanking. Men, we must turn and fight the enemy behind us or risk losing our entire village."

Umbert gave his attention back to the girl, who hurriedly looked away. It did not matter to him where he fought and, probably, died.

"Umbert!" the commander's voice drew Umbert to instant attention, and he whirled to face the man who now stood nearly on top of him. "I want you to stay and guard the prisoners." He handed Umbert an iron-tipped spear.

Shocked, Umbert accepted his first weapon, stammering, "Y–y–yes, sir." He could not keep himself from blurting, "Wouldn't someone with more experience do a better job?"

The commander's head lowered, snakelike. He was clearly unused to being challenged.

Umbert swallowed hard, anticipating a lecture on obedience.

But the commander's features turned as fatherly as Oslan's. "Umbert, I need every experienced spearman to handle the threat behind us. You're safest here. Do you understand?"

"Yes, sir." Umbert believed he did. The commander had given him the most secure assignment to keep him alive longer, a gesture of mercy not mistrust. "Thank you, sir." Only then, he thought to wonder if the choice had more to do with the other men's safety, relieving them of their youngest, least competent member.

"Good luck." The commander stormed off, shouting orders to the other men. Within moments, he had them all massed and marching, including the injured, leaving Umbert and the women alone.

Umbert stared after the retreating soldiers, scarcely daring to believe they could mobilize so quickly. Dragged into an unwelcome apprenticeship, he found himself alone in enemy territory with absolutely no clue as to how to handle the situation. His mind felt numb, blank. A chill spiraled through him, followed by episodic shaking that made his teeth chatter and his hands tremble in wild, uncontrollable arcs. He fought for control. *Just wait and hide until they come for me.* The whole thing seemed madness, one day celebrating his birthday and savoring the beginning of his last year of childish freedom, the next swept into a nonsensical war. Alone. Untrained. Apparently, surrounded. Weak-kneed, he slid down the shaft of the spear to huddle in a heap on the ground.

A sound at Umbert's back mobilized him. He sprang to his feet, whirling, and the spear collapsed to the forest's leafy floor. He found himself suddenly confronted by the frightened faces of twenty women. Helplessly bound to one another in a chain that stretched from one sturdy oak to another, they watched his every move in silence. Most reminded him of the women who had raised him and the other children: dark, silky-haired, doe-eyed women with broad hips and pendulous breasts. Though merely one of the group, his mother had quietly and proudly claimed him, though she could not pick out his father for certain. His gaze went naturally to the youngest and remained there, spellbound.

The woman looked bravely back at him. "Are you going to rape me?"

Her question shattered the silence, and Umbert back-stepped in surprise. "Wh–what?" he stammered, though he had heard her words clearly enough.

Another spat at him. "You heard her, white dog! What do you plan to do with us?"

Umbert continued to stare. He could imagine the Hurrdu children crying for their mothers and sisters, the men separated from their wives, mothers, and daughters. "I'm going," he said softly, "to release you."

The loathing and terror disappeared from their faces. The youngest woman smiled at Umbert. Despite her age, she clearly spoke for all of them. "Release us? Why?"

"Because." Umbert summoned courage from a depth he never knew he had. "Because I don't understand this war or why we're fighting it. Because you call me a white dog, though I'm as dark as you. Because . . . I'm too young . . . too inexperienced, perhaps too stupid to understand any reason to keep you from your loved ones when I miss my own so terribly." Umbert raised his knife.

Most of the women flinched, rearing backward, though the one he addressed did not. She watched in fascination as the blade hacked at the restraining ropes again and again. Each attack parted a few strands and sent the knife bouncing back toward Umbert. He settled for a slower sawing motion, and the rope parted, dividing the women into two lines.

Several still stared at Umbert with dark suspicion. Others set to trying to fully free themselves from the bindings, while Umbert chopped them into smaller groups until, finally, they all stood as individuals, some bound and some free. Most took off running toward their tribal grounds, even with frayed ropes still wrapped around their wrists or ankles. Others stayed where they were, unwinding the tattered hemp. The youngest remained still, allowing Umbert to cautiously cut around the loops until the two of them stood, alone and unfettered, in the clearing.

"Thank you," the woman said.

Guilt assailed Umbert, and he lowered his head. So many men had spent their lives for these captives he had cut loose on a whim. He could not help considering Oslan's words. His tribe needed those women to replace the ones the Hurrdu had taken, to assure future generations, to merely keep them alive. Yet, when these frightened women had stood before him, all he could see was the agony of their own people, the families who would so desperately miss them. "My name is Umbert."

"Mine's Kaliah," she replied. "You're not safe here."

Her words seemed like gross understatement. Umbert forced a smile. "Run with the others," he said. "I am already dead." Surrounded by the enemy, he doubted he had much chance for survival, even if his own allies did not kill him for his treachery. "My life ended the moment they conscripted me."

"Come with me." Kaliah offered her hand.

Umbert stared, her request utter nonsense. Sunlight gleamed from her jet-black hair, drawing out highlights of sienna and red mahogany. "Come . . ."

". . . with me," Kaliah finished again, holding out a hand. "Come."

Umbert found his hand edging toward hers, beyond his control. "Am I a prisoner?" Males caught in the war were usually executed, though both sides took occasional slaves. The danger of the men banding together in the fields or escaping with significant information seemed too great to risk. The women appeared to understand and accept their roles in the process, whether as warriors or prisoners. He had always believed that a sign of their passivity, though now he wondered whether the women just had a better, calmer approach to a horrible situation.

Kaliah laughed, the sound high and musical. "You're not a prisoner. You're . . . my friend. My guest."

Umbert accepted her hand, though he wondered what it truly meant. He doubted the men of her tribe would prove as welcoming. They might take his youth into account and try to retrain him to fight for their cause, which seemed like an astounding irony. More likely, they would execute him. Nevertheless, he went. At least, he might have a few hours in exquisite company before he died, whether in war, for treason, or as a hated tribal enemy. Neither of those ends would likely be quick or painless.

Hand in hand, the two walked through the *aldona* in silence. Though crisscrossed with boot tracks and stinking from decades of blood and death, the forest still seemed beautiful. Sunbeams stabbed or glared through the canopy, making the hand-shaped leaves appear to glow. Sparse undergrowth fought the ravages of eternal shadow and stomping columns of warriors. Deadfalls lay scattered through the forest, the dusty remains of roads crushed beneath them, notches cut in wild patterns that had once marked trails or served as targets for testing or nervous sword arms.

Kaliah eased Umbert around encampments he might have blindly blundered into without her steady guidance. No one paid them any heed, which surprised Umbert. Even with Kaliah's reassuring company, he felt nervous as a hunted squirrel. The camps clearly belonged to the Hurrdu, yet they did not leap up at the sight of him, eager for destruction. Instead, they gave the two youngsters the meaningful smiles of grown-ups watching children play at love. In those moments, Umbert clung to Kaliah's hand like the lifeline it appeared to be.

At length, forest gave way to a village remarkably similar to that of the Arsie, his own people. Tents dotted the outskirts, where olive-skinned women swept doorways, sewed, or pounded foodstuffs. Children raced along the dirt pathways, the younger ones engaged in the rough-and-tumble of play-fighting, the older ones assisting their mothers.

Kaliah drew Umbert past these to the village shops and cottages, then straight to a walled mansion in the center. There, a pair of female guards met them. Without word or question, the women opened the gates and gestured them through the opening.

Stunned by the whole process, Umbert continued to walk with Kaliah, scarcely believing a prisoner would be accorded such treatment. The king of the Arsie lived in a castle in the middle of their tribal lands, and he had similar fortifications, breached by peasants only in times of desperate need, for example, if the Hurrdu penetrated deep into their lands. He could not understand why these guards would grant access to an enemy without the slightest challenge, without interrogation.

At any moment, Umbert expected a spear through his back or a horde of armed men to descend upon him. As if awakening from a dream, he wondered what had possessed him to come. Surely, the Hurrdu would hack him to pieces once they realized what he was; he wondered why it had taken them this long. The Arsie always knew one of their own at a glance, and he doubted the Hurrdu would have any more trouble. Dark devils, white dogs, they called one another; yet, Umbert had never understood the difference.

At the door to the mansion, another pair of guards, men this time, let them through without a word. One did give Kaliah a smile and a bow of greeting before opening the door. Avoiding looking at them, for fear they might examine him, Umbert continued to shamble along at Kaliah's side. Once past the guards and into an airy hallway, he finally whispered his concern. "Kaliah, what's going on?"

"I want you to meet my father."

"All right." It seemed a proper request, especially given the feelings stirring inside him. He enjoyed holding her warm hand in his, staring into her beautiful eyes. "But isn't this . . . incredibly dangerous?"

Kaliah slowed her pace only long enough to steer Umbert from room to room. Though sparse, the furnishings spoke of ancient elegance and wealth. The worn chairs nestled into intricately carved frames, their fraying fabric silk and velvet. Desks and cabinets, though split and notched, perfectly matched. "No battle was ever won without courage." She paused to knock on a massive, wooden door. "You displayed more today than any man I've met."

"I only did what was right." Umbert confessed, "And right now, I'm very much afraid."

"I would worry," Kaliah said, "if you weren't."

The door wrenched open. A skinny, middle-aged woman in patched and faded finery opened the door and gasped. "Kaliah!" She caught the girl into an embrace, her hazel eyes shining with delight, her rich brown hair like a shimmering cascade between her narrow shoulders. "Kaliah, they told us—"

Umbert lost the rest beneath a rush of desperate worry. His own attention went to the gray-bearded man who occupied a gem-encrusted chair at the farther end of the room. Two boys attended him, and a guard snapped to attention between the sitting Hurrdu and the door. Clearly a man of station, Kaliah's father spoke in a booming voice. "Kaliah! It's so wonderful to see you. They told us the Arsie had captured you."

Kaliah wriggled free of the woman's grip. "They had. But this brave man rescued me." She took Umbert's hand again.

Umbert glanced behind himself before realizing she meant him. Suddenly, he found all eyes precisely where he did not want them: on him. He flushed. "I . . . it . . . was nothing."

The father's face went stern. "My daughter's freedom is not nothing."

Terror ground through Umbert. "I didn't mean . . . I mean I wouldn't . . ."

Kaliah squeezed Umbert's hand.

The father laughed. "Your bravery pleases me. And your modesty. What's your name, young man?"

"Umbert," Umbert said, very aware of his gaze. He worried the older man might find it too evasive or intense, and he found it hard to manage anything in between.

"Umbert," the king repeated. "Thank you for saving my daughter." He added carefully, "How goes the battle?"

"Wretchedly, sir." Umbert answered without thought, studying his hands to avoid the man's probing gaze.

The squeak of chair legs brought Umbert's regard back to the older man, who had risen and taken a step toward them. "Wretchedly, but I had heard—" He took another step toward Umbert, the boys hanging back, the guard hurriedly moving ahead of him. "I was told we had managed a flanking maneuver, that my daughter would be rescued in no time. And here she is to prove it so."

Umbert did not know what to say. Clearly, this man possessed great status in the Hurrdu tribe and believed Umbert one of them. The wrong words would seal his doom, so he chose them as carefully as possible. "Sir, the war goes wretchedly for me, because I do not wish to fight. I was to be trained as a blacksmith's apprentice, not a warrior's."

Kaliah gave Umbert's hand another squeeze. The woman, by appearance Kaliah's mother, retreated.

"You do not wish to fight?" The gray-haired man seemed taken aback.

"No."

"Not even for the good of the Hurrdu? To keep our women, like my daughter, safe?"

Though Umbert knew it a dangerous answer, he gave the honest one. "No." He added cautiously. "But perhaps I would change my mind if I understood the reason for this war."

The father's nostrils flared, but he gathered patience for his daughter's savior. "We fight for the honor of our people, to protect our lands, our homes, our property, and our womenfolk."

The answer sounded astonishingly familiar. Umbert might as well be back in the camp, listening to Oslan. "But we could spare all that, and our men, too, if we simply stopped the battle."

The older man returned to his chair, eyes rolling. "Yes, that would be simple. Sometimes I forget how the young think." He shook his head, glancing at his guard. "How does one define patriotism to a child? How can I explain the significance of racial pride?"

The guard merely shrugged, the questions clearly rhetorical.

"Tell him," Kaliah said softly, and suddenly Umbert understood. She had recognized in him the same youthful innocence and wonder that spurred her, the same driving need to end a conflict that had spanned more decades than they would ever see. Generations had come and gone through a war that simply was and would remain until one side or the other disappeared or came to understand. The abject hatred driven into all of them at birth had become consummate, an understanding as old and certain as life itself. "My tribe good; your tribe bad." Yet, the very details that defined those differences had disappeared, lost in the need for a tribal future: offspring, new warriors to replace the old, the ancient hatreds fed anew.

Kaliah had placed his life at ultimate risk; yet, at the same time, granted Umbert exactly what he wanted: one chance to save both worlds.

Umbert cleared his throat. "Sir," he started, hoping the proper words would come. "There are no more white dogs or dark devils. The capture and breeding of one another's women has seen to that." He glanced at Kaliah, who tightened her grip in his and gave him an encouraging look. "Kaliah and I could pass for siblings, which seems absurd when you realize that she is Hurrdu." Umbert met the king's deeply set brown eyes. "And I am Arsie."

The guard stiffened, hand gliding to his sword. He looked askance at the older man, who sat in a stunned silence.

Kaliah grabbed her mother's arm. "Please," she said softly.

The woman spoke. "Mylian, I am half Arsie, by blood." She added carefully, "And so are you."

"No." Mylian pounded his fist on the chair. "No!"

The woman gave no ground. "Look at our daughter, and tell me otherwise."

Mylian did as the woman bade, studying Kaliah as if for the first time. His gaze traveled over the auburn hair, the hazel eyes, the skin with just a hint of her parents' swarthiness. A smile eased onto his face, then split wide open into great, pealing guffaws. He whirled back to face the youngsters in the doorway. "Do you think you can convince the leader of the Arsie as you have me?"

Umbert did not know, but Kaliah never hesitated. "I'm certain of it."

A great respect welled up in Umbert now that Kaliah had proved willing to risk her own life the same way she had his. Her certainty proved contagious, and he knew that one day the great tribe of the Hurrsie-Ardu would bring prosperity to a territory once ravaged by war. And Kaliah would marry Horton Blacksmith's apprentice.

THE MUSES' DARLING

by Sarah A. Hoyt

Sarah A. Hoyt lives in Colorado with her husband, two sons, and five cats. She has sold over two dozen short stories to markets as varied as *Weird Tales* and *Analog*. Her Shakespearean fantasy novel, *Ill Met By Moonlight*, has recently been published and she is currently at work on the sequel.

"EVERYONE," Kit Marlowe proclaimed loudly, standing on the threshold of his open door, "who doesn't like boys and tobacco is a fool."

A few steps away, halfway across the sparsely furnished room, Will woke up and raised his head from the small oak table on which it had rested. Will had fallen asleep in Marlowe's room, waiting for Marlowe to return and read Will's first attempt at writing a play.

The candle Will had lit on entering the room was almost burned out. It would be near midnight.

Marlowe looked drunk. He grinned and said, "There is nothing to religion, you know. Just tricks and—"

Will rushed forward, toppling the stool on which he'd sat. He pulled his friend into the room and shut the door, before someone outside overheard words that could have them both jailed by tomorrow and executed the day after. In the England of Queen Elizabeth, the Protestant religion was mandatory, church services compulsory, and blasphemy or vocal dissent a capital matter.

"Ah, friend Will," Kit Marlowe said, and turned a dazzling smile in Will's direction, at the same time drowning Will in the vapors of expensive Spanish wine from Kit's breath.

He reeled, and Will caught him and supported him.

"You came," Marlowe said, then hiccuped and giggled. "As you said you would, that I might look at your excellent . . . your excellent . . . what's name? Play? Titus whatsis? Andronic . . . nic . . . nic."

Will flinched. He'd come, indeed, as Kit Marlowe had bid him, searching for instruction from Kit, the great playwright, the muses' darling, the toast of the London stage. Kit's landlady had let Will in. Will was a constant presence, a habitual petitioner of Marlowe's.

But Kit obviously had forgotten his promise to look at *Titus Andronicus,* the fifty mangled pages that lay where Will's head had rested.

Will supported Marlowe all the way to the inner door of the room. He put his hand on the knob, but it would not turn.

"Have you a key to this door?" he asked Marlowe.

Marlowe giggled and said, confidentially, "Know you that I studied theology, Will? At—" Hiccup. "Bloody Cambridge. And now I write plays. Bloody plays. Great work for a scholar, is it not? Doubtless my masters are astonished."

Will cursed under his breath. It was obvious he would get no answer about the key. He felt Kit's sleeves for the key the playwright must have secreted somewhere about himself.

He knew well enough that Marlowe had attended Cambridge. It was one of the many things he envied his friend and mentor.

Though they were both the sons of respectable craftsmen, Kit had attended university on a scholarship, a luxury Will could not afford.

And though they were both of an age, Kit Marlowe's plays—*Tamburlaine* and *Faustus* and *Dido*—were the talk of London, the delight of all. Meanwhile, Will, despite his earnest attempts to write for the theater, had got no nearer it than guarding the horses of theatergoers.

Even their appearances were unequal. Kit, slim and good-looking, with his russet hair caught back in a pony-tail, his sculpted beard, his thin mustache, wore pearly-gray velvet doublet and pants, the sleeves slashed through to show golden silk beneath. At collar and cuffs, lace peeked.

Will, ruddy and strong, with black hair already receding at the temples, had nothing to wear but the same old, much mended wool suit he'd brought with him from Stratford-upon-Avon, three years ago.

Yet, truly, Will didn't resent Marlowe. He was grateful that Kit was willing to help him, that Kit was willing to teach him.

Finding the key to the locked door dangling from a chain at Marlowe's neck, Will pulled the chain over Marlowe's head.

"St. Paul," Kit whispered confidentially, "was a juggler, a fraud, the only educated man among the apostles, who were all rude fellows of the lowest class. He blinkered them with tricks. He—"

Will shivered at Kit's dangerous talk. Kit was mad. The small, golden key he'd got from around Kit's neck fit the keyhole on the door. Whether Kit knew it or not, Kit courted death. Aye, and he would win her, if he persisted.

Will turned the key in the lock and opened the door. In the dark space beyond, Will could distinguish nothing, save some shining dust twirling in midair—magical fireflies in the gloom.

What was this? What enchantment was here?

Kit shook himself, as though waking. He stood on his own two feet, not leaning on Will, and put an arm in front of Will to prevent his entering the room. "Thank you, friend Will. Thank you, but I'll go into my room by myself." Thus speaking, still unsteady on his feet, he skipped into his room, retrieving the golden key from the lock in passing. In a swift movement, he slammed the thick oak door in Will's face.

Will jumped back, startled. The devil take the man. The devil take Kit Marlowe, great poet or not.

In his three years in London, Will had made but two friends who could be called such. One was a former Franciscan friar who dabbled in herbs and philosophy and whom people called mad. The other was Kit Marlowe, apparently the madder of the two.

Will had waited for Kit, for a moment of attention, for his cursory reading of Will's lines and perhaps his giving Will a word of encouragement or two. Instead, he got this—the risk of being taken in for listening to blasphemous words and a door shut in his face. Even if Kit were too drunk to read, he could have behaved more courteously.

Will picked up his manuscript.

From Marlowe's room, all the while, came a low, steady muttering, the continuous, senseless monologue of a drunken man.

Will tightened his hand around the pages of *Titus Andronicus,* the play he hoped would rival Marlowe's *Tamburlaine.* He'd talk to Marlowe tomorrow when he hoped the man would have come to his senses.

A sound like that of new, strong cloth ripping under great force came from the bedroom. Its intensity was such that the only cloth that could make that sound would be the size of the world—a winding sheet for the universe.

Will stopped, hesitated, turned to look at the locked door. Did Kit need help?

"At Sestos, Hero dwelt; Hero the fair, whom young Apollo courted for her hair," a woman's voice said. "And offered as a dower his burning throne, Where she should sit for men to gaze upon."

No. Not a woman's voice. The creature uttering those words sounded like liquid fire and fluid ice. A female it must be, yes, but a female angel, the queen of fairies, a creature of primeval force, of undying passion.

It went on speaking, while Will listened.

In such a voice had Eve, sweetly, convinced Adam to taste the fatal apple. In such a voice had the sirens called to Ulysses whilst, tied to the mast, he steered his ship past their temptations.

"Some say for her the fairest Cupid pined and looking in her face was stricken blind."

The words, beautiful enough in themselves, said in that voice, became pure ambrosia that flowed through Will's ears to his mind, and gave him a taste of heaven and immortality.

Tears of joy and confusion flowed down Will's face.

When the voice stopped talking, when the room was silent, he woke as a man who opens his eyes from a beautiful dream and knows not where he is.

Had he been awake or sleeping?

"I have had," he whispered to himself. "A most rare vision. I have had a dream—past the wit of man to say what dream it was. Man's hand is not able to taste, his tongue to conceive, nor his heart to report what my dream was."

Yet, how could Will have slept? He'd never before slept standing up, and he still stood in front of Marlowe's door.

What man sleeps standing? And what man, further, holds a manuscript in his hand while he sleeps?

Still, Will must have been sleeping. For how else could these wonders be? Oh, surely he'd been asleep and that dreamed voice must be an echo of paradise lost, remaining in the heart of fallen man.

The room was quiet. Marlowe must be asleep. Will rushed out of the room, closing the door behind himself. He hurried past the door of Marlowe's landlady, firmly closed at this late an hour, and out of the house.

Outside the front door lay a narrow lane, paved in beaten

dirt mixed in with refuse thrown down by generations to form a dark, foul-smelling mud. Night was advanced, but here in Shoreditch, it might have been full day. No, better than day, for in the day the inhabitants of this newest and shoddiest of London suburbs slept. At night they crept out of their dens and plied their trades.

Through the open doors of the taverns that dotted the area, the light of many candles and the smell of roasted mutton spilled. Apprentices in large, noisy groups, walked by. Whores, in bright clothing, laughed and sang. The smell of ale cloaked the area like a fog. Outside a tavern a man shouted loudly for one and all to come and watch the whipping of the blind bear—*till the blood runs down his hoary sides, a most entertaining and amusing spectacle.*

What if Will hadn't dreamed the voice? What if what he'd heard was true? What if Marlowe had someone in there? A woman?

It was fantastical. It was impossible.

Yet, now calmer, he knew that the poetry he'd heard had the ring and sound of Marlowe's own creation.

While he walked the narrow streets of Shoreditch, five-story buildings on either side of him blocking all sight of the sky and penning smells of sweat and rancid food and old ale all around him, Will couldn't help forming a very strange idea in his mind.

What if Marlowe weren't the one who wrote Marlowe's plays? What if they were the work of some noblewoman, some female scholar that Marlowe kept in his room, writing plays for Marlowe's credit and profit?

Part of Will protested that Marlowe would never do that. Madcap and sometimes dangerous Marlowe might be, but his sins were those of the hothead, of the intemperate, sanguine man. He pulled knives on men in the heat of argument, or he made devastatingly cutting statements about this one's mother and that one's wife. Or boys and tobacco.

But he'd been kind to Will and, more than anyone else in the theater, had treated Will as an equal, offered him help with his poetry and aid in storming the stage where Marlowe's words ruled supreme.

Surely he couldn't be an evil man.

And yet, wasn't it strange how Marlowe never worked at his writing? He never seemed to make an effort at anything. His life, such as Will saw it, was one long feast. Kit caroused with artists and got drunk with noblemen. Where did he find time for the prodigious reading, the careful editing required by his monumental historical plays that beggared the Earth and stormed the skies? While Will read and studied and applied his every waking moment to his work and yet had trouble giving wings to his leaden prose.

Will shook his head. Baseless envy. Let it be his own baseless envy engendering these wretched thoughts.

Yet the worm of suspicion gnawed at his heart.

When he gained his lodging, and in his single, small room, lay down upon his pallet and covered himself with his worn blanket, he found that sleep eluded his belabored mind.

Tossing and turning, between exhaustion and dream, well past one and shy of the other he knew that he must find what Marlowe kept in that locked room.

He must *know*.

In the morning, Kit Marlowe would go out, to break his fast at the Mermaid, the tavern where actors and theater people gathered.

Then, Will could look inside and bid to satisfy his curiosity.

The lock was a problem, but Will would try to conquer it with the tip of his old dagger. If he failed, then curiosity would have to rest unsatisfied. But if he managed to spring the lock and open the door, then he would know for sure whether his mentor was a monster or whether Will, himself, had become as mad as those around him.

On that thought, he fell asleep and dreamed of the liquid-fire voice reciting divine poetry.

*   *   *

Morning found Will standing across from Marlowe's lodging, in the narrow space between two buildings, his dark hat pulled down over his face—trying to meld with the surroundings and vanish. After a short wait, he saw Marlowe come out of his lodgings, resplendent in violet velvet and brand-new lace. Marlowe turned left to the Mermaid, and Will hurried across the street.

Convincing Marlowe's landlady, who, from her open room, watched, that he had been told to wait here for the great playwright was the work of a moment.

Will stole up the stairs on winged feet, his heart beating within his chest like a hammer upon a great anvil. In Marlowe's antechamber, the outer door closed, Will drew his dagger and knelt in front of the inner door.

He had an hour, maybe. No more.

Will should be there when Marlowe came back, since the landlady might talk. But he should be but sitting at the table, ready to drink the muses' wisdom from his teacher's lips. He should not be caught attempting to violate Marlowe's privacy.

Will inserted the dagger in the keyhole and moved it around, trying to loosen the lock. At first, it seemed his efforts were vain. Just when he was about to give up—sweat flowing down his fast-balding head to sting his eyes—the lock sprang and the room opened.

Will's first thought was disappointment. He could not account for the golden firefly lights he'd thought he'd seen the night before.

This room—what he could see of it through the half-open door—looked all too normal. A narrow bed lay beneath the lead-paned window and dust motes danced in the shaft of morning light that revealed disarrayed blankets on the bed and dusty rushes upon the floor.

The only thing that made it Marlowe's room and not an anonymous lodging was an assortment of suits hanging from the far wall—velvet and satin and silk, each in a more vivid color than the one next to it. Will smiled at his friend's vanity and pushed the door wholly open, to satisfy himself.

On opening the door fully, he saw to his left a bookstand. Not a desk, but a bookstand, tall and narrow and golden, with a single, thick and ancient-looking book open atop it.

Will crept into the room and read the words written in faded ink on the open page: *Spell to summon the muses.*

What was this? What sorcery?

His heart pounding, his vision blurring, Will read on, a string of senseless words, whispering them to himself as he read. At the senseless but well-sounding words, the air in front of Will shimmered as it had the night before. Had he heard the voice of a muse, then? The voice of one of those goddesses of antiquity who could bring life and glory to any poet's words, any musician's music, any sculptor's chisel?

As he dreamed and spoke half enthralled, the air in front of him shimmered and roiled until from the maelstrom three women formed, dressed in Greek fashion.

"Hail, stranger," one of them said—a creature with the face of an angel and golden hair flowing on either side of her smiling face. "Hail stranger, well met."

"Hail our deliverer," a dark-haired woman who stood shoulder to shoulder with the blonde said. Her tresses were braided, framing a face steady and grave.

"Hail the man who's freed us from ignoble slavery. Hail," a third muse said. Her chestnut hair lent a soft appearance to her sad features.

"Slavery?" Will asked.

"For ten years, that man Marlowe has kept us in his thrall. He knows magic enough that he only calls us when he is protected by powerful spells inherited from his forefathers. Thus we must work for him, but we get not the payment prescribed in the ancient laws. Like slaves we toil, with no reward," the third woman said.

Will trembled. These women were so fair, their voices so harmonious. Artistically draped tunics hid bodies such as men dreamed of but seldom saw. Their high breasts, their soft curves made Will weak with desire. They sounded like angels. How could Kit have borne to keep them thus enslaved? For his base gain.

Oh, miserable wretch, who kept angels in chains.

"But you, by summoning us without baseless tricks or evil protection spells, have opened the shackles of our magical servitude," the blonde said.

"We are grateful to you, Master Will," the grave woman said.

"And for your help we'll give you reward," the brown-haired one said.

The blonde advanced, flowing, and handed Will something—a small square of paper.

A glance at it and Will could see, written upon the paper cabalistic incantations and strange symbols.

"If you call on us with those words," the brunette said. "We'll come. Call us if you need help writing plays that inflame men's minds."

"But I thought," Will said, "that you despised helping write—"

The blonde smiled. "You're not like *him,* who has so long avoided paying the price for what we generously provided." Her voice, still liquid fire, acquired a cutting edge, like a blade drawn and glinting in the sun.

Will took a step back, surprised at the change.

And saw the brunette smile and say. "*Now, he* will pay, sisters. Kit will pay."

And on that word, they all smiled and Will noticed for the first time that all three classical beauties had teeth as sharp and pointy as a wild animal's, ready to bite and gnaw and tear.

Will didn't remember returning to the antechamber, but he was there, sitting at the table, when Marlowe came in.

Were those the muses? Had Marlowe summoned them? What was the price they spoke of?

"Will, you do not look well," Kit said, coming in the door. "You're pale as milk curd and twice as wan."

Kit closed the door behind himself, self-assured and looking, for all the world, like a new man in this light of day.

His narrow, long hand clad in a white suede glove that Will knew cost a small fortune, came to rest on Will's shoulder. "You must take care. I hear the plague is abroad and people dying of it. Would you like something? Some wine? I have some cherry sack arrived only yesterday in a ship from Spain."

Will nodded, not knowing what he did. Should he tell Marlowe? Should he tell him what he'd done and thus prevent whatever horrible consequences would come from Will's transgression?

But if he told, what would Kit do? At best, Kit would grow violent. Will eyed the bright handle of the expensive dagger whose sheath hung from Marlowe's belt. At worst . . . at worst Kit would stop all the help he'd given Will.

No more listening to and correcting Will's poetry, no more talks about the theater and its ways, no more introductions to theater owners and actors. And then there was the paper from the muses. Would it not be worth it to use magic, to have words such as Marlowe's credited to one's fame and glory?

The price might be nothing at all, compared to such poetry. But if Will spoke, he'd lose the paper.

Will couldn't bear the thought. He remained quiet.

"Ah, wait till you taste this. It could revive the dead." On that, Kit opened the small trunk by the window and brought out a bottle and two cups, poured bright red wine into each cup, and set one in front of Will.

"Partake of my wine," he said. "I'll be gone out of the town for a while, for a holiday. But I'll return in time, and we'll look at your play together, your magnificent *Titus Andronicus.*" He smiled, a kindly smile that made his small, impish face look innocent and too young. "I'll tell you, it will well outshine my *Tamburlaine.*"

Will wanted to believe Marlowe. But what did Marlowe know of human effort and human art, if the muses wrote for him?

The wine seemed to warm Will's frozen body, but his heart remained encased in cold and distance. If he'd brought real danger on Marlowe, Will should warn him. Yet how could he warn him when he didn't know what the women meant by payment? Nothing in the old writings spoke of vengeful nymphs or hungry muses, did it? Here Will's small learning failed him and he wished he knew.

Friar Laurence would know, he thought. The friar knew more mythology and legends than anyone living. And he lived a few streets away, here in Shoreditch, where he used his herbal remedies to help the poor. So, Will would go to him and ask what such creatures were and what they might want for payment.

If they meant ill to Marlowe, Will would spend all his money—all of it, that he had saved to send home to Anne and his three children—and rent a horse to follow Marlowe and warn him of the danger.

"Where are you going today?" he asked Kit. He must know, in case he had to catch up with Kit.

Marlowe, ready to leave, cleared away the wine and cups and half pushed Will out the door ahead of him.

"Oh, to Deptford." Kit smiled. "Just games of tables with some friends, in a boarding house—Mistress Bull's."

Outside, in the busy, bustling street, Kit offered Will his hand. "I'm tired. Run down from all the work and bustle of the city. A day of gaming and drinking and friendly conversation will replenish my heart and soul. You take the like remedy, friend Will, and I'll talk to you of *Titus* as soon as I return."

Marlowe smiled and waved and thus they parted.

Friar Laurence's den was a long, dark room that smelled green and spicy. When Will came in, he heard scraping sounds from the back room, and the friar's voice called out, "Hello?"

"It's Will, Father."

"Ah, Will." The friar came to the middle of the room to welcome him. He was a small, smiling man so thin that his cheekbones seemed to peek—a skeletal forewarning of death—through his parchment-thin skin. "Come in, come in." He wore his old habit still, now gray and sooty with ash and dirt. That he dared wear it in these times, was a mark of the man he was and the respect in which the locals held him.

In the inner sanctum, to which Will had often been admitted, retorts bubbled and spirit lamps glowed and all the equipment of alchemical work lay on a long bench. Friar Laurence picked up some herbs and commenced chopping them.

Will sat upon a stool.

"Morrow, Will," the friar said. "The gray-eyed morn smiles on the frowning night. Now, 'ere the sun advance his burning eye, the day to cheer and night's dank dew to dry, I must fill this osier cage of ours with baleful weeds and precious-juiced flowers. Oh, mickle is the precious grace that lies in plants, herbs, and stones, their true qualities, for nothing so vile on the Earth doth live but to the Earth some special good give." The friar picked up a bulb and showed it to Will. "Nor aught so good but strayed from that fair use, revolts from true birth, stumbling on abuse; virtue itself turns vice being misapplied. And vice sometime by action is dignified. Within the infant rind of this weak flower poison hath residence and medicine power."

Will endured like chatter, but his thoughts dwelt on Kit. Had Will, like the innocent flower, harbored poison to kill his friend?

No, it could not be. There must be another, simpler explanation. Could Will have dreamed it all?

He felt the square of paper within his sleeve. No. He hadn't dreamed it.

Perhaps he was going mad.

Upon the friar's drawing breath, Will said, "Father, I must

ask you what you think. Did the gods of old ever exist? We have such detailed records of their existence . . . their help to both sides in the war at Troy, for instance. All written down by reputable historians, men of much learning."

The friar turned baleful green eyes on Will and for a moment seemed to stare through the young man. "The church," he said, as though speaking out of a dream, "would say that they existed, but they were all demons, tempting men to perdition. Why ask you?"

"Oh," Will said, forcing his voice to lightness. "Everyone calls Kit Marlowe the muses' darling, and I wondered if it might be true, if there were indeed such creatures and what kind of sprites they might be."

This time the friar's gaze fixed intently indeed on Will. "Aye, and Marlowe would be fool enough to trifle with the muses, too. I've heard of him. He is said to be a madman. Besides, it is said he is descended from Merlin himself, the heir, no doubt, of foul books. While at Cambridge, he ever signed himself Merlin, of which Marlowe is but the corruption. And there's no worse thing than dabbling in magic without sufficient knowledge and with no protection." His gaze became softer. "But I see you're troubled. What brings this question on, Will? What makes you think on muses and on gods, aspire to supernatural not of religion?"

Will sighed.

Friar Lawrence had such eyes—green as leeks and shining, like the eyes of a cat that peeks out of the dark and spies a mouse. The friar threw some seeds down into a glass tube wherein the transparent liquid bubbled bright green. "Out with it, Will. Though you're not of the old religion and wouldn't trust me with your confession, I warrant you can trust in me."

Will sighed again and out it came—the glimmer in the air, and the muses with their sharp, odd teeth.

When he talked of the muses saying that Marlowe would pay, Friar Lawrence drew a sharp breath, like a man suddenly stricken. "There's no time to lose," he said. "You've freed the evil creatures into the ether, Will. They will find him and collect their fee and the fee of old pagan gods is always life. They take your life to feed their strength and with that strength they grant you boons." Thus speaking, he extinguished all flames from beneath the various tubes, sealed a few containers. "Aye, there's no time to lose. The thing to remember with them, Will, is that they ever require payment for their boons. And that payment is always life. Think you on all the sacrifices of old. They were payment for the favors of the gods."

Now Will's throat constricted. He saw in his mind the nymphs saying now they'd get their payment from Marlowe. "Thank you, Father," he said.

"Give me the paper, Will," the friar said softly. "Give me the paper they gave you."

Will reached into his sleeve, but on touching the paper, again felt the odd reluctance he'd felt about telling Marlowe what he'd done.

He had worked at his craft so many years, and yet his words remained slow and lifeless upon the paper on which he wrote them. With this paper, he could be the best playwright of London, and his plays could make money to send home, to buy a better house for his family and honor and power for himself.

He felt the paper, but he let it go. What did the friar know? Perhaps he was wrong about the price.

"I see," the friar said. "I see." He looked sad, like a child betrayed.

Will thought of Marlowe. He must go and save Marlowe, if Marlowe needed saving. And if not, Will must go and ascertain for himself what the price of the muses' words was and if he wished to pay it.

Pursued by Friar Lawrence's, "Wait, Will, I must . . ." Will ran out the door to hire a horse.

But when, having hired his horse—a mere bag of bones, the best he could afford—Will took the road to Deptford, he found Friar Lawrence waiting at the city gates.

Riding an old, broken-down donkey and still clad in his

banned habit, the friar looked like something out of the Middle Ages, a creature who went through centuries undisturbed and brought a touch of the past to the present enlightened age.

"I'll go with you," he said, "as you might need my help."

Will could not imagine why a man such as he should need the help of this decrepit friar. He also could not remember having told the friar where Marlowe had gone. But perhaps Friar Lawrence had heard of it elsewhere.

The best horse Will's money could buy was slow. Night had fallen when Will tied his horse in front of Mistress Bull's house, a broad and sprawling inhabitation facing the river in Deptford.

Friar Lawrence remained on his donkey, beside the horse, and made no move to dismount. His brow knit in a frown. "We came too late," he said.

Will shivered at those words, so sepulchrally pronounced, but shook his head. The friar was mad. What could he know?

Will turned his back on his travel companion and knocked at the door.

A woman, still buxom but doubtless past forty, answered.

"I must see Master Marlowe," Will said, his tiredness letting no more than those words forth.

At this, the woman gave a little cry. "Aye, Master Marlowe, poor Master Marlowe, the grave diggers have taken him already."

The world seemed to circle 'round Will, like the stars around the fixed Earth, as his head went faint. "Grave diggers?"

The woman produced a handkerchief from her sleeve and touched her dry eyes with it. "Aye, the poor man. So quiet, he was, and his friends, Master Frizer, and Master Skeres and Master Poley, drinking and playing tables all day. And then, over the reckoning, Master Marlowe grew enraged and pulled his dagger, and Master Frizer, defending himself, stabbed

Master Marlowe through the eye and thus he died, the great playwright, the muses' darling." She looked worried. "And his friends all say they don't know what came over any of them to end the day thus, in fighting and sudden death."

She twisted her handkerchief in her hands still, as Will turned away.

The muses' darling.

In his mind, Will saw the muses, freed and wild, unseen, provoking the tempers of Marlowe's gaming companions and Marlowe's quick-fire rage. He could see them, with their sharp teeth and lapping tongues savoring the blood that spilled like red wine from Marlowe's pierced eye to tinge with red his violet velvet suit.

He turned his back on the woman, discourteously, and returned to the friar. "He's paid," he said, in a voice that didn't sound like his own. "He's already paid."

"Yes," Friar Lawrence said.

He didn't sound surprised. He wasn't surprised. Will's mind put together facts, sluggishly. Friar Lawrence had known Marlowe was dead when they got to the house. He'd known where Marlowe had gone without asking. He'd known.

This revelation was like the sudden, sharp-toothed smile of the muses. Will felt sick. "Who are you?"

The friar opened his hands, displaying his palms in the old gesture of nonaggression. "I am who I am," he said. "I am Friar Lawrence."

Will's throat felt dry. He swallowed, but could get no moisture. "But you knew all about this grief in advance. How did you know?"

Friar Lawrence smiled. "There are certain studies that go with my avocation of alchemy, Will. There are more things in heaven and Earth, Will, than are dreamt of in your philosophy."

Will felt the square of paper in his sleeve. The muses' paper.

"Aye, your gift," Friar Lawrence said. "If you want to

use it, Will, there are things you can do to avoid payment." Friar Lawrence's eyes looked more like a cat's eyes, spying, spying, hoping to catch something. "I could teach you those things, if you wish to know."

But Will thought of Marlowe's curses, his heretical talk, his restless search for untimely death.

Had the muses' price been more terrible than their gift? Or had their gift, itself, made Marlowe long to die?

How would it feel to be acclaimed for words you knew were not truly yours? How would it feel to see your fame grow, lie on lie, and to know yourself small and empty beside the works the world accounted your own?

"No," Will said. "No. Of certain things, I can't know too little."

The friar smiled, as if, somehow, Will's decision pleased him.

Will didn't care. He knew his decision was right. His guilt over Marlowe's death, Will would never forget. But he could avoid a like fate. There were prices not worth paying, not even for words like Marlowe's.

As soon as he got back to London, Will would burn the paper.

Will had rather spend his life holding horses outside the theater, than bargain with his life for words with which to conquer the stage.

William Shakespeare would become a great playwright on the strength of his own talent and work or not at all.

BLOOD AND SCALE

by John Helfers

John Helfers is a writer and editor currently living in Green Bay, Wisconsin. A graduate of the
University of Wisconsin-Green Bay, his fiction
appears in more than thirty anthologies. His first
anthology, *Black Cats and Broken Mirrors*, was
published by DAW Books in 1998 and has been
followed by several more, including *Alien Ab-
ductions, Star Colonies, Warrior Fantastic, Knight
Fantastic, The Mutant Files* and *Villains Victorious*.
Future projects include editing more anthologies
as well as a novel in progress.

D*ON'T move . . .*
    . . . don't speak . . .
  . . . don't breathe . . .
The world came back in fragments as I returned to consciousness. I felt rough stone floor against my back and
head, heard the *pop* of hot metal cooling, and smelled the
distinct odor of cold piss soaking my groin and legs.

I sucked in a shallow breath, aware of a heavy weight
crushing my chest. The air was redolent of sulfur, rock, and an
unfamiliar burnt-copper smell. I tried to move, but only
awaked a searing pain along my left arm, fingers, and wrist.

Where am I? What's happened? Where's Masteol? I lay
still, fighting my sudden panic, and opened my eyes.

The first thing I saw was a stone roof, jagged and uneven, with pointed stalactite spears jutting down toward my
head. Looking around, I was in a narrow cave, the stone
walls illuminated by a rich, crimson-orange glow emanating from farther down the narrow passageway. My next
thought for was my throbbing arm. I glanced down and saw
a mass of huge, swollen blisters covering my limb from
hand to shoulder. It hurt when I just thought about moving
it, so I brought my other arm inch by inch up to the weight
on my chest. My exploring fingers encountered soft cloth,
the coolness of interlocking rings of chain mail, and then a
hot sheath of metal armor.

The Templar, he was right in front of me, I thought. The
last things I remembered were the heavy gauntleted hand of
the holy knight pushing me down, then the world exploding
in screams and red-gold fire, followed by darkness. . . . I
lifted my head to look.

The holy knight was sprawled over me, the top of his
helm resting on my chest. The coppery smell was coming
from him, along with the unique odor of hot steel. Only my
thick robes saved me from being burned by the heat con-
ducted through his armor.

With the last of my strength, I shoved the unmoving
body over, the man's torso thudding to the floor with a
scrape of steel against stone. Craning my neck, I peered
over the side of the helm and beheld a nightmare.

The knight's face and chest had been seared away, as if
he had fallen against a white-hot forge which had eaten
away the heavy mail and vital organs underneath. Of his
shield arm, there was nothing left, only a smear of metal
and blackened blood. His face was obliterated, with not
even the skull intact, just blood, bone, and brain fused into
an unrecognizable puddle in the great helm. The upper part
of his left torso was now a gaping hole, with nothing left of
the rest of his chest but a blackened mass of flesh and viscera. The remaining pieces of the breastplate glowed

cherry-red around the misshapen edges, slagged and charred from the heat of—

By the gods, I thought, scrambling away from what was left of the knight's body, heedless of the pain in my left arm. My hand came down in something hot and wet, and I stifled the scream that threatened to burst from my mouth—

—because I knew that whatever did this is still here.

I looked over my shoulder at the remnants of the man I had just put my hand through. This one had been partially hit as well, burning away robes and skin and muscles and leaving a charred lump of bone and sinew in its wake. The man's arms were outflung, as if trying to shield himself from the terrible flames.

Or spellwielding . . . I thought. Gritting my teeth, I lifted what was left of the corpse's head off its shoulders, trying to favor my burned left arm, which stretched in agony. The hair and scalp had been burned away, but at the base of his neck, I found it. An unrecognizable metal blob fused to the man's skull, a once-magical focus the wizard had used to channel his arcane powers.

Masteol is dead, I thought, laying the skull back down. A lump rose in my throat, but I pushed it back down, knowing I had no time to grieve. *If the focus had survived, I might have been able to use it to escape. My mentor is gone, the Templar is dead,* I thought, looking around at the twisted and blackened bodies of the rest of our exploration group. *Everyone is dead but me. . . .*

I crawled back down the tunnel. After a few dozen yards, I came to the mouth of the passage, blocked by several tons of boulders that had trapped us in here. *By now the rest of the expedition has probably given us up for dead,* I thought. Turning around, I stared at the glow at the tunnel's far end. *Nowhere to go but forward.*

Cradling my injured arm, I rose to my feet and began walking, stepping around the bodies scattered along the hallway. As I went down the hallway, I looked around for a weapon, armor, anything I could use to protect myself. But all that was left of the forward vanguard was the scorched remains of the soldiers.

I was about to round an outcropping of rock that jutted into the passageway when I heard a noise. The distinctive scrape of something moving along the cave floor. Something coming down the passageway toward me.

Something huge.

Flattening myself against the damp rock wall, I held my breath and listened, trying to figure out what was out there. The sibilant rustling continued, then I heard the clank of metal. A hideous screeching noise reverberated through the chamber. I couldn't stand it any longer.

I looked around the corner just in time to see the upper half of a soldier's body, armor and all, being dragged toward the light. I remained frozen there for long seconds, unable to move or tear my eyes away from the spot where I had last seen the body. *There is no hope for me now,* I thought. *No way out behind me, and—whatever is out there—in front of me.*

The clatter of metal against rock snapped me out of my reverie. It was followed by a thick tearing noise, as of heavy cloth ripping. I strained to hear, trying to discern what was going on in the cavern ahead. *If I can figure out what's out there, maybe I can figure out a way to escape.*

The jingling of steel chain filled the chamber. *Sounds like chain mail,* I thought. A moment later, something flew through the air past me and slammed into the wall with a wet slap. I stared at the shredded piece of mail that stuck there for a moment, then slid down the rock, leaving a blood-red trail in its wake. Stuck where I was, I listened as a crunching, snapping sound echoed in the cavern, followed by a loud snort of something breathing. Again I heard the ponderous sounds of massive bulk shifting in the cave. And growing louder.

It's coming back, I thought, flattening myself against the cave wall. The movement stopped right outside the entrance to the passageway. I held every muscle taut, grimacing at the sudden pain in my left arm, but still not daring to move.

A curved gray-brown claw the length of a short-sword blade reached into the corridor past me. It paused, as if scenting the air, then continued on into the hallway. It was attached to a finger that was as long as I was tall. The claw-tipped digit stabbed downward, impaling the Templar's body and dragging it back out of the smaller cave.

I stood pressed against the cool stone of the wall, my mouth locked open in a soundless scream. Then I heard a sound I never expected.

"Sca'less," rumbled a voice that sounded like boulders being boiled in oil. "I know you are in there. I smell your moving blood. Come out where I can see you."

I didn't say a word, but clung to the wall with my free arm, trying not to make a sound.

"Sca'less, don't make me come in and get you. I would be most displeased. I merely want to see what has survived my welcome," the voice continued. "If you do not come out, you leave me with no choice." To illustrate what he meant, a small burst of flame roared into the entrance of the passageway, making me turn my head away from the intense heat.

Either it roasts me now or kills me when I step out, I thought. *Die now or die later, what's the difference?* Yet, deep down, I knew the difference, and after seeing what had become of the others, I knew I'd rather take my chances trying to talk to whatever had me trapped in here.

Before I could move, the wall behind me burst inward, throwing me to the ground. Sharp fragments of rock rained down on me, pummeling my already battered body. *What in the name of Ehal'ost was that?* Before I could regain my feet, I saw the floor fall away, as if I was suddenly flying. Looking around, I saw the small cavern receding from me. I twisted my head around just in time to catch a blast of hot, rotten-smelling air as I found myself hanging in midair, several dozen feet off the ground.

The cave I found myself in was huge, the walls stretching upward until they were swallowed by darkness. The red-gold glow radiated from the walls themselves, throwing off enough light to illuminate the area. I heard the gurgling of water nearby, and smelled the overwhelming odor of sulfur and copper permeating the cavern. But my gaze was drawn back to the face of the creature I was dangling in front of, its huge gold-green eyes level with my own.

I stared back into the inhuman face of something that could only have come from the deepest pits of hell, somewhere beyond evil or chaos. Its head was framed by a spiked fan of bone and sinew that radiated out from its neck, the ruff pulsing in and out with each rasping breath. Its features were a cross between a pig, a dog, and something indescribable, with those mesmerizing eyes protruding out from under a bony brow studded with small horns running from one side to the other. Its snout, which could easily swallow me without having to bite once, tapered to large, flaring nostrils and a pointed tip of a mouth from which dozens of curved fangs protruded, the top ones interlocking with the rows on the bottom in a white wall of bone. The entire face was covered in tiny rows of overlapping rust-colored scales, providing what looked like natural armor. Its nostrils inhaled, pulling my scent to it. The mouth cracked open, and I thought I saw a glimmer of light coming from inside the creature's throat.

I tore my gaze away from it to see what was holding me up and found one of its claw-tipped fingers, as thick around as my chest, curled around my body. I was being held in its hand, my arms pinned to my sides, only my head and shoulders emerging from the top of the thing's gargantuan paw. I could feel the warm wetness of blisters popping on my arm, and each time I breathed, my left side was in torment. But that was the least of my worries now.

"*Sca'less,* you come when I call you!" the monster said, its rasping voice washing over me along with the overpowering scent of cooked meat. My ears ached from the timbre of the words, to say nothing of the volume, which almost shattered my already-aching head.

I was too frozen by fear to speak, or even think. I just stared, mute, stunned at the monstrosity that was holding my life in its hand.

"So you came to find the legend, and now you have," it said, bringing me even closer to its face for inspection. "Get a good look. I hope it was worth it."

I hadn't thought there was anything left in me, but the pungent bloom of a new befoulment spreading down my tattered breeches proved me wrong.

"Ugh, I had forgotten how bad you *sca'less* can smell. Maybe your tongue will be looser in a few hours." The creature whirled around and padded across the cavern, making very little noise for its size, which, now that I could see the rest of it, was huge. It was threescore feet long, with a narrow neck flowing down into its massive body. One of its powerful forearms held me prisoner, the other traversed the cave floor with ease. Its rear legs were three times as large as the front ones, thickly-muscled, with each of the three toes tipped with claws like scythe blades that clicked on the stone. A tail easily half as long as its body curled around it, the spiked tip weaving and swaying.

At the far side of the cavern, it stopped at a hole in the wall perhaps ten feet high and twice as long. Without another word, it rolled me into the stone cell. I landed on my burned arm, which sent a flare of agony through my body culminating in bright flashes of pain exploding behind my eyes.

Somehow I rolled onto my back and looked toward the opening just in time to see a massive wedge of stone sliding into place, cutting off the light from the cavern outside.

"No," I gasped as I staggered to my feet and lunged for the entrance. The stone thudded into place before I got there, leaving me in complete darkness. My right hand cracked into the stone, skinning my knuckles. I felt along the edges, searching for a crack, an opening, anything I could get my fingers into. My quest revealed nothing.

I sank to the floor, the pain of my arm and body all but forgotten in my new predicament. With the absence of light, I felt as if I might go mad. The boulder blocking the entrance was thick enough to keep sound out as well, so there I was, stuck in a silent, stifling death-black cube. My whole world had shrunk to this.

And that was what pulled me back from the mental abyss I teetered on the brink of. A saying of Masteol's came back to me: *"If you are still alive, Chavaen, there are always options."* He'd known about survival, having served several years as a battlewielder during the Kingdom Wars.

The thought of Masteol again brought a lump to my throat. Although he had been a harsh taskmaster, he had also rewarded my insatiable curiosity with a glimpse into a world beyond anything I had ever known. He'd also been the closest thing to a father that I'd ever had. I brushed away the wetness pooling in my eyes, not wanting to give in to despair.

Another saying of his echoed through my memory as if I could hear his reedy voice beside me. *"Time marches on, Chavaen, whether we travel with it or not. Always look ahead of you to see what is coming on the horizon."*

Well, I certainly didn't expect this, I thought. But Masteol was right, my time with him was done, before either of us would have liked, true, but it was done all the same. The important thing was to figure out what to do now.

I'm at the mercy of a creature twenty times larger than myself which has just killed a large, heavily armed group of mercenaries and has an appetite for human flesh. Yet it did not kill me when it had me at its mercy. It must be saving me for something. But for what? A snack? I must keep my wits about me, and keep it talking to observe its behavior. Perhaps I can find a weakness to exploit.

Satisfied that I wasn't going to lose my mind, and relatively pleased for coming up with what seemed like a work-

able plan (and the only chance I had of not becoming its
next meal), I lay myself down on the stone floor, and
cradling my head in the crook of my unburned arm, tried to
rest. I had thought that sleep would be hard coming, but
fortunately I was wrong.

I was awakened by the sound of rock scraping against
rock. Blinking in the sudden light, I saw the silhouette of
the creature peering in at me. It sniffed the air, then wrinkled its large nostrils.

"Paugh, you *sca'less*. How you drove us underground,
I'll never know." Before I could digest its statement, it
reached into the room and plucked me off the floor. "I can't
decide which smells worse, those which have been dead for
months or—" it sniffed and wrinkled its nose, "—you who
are still living. You must be cleaned," it said.

It carried me over to the burbling stream, and dunked me
in, the water shocking me back to full consciousness. It
shook me as a terrier does a rat, then dunked me again, then
a third time. While the water on my burned arm was
heaven, it was mitigated somewhat by my not being able to
breathe underwater. I spluttered and screamed after the
third dunking, only then getting its attention long enough to
make it stop.

"This is not acceptable?" it asked, still holding me in its
clawed hand.

"Sure, if you want to make my arm feel like it's being
torn out of the socket," I gasped, shaking the water out of
my eyes. "I don't know how—whatever it is you are—
wash yourself, but we humans prefer to do it in a more
leisurely fashion."

"If you wish to live, you will be clean," the creature said,
bending its head down to stare into my eyes.

Masteol used to say my tongue often operated indepen-
dently of my brain, especially when I was scared. This trait
had never served me well, and it wasn't going to this time
either.

"Why, so I can be washed up when you devour me like the rest!" I replied, then closed my eyes and turned my head, waiting for my all-too-brief life to come to an end. I figured it was only a question of whether I would be thrown into its gaping maw or have every bone in my body broken when it threw me against the wall.

I heard a dull rumbling, and felt another hot, stale blast of air envelop me. Opening my eyes, I saw the creature making an odd, somehow familiar noise with its mouth. *It's laughing! It's laughing at me!*

"*Sca'less,* you have *rel'tangh.* Your kind would call it spirit. It has been so long since I have seen one of you, I have forgotten how . . . brash you can be." A long, pink tongue edged with black curled out of its mouth and ran along the row of teeth. "It is fortunate for you that the others have sated my appetite for now."

"Then why you did bring me out here? Am I next?" I said, squirming in its immovable grip.

"If I had wanted to consume you, I already would have. But there are two things that keep me from that. First, you're not cooked. Second, what we are doing right now."

Through the combination of anger and terror coursing inside my head, some part of my mind managed to comprehend what the creature was saying. It was bored. It wanted someone (something, I supposed at the time) to talk to. And I was it.

Now that my demise didn't seem quite so imminent, I managed to meet his unwavering gaze again. "So why did you kill the rest?" I asked.

"You were trespassing in my home. I saw no reason why I shouldn't repel you in the most . . . permanent fashion. After all, if anyone else in your group had escaped my trap, they no doubt would be raising an army to come back here and discover what had killed the rest of them. You should count yourself fortunate, as it was only luck that you survived in the first place."

Or they would have warned everybody away, I thought. "So what is to become of me now?"

"No doubt the rest of your group believes you have all perished in my rockslide." The creature's mouth turned up in what could have been called a smile, which made him look even more terrifying than when he had roared at me. "Don't look so surprised. After living here for a few hundred years, I've made a few improvements to keep your kind out. However, it seems I wasn't careful enough, as the rest of you made it past. We will fix that for next time. You, however, cannot leave, as you are the only *sca'less* that knows of my existence. Not only that, but you also know where I dwell. Exactly where I dwell."

"I'm to be kept here for the rest of my life?" I asked.

Its mouth opened again in that hideous parody of a smile. "There is another alternative," it said, nodding with its head back toward the hole I had been pulled through, and the rest of the bodies there.

"But . . . you might decide to just be saving me for later. A . . ." I shuddered at the thought, ". . . meal on the hoof, so to speak."

The creature cocked its head, as if considering my statement. "True enough. How you fare here will depend on you as well. You will find I am not . . . unkind."

Given the fact that you can squash me like a fly if I displease you, I suppose you've been as kind to me as I could expect. A choice like that isn't any choice at all, I thought. "It would seem I am to be your guest." *At least if I want to live.*

And, despite the circumstances, I still so wanted to live.

"Very well." The creature set me down on the stone floor next to the stream. I tried not to wince as it let go of me, then I examined my arm for further damage.

"It seems you did not escape injury after all."

"It's—I'll be all right," I said, although I felt just the opposite. All of the movement I had been put through had stretched and weakened the burned skin. I felt light-headed and dizzy, and just standing was an effort.

"Hold still," it said. I looked up to see the monster's massive hand descending on me again. Before I could move, it had pinned me to the ground, its fingers surrounding me like the scaled bars of a cage.

"What—what are you doi—"

"Don't speak," it said. I saw its index finger rise, then spear down toward my chest. There was a brief crushing impact which knocked the breath out of me, then the digit retracted again. I sobbed for air, each breath feeling like I had a vise on my stomach. Looking down at my chest, I saw blood welling from a puncture wound. Through my pain and fear I heard the creature coming closer to me. I looked around trying to see what was happening.

Its other hand hovered over me, then began to descend, its fingers covered in a black ichorous substance. Before I could protest, it smeared the gummy sludge on my chest. It was uncomfortable, but not unpleasant, at least, until the stuff contacted the open wound.

Every muscle, every limb, every inch of me felt like it had been bathed in that fountain of fire that had killed the rest of my companions. Unable to think or move, I opened my mouth to scream out the last of my breath—

—and as suddenly as it had come, the pain was gone. I looked down at my burned arm. Save for the charred scraps of my shirt, my limb was whole and unmarked. I flexed my fingers, my wrist, elbow, and shoulder, all of which moved with ease.

Along with my miraculous healing, I became aware of another presence at the back of my mind, a separate consciousness at the base of my skull. It just . . . rested there, aware of me, but not doing anything. I looked up at my captor.

"You could have at least told me you were going to do that!" I shouted.

"If I had, would you have let me?" it asked.

"Well . . . probably not," I said, taking a deep breath and realizing that I felt better than I ever had. "How—how did—what are you—"

Towering over me, the creature reared back on its haunches. "My name is Sar'ghain'ailshon'aig, and I am *Dhyragonais.* The last *Dhyragonais,* to be precise. I have existed in this world for more than six hundred of your years, survived the Age of Blackness, fought in the War Beneath, and escaped in the Banishment. I have not spoken to another being, human or otherwise, in more than threescore years. Now, Chavaen, you know who I am, and now," he tapped my chest, "You know why I am here."

"You're—in hiding?" I asked.

He nodded. "Yes, as I have been for more than a hundred years. You do know what I am now, correct?"

I nodded, almost afraid to answer him. "You are D–Dragon."

"Ah, I see the word, while corrupted, has not been lost from your kind yet," he said.

"But—but the legends—" I stammered. "I mean—"

"Say that we dine on human flesh? That we are rapacious killers, existing only to kill and destroy? Well, some of those stories are true. After all, how do you think legends get started in the first place?" the Dragon said, favoring me with another fang-filled grin.

"So, you are just going to—to—" I said, taking a step backward.

The Dragon rolled its eyes. "If I was going to, why would I have healed you? My *vhatiae* is not a boon bestowed lightly, you know."

"Actually, I didn't, having never seen one of you . . . r kind except in books. Actually, I had only seen one book, and when Masteol had caught me, he had whacked my fingers so hard they had been numb for a day afterward. *Well, Masteol,* I thought, *I've finally seen something that you . . . never . . . will.*

"Is something wrong, Chavaen?" he asked.

Other than the fact I will never see another human again, nothing. I thought, wiping my eyes. I needed to distract him from that, however, not wanting to show any weakness. "How do you know my name?"

"The liquid that flows through your body is partly my blood now. There is . . . a bond between us now, a linking of your mind and mine. Granted, it is more from me to you, but, in time, that will grow stronger both ways. I am also able to . . . communicate with you at a distance."

As well as keep track of me? I thought. "But how am I to live down here? What will I eat?"

"You will have to grow adept at a few different skills down here," it said. "There is plenty of game, lizards and such, fish in the stream, and the mosses and lichens are edible. Probably not exactly what you're used to, but it will do. Later, I imagine you will be able to hunt. As I had mentioned, a bit of game would spice up my diet as well."

"Umm . . . don't you just eat . . ." I motioned with my thumb toward the cave, wincing.

"Chavaen, I am fifty-five claws long, and weigh more than twenty-five oxen. While your kind make a tasty morsel now and again, if I ate only . . . *sca'less,* I would soon starve to death in here." The Dragon reached up and plucked a stalactite from the cavern ceiling. It examined it, then popped it in its mouth. "It has taken many meals to get this cave to the proper size," he said after swallowing his snack.

"As well as get you to the, uh, proper size," I said.

The Dragon's laughter rumbled through the cave again. "Now that's more like it." It regarded me for a moment. "I want to show you something, Chavaen."

He tossed something down at my feet. "Pick it up."

I reached down and picked up the gleaming sword with both hands. Despite its size, it was well-balanced, and I was able to hold it with ease, the hilt fitting well under my fingers. I looked up at him, the question evident on my face.

The Dragon spread his arms out. "Have at me, then."

"What?" I couldn't believe my ears.

"Here is your chance to be free. All you have to do is run me through." He shifted position, exposing more of his stomach.

"But you're the last one . . . of your kind," I said.

"And you want to be free, yes?"

"Well, yes, but . . ." I trailed off. *Why is he doing this? It has to be a trick of some kind. He's trying to lure me in. But if that's so, why did he heal me?*

I heard an echo in my mind, as if that alien presence at the base of my skull was trying to whisper something to me. I stood still, listening.

I . . . cannot lie . . . our blood is one now. . . .

A test, then? For the first time since I had entered the caverns, the student in me rose to argue with the scared boy that I had been for the past few hours. *Masteol always told me to evaluate the situation from all sides. Would I destroy him to set myself free?*

I thought of the promises I could make, the oaths I could swear, the vow to keep what I had seen here a secret I would carry to my grave. As soon as the idea came, I dismissed it. *If the situation were reversed, I'd be doing the same thing. No, if I was in his position, I probably would have eaten me by now. I know how base sca'l— I mean humans are.*

Besides, what exactly do I have to go back to? Masteol is dead, and an apprentice without a wizard isn't suited to much of anything else. Sure, I could mix a few herbal brews, but wisewomen were a farthing a dozen. It seemed like even the smallest villages had them nowadays. And besides, I was still just a youth. *Even if I did manage to set up shop somewhere, no one would trust that I could mix anything worth drinking.*

Masteol also said that everything happens for a reason, that there truly is no luck or chance or coincidence. He claimed he had learned that from his studies, and maybe he had, but then, he'd also claimed that the caves were empty, and look where that had gotten us. Still, it was a more attractive way of looking at my situation than "Dragon pet."

I locked gazes with the Dragon and lowered the sword to the ground. "If you are what you say you are, then I cannot. You have treated me with honor, albeit your own kind—" The Dragon raised a horned eyebrow at this, and I quickly continued, "—and have helped me—" I shrugged my healed shoulder, "—and to attack you now would be an insult."

The Dragon nodded in satisfaction. "Then it is agreed."

And so began the third phase of my life. I had been apprenticed, actually I suppose purchased would be a better word, by Masteol as a spellwielder's apprentice when I was eleven. By the time we were so forcefully parted, I had learned reading, writing, and sums, had been trained in the arts of alchemy, brewing, and distilling, and had been on my way to learning the art of spellwielding when we had gone on this damnfool adventure.

Now Masteol was gone, and I was left here in this cave with the last (if I could believe him, which I did) living Dragon in existence.

After I had cleaned up, I said that the room Sar'gaith, as I called him, had put me in when I . . . arrived would make fine quarters for my stay here. He agreed and told me to go to the back of the cave and take a look inside the second passageway.

I did so, and found myself standing in a room filled with everything from wagons and carts to weapons and chests and barrels and crates. The hallway stretched on for several dozen feet, and was filled with just about anything I could use. Most of the supplies and equipment looked old. I even recognized a treasury wagon that had the seal of King Thadvael the Second on it, which made it about seventy years old. *He was telling the truth about that, at least,* I thought. *I wonder where all this came from.* I wasn't about to ask, however.

I rummaged around until I found a set of clothes that looked about my size, dressed, and went back to the larger cave.

As career changes went, it actually wasn't bad, once I got used to the idea. After all, it wasn't like I had any duties to attend to. As I had noticed before, Sar'ghain was bored. My primary task, I soon learned, was simply to sit and listen to him talk.

I suppose you're probably wondering why I didn't try to escape. After all, Sar'ghain didn't have his eye on me every second of the day. After a while, when I had gained his trust, I'd certainly thought about leaving.

Most humans wouldn't have even considered what Sar'ghain had proposed. I suppose they would be dead right now. He was inside me, a part of me. I had the opportunity, many times, but I knew I would never survive away from the cave. I just . . . had a feeling I wouldn't make it down the first hill.

So it was the best choice, the only choice I could make. And after a month down there with him, I didn't want to leave.

I was still only an apprentice after five years of working for Masteol because of my insatiable curiosity. I was always poking my nose in where it didn't belong, which had never sat well with him. He had felt I had strong potential, but I was forever getting ahead of myself. I would try a spell or potion I wasn't ready for, screw it up, usually with spectacularly bad results, and have to wait six more months until I could try again.

With Sar'ghain, there were no secrets, nothing he wouldn't reveal to me, well, except for certain aspects of Dragonish existence, that is. He had lived hundreds of years, and was there when Dragons walked the Earth among men. Several weeks into my stay, over a meal of roasted lizard, he told me the other side of the story.

During those years, men and Dragons were allied, working together toward common goals. It was an amazing time of peace and prosperity for all. Then, a Dragon made a mistake.

Having grown fond of a human who was old and dying, she gave him a drop of her blood. Of course, it revitalized him, and the only thing faster than his recovery was the speed at which the news spread throughout the land. Other men, not understanding how the gift of *vhatiae* worked, thought a way had been found to control Dragons, and so began a campaign to enslave them. Unfortunately, there were many humans, and not many Dragons and, Sar'ghain said, "even though we are well-armored against most forms of attack, you humans are persistent and very single-minded."

The Dragons, not wanting to harm the humans, and realizing that there were those would continue their crusade to control the Dragons until all of them were enslaved, left. They disappeared, going deep underground or high in the mountains, or deep below the surface of the oceans. They called it the Banishment.

On the surface, the humans rewrote their history, claiming that the Dragons were evil, and had been driven off, foiled in their quest to conquer humankind. Dragons passed into legend, and, as generation begat generation, that's what they remained, fairy tales to scare children with. Since then, they had lived their hidden lives, while all around them, the world moved on.

"I do not believe any of my kind are still alive," Sar'ghain said as he finished his tale. "In the beginning, we could keep in touch with each other, but as the years passed, and more and more of us moved around, the communication was not kept up. I was the youngest of them when we went into hiding. Now, I believe I am the last."

I sat there for a moment, lost in his tale. Although his story went against everything I had been taught, I knew he wasn't lying, his blood running through my veins told me that. *History truly is written by the winners,* I thought.

Or those who think they won, Sar'ghain replied.

"But, if giving your *vhatiae* to a human was a mistake in the first place, why did you do it for me?" I asked.

The Dragon looked wistful for a moment, then smiled down at me. "Every living creature needs companionship. As the decades passed, I grew more and more anxious for someone to talk to. But I knew how impossible it was that something like . . . you would happen upon here. And yet here you are."

"Yeah, well, you have a hell of a way of introducing yourself," I said, looking at the hole in the wall he had pulled me through.

Sar'ghain chuckled, jets of smoke puffing from his nostrils. "I had to make sure you were . . . suitably impressed before I tendered my offer."

"Believe me, I was more than impressed," I replied. "You nearly caused my heart to burst out of my chest when you reached through that rock wall."

"It's good to know I haven't lost my touch," he said. "Now, perhaps you will tell me of the world outside, and what has happened since we left all those centuries ago."

And so I did. I confirmed that yes, humans did view Dragons as evil, cunning, treacherous predators who only lived to destroy, and were the sworn enemy of mankind. I told him of the new dark age we had entered, how one king had squabbled with another, until soon the entire continent was embroiled in war, kingdoms raising armies against each other, until the flames of battle reached from one ocean to the other. After more than a dozen years of vicious combat, the principal leaders had run out of men and supplies, and their own kingdoms had refused to fight anymore, exiling one monarch and beheading the other. With those two gone, the rest of the kingdoms had settled down and begun the arduous task of rebuilding.

"Hmm," mused Sar'ghain, "if we had still been around, it probably wouldn't have happened. We were peacemakers, not just for one side or another, but because we genuinely desired peace for the land and people. We never advanced one cause or kingdom over another. We helped the humans temper their quick judgment with wisdom. It is sad to think of what has become of your race since we left."

"Well, perhaps if you were to return, then you could teach the humans again," I said. "After all, it has been many years . . ."

"Perhaps I could have at one time, but . . . I am too old to undertake something of that magnitude," Sar'ghain said. "It would take decades to overcome the hatred humans have for us."

He never spoke of the matter after that, and I never brought it up again. But the more we spoke, the more I realized how wrong we humans had been to turn against these noble creatures, and just what it had cost us.

The months settled into years, and Sar'ghain and I lived in relative peace together. My room was outfitted in a style fit for a king, and after several months, I was allowed to go back to the surface. I spent most of that first day trying to get used to the sun, which was more bright and searing than I had ever remembered. Although I enjoyed my time outside, I had less and less affinity for it as the years went on, preferring the comfortableness of the cave and my friend.

Together we reset the traps, and I created new ones, using the weapons that had been stored in the side cave. I also used some of those tools to make life easier for both Sar'ghain and myself.

Granted, it wasn't always easy. Sar'ghain hadn't had any "company" for more than sixty years, not since a monastic priest had wandered into his cave by accident and stayed until his natural end. I, on the other hand, took several weeks to acclimatize myself to the idea of sharing a living space with a hundred-foot-long, fire-breathing—well, Dragon. That first winter, "cave fever" as I termed it later, nearly did me in. Luckily, Sar'ghain found the solution, which was to toss me outside for a few hours, at the end of which time I was half-frozen and completely purged of my irritability. There were a few minor incidents such as that, but once we grew used to each other, we actually got along very well.

One day during a particularly cold winter, while walking along his back with the "scratcher," a rack of four spearheads lashed to a rod and attached to a six-foot-long handle, I found something on his back that I had never seen before.

"Sar'ghain? Sar'ghain!" I shouted, waking him from the lethargy I had induced by scratching his back, "What are these lumps on your shoulders?"

"Hmm?" his head twisted around, and he looked at the pony-sized bumps on his upper back. "Ahh, it has begun. It is just part of a Dragon's growth cycle. They will take many months to finish, so do not worry. I am fine."

"But what are they?" I asked, reaching for a spot just under his right foreleg with my back scratcher. I tapped one bump with my foot, feeling it give a few inches under my weight. Although the scales were still as hard as ever, what was underneath was soft and more flexible than the rest of him.

"As Dragons grow . . . older, their bodies alter . . . to prepare themselves for the changes that occur," Sar'ghain said, yawning. "This is just . . . one aspect of that change."

Although Sar'ghain would always answer my questions, the way he answered them could be maddening sometimes. That he was in semihibernation, sleeping the winter away weeks at a time, didn't help any either. Knowing I wouldn't be getting any more information from him, I grabbed my bow and quiver of arrows and announced that I was going hunting. A satisfied grunt and rumbling snore was the only the response I got.

Shaking my head, I clambered through the cave tunnels until I came to the small hole I used to climb in and out of the cave network. Although by now I was very comfortable in the cave, there were times when the open sky still beckoned me.

I sniffed the air, and, not smelling anything unusual, scrambled out of the cavern. One of the changes I had noticed was that my senses had become much more acute over the past few years. Sar'ghain told me that his blood also bestowed other beneficial side effects, such as the ability to see in near total darkness, among others. I healed more quickly as well, although I had already seen proof of that.

I had also changed physically as well, growing lean and hard from the effort of providing food for myself. Through trial and error, I had created traps and snares to catch the wild game that abounded in the hills below. I had also explored the cave system until I knew it like the back of my hand, and could get from one area to another in a twinkling.

But for all my senses and abilities, I was unprepared for what happened next. As I came up out of the hole, something dropped over my head, and I found myself caught in a woven net. Before I could even begin to try and untangle myself, something that felt like a charging bull hit me from behind, sending me tumbling down the side of the hill.

I landed in a bruised heap at the bottom. A shadow fell over me. I looked up to see a burly man swathed in furs and wielding a spike-studded club, a feral snarl on his face. He raised his weapon, about to dash my brains out—

"Tovath! Stop right there!" a human voice rang out.

Several people were coming down the hill toward me, but it was the man who had spoken I was most interested in. He didn't look like the usual rabble, dressed as he was in a chain-mail hauberk that hung to his thighs, with leather breeches, fur-lined boots, and a heavy woolen winter cloak that snapped in the stiff wind. His left hand rested on the hilt of a short sword at his side, and his right held a thick shaft of wood twice as tall as he was, topped with a steel-tipped point. I recognized the weapon immediately, having seen it carried by others of his kind. That, and the crimson-and-silver beaten metal pin adorning his cloak left no doubt in my mind who these people were.

Slayers, I thought. *But how could they know what's up here?*

"Lyonais, let me search him! He will know if what we seek is in there. Look at him. He is the one who has set the traps we found!" This came from a tall, thin man shrouded in dark blue robes who was swaying back and forth. His face was hidden by a deep hood, but I thought I glimpsed a red gleam emanating from the darkness. Nobody was standing within ten feet of him.

"Just a moment, Khar'adelen." The leader walked down and stood over me. I smelled the tang of woodsmoke and sweat on his body, along with the scent of fresh-killed deer. "We've been freezing our arses off for two days by that cave, waiting for you to stick your head up, boy."

Stupid. After years of not seeing any sign of humans around, I had grown sloppy, leaving tracks in the snow a youngling could follow, even without using his nose. If I could have moved, I would have shaken my head in disgust.

"Judging by the look of this—thing, I'd say we've definitely come to the right place," the barbarian said.

"Yeah, ain't never seen one like you before," the leader said, squatting down next to me.

"Like . . . what?" I asked.

My question was answered by chuckles from the rest of the warriors, except for a few who looked away, and the robed man, who kept watching me in silence.

"I guess there aren't many mirrors underground," the leader said. "Here, take a look for yourself."

He held up a small piece of polished steel, and I gaped at what I saw. It wasn't the long hair, or the dirt on my face, it was the face itself.

My eyes were an unearthly golden-green, and the pupils were now narrow vertical slits, much like a cat's. The skin of my face was a burnished dark brown, with a patterning of scales overlaying my features. My nose had receded into my face, the nostrils closing to slits. My brow had grown heavy and thick, jutting out over my eyes. I stared in shock, much to the amusement of my captors.

"I guess you haven't seen yourself in a while," the one called Lyonais said.

"We should kill the dragonthrall now, before it warns its master," Torvath said, hefting his club.

"Just a minute, Tor. I think there's someone who will want to speak with our prisoner."

The robed man nodded so hard I thought his hood was going to fly off. "Yesssss . . ."

"Khar, he's yours. Don't worry about being gentle, either," Lyonais said.

The hooded, robed man walked down the snowy slope toward me. Unlike the others, he didn't sink into the snow, and he left no footprints behind him as he came closer. The rest of the men, a dozen or so, gave him a wide berth as he passed them, some of them making various signs to whichever god they worshiped.

I wriggled and stretched, trying to free my arms or even a hand, but to no avail. Tovath blocked the robed man's way for a moment, but the man hissed something at him, or maybe just hissed at him in general, I couldn't tell, and the taller warrior stepped to the side.

Khar'adelen leaned over me, and I learned then why the rest of the men kept their distance. I first saw his eyes, glowing dark red with dancing black pupils. His skin was flushed, mottled with shifting patterns of bright red, as if he had spent all day in the summer sun. Even from this far away, I felt an unnatural heat radiating from him, a fever that could not be controlled. His crimson lips parted, and I saw his mouth was full of pointed teeth, every one of them tapering to needle-sharp tips.

Gods help me, I thought, *a demonthrall.* Masteol had told me about this kind of sorcerer once when he had been feeling talkative, but I'd never expected to see one.

Demonthralls were people who had little or no magical ability of their own, but wanted that power more than anything else in the world. Through forbidden arcane rituals, they summoned beings from other planes and bargained with them to have these creatures inhabit their bodies, granting the host a portion of their power. Of course, the human body was not meant to contain this power for a long period of time, so the average demonthrall died (from what Masteol told me) an agonzing, painful death after four or five years of servitude, the demon having gradually used up the host body and left a useless husk. What happened to the soul of the bargainer, on the other hand, that was another matter.

Sar'ghain! Wake up! I'm in a lot of trouble here! I thought with all my might. Over the years, the bond between us had grown stronger, so much so that Sar'ghain could see places and events through my eyes. If he was awake, that is. During winter, especially during the coldest months, it was almost impossible to wake him. Which meant my biggest weapon was snoring away while a well equipped party of slayers was about to brace him in his lair.

"Don't try to fight, it will go sssso much easier if you don't fight," the demonthrall hissed. He reached out with a black-clawed hand and touched my cheek.

I had a pretty good idea of what he was going to do, so I had tried to prepare myself as best I could. One of the most common powers among mages of all types was the ability to read thoughts. Only another spellwielder could defend against this invasion by putting up a thought barrier in his mind. Of course, Masteol hadn't even gotten close to teaching me that. But that was all right, I had my own plan.

When the demonthrall touched me, it felt like his claws sank through my skin and into my mind, tearing through my memories, searching for what he wanted. He wasn't subtle about it, and it hurt. A lot.

Growling low in my throat, I let him have what he wanted. Summoning all my fearful memories of Sar'ghain, I unleashed them, letting them fly through my mind. The terror at the flames consuming my group, the overwhelming fear

as he held me in his clawed hand, the impotent rage I felt
after one of our arguments, when he had tossed me outside.
I focused those thoughts into a whirling ball of fear, suffering, and anger, and let the demonthrall feed on that. I also
made Sar'ghain larger in my mind, a colossal creature that
dwarfed any human (that part wasn't hard at all).

The demonthrall gasped and jerked his hand back after
only a few seconds. "It's here!" His voice cracked with
glee. "It is below, even now. He fears it."

When my first idea didn't work, I went to my backup
plan, the truth, modified for my audience. "Look, if you go
into that cave, you're not going to come out again. If
you've done your homework, then you must have heard
about the group that disappeared up here what, five years
ago?"

"Try seven," the leader replied.

"Yes, yes. I was part of that group. It slaughtered the rest
of them, and left me alive as its plaything. Whatever you
think is up there, I can tell you, it's worse than your darkest
nightmares."

My words didn't have the effect I was hoping for. The
rest of the group muttered among themselves with excitement, while the leader smiled and nodded. "All right, boys,
this is what we've been searching for. Let's get ready. Bring
him."

The one they called Tovath grabbed the net around me
and pulled me up. He slung me over his shoulder and followed the rest of the slayers back up the hill.

As we walked, I found myself looking into the face of
the leader, who was watching me, frowning.

"Your best bet is to leave now," I said, trying to reason
with him one last time. "You don't know what you're going
after down there."

"Oh, I don't know about that. I think you'll find that
we've come more prepared than you did," Lyonais said.
"However, you're an added bonus. Don't worry, if you help
us, when we're done in there, we'll let you free."

Yeah, right, I thought. *SAR'GHAIN!* I'm surprised my brain didn't burst with the force of my mental scream. Still hearing no answer, I turned my attention back to my captor. "What made you think something was up here?"

"Besides finding you, you mean?" the leader asked, opening a leather pouch on his belt and drawing a glass ball from it. "Your master kept good records."

When his hand touched the glass, the ball flared with sudden light, and I saw pictures inside it. Someone was looking at the rest of the group I had come here with, and I saw myself looking back at the person whose gaze had been captured by this device.

Masteol! I thought. Another item I had seen but never used, he had spoken of it more than once, a device that imprinted whatever he looked at, storing the sights he saw for as long as he wanted, once he activated it.

As I watched, our group trekked through the hill lands, to the cave entrance, past the rockslide, and into the corridor. There was no sound, but the last thing he saw was a burst of brilliant red-gold flame shooting toward him. . . .

So that's what happened, I thought. I tore my eyes away from the ball and looked back at the leader.

"This is what I've been searching for my whole life," he said, smiling as he tucked the bauble away. "This will make me known throughout the kingdoms."

By now we had reached the top of the hill, and the rest of the men were busy uncovering several snow-covered lumps in the snow, revealing tarpaulin-wrapped supplies. Several of the men began assembling weapons, while others removed leather-covered boxes, which, when opened, revealed sealed glass jars filled with a thick liquid.

"Free him, but bind his hands and feet," Lyonais said. Tovath did so and also searched me as well. Finding nothing, he left me on the frozen ground and joined the rest of the slayers. The first thing I did was shrug off my gloves and feel my face. To my surprise, my features felt normal, skin, hair, everything. I couldn't explain it.

The rest of the men were pouring the liquid into the shafts of what I had recognized earlier as lances, only these had hollow centers, which they plugged with wooden stoppers. Lyonais noticed my interest.

"You'd be surprised how much we know about what's in there," he said, tapping the lance shaft. "A strong base, to counteract its fire. When we break off a couple of these in its body, we'll be able to finish it off quick."

The men were dividing into teams of four, each one carrying a piece of the lance, which I assumed would be screwed together just before reaching the main cave. Several of the men also carried bows and arrows with forged steel heads, which they dipped into the base liquid as well. Torches were readied, packs were wrapped and buried.

I had spent this preparation time yelling to Sar'ghain in my mind, but there was no response. Even the presence that usually lay coiled in my head was unconscious, dead to the world. Now, when I needed him the most, I could not wake him.

When everyone was ready, Lyonais jerked me to my feet. He slashed the ropes binding my feet and hands, then looped a noose around my neck and cinched it tight, holding the other end in his hand. "I suppose you'll need your hands free, but I warn you, lead us into any traps, and you die first."

Khar'adelen was peering into the cave opening. "Yesss, it's in there, deep in the ground. Now that I have tasted that one's mind, I know what to look for."

Lyonais shoved me forward. "Let's go."

With no other choice, I began to descend into the caves. Although I respected and admired Sar'ghain, I wasn't about to sacrifice my life for him. I was hoping that there would be a way to warn him of the trouble invading our home, or that maybe he was playing possum, waiting for them without my knowledge, just like that first time I had come down into the caves, all those years ago.

I led the slayers down the twisting tunnels, through the

winding caves filled with stalactites and stalagmites that resembled Sar'ghain's fangs. All the while I kept trying to wake him, pleading, begging, cursing, but I heard no answer.

I delayed them as long as possible, but that damned demonthrall was keeping his eye on me. Apparently he could sense the proximity of the Dragon, and when I tried to lead them away, he would mutter to the leader, who would jerk me back and make me take the correct path. I managed to throw them off twice, but I always ran out of tunnel, and had to keep going down.

At last we reached the passage where I had first come in. It was clean, of course, as we had removed all traces of the first party years ago. Lyonais signaled his men to stop here, and they assembled the lances. The weapons were wielded by two-men teams, with all the rest nocking dripping arrows to their bows. The demonthrall whispered a brief spell over the weapons, and they glowed for a moment with a wicked red gleam. All this time their leader kept his hand over my mouth, making sure I didn't make a sound. When everyone was ready, the leader, who had replaced his short sword with a longer blade, led the advance with his weapon ready.

Sar'ghain's snores echoed throughout the cavern, sounding like an avalanche rumbling down a mountain over and over again. I was standing right next to the leader, who had just advanced far enough to be able to see into the main cavern. He stopped for just a second when he first saw the magnificent creature stretched out before him. His sword drooped in his hand, forgotten for the moment.

But not by me.

Grabbing the blade with one hand, I rammed my other palm onto its point, impaling myself on the slayer's sword. The pain shot up my arm and into my head, but more important, the steel touched the Dragon blood running through my veins.

Sar'ghain's gold-green eye flicked open.

Cursing, Lyonais shoved me to the ground and screamed at his men to attack. The lancers hefted their weapons, and hit the cavern running, splitting up as soon as they could get outside the hallway. Two archers leaped through the doorway right after them, bows drawn.

The pain in my hand blocked everything else out, I couldn't see, couldn't move. The slayer was on top of me, and, judging from the new stabs of agony in my hand, he was trying to free his sword. All I knew was that I had to keep hold of it, that I couldn't let him get away. I felt someone step on my leg, then another boot slammed into my head as the rest of the group climbed over both of us to enter the cavern. My whole world shrank to that sword, the slayer, and me. Far off somewhere I heard Sar'ghain's bellows mixing with the screams and shrieks of dying men. Then I heard a coughing roar that could have only been Dragonfire, and the dark cave lit up like it was midday in summer.

With a twist that split my hand open, Lyonais pulled his sword free and lashed out with it, catching me across the face. "I'll deal with you later," he snarled, then scrambled through the opening into the larger cave.

I dragged myself through the narrow entrance just in time to see the leader charge at Sar'ghain, his sword held high. Sar'ghain had the broken end of one of the lances protruding from his breast, and his neck and side were peppered with arrows, dark blood streaming down his side. One of the lancer teams had been flamed into unrecognizable lumps of melted flesh, and he was disposing of the rest of them with his natural weaponry. I saw his tail lash out, a screaming and struggling archer impaled on the end spike, which he promptly dashed against the wall, pulping the man's skull. There were wet red smears on his body where he had rolled over other men, and his claws and mouth were all dripping with gore and viscera.

"Sar'ghain, behind you!" I screamed. Having seen the

effect of the other spellbound weapons, I didn't want to find out what the sword could do.

Sar'ghain whipped his head around, spotted Lyonais, and shot his left hand forward, impaling the man on his foreclaw. The dying man dropped his sword as the Dragon brought him up to his face, then bit his head off.

I surveyed the carnage left over from the brief albeit vicious battle. The cave was a mess, with broken bodies and weapons strewn everywhere. Sar'ghain stood in the middle of it all, breathing hard, his tail whipping from side to side. A prone slayer, his face a red ruin, whimpered and attempted to crawl away. Without looking, Sar'ghain stabbed down with his claw. The whimpering stopped.

"Chavaen," he rumbled, more angry than I had ever seen him, even when I had first come here. "What happened?"

"I was captured outsi—" I began, when I felt a sudden impact slam me from behind. Looking down, I saw a foot of steel lance sticking out of my chest, shiny wet with my blood. I touched it with my fingers, not believing what I was seeing.

Turning around, I saw Khar'adelen standing behind me, a crazed grin on his flame-red face. Before my world went black, I watched him pull a curved dagger from behind his back and come at me, the blade descending toward my throat. Then all was darkness.

I awoke feeling like a red-hot anvil was sitting on my chest. My sides and stomach pulsed with burning pain every time I took a breath. My mouth was dry cotton, my body consumed by an all-encompassing thirst. When I tried to open my eyes, I saw three ceilings above me, which slowly melded into one.

Looking around, I saw that I was lying in my bed, which had been moved into the main cave.

"It is good to see you awake, Cha'vaen. I wasn't sure you were going to make it, even with my help," a familiar voice rumbled above me. Sar'ghain was there next to me, nudging a barrel of water toward me. I drank until I felt I would burst, then drank some more. The barrel was half empty when I finished.

"What happened? The last thing I remember was that demon . . . thrall coming after me."

"It has all been taken care of," Sar'ghain said, wincing as he shifted his weight. "You were asleep for a long time, even to me. I worried that you were not going to wake again."

"Well, we humans are tougher to kill than you'd think, although I noticed you didn't seem to have too much difficulty. How are you doing?"

"I . . . am all right. The wounds, they were not . . . deep."

"Yes, but what about the . . . liquid they used on you. The . . . leader said it would quench your fire," I said.

The dragon chuckled. "As I said before, not everything in those legends is true." He paused for a moment. "About what happened—"

"Yes, I led them here . . . I had no choice," I began. "I tried to reach you, all the way down—"

"But you warned me in time. Another may not have been so kind, after what I did to you, keeping you here."

"But . . . you're my friend. I wasn't going to let them do . . . anything to you," I said, gasping with the effort.

"I know. And in the years you have been here, you have become my friend, which is why I could not let anything happen to you either." Sar'ghain reached out and pulled the blanket down from my body with his claw. I looked down and saw what he meant.

In the middle of my chest, covering a space from just below my breastbone to the top of my waist, was a single, large, red-brown Dragonscale, rising and falling with each breath. The scale was not resting on my skin, like a bandage or covering, but had melded into my flesh, becoming one with me. I reached out to touch it, feeling as though I was not looking at my own body, but someone else's. My fingers encountered my own skin and muscles, then moved

down to feel the texture of the scale, hot, but yielding, flexible, a part of me now. I looked up at Sar'ghain, unable to
speak.

"The *vhiatae* in you could not repair such a mortal
wound without . . . assistance," he said, smiling down on
me. "There is another one, on your back as well, where the
lance entered your body. These saved your life. You will
adjust to them in time, but there will be some . . . discom-
fort.

"I saw . . . what I looked like . . . to them," I gasped.
"But my face . . . feels no different. How is this possible?"

"At last, it has begun," he said, smiling. "I had hoped for
this . . . but that is for another time. I had told you that my
blood would . . . change you, and it has. You are now becoming a combination of *Dhyragonais* and human. What
those other humans saw that day was your essence, it was
what you are becoming now. It was what happened to that
other human long ago. It was why . . . the other humans
feared us, drove us away. They feared that we would take
over."

"But . . . I know that is not so," I replied. "I know that it
is a melding of—of—both sides . . . the wisdom of your
kind . . . the drive that pushes us to excel . . ."

"Yes, you understand. Now you know why I could not
let you die, Chavaen, for you are more important than you
could have known," the Dragon said.

"I—I don't know what to say—I don't know what to
think," I stammered.

"It is—hard to comprehend now. Rest, and we will speak
later." Sar'ghain moved away, toward the back part of the
cave, leaving me alone with my whirling thoughts and the
new addition to my anatomy. I tried to make sense of it all,
but before I could, sleep claimed me one more.

When I awoke again, the fever had broken, and I felt
more or less human again. After another day of rest, I was
strong enough to move around. After a week, I felt like I

could have taken on that entire group of slayers and defeated them all. The scale in my chest was changing me further, taking me to the next plateau.

I did not bring up what Sar'ghain had done for me again, figuring that he would do so in his own time. However, this did not happen, for even before I was fully recovered, he resumed his hibernation again, sleeping even deeper and longer this time, until I began to worry about his health. Every time I tried to check on him, the bond in my head, which was much stronger now, would reassure me, telling me he was all right.

The months passed again, and the seasons changed, as did I. I no longer bothered with clothes, as I didn't seem to be affected by temperature extremes anymore. I was stronger, faster, and more dangerous than any human, armed or otherwise. I had given up weapons for hunting, preferring to use my natural strength and speed to chase down prey.

As I transformed, I found my thoughts and actions changing as well. Now, if I had been accosted by a group of men, I would have felt no compunction about tearing them to pieces. My life was here, and it was as if I had never known any other. I was becoming more *Dhyragonais* with each month. In this way, I continued day to day.

And still Sar'ghain slept on, the lumps on his back growing ever larger.

A year later, spring had come to the mountain again, bringing with it the fresh game I had desired for several months. I had just returned to the cave with a dozen rabbits when I saw Sar'ghain sitting up, awake and alert.

"Chavaen, I see hunting has been good."

"Yes, the mountains are awake again. We will eat well tonight," I replied.

"No . . . not tonight. Chavaen, I have something to show you. I wanted to wait until you returned to see this."

Sar'ghain turned around so that I could see his back. The lumps were huge now, and had grown together into one

massive hump that spread across his shoulders. As I
watched, I could see it shift and move. Then, with a sound
like chains snapping, the bulge split down the middle.

Sar'ghain flexed his shoulders, wriggling his back and
neck, causing a diaphanous membrane to emerge from the
deflating sac. Large scale-covered muscles peeled away
from his back, forming a frame upon which the membrane
unfurled, spreading apart, stretching out to span the length
of the cave. Sar'ghain flapped his new wings, the wind created by their lifting and lowering fanning my long hair. He
stood on his haunches and reached out with his wings to
their fullest extent, spreading his arms out as well. I could
see the exultation on his face as his blood spread into his
new appendages, the muscles, long dormant while they
formed, flexing with new movement.

"You are . . . magnificent," I said.

"Thank you. Unfortunately, I cannot remain here much
longer. Now that my wings are grown, it is time for me to
take the final journey, the first and last flight of my life.
Soon I will leave this plane, and go to meet my ancestors in
the sky."

I started to speak, but was stopped by Sar'ghain.
"Chavaen, everything I have told you about the relationship
between Dragons and men has been true, but it hasn't been
the whole truth.

"The female Dragon did give her blood to her friend, but
that was not all she gave. She gave him a scale as well, to
prolong his life, and, if he had so chosen, to eventually become *Dhyragonais* himself."

He stopped, letting the import of his words sink in.

"You mean . . . this—" I pointed at the scale rising and
falling in my chest. "—can transform me into . . . you?"

Sar'ghain nodded. "When I . . . caught you, for lack of a
better word, all those years ago, it was with a thought toward this moment. I had felt the wings beginning to grow
not long before your group came here, and I wanted to find
a suitable . . . apprentice. I have seen the honor in you,

and know that you would keep our memory and history alive. We *Dhyragonais* do not have to do this, but choose to only if we find someone who is worthy of it. I have chosen you to receive this."

By now the Dragon in me was as strong as my human side had ever been, so it did not come as a shock to me. Instead, I bowed to him. "Twice now you have saved my life, and have opened up a world to me that I did not know existed. I am honored to accept this responsibility you have bestowed on me."

Sar'ghain roared with pleasure, his cry echoing off the cavern walls. "Come then, I would walk with you one last time." He went with me to the back of the cavern again, only this time to the other side, away from the storeroom. He moved a boulder that I could never have lifted, revealing a large carved passageway, large enough for him to enter, that smelled of outside air. Folding his wings, Sar'ghain walked inside, with me beside him. He replaced the rock behind us, saying to me with a smile, "Someday you will be able to move this yourself."

Together we walked down the corridor, until we came to the other end, which was also blocked off by rock. Sar'ghain rolled this one aside as well, letting me exit, then closed it behind us.

"Later, that will make an excellent cavern for you, as mine will be too large for a few centuries," he said.

I nodded, looking out at the wide expanse of sky. I did not trust my voice just then.

"*Sca'less* . . . Chavaen . . . I have enjoyed our time together. Remember it, and us, when you Become."

"I will, Sar'ghain'ailshon'aig," I said. "May your flight be straight and true, and may you meet your ancestors with honor."

For the first and last time, Sar'ghain bowed to me. "And may your journey be successful, *Dhyragonais,* and I hope to see you many years hence, in the sky above."

With that he leaped into the air, his wings flapping as if he had been flying his entire life. He wheeled in the air once over my head, dipped his wings in salute, and rose up into the sky until he was a distant spot. Then he disappeared.

I have moved into the main cave for now, and have begun work on my own quarters. Sar'ghain was right, the long hall will make an excellent living space.

I still feel Sar'ghain's presence within me, coiled in the back of my skull. The day after he left, it said it would be with me always. He will guide me on this new journey, teach me what I need to know, impart to me the wisdom I will need in the future.

I can feel the changes beginning within me, changes that will take me the rest of the way out of the human world, and into that of the *Dhyragonais*. I look forward to it with a bit of fear, for leaving my old self behind, and anticipation, for the future that stretches out before me. I know I will have a lot to do, for I know what my role will be as *Dhyragonais*. When the time is right, I will make my presence known among the humans. Once men and Dragons worked together. I will bring back that age again.

It will take many years, but I have nothing if not time. After all, I have much to learn from my mentor. My new mentor.